She's in his home and becoming indispensable,
but what does he really want from her?

Housekeeper
at His
Command

Three great romances from three favourite
Mills & Boon authors!

Housekeeper at His Command

DIANA HAMILTON
CAROLINE ANDERSON
MYRNA MACKENZIE

All the characters in this book have no existence outside the imagination of the author, and have no relation whatsoever to anyone bearing the same name or names. They are not even distantly inspired by any individual known or unknown to the author, and all the incidents are pure invention.

First published in Great Britain 2011
by Mills & Boon, an imprint of Harlequin (UK) Limited,
Eton House, 18-24 Paradise Road, Richmond, Surrey TW9 1SR

HOUSEKEEPER AT HIS COMMAND
© by Harlequin Enterprises II B.V./S.à.r.l 2011

The Spaniard's Virgin Housekeeper, His Pregnant Housekeeper and *The Maid and the Millionaire* were first published in Great Britain by Harlequin Mills & Boon Limited.

The Spaniard's Virgin Housekeeper © Diana Hamilton 2008
His Pregnant Housekeeper © Caroline Anderson 2008
The Maid and the Millionaire © Myrna Topol 2007

ISBN: 978 0 263 88445 6

05-0911

Printed and bound in Spain
by Blackprint CPI, Barcelona

THE SPANIARD'S VIRGIN HOUSEKEEPER

BY
DIANA HAMILTON

Diana Hamilton is a true romantic, and fell in love with her husband at first sight. They still live in the fairytale Tudor house where they raised their three children. Now the idyll is shared with eight rescued cats and a puppy. But despite an often chaotic lifestyle, ever since she learned to read and write Diana has had her nose in a book—either reading or writing one—and plans to go on doing just that for a very long time to come.

CHAPTER ONE

ISABEL MAKEPEACE, mostly known as Izzy, sank down onto a bench beneath an arching tree that would shade her from the fierce midday Spanish sun and blinked furiously at the crystal-clear blue waters of the Atlantic. She would not cry. She would *not*!

Thrusting out her full lower lip, she huffed at the fall of gossamer-fine, silvery blond unmanageable hair that was obscuring her vision and wished she wasn't such a monumental failure—wished her feet didn't hurt so much when she could envisage having to walk miles and miles in search of somewhere dirt-cheap to stay while she looked for work.

Trouble was, being a scant five feet tall, she always wore killingly high heels, no matter what. Distinctly lacking stature, in the height department she needed all the help she could get.

Not that her family had ever commented on that—to her—vitally important lack. Lacking in brains, as her much older brilliant brother had cuttingly remarked on more occasions than she cared to remember. And lacking in common sense, as her father would sigh in exasperation while her mother merely shook her head sadly at the daughter who had been a surprise late arrival. An unpleasant surprise, Izzy sometimes feared, while vowing to try harder to live up to her brilliant brother, who was the golden apple of her parents' eyes.

The phone line from New Zealand had crackled with her father's displeasure when she'd told him she had left her job back in England—the job, moreover, that he had created for her amongst, as she strongly suspected, opposition from the other senior partners—and was taking another as an English-speaking mother's help to a wealthy Spanish couple in Cadiz.

He'd forecast that it would end in tears and he'd been right. It had.

The difference being she was not going to shed them!

The advertisement she'd seen in one of the national dailies had seemed heaven-sent. The successful applicant's duties would include looking after six-year-old twin girls and practising English with them, plus a little light housework. It had seemed like the answer to her prayers—the perfect way to start a new life.

That she'd actually landed the job had been a huge boost to her self-esteem—especially after the humiliation dealt her by the man she had adored with more romantic yearning than good old-fashioned common sense. Determined to forget Marcus and her broken heart, to prove herself to be the best ever mother's help and to show big brother James and her long-suffering parents that she didn't fail at everything she turned her hand to, she'd embarked on her new career with energy and goodwill.

She'd cheerfully swallowed the fact that although her new employers, Señor and Señora del Amo, occupied a large, opulent villa on the outskirts of the city, the room she'd been given was not much larger than a cupboard, with a small skylight, an iron-hard narrow bed, and a rickety chest of drawers that she'd banged her shins on every time she'd had to squirm past it to get into or out of bed.

The twins had been a nightmare, refusing to do a single thing she asked of them, and pretending they understood not a single word of English when their mother had proudly claimed the opposite. They had given her either blank stares or shrill giggles when she had attempted, with the help of a phrasebook, to speak to them in their own language.

It had soon dawned on Izzy that she was regarded as a low-paid skivvy. Her day off had been cancelled more often than not, and the 'light housework'—piled onto her between taking the girls to school and escorting them home again—had translated into anything from sweltering over an Everest of ironing to scrubbing the marble paving of the immense entrance hall. But she'd got on with it because she'd been determined she wasn't going to walk out and admit yet another failure.

She had quickly learned to keep out of Señor del Amo's way as much as humanly possible because he— sixteen flabby stones of oiliness—had seemed to think that because he was a wealthy banker and paid her paltry wages he was entitled to paw her whenever he felt like it.

Izzy had made up her mind to save as much as she

possibly could to fund her escape. She'd planned to save the means of paying her way on public transport to one of the busy holiday *costas*, where her poor grasp of Spanish wouldn't be a problem, and finding somewhere cheap to stay while she looked for work in a hotel or bar. But it was a plan that had rapidly hit the dust this morning, when Señor del Amo had sneaked up on her while she'd been loading the washing machine.

Struggling to extricate herself from what had seemed to be an octopus's complement of arms, she'd been unaware that the Señora had walked in on the torrid scene until a shrill stacatto of Spanish had brought merciful release. Rubbing her mouth with the back of her hand to rid it of the shudder-making assault of wet, blubbery lips, she hadn't even tried to translate Señor del Amo's response to his wife. But her pansy-blue eyes had sparked with outrage when the Señora had turned her hard black eyes on her and ordered, 'Get out of our home immediately! How dare you try to seduce an honorable family man—a husband and the father of two innocent girls?'

Stunned by the horrible injustice, Izzy had only been able to gasp with disbelief as her enraged employer had imparted with relish, 'From me you will have no references, and any money owing to you will not be paid. Your name will be forever linked with lewd behaviour among the civilised circles we move in!'

To have sprung to her own defence would have been a waste of breath, Izzy knew. Señora del Amo would believe what she wanted to believe, what made her feel comfortable, and even without looking at him she had known the Señor would be looking smugly triumphant.

There had been nothing for it but to pack her bags and go.

Looking on the bright side, she was glad to be away from the Señor's wandering hands and leery smiles, from the Señora's bossy, unrelenting demands and the terrible twins.

Her dignity restored, she had turned pitying eyes on the Spanish woman and told her, 'If you believe a word your husband says you're a bigger fool than I took you for.'

As Izzy had clipped out she'd almost felt daggers in her back, and she knew she'd made herself an enemy for life.

So here she was: no roof over her head, no job, and little likelihood of landing one in Cadiz with her scant knowledge of Spanish and not enough money to get her to the nearest busy holiday resort, where the language barrier wouldn't be such a problem, and where there would be plenty of bars and hotels looking for staff at the height of the season.

She wasn't going to break into her pitifully few euros to phone her parents in New Zealand, where they'd moved to be with her brother on her father's retirement, and ask to be rescued. To have to admit to yet another failure would be the final straw.

Her small chin firming, Izzy gathered her suitcase and slung her rucksack over her shoulders. Something would turn up. Maybe someone in the dockland area wanted someone to clean offices. It was worth consulting her phrasebook and asking, wasn't it?

An hour later—still jobless, her feet killing her—

Izzy left the fascinating commercial docks with their huge cargo vessels, busy tugs, gleaming cruise liners and little fishing boats behind her and headed towards the old town. She wandered through the maze of narrow shade-darkened streets, where projecting balconies almost met overhead, giving respite from the blazing heat, seeking a café where the price of a cold drink would be much lower than she could hope to find in the smarter, newer part of town.

The irritating mass of her hair was dragging in her eyes, and her cotton T-shirt and skirt were sticking to her overheated body. She wondered if she took her shoes off to give her poor feet a rest she'd ever get them back on again.

But her self-pity vanished as the only other occupant of the narrow street—a frail, shabbily dressed old man—tottered and collapsed. Concern tightening her soft mouth, Izzy dropped her luggage, ignored her protesting feet and sprinted forward to help.

His tough jaw set at a pugnacious angle, Cayo Angel Garcia descended from the penthouse suite he occupied when business demanded he spent time in Cadiz and exited the lift on the ground floor, instead of going down to the underground residents' car park and collecting the Merc.

He would walk—burn off some of his anger.

Impatiently he ran long tanned fingers through his short, expertly cut midnight hair and lengthened his stride, his dark eyes narrowed against the white light of the morning sun.

Returning briefly to the *castillo* after two months out of the country on business, he'd found amongst his personal post a letter from Tio Miguel. Skimming it, he'd felt the usual mixture of deep affection and exasperation. The old guy was the nearest thing to a real father he'd ever had. Cayo's own father, Roman, had wanted little to do with him, blaming him for the untimely death of his adored wife when his baby son had been barely two months old.

It had been Miguel who had shown him the only familial affection he had known—who had spent time with him, advised him. But when it came to taking advice Miguel closed his ears!

The elder of the two brothers, Miguel had inherited the vast family estates, while Roman had inherited the family-founded export empire—an empire Cayo had then inherited on his father's death five years ago.

Cutting across the busy Avenida del Puerto, he entered the narrow, warren-like streets of the old city. He blamed himself for not putting his foot down. Firmly. His uncle, a lovable old eccentric, owned vast wealth, but he insisted on living like a pauper in a mean dwelling, uninterested in what he wore or the food he ate—if he remembered to eat. His whole life revolved around his books. Cayo loved the old man dearly, but his unnecessarily austere lifestyle exasperated and worried him. He should have had him removed—forcibly, if necessary—to the *castillo*, where he would be looked after properly.

But, believing that a man had the right to live his life as he saw fit, providing he did no harm—and no man was more harmless and gentle than his uncle—Cayo had done nothing.

And look what had happened! Strong white teeth ground together in an excess of self-castigation.

The letter that had been waiting for him hadn't rung alarm bells. In fact he'd been pleased to learn that Tío Miguel had finally employed a new housekeeper. A young English girl, Izzy Makepeace, to take the place of the old crone who, it had always appeared to Cayo, had done little more than shuffle around the kitchen. And even there, he strongly suspected, she'd done nothing more energetic than lift a glass or six of manzanilla and spend time gossiping with the neighbours on the doorstep.

When Cayo had voiced a strong suggestion that the crone be given her marching orders it had brought the inevitable mild response. 'Like me, Benita is old. She can't be expected to leap around like a teenager. We manage well enough. Besides, she relies on me for a roof over her head.'

Therefore Cayo had been gratified to read that the crone had left, to be a burden on her probably unsuspecting grandson and his young wife, and that his uncle had managed to find a young woman to take over her duties.

Skipping over the neat copperplate paean praising the new paragon's general excellence, Cayo had thankfully said goodbye to his growing unease over his uncle's domestic arrangements.

Until.

Until last night.

Cayo had combined a visit to his offices in the commercial docks here in Cadiz with a tedious but necessary dinner with business associates, and had planned a long overdue and pleasurable visit to his uncle the following day.

He had sat through the dinner last night, hosted by the banker Augustin del Amo and his wife Carmela, wondering which of the city's fine restaurants would be most to his uncle's liking when he took him to lunch the following day—after Cayo had given the new housekeeper the once-over and made sure she knew her duties. First among these was the need to make sure the old gentleman ate regularly and well, of course. And then something said by the regrettably detestable Carmela del Amo had gained his full and riveted attention.

'It is impossible to get decent domestic help—my poor children have been without a nanny for over a month now, ever since we had to tell the last one to leave. Izzy Makepeace—an English girl. Such a mistake to hire her in the first place!' She had rolled her hard black eyes dramatically, managing to look martyred, and announced, 'I overlooked her slovenly laziness. I am a realist, and one cannot expect perfection no matter how much one pays. But when it comes to contaminating my dear, innocent girls I draw the line. The creature was little better than a *puta*.' Preening in the undivided attention of her guests, she had tipped her expertly coiffured head in her husband's direction. 'You know better than I, Augustin.'

The banker had looked smug as he'd leaned back in

his chair, lifting his wine glass. 'You know how it is. Money is an aphrodisiac. I didn't dare be alone with her for one second—offered herself on a plate. For a financial consideration, naturally. If I'd been the type to take a mistress then I might have been tempted. A lush little package if ever I saw one!'

In receipt of a look that would have wilted an oak in the prime of life, he had added quickly, 'But, as I'm a faithful family man, I—we—told her to pack her bags and leave.'

The anger that had been building ever since he'd received that unwelcome information made Cayo feel as if he were about to explode. The smallest amount of research would have given his uncle's new housekeeper the information that Miguel Garcia—scholar and local eccentric—was, to use her probable terminology, filthy rotten rich.

Izzy Makepeace, with the morals of an alley cat, had successfully got her greedy claws in one of the kindest, most innocent old gentlemen ever to inhabit the planet. But he, Cayo Angel Garcia, was about to ensure that this situation was sorted out immediately!

Izzy Makepeace.

Make *war* was more like it!

CHAPTER TWO

'I'M BACK from market, *señor*,' Izzy announced cheerfully as she entered the cramped ground-floor room her new employer used as his study. A wayward strand of silky blond hair had escaped from the ribbon she'd used to anchor the unruly mass on top of her head, and she pushed it out of her eyes with the back of her hand. 'We have fresh-caught pilchards for lunch, and green beans.'

Cheap, but nourishing.

The housekeeping allowance was astonishingly small, and most of her unremarkable weekly wage went on supplementing it—but she wasn't complaining because her employer was so obviously poor and in no position to pay the going rate. It was immensely gratifying to see the old gentleman looking less frail than he had when she'd helped him when he'd fallen in the street, thankful that he spoke her language and had been able to direct her when she'd offered to see him to his home.

'And peaches—they looked so scrummy I couldn't resist!'

'Scrummy?' Miguel Garcia looked up from his seat

at the desk that was half buried beneath tottering piles of books and papers, his lean, ascetic, once-handsome face breaking into a warm smile as he peered at her over the top of his spectacles, stuck together with sticky tape.

'Delicious.' Izzy grinned back at him, translating from the vernacular.

'Ah. I understand!' He leaned back in his chair, steepling his fingers, his dark eyes kind. 'Then I shall enjoy our lunch. While I think of it—I have asked you before, and as you've been with me for five weeks now I no longer ask. I *insist* you address me by my given name. Miguel. It will be more companionable.'

'Okay,' she agreed blithely. 'But only if you drop what you're doing and come out with me for a little fresh air and exercise.'

He was researching the life of some obscure saint or other, he'd told her, and it was her gladly embraced mission to ensure he remembered to eat and forgot his work long enough to take a short stroll each morning and evening.

'You bully me!' But his gentle smile as he laid down his pen told her he didn't object in the least. 'May I claim an old man's privilege and say how pretty you look this morning?'

'Oh!' Izzy's face was bright pink. He was good for her confidence—at one time flat on the floor! So good, in fact, that she no longer needed the boost of killingly high heels, and had bought flat sandals from the open-air market. She had to admit they made her feel as wide as she was high—but, hey, it made walking so much more comfortable!

And the old gentleman was so *grateful* for everything she did. She was sure he'd never noticed the squalor he lived in until she'd got rid of it—washing, scrubbing and polishing until the humble little house positively gleamed. The praises following his initial stunned surprise at the transformation had come thick and fast, making her head spin. Because she couldn't remember being praised for anything before in the whole of her twenty-two years.

Their separate guardian angels must have put their heads together on the day the del Amos had thrown her out and Señor Garcia had collapsed on the street. Both being in the right place at the right time had been really fortunate. The old gentleman was now looking much better, and she was thankful to have found a new job and a roof over her head so quickly, happy to be doing something worthwhile.

Remembering the ear-bending she'd received when she'd phoned her parents to tell them she'd quit her first job and landed another as a mother's help in Cadiz, she didn't want to repeat the experience. She had got around to writing last week instead, giving them her new address. That done, she wasn't going to think about the kind of nagging reply she'd get when she could enjoy being appreciated for once.

'I'll put the shopping away,' she told her employer, 'then we'll go out and enjoy the air before it gets too hot.'

Closing the study door behind her, she headed for the kitchen, her cool, brightly patterned cotton skirt swirling around her bare legs. She swung round as the street door opened to reveal a tall, dark stranger.

An impressively handsome stranger.

Her pansy-blue eyes widened as she took in his height and the breadth of shoulder beneath a stone-coloured fine cotton shirt tucked into the narrow waistband of obviously designer chinos. They clothed long, athletic legs, and ended in shoes that, at a guess, had to have been hand-made from the finest, most supple leather.

Slowly raising her eyes, she was stunned by the impact of sculpted high cheekbones, an aristocratic blade of a nose, and dark-as-night eyes fringed by lashes that were as soft and black as his expensively styled hair—eyes that were looking at her with blatant hostility.

'Izzy Makepeace?'

The beautiful, sensual male mouth curved with what she could only translate as derision. Her heart thumped a warning.

Who was he? Surely not a plain-clothes policeman, sent to arrest her because Señora del Amo had reported her alleged lewd behaviour, calling her a danger to all innocent children and middle-aged married million-aires in Cadiz—if not the whole of Spain? But police-men couldn't afford to dress in designer clothes that would have cost them the equivalent of a year's wages. Nor would they wear anything like the slim gold watch that banded his angular wrist—that would have cost them their pension!

Stifling hysteria—she mustn't let herself get para-noid over the gross injustice done her by the powerful del Amos—Izzy crossed her arms defensively over her midriff, lifted her neat chin and demanded, 'Who wants to know?'

And she cringed with helpless inadequacy as he swept her a look of chilling contempt, making her feel several centimetres short of two inches tall.

'Cayo!'

At the sound of her employer's voice Izzy let her tautly held spine relax just a little. Señor Garcia—or Miguel, as she must now get used to calling him—knew this person. The sensation of threat that had been present ever since the stranger had spoken dissipated just a little, too. Perhaps, being so impressive in every detectable department, this haughty creature found it normal to look at lesser beings as if they were beneath his lofty contempt.

Her mouth softening with relief at having sorted out the less than flattering vibes winging in her direction from what had to be the most spectacularly handsome guy she'd ever seen, she moved closer to the old gentleman, as if for protection, as he proclaimed with enthusiasm, 'It's so good to see you—it's been a long time! How long are you staying in Cadiz?'

'Long enough to take you to lunch, Tio.' Long enough to warn him of the type of creature he had taken into his home, to redouble his efforts to persuade him to move into the family country home, or at the very least to move into his luxurious apartment here in Cadiz.

Studiously ignoring the new 'housekeeper', Cayo extended a lean, tanned hand. 'Shall we go?' To his amazed annoyance he received a decisive shake of his uncle's head. Until now Tio Miguel had always pandered to his every request or suggestion—except, of course, over the vexed question of his lifestyle.

'We shall lunch here,' Miguel stated with firm good humour. 'Izzy shall cook for us. We have pilchards, I'm told. And peaches.' He smiled down at her and laid a hand on her shoulder. 'Izzy, may I introduce my workaholic nephew, Cayo?'

His nephew! Not in the least impressed now, Izzy shot the poor old gentleman's uncaring relative a withering glance. If he could afford to dress himself in designer gear and sport a watch that must have cost thousands—and she knew about that sort of stuff because her brilliant, well-heeled big brother always dressed in the best, proclaiming that his position demanded it and that quality always counted—then surely he could alleviate his uncle's hand-to-mouth existence and visit more often to check on his welfare? As Miguel had said, it had been a long time.

Barely registering Cayo's response to the introduction, she drew herself up to her unspectacular height and stated, 'I'll start preparing lunch, Miguel.'

She headed for the kitchen, hoping the pilchards would stretch to feed three and not much caring for the idea of cooking for someone who had looked at her as if she were dirt. And how had he known her name? She should have asked—would have done if his chilling look hadn't frozen her vocal cords. It was an omission she would rectify over lunch. Unless he refused to share a table with a mere menial.

Watching her go through narrowed eyes, Cayo recalled how Augustin del Amo had described her. *A lush little package.* Very apt indeed.

The top of her silvery blond head might reach the top of his chest—or almost. And the descriptive 'lush' perfectly suited the ripe curves, full lips and eyes like bruised pansies. She found money an aphrodisiac and despite outward appearances she would know Miguel was rolling in the stuff. After all, she was already intimate enough to call Miguel by his given name!

Reining back the fiery impulse to go after her, take her by the scruff of her neck and tip her into the gutter where she clearly belonged, he turned to his uncle. 'I need to talk to you.'

The sight of the tiny kitchen, with its old-fashioned iron range, arrays of gleaming copper pans hanging from hooks on roughly plastered walls, earthenware platters and bowls perched on shelves, and the chunky wooden table that served as the only work surface always cheered Izzy, and today went some way to smooth her ruffled feathers.

Five weeks ago, when she'd walked in here for the first time to fetch the frail old gentleman a glass of water, she'd been horrified. Evidence of neglect had hit her from every side. Grease and dust had covered every surface, and the copper pans had been green with verdigris. Empty sherry bottles had been piled in one corner, and the heel of a mouldy loaf had rested in a bucket beneath the grimy stone sink.

'You live alone?' she'd asked as she'd watched him drink the water and set the mug aside, on top of a cluttered desk.

'Since my housekeeper left two days ago,' he supplied with a weak smile. 'I thought I should make myself something to eat, and I got the range going, but there was nothing to cook. I was on my way to market when I became light-headed. And I thank you,' he added with courtesy, 'for assisting me to my home.'

Definitely not ready to bow out with a *Think nothing of it*, Izzy asked, 'Do you have family I could contact for you?'

'Just a nephew, who I think at the moment is in Britain.' He spread his thin, fine-boned hands. 'In any case, it is not necessary to trouble anyone. Already I am recovered from my giddiness and feel better.'

He certainly didn't look it. Remembering that he'd been on his way to market to buy food, she asked, 'When did you last eat?'

'I don't recall.' He looked as if the question really puzzled him, and explained earnestly, with a frail hand indicating the mass of books and papers on the desk, 'When I'm working I forget time.'

'Then how about I save you the trouble and pop out for some food?' Izzy was back on her tortured feet, not prepared to leave this poor old man to his own ineffectual devices—at least not until he'd been fed and persuaded to give her the name and address of his doctor.

Heading for the nearest shop, she had found her outraged thoughts kept her from dwelling on her burningly painful feet. Deserted by a housekeeper who, from what she'd seen, hadn't been too keen on doing any work, with his only relative obviously not keeping in touch because the old gentleman wasn't sure where he was. She was already feeling anxious and even slightly cross on his behalf.

Raiding her precious euros, she bought eggs, oil and crusty rolls and tottered back. Half an hour later, watching the colour return to his ashen cheeks as he ate the scrambled eggs and one of the rolls, she chatted away. She was concerned that he absolutely refused to see his doctor, but happy to answer his questions because his curiosity must surely mean he was feeling more himself. So she told him exactly how she'd landed up in Spain, and regaled him with her family history. She glossed over the humiliation she'd suffered at Marcus's hands, and when she came to her present unenviable jobless and homeless situation she gave the half-truth that being a mother's help hadn't suited.

'So what will you do now?' Miguel asked.

Izzy twisted her hands together in her lap, her huge eyes clouding. Since helping the old gentleman to his feet she'd actually forgotten her own misery. Deflatedly, she confessed, 'I don't know. I hoped I would find something here in Cadiz to tide me over. But so far—nothing.'

'Couldn't your parents help?'

Izzy shuddered. And then, because his interest was obviously kindly, she admitted, 'They could—and they would. But I can't face telling them I've failed again. When I left school my dad—like I told you, he was a solicitor—sort of made a job for me in his practice. Being senior partner, he swung it. Then when he retired my parents went out to New Zealand to be with James—my brother. They wanted me to go with them but I wouldn't,' she confided earnestly.

She was relieved to be unburdening herself because usually her family and the people she worked with didn't think she had anything worth listening to, and this old gentleman was hanging on every word she said.

'James is so clever, you see. He sailed through every exam he ever took, and now he's a highly regarded surgeon. My parents are hugely proud of him, of course. Not being anything special, *I've* always been a disappointment to them. To make it worse James married a brainy woman—a top lawyer. Being around them always makes me feel squashed. So I stayed back in England. They weren't at all pleased when I gave up my job in the practice and came to Spain. So I want to get back on my feet by my own efforts and not go crawling to them for help.'

He nodded understandingly and asked, 'And you left your work in England because you had a falling-out with a young man? From what you told me earlier you were very fond of him. If you returned to England do you think you could patch things up?'

Izzy went bright pink. She'd been so humiliated she didn't like to think about it. But maybe she should get it out of her system—and it was certainly much easier to talk to a stranger.

'It wasn't like that.' She sighed. 'I feel a real fool. But I had this huge crush on him—Marcus. He's a legal executive in Dad's old practice, really good-looking—good at making a girl feel special. I thought we were close, you know. He asked me to do little things for him—stuff like collecting his dry cleaning in my lunch hour, doing bits of shopping. He took me out once, and bought me a glass of wine. That's when he told me his housekeeper had thrown a wobbly and walked out and left him without a cleaner. When I volunteered to help him out he called me his treasure and held my hand. Said I was special. He made me feel valued for a change. How stupid can a girl get?'

Surreptitiously she eased her shoes off and allowed her agonised toes the freedom to curl with embarrassment. Then she took a deep breath and confided, 'I heard him talking to Molly, one of the secretaries, obviously responding to something she'd said. "Sure, she can't take those big googly eyes off me—but long live the crush if it means I get a free errand girl, laundry service and cleaner! All I have to do is turn on the charm, call her my treasure and she'll walk backwards over hot coals for me!" And Molly just laughed and said, "Not in those scary high heels she wears, she won't!" I felt like the world's biggest idiot.'

His weary eyes on her flushed, embarrassed features, Miguel Garcia said, 'So you need work and I, it would appear, need a housekeeper. The position's yours if you want it—until you get back on your feet. There will be a weekly housekeeping allowance, and you will receive the same wage as Benita did.' He named a sum that was slightly less than the pittance the del Amos had paid her, but beggars couldn't be choosers, and if she was really careful she could save enough over time to fund a transfer to another destination.

In the meantime she could sort the poor old gentleman out, make sure he ate regularly and that his home was clean, and later contact the Spanish equivalent of the British Social Services to keep an eye on him after she'd left.

'Thanks!' she beamed. 'I'd love to work for you!'

And she was loving it, Izzy thought now as she reached for a heavy-bottomed copper pan and the olive oil. Already she was fond of her poor old gentleman, as she always thought of him. The owner of a soft heart, she'd always been on the side of the underdog, and seeing her employer grow stronger and sprightlier every day was, to her, better than winning the Lottery.

'I don't believe a word of it!' Miguel stated with cold fury. 'Izzy is no more an immoral gold-digger than I am! And if you mix with the type of person who would stoop to spread such a calumny then I am disappointed in you.'

'Of necessity, Tio.' Cayo received the reprimand with a slight upward shift of one wide shoulder. 'Augustin del Amo is a highly respected banker. I occasionally do business with him.' Unsurprised by his uncle's defence of Miss Sweetness and Light—as the older man innocently claimed her to be—Cayo leaned back in the chair on the other side of the cluttered desk, the tips of his steepled fingers resting against the hard line of his mouth.

Izzy Makepeace was smart. Smart enough to know she had to tread carefully. Because the stakes were higher this time. She wasn't angling to be a wealthy married man's paid mistress but something else entirely. An indispensable treasure, caring for an even wealthier man as his age advanced. A wife!

The thought made his blood run cold! No way would

he stand by and see his beloved, innocently naïve relative walk into *that* trap!

'How much do you pay her?' he asked with deceptive smoothness. Receiving the information that she earned the same as Benita had done, he dipped his dark head in understanding.

As long as the unlamented Benita had had enough to buy cheap sherry and didn't have to exert herself by so much as an extra intake of breath in the non-commission of her duties she would have been happy enough to receive wages that hadn't increased in the last twenty years. Even she would have known that her so-called services weren't worth any more, and his uncle, unaware of the cost of living because he lived firmly in the past, in the company of long-dead saints, and rarely read a newspaper or listened to a radio, wouldn't know he was paying what amounted to peanuts. He would have been horrified if the fact had been pointed out to him.

But no sane young working woman would accept such low payment. Not unless she had an ulterior motive. If he'd had doubts before—and he hadn't— that would have clinched it. She had her motive!

'Do you realise that what you're paying her is a fraction of the going rate?' Seeing his uncle's brows draw together, Cayo pressed on with barely concealed exasperation. 'Of course you don't. You don't live in the real world—never have done. Since leaving the university where you taught medieval history twenty years ago you've buried yourself in research. You have no idea what goes on in the world. So why would a young healthy woman accept such low pay? Think about it.'

Leaving the older man looking every one of his seventy-six years and more, Cayo strode from the study and flung open the door to the kitchen.

He had to admit that the room had scrubbed up well. But then it would be in her best interests to work her socks off, present herself as an angel of mercy, indispensable, when the glittering prize was a pot of gold at the end of the rainbow, he rationalised with an ingrained cynicism born of having to fight off greedy little gold-diggers ever since he'd reached his late teens.

She had her back to him, was removing a heavy pan from the stove with both hands.

'I'm just about to dish up, Miguel. If you and your nephew would go up to the dining room I'll be with you in a tick.'

Her cheerful words set his teeth on edge.

She turned then, her smile fading fast when she saw him. He noted the way she banged the pan down on the tabletop and hauled her shoulders back, her eyes very bright.

'Right, mister!' she spluttered. 'I've got something to say to you—'

He cut across her, having no interest in hearing anything from her beyond a meekly compliant goodbye.

'How much will it take to make yourself scarce, be out of this house before nightfall and never come near my uncle again?' Cayo demanded, gazing steadily at her, his black-as-midnight eyes as cold as charity, his feet planted firmly apart, his fists pushed into the pockets of his chinos. 'Name your price.'

CHAPTER THREE

'WHAT did you say?'

Momentarily stunned, Izzy released a disbelieving gasp. She planted her hands on the table, leaning forward, and searched his dark eyes for any sign that he could be joking. Finding none, she added at full outraged volume, 'You're offering me money to walk out of my job and leave Miguel in the lurch? I don't believe this!' She huffed out a breath and imparted, 'I'll have you know he's as good at looking after himself as a two-year-old.' Then, introducing a note of scorn, 'You wouldn't know, of course, because it seems you're rarely around, but your uncle collapsed in the street. It took me three weeks to persuade him to go for a check-up. He's got a heart murmur, not helped by borderline malnutrition, so you're off your rocker if you think I'd leave him to fend for himself for a pocketful of euros! What sort of nephew are you?'

'One who wasn't born yesterday.'

Smooth as silk, he slid into the rough grit of her attack. Stopped in her tracks by that weird statement,

Izzy connected with the silver gleam of cynicism in those compelling eyes.

She suppressed a sudden unwelcome shiver as he added, almost purring, 'You have a saying, I believe? A bird in the hand is worth two in the bush. So, I say again, name your price.'

She tossed her silvery blond head high, and her normally water-clear blue eyes were shadowed by a bewildered frown as she demanded tersely, 'Why?'

'Because I know your sort,' Cayo supplied drily. 'And I have confirmation via Augustin del Amo. Remember him?' His own arrogantly held head was high, too. Brilliant eyes narrowed, he reminded her with harsh conviction, 'Instead of looking after his children as you were paid to—highly paid, by all accounts—you spent all your time trying to tempt him into changing your job description to that of paid and pampered mistress.'

Her stomach swooping, looping and finally knotting, her cheeks flaming, Izzy gulped back a yelp of outrage and finally vented, 'That creep!'

Señora del Amo had promised her name would be mud! And she hadn't wasted any time spreading the lies she'd chosen to believe rather than accept that her husband was a real slimeball. She could just about understand that. But this horrible man—neglecter of frail, impoverished old uncles—was choosing to believe the worst of her without doing her the courtesy of asking to hear her side of the story!

As if that wasn't enough, worse was to come. He pointed out with icy cool, 'Get it into your mercenary little head that there's nothing here for you. You may be able to fool an unworldly old man, but you don't fool me. Take cash in hand and leave—or I'll make sure you regret the day you were born.'

He was a maniac! Izzy decided, feeling as if she'd landed in a parallel universe. Okay, so he'd taken the wealthy banker's words at face value and decided she was a mercenary little scrubber, out for all she could get from the male of the species. So why tell her there was nothing for her here, when anyone could see that Miguel barely had two pennies to rub together?

This man might be prime contender in a competition to find the world's most gorgeous male, but the handsome exterior clothed a nasty mind, she decided, straightening her spine. She wasn't going to even begin to plead her case, because she'd be wasting her breath, nor go on to explain that she already got plenty out of working for Miguel. Like making his living conditions more comfortable, seeing his health improve.

She'd leave only when she was sure outside help was forthcoming. So this handsome devil could take his threats and swallow them. And she hoped they choked him!

A saccharine smile hiding her internal boiling fury, she forced herself to unclench her small fists and slid the fish onto the waiting platter. 'Take this up while I tell Miguel lunch is ready,' she instructed snippily. 'And since you ask me to name my price for making myself scarce, then try this for size.' She squared her narrow shoulders and gave him exactly what he deserved. 'Ten billion. Pounds sterling. In cash. All neat and tidy in a gigantic diamond-studded gold crate. And while we're at it, a nice villa in the hills to put it in!'

Mentally adding, *So put that in your pipe and smoke it, señor!* she made a speedy exit.

Lunch was a dismal affair. Izzy was too angry to eat more than a mouthful and Miguel, usually so talkative even if the subject matter was so rarefied it went straight over her head, was preoccupied, barely uttering a word. She had the horrible feeling that Cayo had poured his poison into his elderly relative's ears and that—even worse—the poor old gentleman had believed him!

Only Cayo seemed at ease. The only sign of his deeply unflattering opinion of her, and his stated intent to make her regret the day she'd been born if she didn't do as he'd ordered, was the slight twisting of his sexy mouth whenever she tried to break the uncomfortable silence with some admittedly inane comment or other.

And then he put down his fruit knife, wiped fastidious fingers on one of the fine linen napkins she'd discovered at the bottom of a drawer and carefully laundered, leaned back in his chair and drawled, 'I hear, Tio, that you are unwell?' He raised an imperious silencing hand as Miguel, startled back into the here and now by that unwelcome reminder, opened his mouth to deny any such thing. 'I intend to get all the facts from your doctor this afternoon. So any blustering denials you are preparing will be neither here nor there.'

Catching sight of Miguel's quizzical glance, one brow raised in her direction above deep-set dark eyes, Izzy pinkened and confessed, 'I thought I should mention it.' She aimed an accusing stare at Cayo's tough expression. 'After all, you've been neglected for too long. Someone should take care of you and make sure you eat and rest properly.'

'Something you do to perfection.'

The gentleness of her employer's tone, the warmth of his smile made Izzy feel faint with relief. If his nephew *had* relayed the del Amos' lies then he clearly hadn't believed them.

She would have felt wretched if he had. She had grown fond of her old gentleman, impractical dreamer that he was; looking after him was like looking after an extra clever elderly babe in arms, and this time she hadn't failed—in fact she'd made a success of her current job.

That empowering thought gave her the confidence to stand up from the table and address the brute sitting opposite. 'I insist Miguel rests for an hour in the afternoon. Thank you for dropping by. I'll see you out.'

The older man's low, delighted chuckle had brought a dark, angry flush to his nephew's fiercely handsome features, Izzy noted with immense satisfaction as he got to his feet, towering over her. Neatly sidestepping him, she led the way down the dingy staircase and through a narrow door that led into the tiny cobbled courtyard she longed to brighten with tubs of flowers. But she knew such a luxury was out of the question when money was so obviously tight. Which glaring fact gave her the resolution to turn and face the man as she reached the street door.

My, he was tall! Wishing she had the advantage of a

pair of her highest high heels, now stowed away in the bottom of a cupboard in her small bedroom, she tipped back her head to meet his lethally contemptuous black eyes. She absolutely refused to let herself be intimidated by those powerfully muscled shoulders and chest, or wonder why the eye contact took her breath away and sent a frisson of unwelcome physical awareness shooting deep into her pelvis.

'You obviously believe the worst of everyone,' she stated, doing her best to get her breathing back on an even keel. 'But ask yourself this—if I'm a greedy little scrubber, out for all I can get, why would I be wasting my time here with a man who's as poor as a church mouse? What do you think I'm going to do? Steal his spoons? And, while we're on the subject, you offered me money to make myself scarce, so you've obviously got some to spare. I suggest you use it to give your uncle an allowance—enough to make his existence a little less hand-to-mouth.'

In receipt of his abrupt, tight-lipped, non-verbal departure, Izzy banged the street door shut behind him and jumped up and down, hugging herself. She'd sent him packing with a flea in his ear! She couldn't remember when she'd last felt so alive!

The arrogant so-and-so had walked in, looking oh-so superior, and tried to make her leave because he believed lies. Naturally his sort would take the word of a wealthy banker over any denial that might come from a mere menial!

But she had refused to go. Just thinking of the utterly ridiculous payment she had demanded made her giggle.

And—the icing on the cake—she had lectured him about his neglect of his uncle. With a bit of luck his conscience, if he had one—which was debatable, she conceded—just might move him in the direction of helping the poor old gentleman financially.

She had won the battle!

The fight was well and truly on, Cayo thought grimly as he left the doctor's office, crossed Calle San Francisco Nueva and headed through the maze of narrow streets back towards Miguel's humble dwelling. On two fronts.

Izzy Makepeace might think she was clever, pretending she was unaware that Miguel was an extremely wealthy man, but it was common knowledge that the absent-minded scholar was loaded. He had no interest in material comforts or possessions, and lived only for his painstaking work—information that would have been easy to pick up working for Señora del Amo, who was a notorious gossip and claimed to know everyone who was anyone and exactly what they were worth. A wealthy eccentric, a descendant of one of Spain's oldest and most respected families, would certainly be worth talking about—even boasting, perhaps, of the business connection.

When Isabel Makepeace had failed to establish herself as a wealthy banker's mistress she would have hung around the Topete area, where Miguel had his home. No believer in coincidence, he knew she must have planned on doing her best to get to meet the man she knew as a better-than-well-heeled elderly bachelor, grasping her opportunity when the poor old guy had collapsed virtually under her nose.

That she fully intended to get her claws into his naïve uncle and not let go had been proved a rock-solid fact when she'd answered his invitation to name her price with that ludicrously greedy demand.

She was after a lifetime of financial security. Make herself indispensable, Miss Sweetness and Light, then wheedle an offer of marriage from the wealthy old man and embark on the sort of high living that would leave his uncle floundering and hurt. He could think of no other reason for a mercenary harpie to work so hard for a pittance—and the evidence of the much improved state of his uncle's home suggested that she did work hard.

His jaw hardened with steely determination. Tio Miguel could be exasperating, but he loved him. Far too much to stand by and see that scheming, greedy little blond pocket Venus ruin the years remaining to him and make him a laughing stock. He, Cayo Angel Garcia, would *not* stand by and see that happen.

And the news from Miguel's doctor had been a wake-up call. The heart murmur of itself wasn't too serious. But coupled with his neglected physical condition…

Guilt scored a line between winging black brows. True, he had lost count of the times he'd tried to persuade the elderly man to make his home at the *castillo*, where he could be well looked after. But after continuous polite refusal to take advantage of his nephew's hospitality or to dismiss Benita, who'd been with him for years, Cayo had backed off, believing that every man had the right to live his life as he felt fit.

A mistake he deeply regretted.

One that wouldn't be repeated. Liberal tolerance was now a thing of the past where his uncle's wellbeing was concerned.

'You work too hard,' Miguel chided gently, finding Izzy in the kitchen ironing his shirts after rising from his siesta. 'And, as Cayo pointed out, I pay you far too little.' He shook his grey head, annoyed with himself. 'I was unaware. I should think of things outside my narrow field of interest. I apologise. Cayo can be shortsighted and stubborn in some respects, I fear, but in this instance he is right. You must allow me to make amends. Will you tell me how excellent housekeepers *should* be financially rewarded? And by the same token tell me the modern-day cost of keeping a modest household such as ours running?'

Her soft mouth open, Izzy stared at her employer in shock. Not because he'd actually woken up to the fact that the cost of living had risen in the last twenty or so years, but because his brute of a nephew had actually pointed it out.

If he was so keen to rid his uncle of her contaminating presence, why had he asked what she was earning and given his opinion that it was far too little?

Unless, of course—her smooth brow furrowed—the information gained from his uncle had cemented his distrust of her into rock-hard certainty. He thought she was working for next to nothing because she had some ulterior motive, had something to gain. But what?

'Well?' Miguel broke gently into her puzzled train of thought just as Cayo sauntered into the room, giving her no time to assemble her wits and make a reply, or give her old gentleman information that would make him feel really uncomfortable and put him in a spot—because it was obvious that he wouldn't be able to pay the going rate.

Suddenly the room seemed airless. Cayo's formidable presence dominated the space with the unmistakable aura of the alpha male—born to lead, to take on all comers without batting an eyelid. For some unknown reason it made her feel decidedly dizzy, and she felt herself flush with some strange emotion she couldn't put a name to. She turned away to take another shirt from the laundry basket, with the image of the way he looked—six foot plus of prime Spanish manhood, from the commanding width of his shoulders tapering down to a narrow waist, slinky hips and impressively long, elegantly trousered legs—indelibly printed on her retina.

'I have spoken at length with Dr Menendez, who gave me the results of the tests you underwent, Tio,' he announced, his tone so authoritative she could have smacked him.

Wandering farther into the room, he absorbed the cosy domestic scene. Miguel in the battered old armchair that had stood just inside the door for as long as he could remember, watching the Angel of Mercy ironing his shirts.

She was working to a different agenda from the one she had employed with Augustin del Amo, for sure. A real Miss Goody-Two-Shoes—caring and competent, catering to an elderly man's domestic comforts, delectable, with enticing strands of the spun-silver-gilt hair escaping the ribbon arrangement she'd pinned it back with. Her luscious curves were clad in a bog-standard T-shirt and cotton skirt, not overtly flaunting her steamy sexuality as her clothes would have done when she'd attempted to snare a rich banker, because those tactics wouldn't work with the elderly scholar.

Clever.

But he was smarter. By a cartload he was smarter!

Kill two birds with one stone. First get Tio Miguel to agree to move to the luxurious Castillo de las Palomas, where he could continue his work and be looked after by attentive staff who would cater to his every need. Cayo would suggest he took his housekeeper with him as companion because, judging by what he'd seen and heard, his uncle was already fond of the little tramp. He felt comfortable with her, and in all likelihood would dig his heels in and refuse to go anywhere if it meant his housekeeper was to be cast out on the street.

Then he would seduce Izzy Makepeace away from her intention to get her claws into the older man—no hardship, because the sultry, passionate fullness of her lips belied the wide, childlike innocence of those big blue eyes, and he had never suffered difficulties in that direction. Quite the opposite. The ease with which he seemed to attract simpering females anxious to do anything to please him had bored him since his hormones had run riot in his teens.

He would seduce her, make sure his uncle knew what was happening, and then make sure she was well and truly finished with.

His mouth tightened. He didn't like it. It felt uncomfortably like cruelty, and he had always prided himself on being straightforward in both personal and business dealings. But if he had to fight dirty he would. For his uncle's sake, he would.

Swinging round to face them, he stated, 'In view of what I learned from Menendez, I have a proposition to make.'

CHAPTER FOUR

Izzy folded the last of the shirts as a fierce stab of anxiety skittered its way through her entire body. This darkly handsome thoroughbred male looked as out of place in these shabby surroundings as a brilliant-cut diamond in a sack of potatoes. She was sure that whatever he proposed would bode no good for her. Cayo wanted her out of his uncle's home, and he didn't look the kind of guy who would give up easily.

'Tio—' Half sitting on the chunky table, he was addressing his relative.

Izzy, her ears tingling for the expected list of her supposed and damning sins, embellished with a strongly voiced suggestion that she be thrown back on the street where she belonged, permitted herself a tiny sigh of relief when he said gently, 'Menendez tells me that your heart problem was occasioned by the rheumatic fever you had as a child. At the time, apparently, the condition went unrecognised. You can live with it, he assures me, provided you take care. Something you haven't done for years—'

'Ah, but things have changed,' Miguel interrupted smartly. 'Unlike poor old Benita, whose sins of omission escaped me, Izzy makes sure I am looked after splendidly! Provided she agrees to stay on—at an increased rate of payment—we will be very comfortable together. You mustn't worry.'

'But I do,' Cayo countered firmly. 'Have done for years. You are of my family—blood of my blood. I care about you and I worry,' he incised, with a telling movement of one lean, bronzed hand. 'I have asked before—not with as much vigour as I should have done, perhaps—and this time I will insist. You must move to the cooler air of the mountains, at least during the debilitating heat of the summer. And who knows? You might be sensible enough to make it your permanent home. At the Castillo de las Palomas you will enjoy every comfort and luxury. As you well know, there are willing staff to cater to your every need. And there is also an excellent library, so you may continue your work, if you wish, in guaranteed privacy and peace. As far as I can see there is nothing, apart from your pig-headedness, to stop you behaving sensibly and in your own best interests.'

Grateful for the absence—so far—of the verbal assault she'd been expecting, and amazed that her slating opinion had actually moved Cayo to doing something about his uncle's wellbeing, Izzy held her breath.

She was unprepared for the elderly man's stubbornness. Despite being obviously touched by his nephew's offer, evidenced by the sudden moistness of his dark eyes, he declined. 'I'm grateful for your concern, Cayo.

Truly. But we are comfortable here, and you know how I dislike any kind of upheaval.'

Emboldened by the look Cayo turned to give her—his brows lifting in obvious frustration, his smile wry, as if they were on the same side for once—Izzy put in, 'Can I say something? It sounds just what the doctor ordered, Miguel—honestly.'

Feeling Cayo's gaze upon her, she met the flash of a very definite query in his spectacularly eloquent eyes and ignored it. That she would be jobless and homeless again didn't count against the old gentleman being properly looked after. She'd manage somehow. Miguel would have no need of a housekeeper—not with Cayo's 'willing staff'—and if his uncle could be persuaded to make the move he would have won, got rid of her supposedly poisonous presence without the outlay of a single euro of the bribe he'd so insultingly offered her.

The thought of him winning made her want to stamp her feet and scream! Yet despite that she knew that urging Miguel to accept the offer was the right thing to do.

She'd risen to the challenge of her present job—warmed to the concept of being a real help, useful and valued for once in her life—but she'd always meant to leave when she was satisfied that her old gentleman would be looked after and not left alone to his own absent-minded devices.

She was stunned when the man who had vowed to make her regret the day she was born now imparted, with the silken confidence of one who knew a weak spot when he saw one and had no hesitation in going straight for it, 'I know you better than you realise, Tio. In the past you have always refused my repeated offers because you have a kind heart—one of the gentlest and kindest, I know. To have availed yourself of comfortable surroundings and the best care would have meant dismissing Benita. So I suggest—urge—that you now bring Izzy with you, as your paid companion.'

Stunned by his suggestion, Izzy was left breathless when he turned again to her and gave her a smile of such dazzling brilliance that she came over all feverish. She could hardly believe what she was hearing as he continued, 'That way you won't be throwing her out of work and making her homeless, so your conscience won't give you indigestion! And I will be more than happy to welcome her as a guest in my home.'

Her mouth made an O of sheer astonishment as she stared at his dark, strong and shatteringly sexy features, searching for clues to his totally out-of-character behaviour. Her jumbled brain cells barely registered Miguel's amused reply. 'In that case, I agree. My hardworking housekeeper deserves a summer break after all her kindness to a foolish old man.'

She only scrambled for her senses after Cayo's elegantly long legs had carried him to the door, with the information that he was heading back to his apartment to await an expected fax from Hong Kong, but would be in touch later to make the necessary arrangements for their removal to his mountain home.

Closing her still gaping mouth, she watched him leave. He was up to something. Something devious. And that was scary. He'd offered her money to leave,

called her names, and made it plain that he thought her
a species of low-life—and yet here he was, actually
smiling at her, saying he'd welcome her as a guest in
his no-doubt palatial home. A castle, no less. It made
no sense at all.

'You've made the right decision,' she told the older
man. 'From what your nephew said it sounds as if you'll
have every comfort and care, and he seems genuinely
fond of you.' She conceded this somewhat unwillingly,
because she didn't want to admit there was anything
remotely human or caring about the guy—at least where
she was concerned. 'He'll be glad to provide for you,'
she went on, 'but count me out. I can't go with you. You
won't need a housekeeper. I'd only be a freeloader. I'd
rather earn an honest crust, and I'll soon find another
job, you'll see,' she ended, hoping she sounded more
confident than she felt.

'I understand,' Miguel responded flatly. 'But if that's
your decision I won't go either. We'll carry on as we
are.' His angular face softened in a smile. 'In fact, now
I come to think of it, I'm perfectly happy where I am.'

The penny dropped. Cayo must have foreseen this,
she realised sinkingly. After all, he had to know his
relative far better than she did. Hadn't he intimated that
the only reason the old gentleman hadn't taken up his
offer before had been because his uncle's tender conscience wouldn't have been easy if he'd made his
previous housekeeper unemployed? Probably unem-
ployable, judging by the state his humble little home
had been in when Izzy had first set eyes on it.

In all probability Miguel would have confided in his

nephew—told him of her own sorry circumstances when they'd first met—leading the younger man to realise that, having taken in a waif and stray, his gentle, soft-hearted uncle wasn't about to throw her out on the street!

Hence the amazing suggestion that she tag along, too, until he thought up some spectacularly nasty way to get rid of her! It made perfect sense.

Nothing else for it in the circumstances. But she was confident that once her old gentleman got settled in comfortable surroundings, with three good meals a day produced like clockwork, and no more scrimping and scraping, he would accept a sudden bout of homesickness, or a fictitious job offer back in her own country. Her decision to leave would be made before Cayo had worked out how to get her thrown out of his aristocratic home and probably out of the country. So, ignoring her better judgement, she told him breezily, 'If you insist on being stubborn then, okay—I'll go along, too. I've never lived in a castle before—should be fun. When do we go? Did he say?'

The opulent chauffeur-driven car took the steep gradients with effortless ease and, having finally overcome her fear of the hairpin bends and terrifying sheer drops, Izzy began to relax and enjoy the ever-changing vista. Precipitous mountains dropped to deep river valleys hazed over with the silvery green of olive groves and the deeper green of forest trees, occasionally broken by the clustered rooftops of picturesque villages.

She would relax and go with the flow, she decided.

Something she was good at, apparently. Her full lips curved into an amused smile as she recalled one of many lectures delivered by her father. 'Unlike James, you have no direction! You meander through life, drifting from one dead-end job to another—have you no ambition?'

Not of the academic kind. There was no way she could compete with her older, cleverer, much praised and doted-upon brother, so she didn't even try.

What her parents had never understood was that she *did* have an ambition. To fall in love, marry the man she loved, create a home together filled with warmth and love, and have children together. Children who would be equally adored and cherished, regardless of talent or lack thereof.

So far it was an unfulfilled ambition. The boys she'd dated in her teens had only been interested in one thing. Suspecting that because of her generous curves, and what James had once scathingly described as her 'blond bimbo looks', they'd clearly thought she would have been easy to get into bed and she'd steered clear, and put her secret ambition on hold until she'd met Marcus. She'd believed he was the one—that he really liked her, valued her. And he'd never tried to get her into the bedroom, which surely had to mean he'd respected her? In her mind's eye she had pictured his tall blond figure waiting as she floated up the aisle.

Alarmingly, the remembered and now despised image faded, and a tall dark figure, stiff with Spanish pride, took its place. Izzy gulped, and blinked the fleeting mind picture away with extreme violence.

To add to her discomfiture, Miguel said from beside

her, in an excruciatingly embarrassing coincidence, 'My nephew really should cease his unemotional, business-like arrangements with his occasional mistresses and take a wife. Las Palomas is exquisite, but sterile in its beauty. It needs a family to bring it to life. He will be there, waiting for us, and I shall tell him so. When the time is right.' He chuckled, as if something had amused him.

Too mortified by the mental image her subconscious had thrown up to respond directly, she asked instead, just to change the subject, 'You are familiar with his castle?'

'I was born there,' was his lightly dismissive response. 'It has been in our family for many generations. I left to attend university in England, and after gaining my doctorate I lectured. America, mainly. I rarely visited my family, and after the deaths of my parents—one shortly following the other, sadly—I never went again. Roman, my brother who was Cayo's father, had the use of Las Palomas while I preferred to live the quiet life of a humble scholar. The family have great wealth—'

'Let me get this straight,' Izzy butted in, wriggling round in her seat to face him more squarely, her brow pleated as she tried to follow what he was saying. Her voice was sharp with outrage on her old gentleman's behalf. 'You mean your brother got the lot—wealth and the castle and everything—and you got nothing?'

'Good heavens, child! What gave you that idea? As the oldest son I inherited vast landed estates, while Roman took over the shipping business—which I believe Cayo has expanded massively since his father passed away. He also finds time to manage the income from my estates—investments and suchlike. I have never been interested in the acquisition of material wealth. I have annual meetings with Cayo and his money men, and although I am grateful for my nephew's husbandry I must admit I find it all tedious. In any case,' he added more cheerfully, 'all I own will pass to Cayo in time, which is as it should be. The Garcia estates, properties and businesses will be under one ownership again, not divided.'

Her ready tongue stilled by Miguel's disclosure, Izzy struggled to get her thoughts in order. She ignored her companion's comments on the landmarks they were passing with aristocratic stateliness.

Despite all appearances the elderly man wasn't dirt-poor, struggling to exist on a pittance. He had to be loaded!

For the first time since she had known him she wanted to shake him! So, okay, he wasn't interested in money—given his other-worldliness, she could go along with that—but the thought of the way she'd boasted about her canniness in going to the market minutes before it closed to take advantage of stallhold-ers who were virtually giving produce away made her feel such a fool. He might have taken the opportunity—and there had been many—to tell her that such fru-gality wasn't necessary, or at least to enquire if the housekeeping allowance was so inadequate that it required such desperate measures.

She could forgive all that—laugh about it, even—but the misunderstanding had had dire consequences.

Cayo had believed those lies. Izzy Makepeace had been thrown out on her ear because she'd been trying to seduce a respectable banker and ensconce herself as his paid mistress, and next he'd heard she'd turned up as his wealthy uncle's housekeeper.

Up to no good.

An impression she must have confirmed with her demand for billions of pounds! Letting him think that a mere pay-off wouldn't satisfy her—that she was intent on getting her hands on his uncle's fortune!

Apart from being fond of his elderly relative, and not wanting to see him falling into the clutches of a woman he saw as a mercenary gold-digger, he wouldn't want to lose his inheritance.

Enough motive to explain his chilling threat that he'd make her regret the day she'd been born if she didn't remove herself from his uncle's vicinity. It came back to haunt her. He'd meant it! She was going to have to confront him with the facts—make him understand that she had believed all along that his eccentric uncle had nothing more substantial to live on than some measly pension or other. It was imperative she make him believe that in agreeing to work for the old gentleman she hadn't had designs on a fortune she hadn't even known existed.

'We are arriving.'

The volume at which Miguel's statement was delivered alerted her to the possibility that it wasn't the first time he'd given that snippet of information. Izzy blinked and refocused her eyes. A high stone wall snaked down the mountainside, and they were entering a curving driveway that wound its way to a magnificent fortified palace—a statement of power and wealth if ever she saw one. Her stomach wriggled with a flock of hyperactive butterflies.

How was she going to convince the cynical owner of this lot that she was innocent of all accusations? Convince him so thoroughly that he'd rethink whatever devious plans he'd made in order to carry out his earlier threat when she'd already dug her grave with her too-ready tongue?

CHAPTER FIVE

AS THE stately car passed through a massive stone arch and drew to a well-bred halt in the inner courtyard, Cayo got to his feet and left the arbour-shaded carved stone bench, emerging into dazzling sunlight.

Phase one completed. The grim line of his mouth softened. His beloved mule-headed uncle was finally safely back where he belonged, to be surrounded by the comfort and luxury that was his birthright. His conscience could rest easily in that respect.

Phase two was yet to be started. The successful removal of one money-grabbing blonde. His thickly fringed dark eyes sharpened with steely intent, boding ill for anyone with the temerity to cross him.

Advancing, he forced a welcoming smile and watched his chauffeur step round to open a rear door. He handed the little gold-digger out before moving round to perform the same courtesy for his uncle.

Waiting in cynical expectation for her to trip eagerly to Miguel's side, tuck her arm solicitously through his and simper up at him from her diminutive height, Cayo narrowed his eyes as instead of acting out the part he'd mentally assigned her she made a beeline across the courtyard to where he was standing.

Her silvery blond hair was, as usual, artfully tousled in a naturally sexy style that many women would gladly pay top dollar to achieve. She was dressed in a faded top that lovingly cleaved to her bountiful breasts, and cotton trousers that tantalisingly moulded her thighs and ended just below her knees. As his body reacted in a despised surge of lust, he wondered, at a tangent, how such bog-standard clothes could make her look so provocatively sensual, when the groomed and expertly painted women who circled like hopeful sharks on the periphery of his life could spend thousands on designer exclusives and leave his libido stone-cold.

He shouldn't knock his primitive response to what Augustin del Amo had lip-lickingly described as 'a lush little package', he supposed acidly, given the task ahead of him.

She had refused to accept a financial inducement to leave his uncle alone, therefore it was up to him to seduce her away from any thought of getting her claws into the older man. A task that sat ill with his ingrained sense of chivalry and honour, honed by centuries of ancestral Spanish pride.

He kept his smile in place with difficulty, hiding the grim, distasteful thoughts that occupied his mind as she pattered up to him. Her delicate cheekbones flushed a soft rose colour as she came to a halt and planted her hands on her curvaceous hips, and her neat chin tilted upwards as she demanded breathily, 'I need to talk to you. Now. In private.'

The smile vanished. His black eyes were cool and distant. She was in no position to make demands of him. 'If you will excuse me, it is my custom to see my guests settled.'

Ignoring her agitated, 'Oh—but listen—' he strode past her, and Izzy swung round to watch him greet his uncle, one arm around the older, shorter man's shoulders. For some reason she wished he could have greeted her that way, with obvious affection and warmth, and then she wished she hadn't wished that at all—because it showed her up as being really stupid.

And maybe she shouldn't have demanded they talk just like that, she decided, feeling flattened. He was obviously adding a total lack of manners to his tally of her sins, branding her as not fit for polite company. But she'd been so anxious to put him straight about her ignorance of Miguel's true financial situation that she had been able to think of nothing else since the shattering revelation that, far from living a hand-to-mouth existence out of financial necessity, Miguel had no idea, and no interest in, how much he was worth.

Just like her to open her big mouth and put her foot in it!

Embarrassment painted her heart-shaped face with a hot flood of fiery colour as the two men joined her. Miguel flung an arm wide, encompassing the courtyard, the magnificent central fountain, the tubs of exotic flowering shrubs and the white doves fluttering from the shady stone arcades that led through to the no-doubt sumptuous living quarters, and asked, 'You approve, Izzy?'

'I'm sure your companion is most suitably impressed,' Cayo said drily, before she could respond, and immediately cursed himself for the sarcastic tone. He was going to have to try harder—to act in a duplicitous manner completely foreign to his straightforward nature if he was to have a hope in hell of persuading her that of the two vast fortunes she could see dangling in front of her greedy eyes *his* was the one to aim for.

'Ramona—my housekeeper—will show you to the rooms that have been readied for you, Tio,' Cayo imparted. Izzy trailed after them as they entered a vast marble-paved hall. 'They are on the ground floor, close to the library. You will have no need to use stairs or find your way about the warren of passages—unless you wish to reacquaint yourself with your childhood home.' His austere features softened in a smile that made him seem human and just impossibly handsome, Izzy thought, deploring the toe-curling effect it had on her as he went on, 'And don't worry. Your books and papers have not been unpacked. No one will touch or muddle them,' he assured the older man gently. 'You may arrange them in the library at your leisure.'

He really cared about his uncle, Izzy granted as introductions were made to the housekeeper and a handful of wide-eyed maids. Cayo gave instructions in rapid Spanish which sent the super-efficient-looking housekeeper leading Miguel to an arched doorway at the far side of the great hall and the maids scurrying to do his bidding. He spoke and things happened.

He firmly believed that she was up to no good—had attached herself to his uncle for mercenary reasons— and he cared enough for the old gentleman to make sure she took herself off with her tail between her legs. Now that she knew that her impoverished and neglected old gentleman was nothing of the sort, she could understand where he was coming from. Especially since he'd heard the del Amos' lies.

She shivered, and nearly leapt out of her skin when he touched the bare flesh of her arm, making her feel as if she'd been prodded by an electrically charged pin. It fuzzed up her brain to such an extent that she couldn't take in what he was saying until the pressure of those lean bronzed fingers around her arm increased and he repeated, 'I will show you to your suite of rooms and see you settled.'

'What? Oh, right—' She attempted to claim back her arm, but the pressure of his fingers simply increased as he led her to an enormous stone staircase. Mounting it, she felt like a prisoner being led to a cell and her mouth went dry. She had to explain. Had to. But, remembering her earlier *faux-pas*, she knew she had to wait and not launch forth when members of his staff were criss-crossing the hall below, well within earshot.

Partway up the soaring staircase, a corridor led off to the right, dimly lit, its stone walls hung with ancient and probably priceless tapestries. Ahead, the corridor branched in three directions. The whole place was an intimidating mystery.

Izzy wished she'd never agreed to come here. She only had because she had thought then that it was the right thing to do for the sake of Miguel and his future wellbeing, believing as she had that he was existing on a mere pittance and it was time that his selfish, wealthy nephew took care of him.

But it hadn't been necessary. Miguel, had he been so minded, could have lived in luxury. She knew that now. Too late.

A blinding flash of insight had her digging her heels into the cool marble flooring and accusing, 'As you're so fond of calling the shots, why didn't you just go ahead and arrange for your uncle to have a properly paid, decent housekeeper years ago? You pretend to care for him, so you could have done that. It took me, a total stranger, about ten minutes to realise he's so wrapped up in his work he can't be bothered about taking proper care of himself!'

She met his black gaze without flinching. She knew the answer—didn't she just! He'd only muscled into his relative's life now, taken over, because he believed— wrongly—that she was about to weasel her way into taking his inheritance. As if he weren't already eye-wateringly wealthy in his own right! Greedy, or what?

He lifted his proud head, centuries of Spanish high breeding carved into the unforgettably handsome features. 'You will moderate your tone and keep your skewed opinions to yourself while you are a guest in my home,' he advised, as smooth and cold as glass.

He did not take personal attacks—especially not from a mouthy little madam who was no better than she should be. Seducing her away from her plans to get the naïve Miguel firmly in her clutches, the devious but necessary assignment he'd set himself, suddenly felt too far beneath his honourable nature to be contemplated. There had to be another way.

Acidly polite, he stepped ahead and suggested, 'Perhaps we may proceed?'

Cringing at that put-down, Izzy followed, engulfed by frustration. He was really good at making out she was an ill-mannered boor—not fit to sully his splendid home, where he was insulated by fabulous wealth and had an army of servants to cater to his slightest whim. But then he was labouring under the misapprehension that she was some sleazy sort of career mistress—that, having failed with the oily banker, she'd set her sights on his uncle.

Time to set the record straight. Convince him that she wasn't what he thought she was. A huge smile wreathed her expressive features as she imagined his grovelling apology—which she would consider and finally accept with dignity, giving herself the high moral ground for once!

On that cheering thought she pattered on, catching up with him as he flung open a door and stepped just inside the threshold of the loveliest room she'd ever set eyes on.

'Wow!' Her big eyes widened. Acres of luxurious white carpet, panelled walls painted a delicate misty primrose-yellow, tall windows with gauzy white drapes, a group of three comfy chairs upholstered in yellow silk placed around a low coffee table, bowls of beautifully arranged roses to perfume the air, and what looked like a fully stocked drinks cabinet.

Cayo dug his hands into the pockets of stylish chinos and drawled, 'Your sitting room. The bedroom is through that door, with *en suite* bathroom, of course. I'll leave you to relax and will see you at dinner.'

Her own bathroom. Of course—what else? The urge to explore was almost overwhelming, but the imperative to put Cayo Garcia straight was stronger. Smartly stepping in front of him, she folded her arms across her slender middle, lifting her face to his. 'Hang on a tick. I have to say something. It's really important.'

'*Sí?*' Strongly marked brows drew together as his eyes met hers. So deep a blue, with the almost childlike clarity of innocence. Deeply misleading. He sucked in a sharp breath. She had an exquisite face. Taken individually, her features were not perfect, but they added up to an exquisitely fascinating whole, framed by wayward strands of silver-gilt that looked as soft as silk.

'Tis a Pity She's a Whore, he thought with mental dryness, then, inexplicably, felt his heart lurch with a spasm of sadness at the waste of all this luscious loveliness, packaging, as it did, a mercenary and immoral soul.

'Listen—' Izzy knew she sounded breathless. She was having difficulty stringing words together in her head, never mind getting them out of her mouth. It was the way he was looking at her that was so dreadfully unsettling. It made her tummy squirm, then tense, her mouth run dry.

'Well?' Cayo murmured without intonation, grimly amused as he pondered on what she was going to come up with—what was now so important. Something as twisted as her last outburst, at a guess.

Izzy just stared, moistening her dry lips with the tip of her tongue, fighting the awful dart of heat in the pit of her tummy that looking into his dark eyes always produced. Eyes as beautiful as his commanding masculine features…

Making a huge effort, she got out, 'I know what you think of me, and I don't blame you. I guess you'd always take the word of a big-wheel banker and his wife over a lowly domestic servant. But I promise you it wasn't like that. I'm sorry to have to say this about your friend, a man you obviously respect, but Señor del Amo was the one trying it on, not the other way around.'

Once she'd launched forth, the words just came tumbling out. 'And I had no idea that Miguel wasn't dirt-poor until he told me on the way here. Truly! He told me that he was born here, that the family wealth had been divided between him and your father. It was the first I knew of it—and you could have knocked me down with a feather!'

Nice try. But not nearly good enough. Cayo's eyes followed the movement as she brushed a silvery strand back from her forehead, pink with effort. His thick black lashes drifted down over sparkling jet eyes as he took in the taut expectancy of her voluptuous body. She was waiting for him to say he believed her, to treat her as if she was all sweetness and light, take the heat off and leave her free to wheedle her way even further into Miguel's affections. Did she think he'd been born yesterday?

'I see.' He was almost purring now. 'So let's recap.' His smile was devastatingly challenging. 'You took pity on a poor old man, and agreed to keep house for him for the sort of miserable wages that would have had any normal working girl heading for the hills, out of the goodness of your heart?'

Izzy shifted uncomfortably. From his point of view her decision would look suspect, she recognised sickly. It was up to her to make him understand. She squared her slim shoulders and said, with far more confidence than she felt, 'I was in a fix, and so was he. He needed someone to keep house. I needed a job and a roof over my head. And, yes, the wages he offered were even less than I received from the del Amos—and, believe me, they were nothing to write home about. I was sorry for him, and anyway I only intended to stay until something could be arranged for his future care. You know how not with-it he is when it comes to noticing what goes on around him—remembering to eat—that sort of stuff.'

'Indeed.'

Izzy let out a huff of relief. He was beginning to believe her. She hated it when people thought badly of her—particularly him. Why him particularly? she wondered dazedly—and then the beginnings of exultation took a smart nose-dive.

'Yet you are here. Still with him. Even though you know his future wellbeing is secure, and when you have already said you intended to leave as soon as that situation arose. I wonder why that is?'

She could recognise the note of sarcasm when she heard it. Izzy felt her skin crawl with the heat of discomfiture. Believing that honesty was the only policy, she mumbled, 'Well, I guess it might look odd. Only you *did* invite me. I told your uncle that as I was no longer needed I wouldn't tag along. But he refused to come if I didn't.' She raised her head, her eyes very wide, willing him to understand. 'You see, as I felt responsible for him, I guess *he* feels responsible for *me*.'

His gaze was calmly assessing. 'I see.'

Izzy swallowed jerkily. Did that mean he believed her? Had decided not to make her regret the day she was born?

Her bones turned to water when he gave her the benefit of his high-voltage smile and told her, 'I suggest you make yourself at home—rest until we meet at dinner. I will have a pot of English tea sent up to you.'

He walked out, his smile vanishing as he closed the door behind him.

She was devious and clever. She'd got her ingenuous patter down to a fine art. She could put on that look of earnest innocence and talk her way out of a double-locked and barred dungeon!

Only he wasn't gullible. His firm jaw set, he strode down to check on how his uncle was settling in, reflecting that her look of wide-eyed innocence didn't gel with the sexy body that oozed temptation.

His mouth tightened. Time to put his plan into action. Show her the sort of luxury she could only have dreamed of. Dangle the prospect of great wealth in front of her pretty nose. No need to actually bed her—just let her believe he wanted to, give her the impression that he was too much of a gentleman to take advantage of his uncle's companion. He would wait for her to get desperate enough to secure a massive fortune and openly encourage him, then make sure Miguel saw and understood what was happening—saw her in her true colours. Saw her as the greedy little sex-pot she was and hardened his highly moralistic heart against her.

Then Izzy Makepeace would be history!

Cayo laid down his dessert fork and leaned back in his chair, his smile just slightly apologetic. 'I asked for a simple meal. It's been a long day for you, Tio. Which is why I decided we wouldn't dress for dinner.'

Izzy, her mouth full of delicious ice cream layer cake, widened her eyes. If this had been a simple meal, then what would a lavish spread have been like?

Too hungry to be nervous—her stomach had been rumbling alarmingly when one of the maids had appeared at nine o'clock to escort her down to dinner— she had tucked in to a salad of roast peppers, then turbot fillets poached in wine, followed by slices of guinea fowl on a bed of tomatoes and onions, and ended with a pudding that had practically made her swoon!

And as for dressing down instead of up, as would seem usual—well, she was already wearing her best: a plain blue cotton shift. Now she did feel nervous—even more so when Cayo remarked, apparently idly, as he toyed with the stem of his wine glass, 'As you might remember, Tio, at the end of this month I host the annual ball for my tenant farmers and estate workers, my business associates and their wives.'

'Indeed.' Miguel pushed his do-it-yourself repaired

spectacles back up his nose. 'Am I expected to—as Izzy would doubtless say—strut my stuff?' He beamed at her and she gave back a hesitant smile, dreading the thought that she would be expected to put in an appearance at what would be a glittering event, and wondering if his High and Mighty Cayoness was busily chalking up another black mark against her for teaching his scholarly relative low-grade slang.

But, far from giving her that look of cold displeasure, he was actually smiling at her—just as he'd done before he'd left her room earlier. Maybe, she thought with a swoop of optimism, he had really thought about what she'd said and did believe her side of the story!

Her optimism increased by leaps and bounds when Cayo informed Miguel gently, 'It would be nice if you showed your face in the afternoon, when the locals are being entertained—you are often in their thoughts, and seeing you in your home setting at long last would give them pleasure. But if the evening events are too much for you to endure you may retire with my blessing.' His smile widened as his stunning eyes sought hers and held. 'No, I was thinking more about Izzy when I mentioned the coming celebrations. With the ball coming up in a fortnight she'll want to choose something glamorous to wear, and I need to be in Madrid tomorrow. I suggest she comes with me to find something suitable— that's if you can spare your companion for a couple of days?'

'Of course—an excellent suggestion! I shall be unpacking my papers and shall neither need nor want any help.'

So he *was* expecting Cinderella to go to the ball! Her heart headed for the soles of her feet, and with difficulty Izzy broke eye contact, biting down on her full lower lip. She could drown in those eyes, and was ashamed of the way he could make something pulse wickedly in the most secret part of her anatomy—especially when he was being nice to her, she thought in consternation as she felt her generous breasts tingle and push against the cotton barrier of her dress.

Aware that she was expected to say something, she wriggled uncomfortably in her chair and mumbled in agitation, 'Nice thought. But I'll pass. Thanks all the same.'

Refusing to be trapped by those dark Spanish eyes again, she gave her attention to Miguel as he asked, with his usual gentle humour, 'And why is that, *cara*? Do you carry a choice of sumptuous ballgowns in your rucksack?'

Mortified, Izzy's face blazed with embarrassed colour. 'You know I don't! I can't afford glamorous gear. But as I'll give the fancy ball a miss, there's no problem.'

Cayo's eyes swept her pink and mutinous face. Still playing games. Waiting for Miguel. He hadn't missed that telltale endearment; it had made his hackles rise. Well, he would give her what she was obviously waiting for. And then some.

He drained the last of his wine and set the glass back on the table, drawling, 'I don't live in the Dark Ages, expecting a relative's companion to be kept firmly out of sight on such an occasion! And as for your lack of funds—' A lean, tanned hand swept dismissively. 'Forget it. All that is necessary will be provided.' He sent her a look of sparkling challenge. 'It will be my pleasure.'

Izzy's tummy looped the loop, her face flushing. By the sound of it he had thought it over and decided to believe her side of the story! The hot surge of relief left her feeling weak. Although, she admitted, she shouldn't really care what he thought of her. They were nothing to each other. But at least it meant that he'd forgotten his hateful threat to make her regret the day she'd been born. He wouldn't be offering to take her to Madrid with him and buy her something suitable to wear if that was still on his agenda, would he?

Even so... 'I don't accept charity, *señor*.' Pride brought her chin up, leading to a collision course with those brilliant dark eyes. She compressed her soft, wide mouth as a throb of sexual awareness pulsed deep within her. She hated the physical effect he was having on her, but knew she could do nothing about it.

Her silly crush on Marcus had never left her feeling so helpless and out of control. Marcus had made her feel soft and gooey—motherly, even—worrying over whether he was feeding himself properly and wrapping up warmly when the north wind blew. She only had to look into Cayo's magnificent eyes to turn into a molten wreck!

'Charity doesn't come into it,' Miguel injected swiftly. 'You have been kind beyond words to a foolish old man. I am in your debt. And as I am still your employer I insist that you accompany my nephew.' He laid a gentle hand over hers in an affectionate gesture not unnoticed by Cayo's darkly glittering eyes. 'When you stepped in as my housekeeper I did you a grave disservice, as Cayo rightly pointed out. I was thoughtless and selfish. You will go to Madrid and allow Cayo to make amends on my behalf—to please me.'

Touched by that entreaty, Izzy felt her spine sag. She had grown very fond of the elderly man, and he was obviously beating himself up over his earlier absent-mindedness. The way she'd had to struggle to keep his household going on a pittance would have made a cat laugh. It had been a situation born not out of necessity or meanness, but out of his lack of interest in or knowledge of the world as it was today.

'Okay,' she agreed grudgingly. 'If it pleases you.' She flushed with discomfiture as Miguel gave her hand a final squeeze and laid aside his linen napkin.

'Excellent! That's settled, then!'

But Izzy felt far from settled. Nerves were tingling all over her body. The prospect of spending time in Cayo's sole company made her feel dreadfully uneasy. And not because he harboured an ill will towards her, as had been the case until they'd had that talk earlier, but because for the first time in her life she was consumed by a deplorable lust for a man who was as far out of her league as the moon!

CHAPTER SIX

LUST could be conquered. Couldn't it?

Of course it could, Izzy reassured herself wildly as Cayo entered the sumptuous suite she'd been given through an interconnecting door that led, presumably, to his rooms. It was an intimacy she wasn't in the least ready for.

No need to get all hot and bothered, she assured herself shakily, trying her best not to look as agitated as she felt. He was now wearing a pale grey silk-sheened suit that screamed top designer and enhanced his wide shoulders, narrow waist, snaky hips and long, powerful legs with classy and understated elegance.

He took her breath away.

Tearing her eyes from him with difficulty, she stared down at her toes. When he'd piloted the helicopter from Las Palomas to a private airstrip on the outskirts of Madrid he'd been wearing cargo pants and a torso-hugging sweatshirt, and she'd thought that she'd never seen a man who exuded such raw sexuality. She had spent most of the flight listening to his occasional comments through the headphones and telling herself to start thinking like a sensible adult. Admiring such a fine specimen of manhood was perfectly natural. But wanting—literally aching—to get up close and personal was right out of order.

Now, dressed as he was, the raw sexuality was still there in spades, but there was something extra. Power. Mastery. And that was scary—especially as her heart was racing, her pulses fluttering alarmingly, shameful hunger coiling deep in her pelvis.

She wished he'd say something to break the tension she could feel all around her, but when he did she wished he hadn't.

'If you're rested and ready, we'll go. I have a car waiting.'

Rested? Some hope!

She'd been pacing her room as if her legs had discovered the secret of perpetual motion ever since she'd arrived at this eye-poppingly luxurious hotel, which he'd casually informed her he owned—among loads of others. Part of his property portfolio, apparently. She'd been wondering what she was doing here, and beating herself up for so weakly agreeing to come in the first place. The leopard, it seemed, had changed his spots, and was being really, really nice to her. And she didn't think she could handle that because she could only just about keep her lustful yearnings under control when he was being vile.

And now he was suggesting—still in that warmly considerate tone—that if she was ready they were to go somewhere together.

She parted her lips to ask where, but all that emerged was an embarrassing croak. She cleared her throat, took a deep breath, avoided his stunning eyes and managed, 'I'll pass. You go. Wherever.'

Nice try, Cayo admitted grudgingly. Conversation had been limited on the helicopter flight, but she'd hung on his every word when he'd pointed out places and buildings of interest as the chauffeur-driven limo had whisked them through the suburbs and into the centre of the city. She had only withdrawn into her secret thoughts when he'd made sure she knew he owned the hotel they were to stay at. One of many throughout the world, and all of the same exquisite quality, he'd told her, as if he were used to vulgar boasting when nothing could be further from the truth.

In any other domestic servant he would have put her current subdued mood down to being out of her depth. But with Izzy Makepeace he knew better. She would be mentally totting up the value of this prime property, multiplying it by many, adding it to his export empire and licking her lips and planning tactics!

His chiselled mouth twisted wryly. But his drawl was smooth and soft as silk as he advanced, 'I don't think Madame Fornier would appreciate if it I attempted to try on the clothes she's laid aside in your stead.'

In dire danger of totally losing it, Izzy struggled to contain a sudden and alarmingly hysterical explosion of giggles at the picture that immediately presented itself—this ultra-masculine Spanish aristo trying to shoehorn himself into something several sizes too small, silky and slinky. Her eyes were sparkling with dancing laughter lights as she plucked her bulgy padded cotton handbag from the bed and slung it over her shoulder, stuffed her feet back into the spiky high heels she'd worn as a much-needed confidence booster, and announced, 'Fine. Let's go.'

Grab the first halfway suitable dress to wear to a ball she didn't want to attend and her ordeal would be over. They could head back to the castle and Miguel's easy, safe company. There was only so much of the magnificent Cayo Garcia's undiluted, sexy presence she could take without turning into a gibbering wreck of raging hormones.

Standing aside as she preceded him through the door, Cayo's eyes narrowed cynically as she swayed ahead of him at speed, on those ridiculously teetering heels. He deplored the way the enticing movement of her shapely backside awoke his most basic primal instincts, harshly reminding himself that the mention of a new wardrobe had got her moving as if she'd been shot from a cannon. Her big blue eyes had lit up like a Christmas tree at the thought of getting her hands on a whole bunch of freebies.

She couldn't hide her greed, he thought with distaste—then promptly reminded himself that her greed was what he was working on. Cocoon her in luxury, shower her with gifts, demonstrate what it was like to live in the lap of luxury, totally spoiled and pampered, and she would switch her avaricious attention from his clueless uncle to him. Mission accomplished.

And then Miss Izzy Makepeace would receive one large and unpleasant surprise.

His wide, sensual mouth quirked with satisfaction as he caught up with her and laid a seemingly friendly arm across her narrow shoulders, guiding her towards the waiting car. 'It's not far. My driver will wait to take us on to the restaurant—we have a table booked for nine o'clock.' He eased her into the rear seat. 'He will then take your purchases back to the hotel.'

Leaning forward, he spoke rapidly in his own language to the driver, and as he settled himself beside her Izzy slid into the far corner. 'I could eat back at the hotel—have something in my room,' she objected.

She was already really, really nervous around him—terrified of the effect he had on her. Sharing dinner with him in some upmarket restaurant would be too much. Besides, dressed as she was, in a crumpled cotton skirt and one of her ordinary old T-shirts, she'd look horribly out of place. An excuse he'd understand, surely?

'I'd rather—honestly. And in any case I'm not dressed to go any place fancy,' she stressed as the car drew out into the early-evening traffic.

She stole a look at him from beneath long, fringing lashes and felt her heart stop, then flutter on. Angled from the corner, his eyes met hers. He was smiling. He was gorgeous! She felt dizzy.

'Nonsense.' His voice was like a slow, sexily warm caress. 'It is your first time in Madrid, yes? I insist you enjoy our city, and you won't do that by hiding in a hotel room.'

She had turned away from him now, her head downbent on the slender stalk of her neck, her glorious hair hiding her profile. But he wasn't falling for the shrinking violet act—just as he hadn't fallen for her story placing Augustin del Amo as the villain of the piece. It hadn't rung true.

He had no liking for the man, but he didn't need a degree in psychology to understand that as a highly respected banker—regardless of his alleged discreet extra-marital tendencies—he would have far too much sense to foul his own nest. And Izzy Makepeace had been working for him, living under his roof.

Del Amo might have described her—accurately—as a 'lush little package', but with his business and social standing, and his wife's gimlet eyes on him, that would have been as far as it went. Del Amo might be many things he disliked, but he wasn't a fool.

Cayo snapped out of his thoughts as the car came to a stop. Relieving his driver of the necessity, he strode round to hand the tricky little madam out, reflecting that she wouldn't be able to hide her true colours when her greedy eyes fell on the delights Madame Fornier would have ready for approval.

His hand curved around her waist, urging her towards an arched doorway set in an elegant neo-classical building that looked nothing like any dress shop she had ever seen. Yet discreet gilded letters over the lintel announced 'Fornier' so she guessed, sinkingly, that it was some really fancy place where only the titled or extremely wealthy were admitted.

Izzy's skin prickled. She wished he wouldn't touch her. It made her feel quite dizzy! But at least, she comforted herself, he now believed her side of the del Amo story. He would still be being vile to her if he didn't—not nice, friendly and courteous, treating her to this trip to Madrid, a night in his fancy hotel and a new dress. The fact that he now didn't think the worst of her made her feel a little warmer inside. She was used to people finding fault—from her family to her past employers—so when someone was being nice to her she felt ridiculously like a tail-wagging, fawning dog!

And thinking of dogs—

Izzy dug her heels into the paving slabs. Not much more than a puppy. A miserable bundle of matted gingery hair and sticking-out ribs, cringing in the shadows of the archway, shivering in spite of the sultry evening heat.

'Oh, you poor little thing!' Izzy met the mournful brown eyes, registered the heart-rending whimper in response to her voice and was totally lost. Leaning forward, she scooped the pathetic little animal up. It wriggled ecstatically against her and nuzzled into the angle of her neck, its long, practically hairless tail furiously wagging.

Turning to Cayo, ignoring his frown, she stated, 'I can feel all his bones—he's starving!'

'And likely to be crawling with fleas. Put it down. Madame Fornier would not appreciate—'

'No.' Izzy stood her ground, her chin lifting stubbornly. No way was he going to make her abandon the needy puppy. 'I'm taking him back with me. He needs a bath and food. I can't just leave him here—pretend I haven't seen him. Even if you can!'

And then, because the Spaniard's frown had deepened she added, less confrontationally, 'Look, don't think I'm not grateful for your offer of a new dress. I am. But I'm not bothered. I can live without a fancy dress, but this little thing won't last long unless someone cares for it. Pop in and apologise to Madame Whatever. Then we can take this poor little scrap back to the hotel.'

She actually meant it.

Cayo's spiralling perplexity deepened his frown still further. Had she been like this—five foot nothing of fierce protectiveness—when she'd stumbled across his uncle and the old man had collapsed? In that case she'd accepted a job at wages that were less than rock bottom in order to care for an old man she'd believed to be neglected and near destitute, caring for him when she'd thought that no one else did.

In this case she wasn't 'bothered' about acquiring a whole new wardrobe of designer gear. The immediate care of a scruffy mutt was of more importance.

Nothing seemed as clear-cut as it formerly had. Had he been wrong about her? Had his famous sound judgement let him down badly?

Moving forward, he set one final test. 'Does it have a collar or name tag?' Receiving a decisive and negative shake of her tousled blond head, he opined, 'Then I'm afraid it's been abandoned. I'll have my driver take it to a vet while we keep our appointment.'

As if the puppy had understood every word, it gave a piteous whimper and began licking Izzy's face. Her hands tightened protectively around the scrawny body. She could feel its little heart beating frantically. 'No!' She could just imagine a huge white-coated man with a lethal injection bending over the poor little thing. 'I can look after it!'

'*Bueno!*' Cayo's mouth firmed decisively. 'Wait in the car—and take that flea-ridden disaster with you.'

The last thing he needed in his life was a mangy puppy that would grow up into a mangy adult mongrel, but he knew when he was beaten and was practical enough to give way with good grace. Besides, for the first time in his adult life he felt as if he was on shaky ground, unsure of himself. He deplored the feeling.

Reaching into an inner pocket for his cellphone, he made three short, tersely specific calls with the utter confidence of a man who was used to getting what he wanted, to having others jump when he told them to. Then he strode towards the waiting car, his eyes glinting narrowly as he sought an answer to the question of whether he'd been catastrophically wrong about Izzy Makepeace.

He was never wrong!

And yet…

Izzy's head was spinning and she couldn't stop grinning. She and the puppy had been treated like royalty ever since they'd arrived back at the hotel.

The manager had been waiting for them. Obsequious and deferential, he had accompanied them up to her suite, barking out rapidfire orders to two of his staff, who had filled a plastic bath with warm water. To demonstrate how important he was, the manager had minutely inspected the bottle of baby shampoo before handing it to her.

Aware of all eyes on her, of Cayo sardonically distant in the background, Izzy had knelt and lowered the puppy into the water. Benji, as she'd already decided to name him, had taken immediate exception to the unfamiliar experience and scrabbled frantically to escape the unwanted dunking, soaking her and the bathroom floor, and venting cross baby yelps as she'd lathered and rinsed him, only subsiding when she had finally lifted him out and wrapped him in the big fluffy towel immediately handed to her.

Leaving his staff to empty and remove the bath, the manager had ushered her through to the opulent sitting room, where a low table had already been laid with a bone china plate of thinly sliced chicken breast meat and a silver bowl of water.

Now, oblivious to the cleaners, who had arrived to put the bathroom back to its former pristine state, Izzy watched the puppy wolf down the chicken with enormous satisfaction, too pleased with the frankly amazing and gratifying outcome of what she had believed would be a huge problem to worry as a vet and his assistant arrived, bowed down with packages.

As Spanish seemed the order of the day, Izzy left the vet and his helper to their examination, contenting herself with exploring the packages, bulky and small. Cayo had arranged for the delivery of everything to make a small puppy happy and comfortable. There was a comfy padded dog bed, a soft blanket, a pack of puppy kibbles, feeding bowls and a minute collar and lead of the softest leather imaginable.

When the vet had finally made his departure Cayo lobbed a look—part exasperated, part amused—at Izzy, as she knelt over the dog bed, where the animal had finally settled.

Smiling, Izzy rose from her knees, turned and faced him, her hands on her curvy hips. 'You don't fool me, Cayo Garcia! You're nothing like as hard-hearted as you try to appear!'

Her huge eyes were glowing. They looked like priceless sapphires. The front of her T-shirt was soaked, moulding the thin fabric to every lethally voluptuous curve of her breasts.

His breath felt hot in his lungs. Whether or not she had mercenary intentions, whether she was a scheming, greedy gold-digger or a soft-hearted innocent in need of protection from her own headstrong, thoughtless altruism he had yet to discover. Only one thing was clear: she was a walking man-trap!

She was moving towards him, her luscious hips a swaying temptation, her smile wide and dazzling enough to make a man believe the sun had come out at darkest midnight. A small hand stretched out to him.

'He's really cute when he's asleep. Come and look. His name's Benji—'

'I'll pass.'

His voice sounded rusty. Something gave a violent wrench deep inside him. His face felt hot. Time to get out of here. Right now! He tore his eyes away from the temperature-raising outline of her nipples, the way the wet fabric clung.

'I suggest you get changed. I'll have dinner brought to you.' And he exited through the door that connected to his suite before he could give in to the shaft of driving sexual need that was invading his entire system.

CHAPTER SEVEN

IT FELT exactly like a blow between the eyes. Izzy
blinked back the sudden sting of tears. For a few
minutes she'd been feeling relaxed, even hopeful that
her volatile relationship with Cayo could be somehow
redefined, that there was at least an outside chance of
an easy friendship between them—and who knew
where that might lead? A girl could dream, couldn't
she?

She'd almost—just fleetingly, of course, in a moment of insanity—believed herself to be falling in love
with him!

How feeble could a girl get?

Disconsolately she plodded to the bathroom,
stripped off her sodden clothes and had a quick shower.
She took ages towelling herself dry, brooding over her
lack of judgement.

The things he'd done to make sure the stray puppy
received all necessary care had made her think that he'd
transmogrified from the kind of guy who would walk
past a starving small animal without batting an eyelash

into someone who cared enough to summon vets, hotel managers and plates of chicken. A man with a kind heart.

How silly!

He'd only done it because he'd seen she'd been adamant about rescuing the puppy, and he hadn't wanted his precious hotel infected with fleas or to have to put up with her loudly wailing recriminations if the 'flea-ridden disaster', as he'd unflatteringly named poor Benji, had died!

And there she'd been, making a first unselfconscious friendly gesture towards him, wanting to share her pleasure with him, making a fool of herself, almost falling in love with him! And what had he done?

Flattened her!

Just as Marcus had done. The only difference being that Marcus had been Mr. Charming to her face, while ridiculing her behind her back and taking really hurtful advantage of her admittedly silly crush, and Cayo had been up-front, letting her know to her face that he wasn't interested in sharing a warm, happy moment with her.

Just what his reaction would be if she inadvertently allowed him to see that she fancied him rotten didn't bear thinking about!

Knowing her, and her inability to hide what she was feeling, that just might happen. She was going to have to be extra careful around him, she stressed firmly as she got into the complimentary bathrobe. She left the *en suite* bathroom to find that a tray of utterly delicious-looking food plus a bottle of wine had been left on one of the tables—a table that fronted one of the delicate antique sofas.

She poked glumly at the food, but she wasn't hungry. So she poured herself some wine and, sipping, took it with her as she went to check on the puppy. He was still asleep. She almost wished he wasn't. She could do with some company.

She almost jumped out of her skin when a knock on the suite's door heralded the arrival of two porters with arms full of boxes which, smiling serenely, they deposited in a mountainous heap.

'For you, *señorita*,' the taller of the two explained, his accent thick. 'With the compliments of Señor Garcia.' They were both grinning at her now. Knowingly? Izzy's face flamed. Did they think she was the hotel owner's bit on the side?

Too mortified to be able to speak, even to say thank you, she watched them leave, swallowed the remainder of her wine in two thirsty gulps, and approached the boxes as if each and every one contained a time bomb.

They were matt black, with 'Fornier' inscribed in elegant gilt lettering. She felt so guilty she needed another gulp of wine. She smothered a giggle. The situation she'd gone and got herself into was turning her—she who rarely drank except the occasional small glass—into an alcoholic!

Poor *madame*! Because they'd failed to keep their appointment, Cayo had made the poor woman pack up the selection of dresses she'd been meant to choose from and had them sent over to the hotel. Didn't he care what trouble he put people to on his behalf?

Probably not.

Definitely not!

Well, the least she could do was make her choice now. Surely one out of what looked like a massive selection would fit? Not having laid eyes on her, *madame* would probably have covered all options, from lofty stick-insect to short, fat dumpling. Into which latter category she was afraid she would slot.

Unprepared for the reality, Izzy felt her eyes widen to saucers and her soft mouth drop open as each lid she lifted revealed something different. From formal wear through to smart-casual, exquisite underwear and dainty, kitten-heeled shoes. Everything in her size. How had *madame* known that? Had Cayo told her? Made a wild and, as it happened, accurate guess?

Costly fabrics, sumptuous colours. Perfectly cut, beautifully styled. The sort of garments that would probably cost a king's ransom!

Her face set, her generous mouth mutinous, she replaced the lids on all the boxes. She could not, *would* not accept them.

Under mental protest she would accept one dress to wear for the dratted ball. She wasn't at all comfortable about that, but had reluctantly gone along with it because Miguel, bless him, wanted her to, and she could understand that he'd been feeling bad about hiring her at slave-labour wages.

Despite the air-conditioning she felt decidedly hot and bothered, and knew she'd never be able to get a wink of sleep if she didn't tell Cayo right now that this was all way over the top. No way was she going to allow anyone to spend such a large amount of money on her.

'You deserve only what you can pay for yourself. Anything else is freeloading. Look at James. He works hard. He's well on the way to being able to have exactly what he wants. The way you're going you'll be lucky to afford to keep yourself in those ridiculous shoes you insisted on wearing.'

It had been constantly drummed into her since she'd been a schoolkid, in an attempt by her parents to get her to achieve the unachievable—in her case high grades at school. Grades that would lead to that glittering goal: a high-paying, ultra-respectable career.

Cayo closed his cellphone, terminating the conversation with his chief accountant, citing the lateness of the hour as his reason for silencing the dry-as-dust voice. In reality he was completely unable to concentrate on the information he had asked for, disturbing the man in whatever he did to relax in the late evening.

Never before had he suffered from an inability to keep his mind on track. It was a first, and he knew who was to blame.

Izzy Makepeace!

His lean, strong features hardened. Had he made a serious error of judgement? To one who prided himself on rock-solid character assessment it was a possibility that sat uneasily on his broad shoulders. Recalling his initial treatment of her, the things he'd said, he flinched.

If he'd been wrong, then his behaviour had been reprehensible.

But had he?

True, earlier this evening she'd passed up acquiring a whole new wardrobe and dining at one of Spain's finest restaurants in favour of rescuing a stray puppy of the un-cute variety. If it had been an act to convince him that his opinion of her as a scheming, money-grubbing slut was way off the radar, then she was obviously a tragic loss to the theatre.

Striving for pragmatism, telling himself that only time would tell, that even now she would be trying on and drooling over the goodies he'd had the Frenchwoman send over, he crossed to the drinks cabinet and poured himself a sparing amount of Scotch.

Only to swing sharply round on the balls of his feet as the connecting door was flung open without ceremony and the object of his uncharacteristically muddled thoughts bounced in.

His grip tightened on his glass. Even with her bright mane of hair tumbling around her flushed face, her startlingly blue eyes narrowed and flashing like an angry cat's, and her luscious body bundled in a silk bathrobe, she was spectacularly sexy. His pulses quickened. He ignored them, deploring his body's sexual reaction to her.

Deplorable if he'd been right about her in the first instance, and just as deplorable if she turned out to be a wronged innocent.

He didn't bed innocents.

But he wanted to bed *her*?

Before that question could lead to an answer he wouldn't like, he lifted his proud dark head and ground out, 'What is it? Did you forget to knock?'

Sarcastic brute! There he stood, in all his male magnificence. Long legs planted firmly apart, his suit jacket shed, shirtsleeves rolled up to display the golden skin of his strong forearms, slightly roughened by fine dark hairs, with a lock of silky black hair falling forward to brush his arched, expressive brows.

Haughtily disdainful eyes.

She would never understand him in a million years! Nice as pie one moment; utterly vile the next. She had to be the world's biggest fool to fancy him. So she wouldn't, she told herself tipsily. She would say what she had come to say and then sweep out with dignity.

Looking at a point beyond his left ear, because she always went peculiar when she looked directly at him, she dragged in a deep breath and blurted, at volume, 'Send that stuff back! I'll pick out something to wear for that dance—sale or return, because I may not be around that long—but the rest's going back! I may not have two pennies to rub together, but I'm not on any registered charity list that I know about! And I'm not a freeloader, either!'

Satisfied that he'd got the message, she twisted round, took a giant stride in her haste to reach the connecting door, caught her bare foot in the hem of the swamping robe and fell on her face.

'Are you hurt?'

Tears of frustration, anger and downright mortification pooled in her eyes as strong hands fastened on either side of her waist and Cayo lifted her back onto her feet. She'd meant to be so dignified and decisive, and all she'd done was fall flat on her face in a heap!

Breath gathered in her lungs and stuck there, burning. Any minute now she was going to put the tin lid on it and burst into loud and messy tears—that was her chagrined thought as he turned her round to face him, repeating, 'Have you hurt yourself?'

His strong hands still steadied her, scorching through the silky fabric. He was so close—too close. She was stingingly aware of his lithe and powerful male body. An awareness that flooded her with tension.

Her heart began to pound heavily and she couldn't breathe. Against all common sense she lifted her eyes to his and felt exactly as if she were drowning in the soft dark depths.

Panicking, her knees threatening to give way under her, she reached out to clasp the strength of his forearms for support—and almost cried out in shock as the touch of warm skin sent a jolt of electrified sensation right through her body. 'I'm fine!' she gasped, dropping her hands and making a futile attempt to move away from him.

His hands tightening, Cayo held her still, his eyes surveying the downbent head with its mass of silky silver, and felt his heart jerk beneath his breastbone.

Her explosive entry into his room, the way she'd shouted at him—something no one had had the temerity to do for as long as he could remember—had forced a crooked smile of unwilling admiration to his sensual lips.

When she felt strongly about something—Tio Miguel, the scruffy mutt, a designer wardrobe most women would give their eye-teeth to be gifted—she stood up to him, waded in, fists metaphorically flying. It was refreshing after the immediate and simpering compliance of the sophisticated women who inhabited his social circle and bored him to distraction.

Gently, he used a long, tanned forefinger to lift her chin, forcing her to meet his eyes. Her full lower lip trembled ominously and the deep blue of her eyes shimmered with unshed tears. Hurt eyes, as clear and innocent as a child's.

Physically she was unharmed. But she was hurting. Self-contempt tightened his gut. He had wronged her, believed lies, dismissed her version of events out of hand, harbouring the unjust opinion that she had set out to weasel herself into his uncle's affections in order to get her hands on his fortune.

In all honour he had to make amends.

'We will sit and talk calmly—clear the air between us,' he announced, dropping his hand and taking one of hers in his. He led her through to the suite she was using, noting the untouched food and the opened bottle of wine. The scruffy puppy snuffling in the padded dog bed was beginning to wake.

Swallowing a sigh, he excused himself momentarily and picked up the house phone, his orders terse and clipped. His brows clenched together when he turned and saw that Izzy had squeezed herself into the corner of one of the sofas, her legs tucked up beneath her, her arms wrapped around her body, as if she were trying to make herself invisible. Her lovely face was troubled.

She was always putting her foot in it, Izzy thought wretchedly. Blindly charging in, all guns blazing, acting without thought—sensible or otherwise—making a great big fool of herself!

Small hands twisting in her lap, she wished she could become invisible. The unaccustomed intake of alcohol and the emotion of the day had heightened her crusading tendencies, and in the aftermath she could see that her wildly inappropriate response to the arrival of a load of horrendously expensive clothes that she would never have been able to afford for herself in a million years had been totally crass.

She should have done nothing, said nothing until the morning. And then informed Cayo—calmly and with dignity—that the gift was unacceptable. Left it at that, without all these diva-like histrionics.

There followed the prompt arrival of two uniformed members of staff—one bearing a loaded coffee tray and a plate of what looked like small crusty filled rolls, the other waiting for orders from Cayo, delivered in rapid-fire Spanish. He lifted Benji from his basket, attaching the collar and lead to his scrawny neck.

'What's he doing?' Snapped out of her miserable introspection, and forgetting her lecture to herself, Izzy scrambled to her feet as the puppy was borne away.

In receipt of that suspicious reaction Cayo lowered his brows in annoyance. 'I think you should begin to trust me. The animal will be perfectly safe,' he informed her, with an extreme dryness that brought a bright flush of colour to Izzy's face. 'It is to be walked in the gardens of the hotel, to avoid accidents, and then taken to the housekeeper's room, where it is to be fed before being brought back.'

'Oh!' Izzy flushed uncomfortably and flopped back on the sofa. 'Sorry.'

'You jump to conclusions that do not flatter,' he imparted wryly as he lowered his lithe frame beside her. 'Why is that?'

'Why do you think?' He actually had the gall to look mystified, Izzy decided. It was enough to make a cat laugh! But then, in his opinion, he could do no wrong. 'You said I should leave him where he was, and then you threatened to have him sent to a vet—probably to be put down. You didn't exactly encourage me to bring Benji back here, did you?'

'But I didn't prevent you,' he pointed out, the corners of his mouth twitching.

His statement floored Izzy, as she had to admit that since she'd refused to abandon the puppy he had done everything to ensure its comfort and wellbeing—even though he was clearly not a fan of small animals with mangy-looking hair and stubby legs.

'Enough of that. We have other, more important things to discuss.' A lean, tanned and beautifully crafted hand sliced dismissively. 'The dog is yours.'

Izzy instinctively turned to thank him, to look directly at him, and her tummy flipped. He was so handsome he took her breath away. She wished quite desperately that he'd take himself off to his own suite, because she so wanted to move closer than the scant inch or two that separated them, to reach up and pull that handsome head down, to feel his beautiful mouth against hers... And if she wasn't very careful she'd find herself doing just that, making a monumental fool of herself...

Cayo shifted uneasily, unable to take his eyes from her lovely face. The beautiful blue eyes no longer looked innocent and childlike but sultry, the dark, gold-tipped lashes lowered. Her soft full lips parted, pink and inviting. The ache at his groin intensified. His pulses went into overdrive. He raised an unsteady hand to brush aside the tendril of silky silver hair that had tumbled over her wide forehead but, appalled by the thoughtless impulse, swiftly dropped it again.

Getting sharply to his feet, he incised, 'As the meal was not to your liking and is now cold you must help yourself to coffee and rolls. I'll see you in the morning. As I said, there are things to discuss.' And he left with as much haste as his condition would allow to seek a long cold shower.

She had her wish, Izzy acknowledged, stunned by his abrupt and curt departure. He was seeking his own suite and no doubt locking the door! So why did it feel as if she'd been drenched with a bucket of freezing water?

He'd probably legged it because she'd been looking at him as if he were a juicy steak and she was starving, she admitted with deep embarrassment. Around him, especially when he was being okay and not calling her names or threatening her with goodness knew what because he thought she was after his uncle's money, she couldn't help herself.

Feeling drained and ridiculous, she wandered over to pour herself a cup of coffee, and sat to await the puppy's return.

The only sensible thing to do was to take herself off, out of his orbit, and find work, hopefully with accommodation thrown in. Some place where a small puppy would be tolerated.

He'd said there were things they had to discuss. Well, her departure, as soon as possible, would be top of the list.

CHAPTER EIGHT

THE second of his two tiresome but apparently necessary business calls returned and completed, Cayo crossed to the bank of tall windows and flung them wide open. At this time of year Madrid sweltered beneath an unforgiving brassy sun, sending those Madrileños who could heading for cooler coastal or mountain climes.

But this early in the morning the temperature was bearable, and he filled his lungs with the last of the cool air he could expect to enjoy today, looking with wry affection out over the rooftops of the uncompromisingly modern city. Big and busy, it offered its fair share of culture in the form of museums, theatres and opera. And the rare treasures of the Royal Palace and its elegant parks, and sophisticated entertainment such as nightclubs and restaurants were second to none.

A consumer's paradise, and a rich feeding ground for the likes of gold-diggers—as he'd first named his uncle's housekeeper.

Unfairly blackening her character?

Maybe.

Almost certainly.

The thought did nothing to make him feel good about himself.

A few days—a week if he stretched it—of allowing Izzy Makepeace to wallow in the best the city had to offer, showing her that at his side the world was her oyster, or could be, was now unthinkable. At least not for the reasons that had led to his initial plan.

But as a way of making amends it was doable. Right. That was if he had anything to make amends for.

He couldn't remember a single time in all of his thirty-three years when he had fallen prey to indecision. He weighed up known facts and made up his mind. And that was that. No ifs and buts.

But in Izzy's case he damn well wasn't sure. He'd lain awake half the night reviewing the known and conflicting facts, and still, to his chagrin, he hadn't reached a rock-solid unarguable conclusion.

Was she, as the events of the last twenty-four hours would appear to suggest, innocent of all he had mentally and verbally accused her of being? Or was she just diabolically clever and a remarkably fine actress into the bargain?

Only time would tell.

Despising himself for what in others he would have named a deplorable weakness of character—an unprecedented and decidedly uncomfortable emotion, and one he wasn't prepared to live with for much longer—he flung open the connecting doors to her suite. They would continue the discussion he'd aborted the previous evening, and he would winkle out as many facts about her as he could.

He stood, straddle-legged, on the threshold of her suite. Of what looked like her *empty* suite, he noted scowlingly.

He called her name. It hung, unanswered, on the still air.

Last night she had approached him with a warm and gorgeous smile that could prove to be an unwary man's downfall, her hand outstretched in invitation. Inviting him to coo over her new pet! The naïve action of an innocent, or a calculated prelude to something far more earthy?

Madre de Dios! All he'd wanted to do, burned to do, was to sweep her into his arms and strip away the silky robe, revealing himself to be as excited as a kid tearing the wrappings from a wickedly tempting package on Christmas morning!

Recognising danger came instinctively to him. He'd made some brusque remark and left her. Likewise, earlier, when he'd escorted her back to her suite, he'd been drawn into the sudden sultry mystery of her eyes and felt himself to be drowning, wanting to explore the mystery, draw her to him, taste her, know her.

Thankfully he'd had the strength of mind to distance himself smartly from temptation, because on the one hand he didn't make love to greedy tramps and on the other he didn't seduce an innocent—especially an innocent he'd already wronged.

Either way, Izzy Makepeace was strictly out of bounds! And this morning they had things to discuss.

She knew that. He'd made it plain. He vented an expletive beneath his breath. When he made arrangements he expected them to be adhered to—to the letter!

That had to be why this almost frantic sense of frustration was claiming him after a search of the entire suite revealed nothing. Apart from the empty dog bed, and the neatly stacked Fornier boxes that had the air of rejection about them, Izzy might never have been anywhere near these rooms.

He ran lean fingers through his midnight hair, his scowl deepening as he reached for the phone and dialed down to the manager—to learn that the Señorita had been seen walking the small dog in the grounds of the hotel. Early. About an hour ago, or maybe longer.

An hour!

The hotel grounds were beautifully tended, tranquil, but nowhere near extensive enough to hold her interest for an hour or possibly more. Had she grown bored and set off into the city with that ridiculous puppy? Totally forgetting that he would be expecting her to be in her suite, waiting for him to join her?

Just another aspect of her thoughtless behaviour.

His features set in grim lines. On the whole, Madrid was a relatively safe place, but there were areas of the city where it was definitely unsafe for a lone female to venture. And this lone, sexy female wouldn't have a clue as to where she was going. She barely spoke half a dozen words of the language, and those in an accent so excruciating as to be unintelligible.

His heart was pumping fit to burst out of his chest as he brushed past a startled waiter and bounded through the wide French windows onto the terrace a scant four minutes later.

Nothing. A couple of early risers drinking coffee at one of the terrace tables. The sweep of emerald-green lawn beyond, empty of any strolling, lush little lady with a ragged, stumpy-legged dog on a lead.

Unless…

His long, loose-limbed stride took him over the immaculate grass in double-quick time, past a stand of oleanders towards the walled perimeter, where a deep belt of parasol pines cast welcome shade and filtered out the noise of traffic.

If she wasn't down here he would have to scour the city streets, and when he found her he would take a great deal of pleasure in wringing her little neck for doling out such unacceptable measures of anxiety!

After the glare of the sunlight the shade was dark as Hades, and he allowed his eyes a few moments to adjust before he strode deeper, calling her name with growing irritation. He swallowed a full-throated, anger-filled roar as a small, sparsely-haired missile hurled itself at him, stubby legs working overtime, lead trailing, and fixed him with bright beady eyes, the tail wagging the body.

Gritting his teeth, Cayo bent to grab the lead. Where the mutt was, its owner wouldn't be far away. Doing what? Wasting his time!

'Find!' he commanded, without much hope. Without any, actually. In his estimation the animal's intelligence would be on a par with its looks. Zilch!

Hanging on to the lead for grim life as the little dog

shot off like a greyhound out of a trap, Cayo wondered if once again he'd been mistaken. Did the animal have enough intelligence to be heading for his mistress, or was it careening off in any direction just for the heck of it? And then he saw her.

Sitting on the bone-dry earth, one leg tucked beneath her, rubbing the ankle of the other. Her washed-out denim skirt was rucked up to thigh level. She had lovely legs, firm rounded thighs—the sort of thighs a man could dream of moving between.

Anger at his entirely inappropriate line of thought made his voice sharp as he lashed out. 'What do you think you're doing? We had things to discuss this morning. Did you forget? Or were you born lacking in common courtesy? And what's wrong with your ankle?' he added after a beat of breath. Eyes narrowing, he moderated his tone—because he recognised that his harsh verbal onslaught stood in the stead of the more physical and metaphorical promised pleasure of wringing her dainty little neck!

He'd been worried about her—anxious on her behalf. The thought that she might have taken herself out of the hotel grounds and got herself lost in a city that could present danger to a solitary and unwary female had she wandered into one of the more unsavoury areas had made him taste fear for the first time in his life.

Over the top, he recognised with shaming hindsight. Totally. He didn't feel *that* protective of her!

Did he?

Madre de Dios, he was losing his marbles! Ever since she'd been around he'd been losing his fabled cool! And now she was just sitting there, cuddling the ugly pup who was frantically licking her face, ignoring *him*!

Planting his feet apart, he bit out in his best board-room-silencing tones, 'I asked you a question. What is wrong with your ankle?'

Emerging from the excess of doggy devotion that had gone some way to compensate for His Lordship's yelling at her, Izzy tossed back her head, setting the wild silky exuberance of her long hair flying, and answered as coolly as her crossness at being unfairly bawled out would permit.

'Nothing much. I tripped, and twisted it a bit. But it's much better now. Thank you for asking,' she added with an injection of sharp sarcasm, setting Benji back on the ground and hoping she could get to her feet without any real lack of dignity. She paused to lob at him, 'I thought it was more than early enough to get a walk in before you surfaced. I didn't twist my ankle on purpose, and I didn't ask you to inconvenience yourself and come to look for me. So don't snap and snarl at me! I can't think what we have to discuss anyway, although I hadn't forgotten. But might I suggest you make a proper appointment in future? You know—state a time and place, for example!'

She glared up into his lean, darkly handsome face and immediately wished she hadn't. He did things to her that should be prohibited by law. And he was trying not to smile. That made it worse—made hot tears of anger well into her eyes. She was telling him off, being serious, and he thought she was funny!

Desperate to hide her reaction—the pulse-racing physical desire that flooded her whenever she was around him, or even thought about him, come to that—she scrabbled awkwardly to her feet, biting her lip and clumsily hopping on one foot. Because her wretched ankle did still hurt. She hoped he didn't see the way her colour came and went. She couldn't control the way heat exploded deep in her pelvis and made her feel weak and fluttery all over. It was a source of shame to her and she'd just die if he guessed what he did to her.

'Here—' Strong hands reached out to steady her, spanning her small waist. Her head was lowered, the silvery blond curls all over the place. He had the finger-itching impulse to run his hands through the shimmering strands, to lift swathes of it to his face and breathe in the faint flowery perfume of it. Instead he asked with commendable, drawling cool, 'Can you put all your weight on that foot?'

Beast! Izzy's head shot up, angry tears once more flooding her eyes. Did he have to state the obvious? That she was overweight! She'd never be a size zero, but did he have to rub her nose in it?

'It really hurts?' Cayo supplied softly. The sight of her tears was making his heart clench, and he surprised himself with a genuine wish that he could take whatever pain she was feeling away from her and bear it himself.

Suddenly his heart felt like marshmallow. Just because there were genuine tears sparkling in her beautiful eyes? Could a man of his age go senile?

'Don't cry.' Where had that husky note come from? A frown darkened his brow. Stamping hard on the pressing urge to drop his head, close her eyelids with his lips, kiss the tears away, then trail a route down to her lush pink mouth, feel her lips parting for him, inviting him, to touch her with his hands, all of her, he gritted his teeth. He ignored the insistent ache in his groin and lifted her into his arms, striding back through the trees, the little dog trotting in his wake.

Izzy gasped as her whole body melted into his strong arms, her breathing shallow and erratic. The huffy disclaimer that her angry tears had nothing to do with the discomfort in her ankle and everything to do with his obliquely pointing out that she was a stranger to any regime of dieting and strenuous work-outs had disappeared at the speed of light.

Held by him, this close to him, their combined body heat seemed to ignite into a violent sexual conflagration, turning her mind to mush and her body to a quivering, needy wreck. She expelled a shaky moan, wound her arms around his neck and snuggled her head into his hard-muscled shoulder, wallowing in illicit sensational excitement, almost exploding with it as they reached the sun-drenched lawns.

He said, with an intensity that scorched what little was left of her brain, 'I'll get someone to look at that ankle.' And then, coming out of nowhere, 'And then I'll kiss it better myself. Would you like that?'

Kiss it better? Would she like that?

Would she like to win the Lottery and as a bonus discover the secret of eternal youth?

She knew to her everlasting shame that she would

like him—absolutely *love* him—to kiss every inch of her body. Her face flamed with acute mental discomfort. She who had never had any trouble holding on to her virginity, never given that state a thought, wanted him, this gorgeous man, to take it from her.

So what did that make her?

Incredibly stupid, she supplied with self-loathing. 'Kiss it better'? Get real, girl! He'd said the sort of thing people the world over said to humour any child suffering some minor hurt.

So he was treating her like a child now, was he? An overweight child! He had the knack of making her so angry she wanted to throw things—straight at his arrogant, too-handsome head, preferably! He was the only person in the whole world who could turn her normally good-natured placid self into a seething, emotional wreck! Reduce her to wanting to boil him in oil and make mad, passionate love to him at the same time!

As far as she was concerned he was incredibly dangerous. How long would it be before she made a monumental fool of herself? Letting him know that she was so in lust with him she didn't know what to do with herself?

He'd either laugh till his head dropped off or shoot her one look of grim distaste and make sure he never came within a hundred miles of her ever again!

True, he seemed to have changed his mind about her being a gold-digger without a moral worth mentioning. But that didn't mean he'd be over the moon if he realised an overweight, poorly dressed domestic servant wanted to get up close and personal with an elevated being such as he.

The only thing to do was take herself off, *pronto*. She would insist Cayo took her back to his lofty luxurious castle and then explain to Miguel that she didn't want to be a companion. If he decided to return to Cadiz at the end of the summer he'd have to find another house-keeper. It would, of course, mean failing at yet another job, she thought disconsolately as she stared at her bound ankle on the footstool.

At least there was no real damage there. Cayo had magicked a doctor out of thin air, seemingly. No surprise there, then. People jumped when he told them to, pausing only to tug at their forelocks and ask, *Please, sir, how high, sir?*

A slight sprain, that was all. The doctor had deftly bound the offending ankle, given instructions that she was to stay off it as much as possible for the remainder of the day, and then Cayo had slid the footstool beneath her foot and left with the elderly medic. Leaving her to stew in her self-declared mania. And fume.

Until: 'We both missed breakfast.'

Izzy's heart thumped wildly as Cayo entered the room, complete with loaded tray, and the simmering, sexy smile that increased her inner turmoil by rocket-propelled miles produced a self-protective snipe. 'Do-it-yourself time, is it? No platoon of waiters and managers and fanfares—?'

'Shut up.'

His dark eyes were liquid. Warm. Dressed now in a fresh, startlingly white shirt, and hip-hugging dark trousers that made his legs look endless, he was a menace to the female sex, Izzy accused mentally as she watched his lithe movements. He placed the tray on a low table by her side and swung a delicate gilded chair to place it within touching distance. There was a trite phrase, wasn't there? 'Poetry in motion'? Trite or not, it just about cut it.

She expelled a long sigh. One minute she'd been a bundle of fuming disgruntlement because he'd left her alone, and the moment he showed his face she went all unnecessary!

Pouring dark, fragrant coffee, Cayo handed her a cup. It rattled on the saucer as she took it. Poor scrap!

Leaving with the doctor, he'd done what he should have done days ago. Put through a call to Augustin del Amo. His tone had held threats that hadn't needed to be voiced—because no one who had a thought for his future peace of mind refused to co-operate when Cayo Angel Garcia demanded it. He had quickly obtained the truth that lay behind Izzy's summary dismissal from the household.

A truth he had been increasingly convinced of himself.

Now all he had to do was try to make amends.

He hooked a chair closer to the one she was using. Sat.

'I have something to tell you, Izzy. And something to ask you.'

CHAPTER NINE

GRITTILY determined not to let him get his word in first, to sidetrack her, Izzy gulped down her coffee without tasting it. One second in his company was enough to knock her common sense clear over the boundary and scatter her resolve to the four winds, so the sooner she made her intentions known the better.

'I'm leaving—can you get me back to Las Palomas, please?' She practically babbled in her haste to get her self-protective, set-in-concrete decision voiced.

She didn't look at him in case she turned to jelly, as she always did. She kept her eyes glued to the puppy, who was lying on his back, snoring, hoping the gods would be kind and help her find a job and a place to live where pets would be welcome.

'So soon?' Cayo disposed of his empty cup with care, one flaring ebony eyebrow lifting. 'But you've seen nothing of the city,' he pointed out mildly, wondering what had brought this on. 'Madrid has much to offer.'

His narrowed dark-as-midnight eyes searched what

he could see of her averted features. He learned nothing beyond the obvious: something had rattled her cage. It was the first time he had encountered a female he couldn't immediately read like a tediously boring book.

Unless, of course, her ankle was still painful. That might explain her grouchy mood. Though he had been assured that the sprain was slight. Or maybe she thought—wrongly—that she was to be incarcerated in this room, with her foot stuck on a stool, for the duration of her visit to the capital.

Satisfied that he had found the answer with his usual incisiveness, he imparted, with the smoothness of silk, 'You don't have to spend all your time cooped up in a hotel room. We'll hit the town later. You won't be up to sightseeing or dancing the night away—not for twenty-four hours, anyway—but a superb meal and a glass or two of fine champagne in one of the city's premier restaurants might put a smile back on your face. And it will give you the opportunity to try out something from your new Fornier wardrobe.' It was the least he could do after what he had learned from the sleazy apology for a man Augustin del Amo.

The smile in his voice curved his mouth as he waited for her response, fully expecting to enjoy the radiance of her gorgeous smile as she accepted that invitation. Of course he wasn't smug! The satisfaction he felt was down to confirming that he hadn't lost his touch. He'd always been able to second-guess what other people were thinking—a knack that had proved its worth in gold in his business dealings.

Had he been standing, he'd have been rocked back

on his heels when she turned her head and gave him a look overflowing with frustration and loathing, and bawled, 'How shallow can you get?'

Telltale patches of hectic colour adorned her cheeks. She felt so wound up she was in danger of exploding. Did he think all she wanted to do was to flounce around in designer dresses and swill champagne? 'I wasn't talking about leaving this *room*! I meant your uncle's employ, and possibly even Spain! Like *now*, or sooner!' Her deep blue eyes were sparkling with tears of rage.

She'd screwed herself up to the point of accepting that she had to do the sensible, properly adult thing and remove herself from his dangerous presence—even though knowing she'd never see him again made her feel sick and empty inside—and his only and no doubt predictable response was to react as though she were the idiotic, empty-headed child he obviously thought she was, easily placated by the offer of a treat!

But he didn't know how she felt, she admitted, subsiding, always the first to see the other side of a story. He didn't know—couldn't know—that she only had to set eyes on him to be wanting to rip his clothes off. And her own!

'I see.' Cayo's eyes narrowed as he swiftly recovered from the shock of having been proved wrong. An event as rare as finding a lap-dancing nun! There had to be some kind of witchery about this lady, because she'd done the unthinkable and proved him wrong all along the line.

So she was definitely planning to walk away from her job as Miguel's housekeeper-cum-companion? So why was his brain already formulating objections when seeing the back of her was what he'd been so desperate to achieve since he'd learned she was working for his uncle?

And why had the bellowed information immediately put him in direct opposition, just as diametrically determined to keep her around?

But wanting to see the back of her had been *then*. This was now, when he knew the truth, he rationalised. He had an international reputation for hard-nosed ruthlessness, but had always believed he was fair-minded. He didn't want her to leave without some recompense for the hard time he'd given her when he'd taken the words of the banker and his wife at face value.

He couldn't forget the way she'd set to and looked after Miguel, working hard for slave-labour wages just to see that an old man she thought was on the breadline was comfortable and cared for. That alone, in his book, demonstrated a rare generosity of spirit, and deserved reciprocal generosity on his part.

Relieved that he'd worked that out, and that his initial shattering reluctance to see her pack her bags and walk away had nothing to do with his regrettable difficulty in keeping his hands off her, he relaxed. Lust he could deal with. No problem. But his conscience wouldn't let him see her leave before he'd made adequate recompense.

Swinging himself to his feet, he removed the breakfast tray. Neither of them had touched the fruit or the linen-wrapped hot crusty rolls. No matter. Eating was low on his list of priorities at the moment. She'd been loudly vehement in her stated desire to leave his uncle's employ—'now or sooner'.

He would change her mind. Tio Miguel would expect it of him. He would be vastly upset if she were to leave with no job to go to and nowhere to live, just her clothes bundled into a rucksack and a scruffy mutt on the end of a lead. Or so he excused his own bone-deep reluctance to wave her off at a bus stop.

'There is surely no hurry?' The words slid out like warm honey as he returned to her side, leaning forward to scoop her effortlessly into his arms. Ignoring her spluttered protest, he strode through the open long windows, out of the air-conditioning and into the blaze of white heat on the wide balcony.

Izzy, her heart beating so fast she felt giddy, pummelled his broad chest with ineffectual fists. Being swept up into his arms twice in one morning was seriously undermining her sanity, and making the secret feminine part of her throb, ache, turn moist and slick. She was so ashamed of herself that an anguished sob escaped her before she could swallow it.

'You are overwrought.' Cayo gentled her into a padded seat. 'There really is no need.' He adjusted the huge sun awning so that she was completely in shade, withdrew his mobile from a pocket at his narrow hips and issued rapidfire orders in his own language, smiling down at her.

His black eyes were liquid with kindness, and Izzy looked quickly away, concentrating on the view out over the gardens until her eyes stung. Because meeting his gaze, holding it, would let him read what was there:

desire, lust, need—the whole package. She wouldn't let that happen.

So she was overwrought! Whose fault was that? The sex-on-legs man who was now telling her, 'Cold drinks will be with us in moments.' That was who!

He was also saying, 'We must talk. But first I want to apologise. I accused you of trying to wheedle your way into Miguel's affections with the intention of getting your hands on his wealth, of having no morals worth mentioning. I was wrong.'

Izzy's soft pink mouth dropped open, her huge eyes wide as she watched him move forward and join her on the padded seat, one arm disposed along the back. She wouldn't have thought his inbred arrogance would permit him *ever* to admit to being in the wrong. She'd assumed that apologies would be a stranger to his tongue—he hadn't apologised when she'd given him her version of the events that had led to her dismissal from her former job, so why was he saying sorry now?

She angled her head to one side, gazing up at that compellingly handsome face, and Cayo caught his breath between his teeth.

Her enchantingly tousled hair was tumbling forward in a tangle of shimmering silver-blond curls. His fingers ached to make exploratory contact. And her parted lips, lush, moist, rose-pink, were an invitation he was hard pushed to resist. And those clear, unbelievably blue eyes—

He cleared his throat roughly, his tone husky and then flattening as he confessed, 'I spoke to Augustin del Amo this morning.' He thought it wise to admit the truth of what really happened. 'Again, I can only apologise, and ask you to allow me to make some reparation.'

His accent was more pronounced than she'd ever heard it, and a lock of silky black hair had fallen forward to brush his arched, expressive brows. He reached out and took her hands. Her ability to breathe vanished. The golden skin of his forearms was slightly roughened by fine dark hairs. So temptingly touchable…

A great choking lump took residence in Izzy's throat. A question burned her tongue. The electrifying touch of his hands on hers sent it flying out of her head.

He repeated his request, 'May I make reparation?'

She could only gasp, 'Such as?'

His mobile mouth twitched. Izzy wanted to kiss it so much it made her insides fizz. Which was why she had come to the grown-up decision to leave as soon as humanly possible, she reminded herself. A decision that was founded on very shaky ground, she discovered, when his long tanned fingers tightened around hers and he supplied, 'A billion sterling in a diamond-encrusted gold crate, perhaps?'

Laughter lights in both dark velvet and sparkling blue eyes met and melded.

'You remembered that!'

'How could I forget? You are the only woman I know to let me feel the sharp edge of her tongue.'

'I bet!' She tugged her hands away from his. The fleeting moment of rapport had vanished. It had felt so very good. But now it might never have happened. She wished it hadn't!

Long, gold-tipped lashes swept down to veil her

eyes, because it really hurt to translate what he meant. Hordes of beautiful, sexy, exquisitely dressed, sophisticated and suitable women flattering him outrageously and hanging on his every word. Not a single one with any reason or desire to even think about bad-mouthing him!

Mental images of some nameless, long-legged lovely wrapped all around him, cooing sweet nothings and purring with pleasure, rose up to choke her, blinding her to the arrival of a waiter with the cold drinks Cayo had ordered.

With a brief nod of thanks he leaned towards her, his eyes soft, and assured her, 'That was a compliment, *amada.*'

Stop it! she shrieked inside her head. When he was nice to her, her emotions went haywire! Her hand shaking, she lifted a glass, her fingers curling around the ice-cold surface. She drank the most refreshing grapefruit juice she'd ever tasted as if she were stranded in a desert and dying of thirst.

Setting the empty glass back on the table with unnecessary vigour, Izzy wished she were impervious to Cayo's charismatic good-looks, but she knew she never would be—not in a million years.

She was thrown completely off-balance when he captured her hand and said, in that slow, sexy drawl, 'Time to talk. As friends.'

Her hand felt so small and delicate within his, her fingers curling in response. He had the unprecedented and urgent need to lift it to his mouth, plant kisses deep within her palm.

He didn't do soppy, romantic gestures!

And he wasn't going to start with Izzy. Izzy was out of bounds!

Which was a pity!

Scrub that thought!

His features as impassive as only he could make them, he gently untwined her fingers from his and carefully replaced her hand back on her lap. 'You up for it?'

'For what?' Her voice sounded funny, as if she were drunk, Izzy decided. Just because he'd briefly held her hand again. Time to get a grip.

'I want to discuss your decision to leave Miguel's employ.'

'Oh. Right.' Izzy perked up. At least she told herself she did. She'd made the perfectly sensible and correct decision to leave, and naturally Cayo would want to discuss the best way to go about getting her back to Las Palomas, as she'd requested, where she could pack the remainder of her gear and say her farewells to Miguel. 'Go ahead.'

'I understand your decision to leave,' Cayo assured her gently, determined to prevent her taking off like a scalded cat. He wanted her to leave Las Palomas only when he had decided his guilt over his shockingly bad judgement had been relieved. 'His work's the only companion Tio Miguel needs, always has been, and as it's my firm intention to get him to agree to make Las Palomas his permanent home he won't need a housekeeper. Staying in his employ would make you feel like a spare part.'

Izzy nodded her agreement, the sudden painful lump

in her throat not allowing her to vocalise. He understood, and he would do everything in his considerable power to facilitate her removal from the lives of the super-elevated Garcias with all haste.

Deflation hit her. A decision made in a blinding moment of unadulterated common sense was one thing. But being faced with the imminence of a very uncertain future, with the responsibility of a small puppy to add to her anxieties, was quite another. Perhaps common sense wasn't all it was cracked up to be.

Sparkling dark eyes enhanced by incredibly thick black lashes rested on her slightly trembling pink mouth. 'I won't ask you to alter your decision, only to delay it.'

He caught his breath as she lifted her eyes to his. So wide, so vulnerable. The thought of her, jobless, homeless, wandering Spain in the hope of picking up work, was inconceivable. He wouldn't let it happen. He might be the tough nut described in the financial papers, but he wasn't a monster.

'Give it a couple of weeks or so—at least until after the Summer Ball. Leave straight away and Miguel's feelings would be hurt—especially if you ungraciously refuse to accept the new wardrobe he specifically wanted you to have. I know he feels badly about the way he so grossly underpaid you, and I know he wants you to have a holiday. And as for me—' he spread his finely made hands expressively '—I owe you. It's not beyond my capabilities to find you suitable work and accommodation within one or other of my companies.' Not a shadow of his ongoing loathing at the thought of seeing her walk off into the sunset with no visible form of support showed on his face as he invited, 'Tell me of your life before you came to Spain.' Miguel had told him what he knew, what she'd confided. He wanted to know more.

'Why?' Izzy swung her legs around and wriggled into a position where she was directly facing the man seated at her side. She caught her breath, mesmerised by the sheer brilliance of his eyes, horribly aware of the tightening tingle of awareness deep in her tummy. Was he, at last, actually interested in her as a human being? A woman?

It was a thought too sweet to be ousted by acknowledging its sheer stupidity—until he countered blandly, 'Think of it as a job interview. If I'm to place you within one of my companies I need to know I'm not trying to push a round peg into a square hole.'

Extreme humiliation claimed her. No wonder her family was irritated by her, called her stupid. Of *course* he wasn't interested in her as a flesh-and-blood woman. Why the heck should he be? She had none of the social graces, the dazzling beauty and sophistication that would raise a flicker of interest in a man such as he.

Squashing the desire to tell him to mind his own business, that she'd find work without his help, she glumly acknowledged that she couldn't afford to be defiant just because her feelings had been hurt. Feelings she had had no right to have in the first place. Talk about cutting her nose off to spite her face! She needed work. He'd promised to place her.

'My CV's nothing to write home about,' she mumbled, her hands twisting in her lap with sheer embarrassment.

Her family had always drummed it into her that unless she applied herself academically she would get nowhere. Wrongly, she decided with hindsight. Because she had always known she could never begin to approach the scholarly brilliance of her older, doted-upon brother, she hadn't even tried. Now she was being obliged to spell it out.

'No qualifications. A string of going-nowhere jobs. And then Dad found me work in his office—he was a solicitor. Just making the tea, really, and running errands. Then he retired—'

'To New Zealand, to be with your doctor brother.'

'James is a brilliant surgeon,' Izzy corrected, knowing full well her brother would have insisted on that distinction. She pinkened because Miguel must have told him this stuff, which reminded her that Cayo would have been checking out his uncle's new and—in his initial opinion—dodgy housekeeper. Miguel would have relayed what he knew about her because she'd confided heaps about her background to explain what she'd been doing in Spain in the first place.

'And you took work in Spain, leaving your job and your home because you and the man you were in love with had a falling out.'

Cayo cut to the chase. It figured. She could be fiery-tempered, headstrong enough to act on impulse without calmly thinking out the consequences. But she was also warm-hearted, and hadn't a mean or ungenerous bone in her delectable body.

'Are you still in love with him?' It was a struggle to keep his tone uninterested when he was illogically incensed by the possibility—for some reason he was totally at a loss to understand.

He was left clenching his teeth against some unwise and possibly ridiculous frustrated outburst when, her chin up, she came back with, 'That is absolutely none of your business!'

Miguel obviously hadn't relayed the whole story of her soppy crush on Marcus, the way he had used her and laughed at her behind her back, and she certainly wasn't going to lay what amounted to her further stupidity and humiliation on the table for him to gloat over or pity her for.

'I take that as a yes.' The dismissive tone he could turn on at will was at odds with what he could only describe as his anger. Miguel had been short on details of the English love of his housekeeper's life, and he hadn't pressed, hadn't been remotely interested, cynically deciding that any male Izzy Makepeace professed to be in love with had to be loaded, and that clearly the English guy had seen through her and given her the elbow—hence her removal to hunting pastures new.

But he knew differently now. She wasn't the avaricious slapper he had named her. She had loved the English guy. Still loved him.

He forced himself to unclench his jaw. As she had said, it was none of his business. So why did the pretty certain knowledge that Izzy would regret her impetuosity and return to her lover, or that he, like any red-blooded male, would track her down and claim her leave him feeling so sour?

Change the subject.

Cool, impersonal tone.

He didn't do staff interviews. His personnel officer handled that. But he'd give it his best shot. It couldn't be too difficult.

'Having seen how you so brilliantly transformed the grotty hovel that was Miguel's home under his unlamented former housekeeper's tenure, I would say your talents lie with the domestic.'

'Talents?' In spite of herself, Izzy went bright pink with pleasure. 'No one's ever linked that word with me before,' she confessed. Praise coming from this elevated being would be pretty rare, and she knew she would always treasure it—which was horribly feeble, and a rather shameful fact that wild horses wouldn't drag from her.

His heart, never the mushiest of organs, seemed to swell with sympathy. He recalled, now, something Miguel had said, that he'd ignored as would-be heart-tugging propaganda.

'Reading between the lines, I'd say her family treated her appallingly. Forever comparing her unfavourably with her brother, making her feel third-rate.'

'I believe you lived in the shadow of your brother, but that doesn't mean you don't have your own strengths. Different, but equal,' he remarked gently.

That brought her head up, and a slight frown to mar the smooth perfection of her brow. Miguel had certainly been giving his tongue full rein! She shrugged, a slight, defeated gesture.

Quite unaccountably, it moved him to say, 'You must have felt unloved. A lonely feeling, as I know. I was six years old when I overheard my father tell Tio Miguel, "If you feel so strongly, you spend time with the *mocoso*. By being born he cost me my adored wife's life. I'll see that my staff feed and clothe him, and he will be educated, but other than that I want nothing to do with him!"' His eyes hardened at the memory, but his voice was still gentle as he admitted, 'Until then I had tried every way I knew to make Papà notice me, love me. After that I stopped trying. I made my own life—with Tio Miguel to guide me when he was around.'

Appalled, Izzy opened her eyes very wide. They flooded with over-emotional tears. What a terrible thing for a lonely, motherless little boy to overhear! Her own nagged-at childhood didn't come near such a truly dreadful trauma.

A frown scoring his brow, Cayo managed to stop his fingers from brushing away the silvery teardrops. 'I'm not looking for sympathy,' he denied shortly, genuinely perplexed by the way he'd opened up to her. He had never repeated what he'd overheard to a living soul— not even Tio Miguel. In fact he hadn't even hung around to hear his uncle's response, he remembered, just run to the stables and sobbed himself to sleep. It was not an episode he had ever wished to talk about. So he didn't understand himself, and thoroughly loathed that state of affairs.

'I am merely pointing out that, regardless of what others might think of you, you do have talents and it's up to you to make something of your life. As I have done,' he proffered on a bite.

Make something of her life—as he had done? Thanks, but no thanks! Her tender heart twisted. Sure, he was a massively successful, wildly wealthy business tycoon, but apart from his uncle he cared for no one. Not even his gloriously beautiful mistresses, whom Miguel had unguardedly described as 'unemotional business arrangements'. His harsh, unloving father had been responsible for turning his son into a stranger to emotion, and that, in her book, made Cayo Angel Garcia a desperately poor man.

And she knew in that moment that she loved him.

Blinking back the annoyance of fresh tears, her heart hurting, she reached out a hand and touched the side of his extravagantly handsome face in an instinctive gesture of compassion.

She heard the catch of his breath. And then his lean, finely boned hands cupped her face, his long fingers splaying in her hair as he brought his dark head down to hers, his lips claiming hers with scorching demand, sending rivers of fire right down to her toes. The level of response she gave back to him as she greedily accepted the plundering of his tongue shocked her by its wild intensity.

His hands were on either side of her head, their hungry lips the only point of contact, and Izzy whimpered deep in her throat with the driving need for so very much more. She found her hands splayed against the breadth of his chest, touching him, and the erotic heat of him sent her out of her mind with need, with craving, with love…

CHAPTER TEN

THE COOL mountain breeze gave welcome relief from the midday heat that was baking the inner courtyard. But out here, beyond the massive castle walls, it danced amongst the high meadow flowers and carried the refreshing scent of pine. And if she closed her eyes Izzy was sure she could smell the sea which, so Miguel had told her, lay beyond the crumpled mountains of western Andalucia.

Dominating the limestone plateau, Las Palomas had to be the most beautiful place in the whole of Spain, Izzy decided as she watched Benji chase his tail in the long seeding grasses.

The little dog had improved almost beyond recognition since she'd found him cowering in that Madrid doorway. His once pitifully thin body was growing strong and sturdy, the mangy coat thicker and sleeker.

Izzy's smile was wistful.

The only opportunity she had to spend quality time with the rescued stray now was when she brought him out here to use up some of his boundless energy. The rest of the time he stuck to Miguel closer than Velcro.

It was amazing how the pup and the elderly man had taken one look at each other and formed an immediate mutual admiration society.

Once, only half joking, she had told Miguel, 'Know something? I'm really jealous! The way Benji's taken to you puts my nose right out of joint!'

The elderly man had simply said, 'Look on the mutual devotion as a bonus. If you insist on leaving me and this beautiful place, and if Cayo insists on finding you paid employment—I guess it will be something truly exciting, like chambermaiding and a nice little room in an attic, if any of his hotels have attics, that is— then you will be pleased to know that your little stray has a happy and secure home here with me. Because, you see, my nephew was right. He always is, of course— and woe betide anyone who tries to tell him differently! I've decided to stay here permanently.'

That was the sensible way of looking at the situation, Izzy knew. Stupid to feel hurt because on learning of her decision to give up her job as his totally unnecessary companion her old gentleman had merely raised one brow, smiled what she had privately thought a suspiciously secret sort of smile and said, 'I see.' Not once had he tried to persuade her to change her mind. And there'd been a marked touch of unusual sarcasm in his voice when he'd mentioned chambermaiding and attics in the same breath!

Stupid to feel hurt. So she wouldn't. She would be sensible. Just as sensible as she'd been ever since Cayo had brought her back to Las Palomas five days ago. Then disappeared.

'Business,' Miguel had said, waving a languid, dismissive hand. 'The man doesn't know how to relax. But he'll be back for the Summer Ball.'

Which was today.

A huge marquee had been erected on one of the fastidiously tended sweeping lawns, and there tenant farmers and the inhabitants of the two sleepy villages which formed part of the vast Las Palomas property would be entertained with flamenco, dancing to a string quartet, and enough food and drink to keep an army going for a month.

Strings of coloured lights festooned the castle walls and every tree and fountain, just waiting for darkness to fall. The kitchens were a hive of activity as the chef and his helpers started preparing the banquet for the company of VIP guests and their wives and partners, who would apparently be arriving any time now to stay overnight, because she'd heard that the dancing would go on until dawn.

And there was still no sign of Cayo.

She chewed on a corner of her lower lip as she watched Benji chase a butterfly. She was being sensible about the future, and her departure from this lovely place, so she could congratulate herself. She was being adult about what had happened, too, she decided, feeling glum.

She'd fallen in love with Cayo—which was a silly thing to do, but she wasn't going to let herself obsess about it. Of course not. She'd get over it, given time. And so what if that kiss had given her a taste of rapture she was sure she would never experience again? She'd get over that, too. Maybe even forget it had ever happened.

Given time.

And time was what she'd had ever since he'd disappeared without so much as a, *see you*.

Time to think. About the way he'd broken that kiss as cataclysmically as he'd started it. Stepping away from her. Apologising! Looking as stiff and granite-faced as a carved effigy before snapping round on his heels and stalking away. Leaving her shuddering with the aftermath of exquisite physical sensation and the earth-shattering revelation of having fallen head over heels in love.

Lunch had been served in the sitting room of her suite that day, and he'd acted as though nothing had happened. The perfect, ultra-considerate gentleman. She'd been disorientated by his annoying behaviour— she'd so wanted him to kiss her again, and he had behaved as if she were a kid sister, leaving her wanting to jump up and slap him. And all of that had been mixed up with the truly awesome bombshell of really falling in love, ensuring that she'd gone along with every last one of his suggestions.

That she allow him to show her something of the city, as formerly arranged. That Miguel's gift of the Fornier wardrobe be accepted, and that she spend some time at Las Palomas with his uncle while he sorted out a suitable occupation and affordable accommodation for her.

All commendably sensible.

And during the days that had followed, as he'd escorted her around Madrid's highspots, he had been the perfect companion—knowledgeable, kind, considerate. Only once, when he'd announced that they'd be dining out and going on to some classy-sounding nightclub, and she'd worn a silky little scarlet Fornier creation, had he taken one glance in her direction and looked as pained as if a hornet had taken a bite out of him. It had left her agonising over whether he'd looked like that because she looked tarty, wondering if the clinging dress was too short, showing too much cleavage to be acceptable in polite society.

She'd noticed that he hadn't really looked at her again, and when they'd hit the nightclub he'd suggested they leave almost immediately. He hadn't said one word to her on the short drive back to the hotel.

But apart from that Cayo's behaviour couldn't be faulted. So why had she swung between feeling dizzy with love for him and feeling so frustrated and miserable she could have screamed?

He had to be deeply ashamed of having kissed her, really regretted it, and was horrified by her more than merely enthusiastic response, she decided. She was deeply mortified as she recalled the way she had clung, squirmed and wriggled against his hard, lean body, as if she could never get close enough until she'd fused their bodies together.

Her hands had taken on a life of their own, touching, revelling in the strongly boned and muscled breadth of his shoulders, the smooth outline of his body where it narrowed to his taut, flat waist, and then moving up again like a heat-seeking missile so that her fingers could tangle in the midnight softness of his hair.

Her face flaming scarlet with humiliation, Izzy busied herself searching for Benji's favourite ball. She'd behaved like a real hussy. No wonder a guy as coolly sophisticated as Cayo had been turned off. If she wanted to do herself a favour she'd do as he had obviously done and put it out of her mind.

Right out.

Because...

Because just possibly there was something entirely different going on here. Suppose kissing her had been part of his plan? That he'd had to really steel himself to do it, and hadn't been able to bring himself to repeat it?

That possible scenario had occurred to her in the small hours of the night, waking her from a dream she'd been having of the first time he'd taken her hands in his.

He'd been apologising for thinking the worst of her, explaining that he had just that morning spoken to her former employer and had the truth from him regarding what had happened, confirming that she'd been blameless.

And all the time she'd been under the impression that he'd believed her side of the story when she'd recounted it much earlier. That impression had been strengthened when he'd immediately started to treat her like a human being—even to the extent of inviting her to accompany him to Madrid for a short holiday. So why, obviously still convinced that she was out to wriggle herself into Miguel's affections, to make herself indispensable and get her hands on his money, had he stopped calling her vile names, threatening her, and started being nice to her?

Her lush mouth wobbled now, as the only viable and most distressing answer that had presented itself in the small hours claimed residential status in her mind.

Miguel's wealth. Which Cayo would inherit. Provided the elderly man didn't marry, or leave it to a sneaky little gold-digger.

To make sure that didn't happen Cayo would have put himself up as a sort of well-heeled diversion, that would make the calculating heart of a career gold-digger beat faster and swiftly change allegiance.

He'd gritted his enviably strong white teeth, taken her hands in his, and acted as if he cared about her. Even kissed her silly to make her think he was more than a little attracted to her. And all the while not trusting her an inch—even though he'd claimed to have had the truth of her innocence from the horse's mouth.

He wouldn't believe in her innocence if the Angel Gabriel himself proclaimed it!

Despising herself for being so slow on the uptake, and falling for a man capable of such devious behaviour, she finally located the gaudy yellow and scarlet ball. She straightened, whistled for Benji, and threw it as far as she could over the tall grasses, watching as the puppy, yelping with excitement, scampered after it. And resolutely blinked the tears from her eyes.

'She is exercising our puppy.' Miguel laid aside the magnifying glass through which he'd been examining an illuminated manuscript and smiled as he answered his nephew's query. 'I believe she takes him beyond the immediate grounds and into the meadows, where he can run wild. You will find her if you look.'

He bit back a chuckle as he encountered the younger man's stony gaze and added, with seeming innocence, 'She will be pleased to see you. I believe she has missed you. She has been *desanimada*, without her usual sunny spirits.'

Deciding he'd said enough on that subject as Cayo's expression darkened, he probed slyly, 'Did you find alternative employment for my soon to be ex little companion?'

'Nothing suitable.' Cayo swung on his heels and exited, his strong, blue-shadowed jaw set at an uncompromising angle. Was his uncle trying to make him feel guilty?

He felt guilty enough without any input from him!

He had kissed her because he hadn't been able to stop himself. His legendary cool had deserted him. His mind, normally as reliable as a calculating machine, had seriously malfunctioned.

Punching a balled fist into the open palm of his other hand, he left the castle by a rarely used side door, to avoid the interminable to-ings and fro-ings of his staff, and took a winding path that led towards the perimeter wall.

He had kissed Izzy and her response had sent what little had been left of his mind hurtling into orbit. The lush perfection of her body had pressed against his with an urgency she hadn't tried to hide, making the imperative to strip away the light barrier of clothes that separated them and make love to her a mere millimetre away from being acceded to.

Only his honour had stopped him in his tracks.

There was the type of women one married. Open, innocent, a little naïve perhaps. Good women. And Izzy, he now strongly suspected, fell into that category. As a confirmed bachelor—with no intention of marrying, not even for dynastic reasons—he avoided women such as these like the plague. There were other women widely available to more than satisfy his physical needs without troubling his conscience.

Beautiful, sophisticated, superficial and knowing women. Totally satisfied with the prospect of a handsome gift at the end of an invariably short and mutually advantageous affair.

Initially he had believed Izzy was another, more dangerous type. The type of woman who would latch on to any wealthy man and bleed him dry. He knew differently now, of course, which was why honour demanded he make full reparation. And keep his lustful thoughts and impulses to himself!

And that was why he was being drawn towards the meadows beyond the perimeter wall, he reasoned. To explain why he had so far failed in his duty to see that she didn't suffer from the loss of her job.

If his enquiries amongst his various personnel officers had raised eyebrows he had disregarded them. Izzy's placement would need to be special. He owed her. Which was why the job of cleaner at his Cadiz offices had been an outrageous suggestion, causing him in a moment of unfair anger to mentally mark down the man offering the available job for instant dismissal. Thankfully it had been a smothered reaction but it had only been topped by his withering scorn when he had been informed that there were openings for kitchen staff and waitresses in a couple of his hotels.

Even a position as an English-speaking trainee receptionist at his latest acquisition, a luxury hotel in Rome, had been deemed not good enough. Not for Izzy. She couldn't make herself understood in Spanish, in spite of the phrasebook which he'd noticed went everywhere with her. How she would manage in Italy was something he couldn't consider without a shudder.

The low wooden door that gave access to the open meadow land creaked as he opened it. Unless Izzy chose to return the long way round—across the fields and the horse paddocks, opening and closing several gates until she hit the long and steep approach road to the castle—she would return this way.

Shielding his eyes from the sun's glare, he scanned the meadow. And saw her. His heart flipped in his deep chest. Her silvery hair was piled in a haphazard mass on top of her head, and she was wearing a pair of lemon-yellow cotton shorts that clipped her curvy hips and displayed those shapely, lightly tanned legs to perfection. These were topped by a well worn and faded skimpy blue T-shirt that clung with loving softness to the enticing swell of her breasts.

And he ached to possess her. To discover, taste, own every last delicious inch of her.

Ignoring his fierce arousal, he clenched his fists at his sides as she approached, the dog dancing at her heels. Her steps slowed when she saw him. Judging by the way she was dressed the Fornier casuals were still languishing in their classy boxes. But she could wear a bin liner and still look delectable, he thought. She was that rarity: a woman who didn't need fancy clothes to make a stunning impact.

Recalling the night she'd worn that scarlet designer gown, he smothered a groan. She had looked sensational. So ravishingly tempting he'd had to use every last ounce of his increasingly shaky self-control to stop himself from seducing her on the spot.

She stopped six feet away, her smile slight, uncertain. Her unadorned lips were the softest pink. They had tasted of heaven.

She was out of bounds. She wasn't the type to indulge in an affair and emerge unscathed. He would cut off his right hand before he caused her any hurt. And he certainly wasn't prepared to tie himself down in marriage just for the mental and physical relief of having her in his bed night after long, blissful night.

The reminder was unnecessary. His teeth clenched with brutal force.

He was glad of the diversion when the little dog hurtled towards him. Picking him up, holding the squirming body firmly while stoically enduring the welcoming slobbery doggy kisses, he reached a solution.

The only solution.

Setting the animal back on its feet, he straightened, and his voice was flat as he told her, 'As you know, I run a highly successful export business out of Cadiz. There are branch offices in the UK. There will be a job waiting for you there.' He'd insist on it. And when he insisted his staff turned themselves inside out to ensure his instructions were followed to the letter. 'Suitable accommodation will be found as part of the employment package.'

He named a salary that took her breath away. Her deep blue eyes widened until they seemed to fill her face. Something as cold and hard as a stone turned over inside her. She had come to love Spain—almost as much as she loved the man who stood before her, mantled in icy reserve. But she was to be packed off back to England.

It was for the best, she assured herself staunchly. She had fallen in love with a man who didn't know the meaning of the word. He had never known love as a child. His mother had died and his father had blamed him, turned his back on him. And, if her suspicions were correct, his intentions towards her were as devious as a pack of monkeys.

His intention had always been to get rid of her. Not quite with the flea in her ear, as he'd initially promised, but with a big fat bribe. Whoever had heard of an unqualified nobody commanding such a high salary, with free accommodation thrown in on top?

There was only one way his tricky mind would be working. He would have seen her demand that he bring her back here and her babbling about finding a job as a ploy to return to the gullible elderly man she'd been working on. Hence his swiftness in spiking her guns, by promising to find her suitable work and accommodation. It was all falling into place.

He hadn't been able to bring himself to carry out his intention to seduce her away from what he believed were her greedy designs on his naïve old uncle, because after that initial kiss the very thought of going further had turned his stomach. But he was still desperate to get her away from his wealthy beloved relative.

Her chin came up. He was so unfairly, incredibly handsome she didn't know whether to slap him or burst into tears.

She did neither. She could be tricky, too.

'Thanks for the offer. I might well take it. Or I might decide to stay on as your uncle's companion.' Completely out of the question, but he wasn't to know that. And the threat should give him a huge dose of indigestion! Her blue eyes sparked. 'I'll let you know.' And she walked away.

Cayo's eyes narrowed as he watched her. Part of him wanted to spank her. Part of him admired the way she always managed to stand up to him. And yet another part, the most insistent of all, wanted to make love to her until she didn't know where she was.

CHAPTER ELEVEN

PRE-DINNER drinks were being served by smoothly circulating white-coated waiters. In the main salon, beneath the breathtakingly beautiful painted ceiling, the A-list guests mingled. The noise level was muted, because these superbly groomed sophisticates didn't do rowdy, full-on partying. And the jewels displayed on pampered pale fingers, around elegant necks and pinned into glossy, expensively styled hair would probably pay off the national debt of any large third-world country.

Izzy shivered. She *so* didn't want to be here.

The sore thumb.

People were looking at her—not ill-bred enough to stare, of course, but sending ever so slightly inquisitive looks in her direction, as if she were a gatecrasher, muscling in where she had no right to be. And it wasn't as if she'd appeared in her oldest jeans and shrunken jumper, either.

The classy floor-length Fornier creation in soft ice-blue satin either skimmed or clung in all the right places, and she'd taken endless pains to anchor her hair securely on top of her head. It was far too early on in the evening for it to be doing its own thing and tumbling all over the place.

Clutching her untouched flute of champagne, she wished she'd stuck to her guns and taken herself off for an early night. But Miguel had made her promise.

She'd spent the late afternoon with him and the tenants, mixing and mingling, entranced by the flamenco display, clapping along with everyone else, and reduced to helpless giggles when she and the fat farmer who'd invited her to dance had fallen over each other's feet. He'd sat on the grass, legs outsplayed, roaring with laughter, and a small crowd had gathered and started clapping and cheering.

She guessed she was good at making a fool of herself, if nothing else! But it had all been good fun, and when Miguel had announced his intention of retiring and skipping the later, more sophisticated banquet and ball, she'd said she'd do the same. But...

'I can plead age and infirmity. And disinclination. You can do no such thing. And you will enjoy it. I want you to promise me you'll attend. To please me? Cayo will look after you.'

But Cayo was doing no such thing. Looking head and shoulders more handsome and charismatic than any other guy in the room, he was circulating, his smile effortlessly charming, the white dinner jacket he was wearing making him look good enough to eat.

Ignoring her.

She sighed. Telling porkies—saying she might after all stay on as Miguel's companion, thus getting her own back on Cayo for his hard-headed intention to get rid of her, get her right out of the country—didn't seem such a brilliant idea right now.

The moment he could drag himself away from the flirtatious Spanish beauty dressed in black and wearing enough diamonds to sink a battleship, she would dive in, tell him she would accept the job back home and leave Spain as soon as it could be arranged. Then she would go to her room with all speed.

And she would never see him again—because she would lose no time, once back in England, in looking for something else—anything. Because he might at some time in the future make a flying visit to the UK office, and she didn't want to be there when he did. It would set her back miles and miles on the road to recovering from her ill-conceived love for the brute.

Itching to act on that decision, she was more dismayed than puzzled when the butler silently advanced on her and told her she had a visitor. 'In the great hall, *señorita*. He is waiting. He says he is your brother.'

Jettisoning her unwanted drink on a convenient table, Izzy hitched up her narrow silk skirts and tottered on the highest heels Madame Fornier had provided after the gliding butler.

What on earth could James be doing here? Half a world away from his important work, the home she'd been told was the last word in refinement, and his clever, sensible wife—all the things that boosted his overblown ego.

Trust him to turn up when she least wanted to see him! He was her brilliant big brother, and she admired him, but he could be a real pain. Like the time when she'd been around eight and he'd found her experimenting with their mother's make-up. Lipstick and mascara, rouge and eyeshadow had been daubed in great clown-like splodges, when she should have been in her own room, as instructed, copying out a list of the kings and queens of England, complete with dates and fates, in her best handwriting.

He'd sneaked on her—of course he had—and got her into boiling hot water! Metaphorically and literally. Her father had grabbed her by the scruff of her neck and scrubbed her face with soap and hot water, and her mother had vented one of her long-suffering, despairing sighs and rushed to try to rescue what she could of her ruined cosmetics.

Now James was here. And she had no idea how or why. Tall, thin, with a long face and light brown hair thinning on top, he looked a decade older than forty. He was like a stark accusation in the perfumed frivolity of the enormous flower-decked space. 'What on earth are you doing here?' she said bluntly.

'Fetching you home,' he snapped back at her. 'When we received your letter breaking the news that you'd left your job as mother's help, and were working for an old man you'd apparently met in some backstreet, we had a family meeting and decided unanimously that you had to be brought away. Either to New Zealand, where we can keep an eye on what you're doing, or more usefully back to the job in Father's old practice you so stupidly left.'

His long features were flushed with barely controlled

anger. His precious dignity must be precariously balanced, Izzy guessed. He would be feeling uncomfortable and stupid—an effect he and, to a slightly lesser degree, her parents had always had on *her*.

'Father's spoken to the new head of practice and he's willing—with certain reservations, naturally—to give you your job back.' He glowered his impatience. 'Do you have any idea how much time I'm wasting on your behalf? How much inconvenience I've been put to? Travelling halfway round the world to drum some sense into your head! You weren't at the address you'd given, but a neighbour told me where you'd gone, and with whom. That you've foisted yourself on the charity of a family of such high social and financial standing leaves me appalled and practically speechless. You've been a nuisance and a disappointment since the day you were born, but this takes the biscuit!'

Izzy cut off her self-destructive impulse to point out that he didn't *sound* speechless, because she knew from unpleasant past experience that answering James back brought swift and usually painful retribution.

'I haven't foisted myself on anyone—' Izzy did her best to defend herself, but her voice was thick with tears. James always made her feel a no-account failure, and he obviously wasn't going to listen to a word she said.

'I have a taxi waiting and our flights back to the UK leave first thing in the morning,' he cut in coldly. 'So I'd appreciate it if you'd pack your things and be quick about it while I find Señor Garcia and apologise on your behalf.'

'No apologies are necessary.' Cayo strode forward.

He'd heard enough. If he heard any more he'd take that long streak of disdain by the scruff of his neck and throw him off his property.

Izzy's bright head was bent, her slender shoulders sagging with humiliation. Anger on her behalf boiled inside him. So this was the brilliant brother who'd always cast such a shadow over her, causing odious comparisons—and being made to feel third-rate, as Miguel had suspected—and blighting her young life.

His mouth tightened in unforgiving lines as, reaching her side, he slid an arm around her tiny waist. He felt her tremble, saw her eyes sweep up to seek his—deepest blue, glittering with unshed tears. Tears of humiliation.

His hand tightened protectively around her. She leaned into him. And his voice was flint, his eyes even harder, as he informed the older man, 'Izzy stays here for precisely as long as she is happy to. She is my welcome guest.' His accent thickened. 'Should I ever hear you speaking like that to her again you will find your teeth at the back of your throat.'

Seeing James Makepeace, brilliant surgeon, turn the colour of an overripe tomato gave him immense satisfaction—although it shouldn't, of course. He had never threatened anyone with physical violence before, or been so deliberately, bluntly rude. He'd always regarded such behaviour as being uncouth. And uncouth he wasn't. Chilling politeness when displeased was more his style. But something about this situation had made him lose his cool. Big-time.

Carefully moderating his tone, reining in his astonishing pugilistic impulses, he imparted, with the calm of a frozen lake, 'Your sister is among friends who value her, who will care for her. I suggest you relay *that* information to your parents.'

Izzy could hardly believe her ears! Or her eyes! Cayo had leapt to her defence! He must have followed her out, heard the bulk of what had been said and waded in to put her brother firmly in his place. Something that, to her knowledge, had never happened to him before. He was more used to being spoiled, praised and listened to as if he were the fount of all wisdom. And now James, who always gave the impression of being vastly superior to anyone in his vicinity, was looking distinctly uncomfortable.

Her soft heart melted. He was her brother, after all. And if he'd come looking for her because he cared for her, was worried for her, then she would have done as he'd said—packed her things and left with him. As it was, all he'd done was make her feel she was a nuisance, that her behaviour in attaching her useless self to such an important family was shameworthy enough to warrant a man-to-man apology.

A lump in her throat, she offered, 'James—I'm really sorry you felt you had to come all this way. There was no need, truly. And tell Dad I'll pass on going back to the practice.' The thought of returning to her one-time work place, where everyone would know of her juvenile crush on Marcus, would be laughing at the way she'd run errands for him, cleaned his flat just for a kind word, made her feel queasy. 'Because Señor Garcia has offered me a job in his UK offices. As soon as I take that up I'll phone and let you know.'

At her side she felt Cayo's lean, muscled body stiffen. Relief because he'd soon see the back of her? Because she wasn't going to do as she'd threatened and stay on for ever as Miguel's totally unnecessary companion with the aim of getting her hands on his wealth as was his impossible-to-shift conviction?

But that didn't fit with the way his arm still curved protectively around her tense body, the way he'd leapt to defend her against James's cutting tongue. Unless he was the type of guy who always took the underdog's side, deserving or not...

She raised a shaky hand to rub at the crease of bewildered confusion between her eyes, and heard Cayo's stiffly polite tones as he offered, 'May we give you some refreshment before you leave?' She looked up to catch her brother's tight-lipped, disapproving expression before he uttered a brief negative, turned and walked out. Not deigning to comment on the new job, not even looking at her. Not saying goodbye.

Tears flooded her eyes. She was ashamed of the weakness. She'd always known her family didn't rate her—and James in particular—so she shouldn't let what had happened upset her so much.

Cayo dropped his arm from her waist. Her body felt icy cold where his touch had been. His voice rough with unconcealed humour, he told her, 'I do believe your very proper brother thinks I'm keeping you here as my paramour, *querida*!'

Izzy's breasts heaved and a hot knot of misery rose in her throat. The idea of being his paramour made her legs go weak, took her breath away, but *he* found it unthinkable enough to be amusing!

And he had probably guessed James's suspicions correctly. After all, Cayo had been very defensive of her—standing up close, sliding his arm around her, proprietorial and protective. And how many times in the past had James accused her of being a brainless blond bimbo? Dozens! Brainless enough to shack up with the first man to ask her?

She shivered. The guests would be being ushered through to be seated at the enormous dining table any time now, to enjoy the sumptuous banquet the chef and his assistants had been preparing all day. She wouldn't be among their number. She had to hole up somewhere quiet, where she could think, try to assess this latest situation, try to work out what Cayo really thought about her.

'You are upset.' Strong hands fastened on her naked shoulders, turning her into him. 'Look at me.'

Hardly daring to, because this close to him it was impossible not to look up into those lean, bronzed features, impossible to slap down the absolute and terrifying need to reach up and cover that charismatically handsome face with fevered, desperate kisses. But he lifted a hand, and the feel of the pads of his long fingers just beneath her chin had her raising her eyes to his, willpower flying.

A tear escaped, trembled on her lashes and fell. He bent his dark head and captured it with his lips. 'Please don't cry. He's not worth it.'

Cayo had never considered the position of his heart

before. It functioned. End of story. But now he definitely felt that reliable organ make itself known, turning to warm, soft marshmallow. A deep breath tugged at his lungs.

He knew exactly what it felt like to grow up without knowing love. Izzy had had her family around her, but all they had done, apparently, was compare her unfavourably with her brainy big brother and make her feel unimportant, a nuisance, a total failure, because she didn't match her brother's brilliant achievements. And she hadn't had a kindly, caring uncle to make her feel valued, as he had.

'You are ten times the human being your brother is. From the little I've seen of him, and heard, he's a cold, pompous, insensitive prig—he may be a clever surgeon, but you are warm, feisty, and you give of yourself. Remember that.'

His voice was so low it was almost a whisper, and Izzy gasped as he swung her into his arms. Still reeling from the light, lingering touch of his lips on the angle of her cheekbone, she could only cling on for dear life as he skirted the newly erected dais where the mini-orchestra would play for those who wished to dance later and effortlessly mounted the ancient stone staircase.

Reaching the room she was using, he slid her to her feet, slid her down the length of his body, shattering the small amount of equilibrium left to her. Her mind went blank, and she was stingingly aware of the heat pulsing through her, pooling deep in her tummy, of the way her unbearably sensitised breasts pushed against the pale blue satin.

Desperately hanging on to the very last scrap of sanity left to her, she turned—turned her back to him. The unpleasant scene with James was forgotten, unimportant. The only feeling to possess her mind, soul and body was her self-destructive love for this urbane, tricky, devastatingly charismatic man, who could have his pick of the world's most beautiful and suitable females.

She should be locked up for her own protection!

'You should go now. Your guests will be missing you.' Her voice was shaking so much she wondered how she'd managed to get the words out.

'Let them. Iglesias—' he named his butler '—is discreet and intelligent, which is why he holds his position here. He will see the banquet runs smoothly without my presence.'

Cayo's brooding eyes caressed the nape of her neck. Pale and vulnerable. One of the shoestring straps had dropped, now lay across the smooth warm flesh of her upper arm. The line of her shoulder and neck was exquisite. His fingers itched to remove the pins that restricted the gloriously untamed tangle of silky silvery curls so he could bury his face in its perfumed softness. She smelled evocatively of sunshine, fresh air and flowers.

Hadn't anyone, at any time, told her how beautiful she was? How special?

He could fully understand now why his uncle was so fond of her, so protective. A sensitive and wise man, he had seen the intrinsic goodness of her caring nature—where he had seen only a devious schemer, believing he was right until Augustin del Amo had admitted the truth.

He should be hung, drawn and quartered—along with her wretched family for their collective criminal blindness. And the idea that manufacturing a job for her in the UK was adequate recompense for his initial behaviour towards her made him cringe with shame.

His body hardened unbearably. He gave a silent groan. He wanted this woman with an urgency he had never fully experienced before.

Therefore, and entirely logically… 'Izzy.' He placed large hands on her slender shoulders and turned her to face him. 'Marry me.'

CHAPTER TWELVE

IN TOTAL tongue-tying shock, Izzy could only stare up into his heartstoppingly beautiful features, her eyes widening until they almost filled her delicate, furiously colouring face. Had she finally lost all of her sanity? Every last, dwindling scrap of it!

Perhaps it was the overwhelming, vital force of the closeness of his lean and fantastic body, the bone-dissolving touch of his hand on her over-sensitised skin. Or maybe it was the headily seductive perfume of the many deep bowls of ghostly white lilies, coupled with the witchy dark shadows that were creeping from the corners of the timelessly elegant room, that had spooked her into totally losing her grip on reality.

She shook her head sharply in a vain attempt to clear it. She felt the mass of her hair start to tumble, and wished he'd move away, stop touching her. And then, chaotically, she wished he'd move even closer.

'Well, *amada*?' Cayo murmured, soft and only just audible, his hands moving to gently cradle her face, his fingers splayed in the silken blond glory of her hair.

He was too bewitched by her brilliant eyes, the slightly trembling, luscious pink and temptingly kissable mouth, to ask himself why a man who had vowed never to marry should do the absolutely unthinkable and shackle himself, while of sound mind, to one woman. A woman who would have the right to make demands on his time, his privacy, his valued independence. But moments ago he had opened his mouth and listened to a proposal come out.

'Sorry.' It was a gigantic effort to speak at all. Scrambling frantically for some shred of down-to-earth reality, Izzy said, 'I guess I didn't hear you too well.' Her voice wobbled disgracefully. He couldn't really have asked her to marry him, could he? Him? It was so unlikely it made her feel really weird.

The pad of one thumb trailed delicately over her parted lips. The other tucked beneath her chin, positioning her mouth beneath his, and his voice was thick as he repeated, 'Marry me, *amada*.' Lowering his head slowly until his lips were a whisper away from the trembling, agonising expectancy of hers, he said, 'Say yes, my Isabella.' Light as silk, soft and warm as melted honey, his mouth touched hers, breathing the imperative deep into her soul. 'Say it. Say yes.'

Reduced to a shivering, clinging mass of dizzy, shameless longing, she breathed her answering mindless affirmative—and gasped with excruciating excitement as he claimed her mouth with unashamed masculine urgency. Her knees gave way beneath her as his tongue plunged with masterful sensuality deep into the moist sweetness of her mouth.

In answer to her suddenly boneless predicament, Cayo lifted her in his arms and carried her to the massive four-poster. Brushing aside the filmy white drapes, he laid her on the ivory silk counterpane, his fierce arousal disordering his breathing. Never before had he felt so hot for a woman, and it felt good—so good.

His body strained to claim hers, to plunge deeply into the hot slickness of her. But this had to be special. For the first time in his life he wanted to give pleasure more than he wanted to take it.

Bending to trail his fingers over her delicate collarbone, he vowed, 'I will make you happy, my Izzy.' He allowed his fingers to trail lower, over the tantalising upper swell of her breasts, until he came to the barrier of satin. He moved them slowly down, over the soft fabric, sucking in a deep breath as his hands cradled the glorious bounty of her breasts, registered the tormenting hardness of her straining nipples.

He breathed something rawly fractured in his own language and then lifted her, his long sure fingers dealing with the back fastening of her dress.

Exultant, Izzy helped him. She loved Cayo with a depth that both shocked and delighted her, and she wanted him with an urgent need that broke the bounds of what she had dreamed possible. Hedonistically she gloried in her nakedness as the last scraps of silk and lace were removed and heedlessly tossed aside. And lay in the misty, bewitching dusk, watching as he dealt summarily with his own clothes, her eyes never leaving him, his eyes never leaving her.

Izzy squirmed impatiently with the flame of greedy excitement. He exuded raw sexual power. The breadth of his magnificent golden-skinned shoulders, the muscular strength of his deep chest, long powerful thighs. Responsive heat engulfed her.

This gorgeous, totally adored man wanted her as his wife!

She lifted welcoming arms as he took the single stride that brought him back to her and slid beside her. His voice was thick as he ground out, 'I've wanted you like this for far too long, *amada*. Every time I looked at you I wanted to take you to bed. Holding back has driven me half crazy!' And his mouth took hers again, with a passion that sent her deep into delirium.

Izzy came awake slowly. The sun was up, golden light spilling in bands over the luxurious carpet. Cradled in Cayo's arms, she stretched languorously and turned glowing eyes to him as he hoisted himself on one elbow, brushed the tangle of curls from her forehead and dropped a light kiss between her brows.

'Buenos días, querida,' he murmured, dark eyes soft and slumbrous. 'Last night was wonderful. All I ever dreamed it could be.'

Her thoughts precisely. Although 'wonderful' seemed an inadequate way to describe what had happened. Fantastic and earth-shattering hit the spot a little more accurately. Though what had happened between them during the night hours had been beyond any words at a mere mortal's command, she decided, feeling distinctly awestruck.

Wrapping her arms around him, she nuzzled into the warm solidity of his chest, a dreamy smile curving her lips as she pleaded softly, 'Tell me you love me?' She wanted to hear those words so badly—wanted to share what she felt with him.

For a moment he seemed to tense. She felt the tightening of the muscles in his back, and then he gave a soft laugh, spread her on her back. He lowered his lips to hers and promised, 'I love your mouth, your hair, your fantastically sexy body.'

He dipped a sure hand between her thighs and she had to fight to stop herself from screaming with ecstasy as he found the slick, pulsating seat of her sex, and stars exploded deep inside her as he proceeded to demonstrate exactly how much he loved her body.

'What are you doing?'

'Getting dressed.'

Well, that was obvious, Izzy thought as she came properly awake, peering at him through lazy, love-drenched eyes. A knot of unbelievable excitement clenched inside her. She was going to be his *wife*! Life simply couldn't get better than this!

Getting dressed... Pushing his dress shirt into the narrow waistband of his beautifully tailored black trousers.

Hoisting herself up against the pillows, she pushed her hair out of her eyes. She might be disappointed, but she wasn't going to show it. 'I had this fantasy of our having breakfast in bed together, and then the two of us having a nice little lie-in,' she confided lightly. Her eyes sparkled. She felt so comfortable with him now—part of him, almost. She could say anything, tease him.

But he wasn't smiling. Indolent dark eyes were fastened on the lushly full globes of her naked breasts, and a muscle at the side of his sensual mouth tightened. 'It is a fantasy I wish I could enjoy, *querida*.' He came to her, touched his lips to each pink crest in turn, and then to her mouth.

Izzy sighed voluptuously, her hands going to his flat waist, tugging him towards her. Would she ever be able to get enough of him? She didn't think so! She had never dreamed such passion could exist.

But he took her hands, laid them at her sides and tucked the sheet up to her chin. 'Don't tempt me,' he growled, but he was smiling. And then he was serious as he told her, 'I want you to promise to say nothing of our betrothal for now—not even to Miguel. In a few days, when your brother has had time to get back to his home and is calmer, we will phone and break the news—invite him, his wife and your parents to our wedding. James and I didn't part on the best of terms,' he understated. 'For your sake I would like things to be on a happier footing. To that end, you must be able to truthfully tell your family that they are the first to hear of our plans.'

He straightened, ruffling his fingers through her hair. 'While I'm anxious for my uncle to share our good news, I really do believe that under the circumstances your family should be the first to know. That is why I don't want any member of my staff to discover me sharing your room. The gossip would spread around the castle like wildfire, and Miguel would be morally outraged if he thought I was taking advantage of you! So until we can break the news to your family it must be our secret. Besides, I need to personally apologise to James for my less than welcoming behaviour—I would hate to cause a rift between our families.'

He grinned disarmingly, running his fingers through his already rumpled midnight hair, and Izzy smiled back. Loving him. It was really good of him to want her family to feel special because they were to be the first to be told of her forthcoming marriage.

Watching him collect last night's discarded white dinner jacket before leaving the room, Izzy felt her heart nearly burst with love. He was such a diplomat! For her sake he would actually apologise to her pompous, ultra-critical brother, and maybe her whole family would for once change their entrenched opinions and admit that in falling in love with Cayo Garcia she hadn't been so stupid, after all!

The stout castle walls seemed to hum with activity when Izzy finally left her room, dressed in a cool cotton skirt and a pretty cropped top—courtesy of Madame Fornier's excellent taste.

Staff were clearing away all signs of last night's festivities and dealing with the aftermath of the buffet breakfast that had apparently been served. Her stomach rumbled—a reminder that she hadn't eaten in ages.

Cayo, casually dressed in cream-coloured chinos and a crisp shirt, was overseeing the exodus of the overnighting guests. Wondering if he was making his excuses for having missed the banquet, or if he was sticking to the alpha male's creed of never explaining, never apologising, she grinned wickedly and headed for the kitchens.

Rodolfo, the chef's assistant, was feeding Benji. He looked up and grinned widely. '*Señorita*, may I get you something? Coffee, perhaps? Or maybe—' he put a doleful expression on his boyish face '—you only come to take this hairy one for the walk?'

Every time she encountered Rodolfo he pretended to try to flirt with her—a habit that would vanish once he learned she was to marry his master. She grinned right back at him. This morning she wanted to smile at everyone. 'Coffee would be lovely.'

Spying a tray of crusty rolls—left over from breakfast service, she guessed—she helped herself. She bit gratefully into the crisp crust and wondered if she would be able to catch Cayo after the last of the guests had left. She knew she would have to avoid Miguel for the rest of the day, because he would be sure to ask how she had enjoyed the ball he'd been so insistent she attended.

Give him twenty-four hours and he would, as usual, be so lost in his work he would have forgotten all about it. Sipping gratefully at the coffee Rodolfo gave her, she watched Benji finish his breakfast and chase his empty bowl over the slabbed floor. She tried to imagine her wedding dress—sleek, sophisticated silk, or frothy in-your-face bridal lace? Picturing herself in either, walking up the aisle on her father's arm to Cayo, who would look devastatingly handsome, made her stomach twist itself into knots.

Unable to stand still a moment longer, she smiled beatifically at nothing in particular, called to Benji and exited by the maze of corridors that brought her out into the service courtyard. She made her way to the perimeter meadows, where the puppy could run and play.

There she sat, in the long seeding grasses, and waited. Waited in a bone-melting, loving trance until Cayo joined her.

'I knew you'd find me.' Eyes sparkling, she gazed up at him with unhidden adoration, reached for his hand as he hunkered down beside her.

Brilliant dark eyes set within heavy black lashes gleamed at her. 'How could I not? Come.' He straightened, whistled for the puppy, who was chasing a bee with no chance of success, and pulled her to her feet. 'There are soft rugs and a large picnic hamper waiting for us in my car. I want you to myself,' he confided thickly. 'Today we find a remote mountain meadow and we make love until the stars shine above us. Do you want that as much as I do, *querida*?'

Want it? Izzy nodded vigorously. She felt as though she were floating in space, her bones and flesh turning to jelly at his words. She wanted him so much she could barely walk, let alone speak!

CHAPTER THIRTEEN

Izzy tucked the hem of a soft sage-green sleeveless blouse into the waistband of a cream-coloured linen skirt. It was surprising how she'd got used to wearing the sort of beautiful, classy clothes she wouldn't have dared to even look at, let alone been able to afford to buy in her previous permanently cash-strapped existence, she mused as she peered in the tall looking glass, trying to bring some semblance of order to her defiantly wayward hair.

The only thing she couldn't get used to was Cayo's absence.

He'd been away for five days, ten hours—she checked her watch—and thirty-five minutes.

She missed him so much that every fibre in her body ached. Missed the nights when he had come to her room, the days spent well away from the castle, exploring the countryside, making love, eating in little out-of-the-way inns, returning late at night to make love again. Missed the sound of his voice, being able to look at him, drink in all that lean and magnificent male beauty.

It had been an idyll. So utterly perfect she'd felt mildly disorientated, as if she were living in a wonderful dream. Until...

'*Querida*, I have to be away for a day or so.'

Coming down for early breakfast one day—discreetly, arriving in the sunny garden room at a different time from him—she had found him swallowing the last of his coffee, dressed in a light grey designer suit and a pristine darker grey shirt. He had taken her breath away. 'I'm sorry, but something's come up that I can't deal with from here.' His dark eyes had been veiled. He hadn't looked at her. Getting to his feet, he had reached for the document case stowed beside his chair. 'I'll be back before you know it.'

Izzy had sat down with a bump.

Running down the massive staircase, dressed the way she knew he liked to see her, in a floaty flowered skirt topped by the bikini top he always said he couldn't resist removing the moment they were assured of privacy, she had been almost bouncing up and down in her impatience to phone her parents in Wellington and break the fantastic news of her forthcoming wedding.

'But it's been four days,' she reminded him in a breathy rush, 'James will be settled back home by now. I thought we could phone them this morning.' She angled a beaming smile at him. 'I can't wait to tell everyone!'

'It can wait for a day or two longer.' He dropped a distracted kiss on the top of her head, straightened, and prepared to leave.

Izzy caught his hand, preventing his departure, deeply

disappointed by the further delay, and even more so by his planned absence. It drained all the joy out of her day, and she queried, 'When did you decide you had to leave?'

Disconcerted, he frowned, removing his hand from her clutching fingers. 'Last night. Does it matter?'

Last night—while they'd been making love? Had his mind been elsewhere, busily planning this morning's departure? She felt her face flush. 'But you said nothing,' she accused miserably. 'If I'd come down half an hour later would you just have left? Without a word?'

Unused to having his actions questioned by anyone, Cayo stifled a snappy response. Some creative thinking was called for here. But making excuses for his behaviour was beyond him. 'Don't be silly. Of course not!' A fleeting smile. 'Don't pick a fight, *querida*!'

Five minutes later, listening to the noise of helicopter rotors beat the air, Izzy felt abandoned and utterly miserable, like a commodity to be used when time allowed and then put aside, forgotten, when something more interesting popped over the horizon. He hadn't even bothered to warn her that he'd have to go away on business.

Then she told herself to grow up. Fast! She was to marry a man who controlled vast wealth, many highly successful business enterprises. Of course there would be times when he had to take off at the drop of a hat. What sort of wife would she make if she sniped at him or sulked whenever that happened?

The sort of wife he would soon wish he'd never met, she informed herself grimly.

So she would take his sudden departures, his obvious concentration on the work at hand, with good grace— accept that his air of abstraction, of distance from her, was because his mind was preoccupied with whatever business dealings lay ahead. She would make him a wife he could be proud of, and not act like a whining child suddenly deprived of its favourite toy!

Now, slipping her feet into low-heeled pumps, she reflected uneasily that it had been almost two weeks since he'd asked her to marry him and it was still a secret.

A secret she was bursting to share!

Yesterday she'd been sorely tempted to phone her family and share the news that was lodged like a great heavy rock in her chest, bursting to get out. A temptation so strong she had found her hand resting on the phone on a couple of occasions.

But she had resisted, albeit with difficulty, and she congratulated herself thinly. Cayo had asked her to wait. He wanted to speak to her parents personally and make his apologies to James—smooth her brother's ruffled feathers, make sure no bad feeling existed between him and her family. So for his sake she'd grit her teeth and keep her impatience under wraps.

Satisfied that she looked reasonably calm and collected, she left her room to join Miguel for afternoon tea. She smiled softly, glad to have something to think of other than Cayo's frustratingly long absence.

It was a ritual the elderly man had insisted on since his nephew's sudden departure. English afternoon tea, complete with tiny triangular cucumber sandwiches and seed cake, was to be served at four every afternoon in the library.

She'd told him that the custom had virtually died out with the Edwardians, but he'd insisted, and always used the occasion to gently quiz her. Was she happy at Las Palomas? Did the heat of high summer make her miss her cooler home climes? And, more pertinently, was she missing the young man she'd left behind? Was she still hurting over him?

She longed, quite desperately, to confide that she and his nephew were to marry, that in the near future she'd be part of the family, and she had to bite her tongue to stop the words bubbling out in an excited torrent. She reminded herself that, nominally at least, she was still supposed to be here as Miguel's companion.

Wondering what gentle questions she would have to parry this afternoon, she approached the partly opened library door. And stopped in her tracks as she heard voices. Delighted colour flooded her cheeks, and her heart leapt wildly.

Cayo was back!

About to push the door fully open, wondering how she would be able to act normally, stop herself from flinging herself into his arms, she froze.

Because Cayo—her adored, soon-to-be-husband— was saying, 'On the subject of marriage, Tio, I have told you—a man would be a fool to settle for one flower when he can flit from one blossom to another with impunity and retain his freedom…'

Smothering a gasp as her heart lurched sickeningly,

Izzy flattened herself against the wall for support, shutting out the excruciating sound of the words that spelled out her betrayal. How could he *say* those things? And sound so amused when saying them? How could he do that to her?

Unaware that her cheeks were wet with tears, she fled back to her room.

Her heart felt as if it had been split in two with a very sharp knife. He'd spelled it out, clear as spring water. He would use a woman when the urge hit him. Move on to the next when the challenge of pursuit was sated. Not caring who got hurt in the process so long as he kept his precious freedom!

Oh, how could he?

He'd had no intention of marrying her, she conceded bitterly. No wonder he'd been so insistent on keeping their phantom wedding plans secret!

Angry colour stung her cheekbones. What had he planned? To distance himself for a few days, thus giving her unashamed ardour time to cool—her face flamed anew at the reminder of just how unashamed she had proved to be—and then on his return calmly inform her that he'd changed his mind? There would be no wedding. He would resurrect the offer of a job in the UK and wave her goodbye at the airport without a flicker of conscience.

Because the high and mighty Cayo Angel Garcia didn't own such an uncomfortable thing!

Recalling how blown away she'd been when he'd confessed that he'd been wanting to get her into bed, had had difficulty holding back, she bared her teeth in a grimace of self-loathing.

She'd already been head over heels in love with him, and—naïve idiot, that she was—his offer of marriage had clinched it. She'd thrown herself body, heart and soul into bed with him. How he would have gloated! And now, having sated his sexual curiosity, he was preparing to ditch her.

Far too late she remembered how she'd been so suspicious of his motives between leaving Madrid and his sudden, out-of-the-blue proposal of marriage, wondering if his bewildering behaviour meant he didn't entirely believe the truth he'd said he'd had from Augustin del Amo. And the way he'd called her *querida*—his translation of the word paramour, which she knew was an outdated term for mistress. How could she have so brainlessly allowed her heart to rule what passed for her brains?

Her family were right.

She was a fool.

Her own worst enemy.

Everything she did crumbled to ignominious failure!

Now she had to decide what to do. Pacing the floor and grinding her teeth would get her nowhere.

Stay and face him? Tell him exactly what she thought of him?

Water off a duck's back.

Besides, she couldn't trust herself not to give herself away—let him see how very much she'd adored him, how the hurt he'd dealt her went so deep she didn't think she'd ever get over it. Such information would fuel his already massive ego. So, no thanks. Such an outpouring of condemnation might bring her temporary relief, but the consequences would be cringe-making, and she couldn't bear to let herself down to that extent.

Or go?

Simply go?

Let him think she'd ditched him before he got the chance to tell her she was history?

Right. As good as done. It was the only way she could hope to salvage something from this ghastly situation.

Flying to the escritoire, she dug out a sheet of headed notepaper, scrabbled for a pen and scrawled.

It was fun while it lasted, and thanks for your offer, but I'll pass.

As a further dig she added:

I'm afraid it would take more than you can offer to tempt me to give up my freedom.

She stuffed it into an envelope, and propped it against the bed pillows before she could change her mind. There was a tight ball of misery in her chest because the thought of marrying him had made her deliriously happy—happier than she'd ever been in her entire life.

Scrambling out of her skirt and blouse, she dragged on a pair of her old jeans and a crumpled T-shirt and pushed the rest of her gear into her rucksack. She would take nothing she hadn't arrived with.

Passport. Purse. Her hand hovered over the cheque Miguel had given her—to make up for the pitifully low wages he had unthinkingly paid her back in Cadiz, he'd told her as he'd pressed it into her hands. A cheque she had had no intention of ever cashing. Reluctantly slipping it into her passport, she closed the straps of her battered rucksack. She had to be practical, even though she felt like having hysterics and breaking things. She would need money to tide her over until she could find work, though she felt horribly uneasy over taking it.

Her mangled heart gave another painful lurch. She would miss her old gentleman, and hated to leave without saying goodbye, giving Benji one last cuddle. At least she was confident that Miguel would look after the little stray. She would write to him when she was settled somewhere. Tell him how fondly she remembered being his housekeeper in Cadiz, and that she would always remember him with affection. To seek him out now would involve making explanations of a sort—which he probably wouldn't believe because she couldn't tell him the truth. And she'd run the risk of bumping into Cayo.

The thought that even now she might not be able to avoid him brought her heart to her mouth. True, she could jump in before he had a chance to open his mouth and tell him she'd decided that no way could she marry him, thanks all the same. But she knew that she would have zero hope of doing that without giving her true feelings of hurt and betrayal away, dissolving into accusations and floods of shaming tears.

Taking a deep breath, she tried to reassure herself that Cayo wouldn't be in a huge hurry to seek her out. He'd been talking to Miguel in the library. To explain the silver teapot, the sandwiches and cake, his uncle would have given him the information that she was due to join him at any moment. So he was probably still there, lounging back in the leather chair opposite the desk his uncle was using, drinking tea and looking forward to telling her she was dumped. Moving on with the rest of his gold-plated life!

Scuttling down the long and empty corridor, down the service staircase, avoiding the main living quarters, she made it to the kitchens. There was usually someone around, even at this quiet time of day, and several of the staff spoke her language. During Cayo's absence, with Miguel's help, she'd been trying to get her head round the basics of theirs. So she'd get by. Just about.

But the cavernous room was empty and silent. Most of the staff lived in, and she should have known they would be relaxing in their rooms or taking advantage of the custom-made gym and swimming pool in the extensive cellar region at this time of day.

Swallowing a frustrated sob, she darted out to the service courtyard, in the forlorn hope of finding someone still busy with some sort of duty. Immediately she spied Rodolfo, sprawled out on a bench in the shade, his nose in a newspaper.

Sending up a prayer of thankfulness for her deliverance, she pulled in a deep, hopefully calming breath and approached him, forcing herself to smile, because he was frowning at her horribly puffy reddened eyes.

'Are you busy?' Obviously he wasn't, but she felt it only polite to ask.

'No, *señorita*. May I help you?'

'I need a lift to the nearest town.'

'A lift?'

He was wrinkling his eyes. Clearly his knowledge of English didn't stretch that far.

'Someone to drive me to the nearest town or village.'

She didn't care where. All she cared about was putting distance between herself and the man who had so cruelly used and betrayed her, taken advantage of her deplorable naïvety. Feeling herself on the brink of tears, she forced her mouth to smile again. And felt weak with relief when he finally understood, folded his newspaper and got to his feet.

'Certainly, *señorita*, if it is possible. If the car for the staff is not in use, then I will drive you where you like. I will see.'

Watching him walk across the courtyard to the row of garages, Izzy held her breath. The appointed time for English afternoon tea was well and truly over. Had Miguel sent Cayo to look for her? Or roused the housekeeper? In either event, her letter would have been found.

How would Cayo explain the contents of the note to his uncle? Perhaps he wouldn't. Would just say she'd left. But Miguel cared about her. He'd insist she was found, question the staff. Any minute now a search party might explode into this courtyard, and she'd be forced to explain herself.

She couldn't face Cayo. She never wanted to have to lay eyes on him again. It would hurt more than her poor battered heart could bear!

Rodolfo had opened the doors of the farthest garage

and disappeared inside. To her tortured mind he seemed to have been out of sight for weeks instead of seconds. When she heard the well-bred purr of an engine she sagged with relief, and expelled the breath she hadn't realised she was holding. She had to force herself to stay where she was and not fly over the cobbles and fling herself into the slowly emerging sleek black car.

When the vehicle eventually sighed to a halt beside her, she made herself stand still while Rodolfo exited, all smiles, and paced round to open the rear door. Then, unable to contain herself a second longer, she was flinging the rucksack on the back seat and was into the front passenger seat before he could blink, fastening the seat belt with hands that felt like a dozen fat fumbling thumbs.

'You want shops?' The chef's assistant still looked puzzled.

Izzy decided hysterically that he probably thought she was unhinged, so she made her voice flat and level as she countered, 'No, I just want to explore a little while I am in your beautiful country.' Inside her head she was screaming, *Go! Go! Go!* But she invented, with a calmness that deeply amazed her, 'I'll find somewhere to stay for two or three nights and phone when I want to return to Las Palomas.'

Which would be never.

Rodolfo shrugged, slanting her a long, assessing look. Praying he didn't find her story so thin he'd feel duty-bound to check with his employers, Izzy said tightly, 'I *am* permitted time out to do my own thing.'

'Then Arcos, I think. Not too far—an hour to drive.

It is a beautiful town, one of the *pueblos blancos*, high on a rock, with a river running round and many places to stay—'

'Sounds perfect,' Izzy said through her teeth. She didn't need the tourist spiel. She would only be in the town for as long as it took to hire a taxi to take her some place else—back to the coast, where, hopefully, she would find work. 'Let's go, shall we?'

As Rodolfo complied, poker-faced, and the car purred towards the wide archway in the stout stone walls, Izzy didn't know how she managed to sit still. She only began to relax just a little when they were on the narrow, winding mountain road, and tried for a whole two seconds at a time to put her disastrous immediate past behind her.

Her uncertain future was something she was going to have to think about when she'd got herself together again—had stopped wanting to rant and rave and throw things and give Cayo Garcia a black eye that would keep him hiding behind shades for weeks, wanting to cry herself sick because she was hurting so badly.

Ten minutes into the journey, Izzy was sinking into a pit of such deep misery she didn't know how she was ever going to climb out of it. The imperious buzz of the in-car phone didn't make an impression until Rodolfo brought the car to a halt on a bend that overhung one of the scariest precipices she had ever seen.

'I must answer this.'

The young chef's assistant unhooked the instrument, listened more than he spoke. Izzy, her brow furrowing, could pick out the affirmatives but little else of the rapid Spanish interchange.

When the call ended he turned big soulful eyes on her. He looked chastened. 'That was *el patrón*,' he told her. 'We are to wait here until he comes.'

Izzy felt distinctly nauseous as her stomach jumped into her throat. 'Cayo?' She could hardly get his name past her shock-frozen lips.

'*Sí*. There is to be trouble.'

CHAPTER FOURTEEN

RAGE was consuming Cayo with a rare ferocity as he swung out of his car and approached the young man standing on the hot, dusty road, his face greenish beneath the olive-toned skin.

Tight-lipped, he issued terse instructions, then swung round and opened the door at Izzy's side. 'Out!'

She didn't look at him, he noted with dark wrathful eyes. Something had happened. He intended to find out what. He watched with barely contained impatience as she left the vehicle with obvious reluctance, her body stiff, her soft mouth set. She looked as if she were about to explode. Having been on the receiving end of her tirades in the past, he waited grimly.

It didn't happen. Like a poorly articulated puppet she allowed him to deposit her in the passenger seat of his car. She said nothing as he started the engine and drove at speed to where the narrow road flattened slightly and widened, permitting him to turn. He checked in his mirror that Rodolfo was following as instructed.

Izzy kept her eyes firmly on the window at her side, seeing nothing. Her heart was thumping. She couldn't look at him. If she did she would totally lose it. As it was, she was holding on to her self-control for grim life.

Clearly he was furious. He must have found her note, read it. It would have taken his analytical brain only one second to send him to check on the garages, to find the car the staff had the use of missing, punch in the numbers of the car phone—and bingo!

Though why he had bothered to drag her back she was too distraught to even begin to fathom. Asked to second-guess his reaction, she would have said that he must have tossed the note aside, shrugged his impressively wide shoulders and considered himself fortunate in being spared her possible recriminations. Or, worse, the unedifying spectacle of a female in messy, noisy tears when he told her he'd changed his mind on the subject of marriage.

Unless, of course, his head was so monumentally huge he couldn't stomach the idea of being given the heave-ho. *He* did the loving and leaving—not the other way round! It had to be a first for him. And he didn't like it. It made him furious.

In that moment she was sure she absolutely hated him. Staring fixedly ahead, she clipped out through a jaw that felt as if it had been set in concrete, 'Don't take your fit of pique out on Rodolfo. He was only following my instructions.' And then she shut up, before the lump in her throat choked her.

'And I intend to discover why you gave those instructions,' he came right back at her as he brought the car to a halt in the inner courtyard. An impatient stride brought him to where she sat, her neck and shoulders aching with tension.

On legs that felt as if they would give way at any moment, Izzy found herself being virtually frog-marched through the impressive main entrance. His fingers bit like a vice into her arm, and he merely dipped his head in cursory acknowledgement of the house-keeper who was refreshing the flower arrangements in the vast main hall. He totally ignored what sounded like some pleasantry coming from the portly woman, sweeping Izzy up the great stone staircase and depos-iting her in the room she had never expected to enter again.

The silence stung and lengthened unbearably. Re-flecting that she was such a failure she couldn't even manage an escape bid without being ignominiously hauled back, and with what passed as her pride in ragged tatters, Izzy swallowed a sob.

Cayo said, with a gentleness that shocked her rigid, 'Why did you write this?'

For the first time her eyes swung to him. Widened. He was holding the note she'd scribbled in such haste. Her heart twisted inside her breast. He'd discarded the jacket of his suit, and his white shirt was open at the base of his tanned throat, tucked into the waistband of his narrow-fitting trousers, dark grey this time. He looked, as always, utterly sensational.

Izzy trembled with the impact, but, straightening her already tense shoulders, told herself with iron determi-nation that she wasn't going to let herself get all moony and feeble over a man who was clearly an out-and-out louse. 'I would have thought it was clear enough,' she uttered thinly.

And he smiled—actually had the gall to smile!—and gave a negative shake of his far-too-handsome head, which sent a lock of his so touchable dark hair tumbling over his forehead.

It made her treacherous fingers ache to push it back, but she puffed out her chest and yelled, 'I don't want to marry you! I *won't*! Can't you understand something that simple?' She was almost hopping on the spot she was so plain cross—with him, with herself, with everything! 'You're just not used to having a marriage proposal flung in your face!' she spluttered.

'No.' His long, sensual mouth quirked unforgivably. 'I have never proposed marriage before, therefore I am a stranger to a refusal.' A graceful stride brought him close enough to cup her chin, to lift her face so that he could look deeply into her wide and now frantic eyes. 'Tell me what is wrong, my Isabella.'

When he used that intimate tone, employed the Spanish version of her name, she always melted in a puddle of goo. Now was no different.

'Don't!' She twisted her head away.

'Don't do what?' He captured her chin again, his thumb stroking her taut jawline. 'This? Touch you?' Taking her strangled groan as confirmation, he delivered, 'The words I read are not those of the woman I have come to know and love—'

That was too much! *Way* too much! 'Don't you *dare*

say that!' she exploded, pummelling his all too solid chest with ineffectual fists.

What was the tricky devil planning? To soft-talk her into bed with him again? To use that magnetic personality, that hypnotic sex appeal, those shatteringly charismatic good-looks, to turn her into a mindless slave all over again? And then, when he considered he'd got his just revenge for her crass impertinence in turning him down, to show her the door?

That wasn't going to happen! Unaccustomed as he was to anyone going against his wishes, this time he would find he'd met his match!

'Don't say what?' He caught her flailing fists between his strong hands, jerking her closer, so that she could feel his body heat, smell his tantalising male scent: fresh air, a faint aroma of lemony cologne. She trembled as he murmured, 'That I love you?'

Closing her eyes and pretending that being this close to him turned her stomach wasn't working. By anyone's reckoning he would come top of the seduction stakes—by a mile—in any league table! So she relaunched into attack mode, huge blue eyes brimming with withering scorn.

'Go to the top of the class! I asked you to tell me that once. You couldn't bring yourself to say it! Just blithered on about loving my body!'

He brought his head down to hers, nuzzling against her ear. His voice was soft with amusement as he told her, 'I didn't know I blithered. I must be getting old! Perhaps I should be careful not to start dribbling, too.'

Definitely against her better judgement, Izzy wanted to giggle.

He said, really soberly, 'I fudged it because I'm a fool. I'd been falling in love with you for weeks, but I was too set against allowing that I could, or ever would, give my future happiness into the hands of any woman to see it.'

Izzy would have given twenty years of her life to be able to believe him! The physical craving to melt into him, to lift her face for his kiss, was torture. But she was going to resist it with all her might.

She was so entangled with her inner battle that before she knew it she'd been led to the fancy empire-style sofa that stood beneath one of the tall windows that marched along the outer bedroom wall.

Cayo angled his lean and superb body beside her, his brilliant eyes narrowed on her pale features, and his voice was like an exquisite physical caress as he relayed, 'When I found that note I was furious enough to pull down the castle walls with my bare hands. Then my brain took over and told me that it made no kind of sense. Something had happened to make a sweet, loving woman on the brink of marriage run from the man she loved.'

His gentle smile, the soft touch of his hand as it briefly closed on hers, sent her into a tailspin.

'Tell me why a woman who'd work for next to nothing to care for an elderly man who, or so she believed, was severely impoverished, who would pass up the opportunity of acquiring an expensive new wardrobe to rescue a stray dog, a generously spirited woman with a heart as big as a bucket, a woman who'd think nothing about saying what she thought, shouting the odds if she felt an injustice had been done, would sneak away and leave such a vicious letter for the man she loves? It is not in character, my Isabella. So tell me the truth.'

She was going to cry!

No—no, she wasn't!

He couldn't blind her with soft soap! She knew the truth—knew what he was really like. He'd condemned himself within her hearing.

'You won't like this,' she pointed out. A man like Cayo Angel Garcia—a big shot in the world of business, top dog in all other spheres of his life—would hate having his shortcoming thrust under his handsome nose. 'You'd been away for longer than you'd said you would be. I was missing you,' she confessed. She'd lost everything when she'd heard the truth, so she might as well lose the last tattered rag of her pride. 'I heard you talking to Miguel and I was ecstatic. You were home. When I heard what you were saying I—' Her eyes flooded with despised tears. Reliving the nightmare brought her loss back to her with hideously savage reality.

'What I was saying?' Cayo prompted swiftly, a frown indenting his smooth brow as he watched the slow fall of her tears.

Furiously swiping at the wetness on her cheeks with the tips of her fingers, she lowered her head. She didn't want him to see the pain she was sure she wouldn't be able to hide. It hurt so badly to remember his words. So much more to actually repeat them. 'You were telling your uncle that you were anti-marriage, saying a man would be a fool to settle for one flower when he could flit from one to the other without losing his freedom.'

Having been found out in his duplicity, Izzy had fully expected him either to bluster or simply shrug and walk away. She certainly didn't expect his lazy reply. 'Do you always act like a headless chicken when faced with a crisis? Didn't it cross your mind to speak to me? Tell me what you thought you'd heard?'

Being compared to a headless chicken was just too much! She'd been called a brainless blond bimbo, a nuisance and a failure, and had taken it on the chin. But a headless chicken!

Her head snapped up, and she met his amused dark gaze with blue shards of ice. 'I didn't want you to see how much you'd hurt me,' she stated between gritted teeth. And if he started to gloat at that snippet of information she would hit him into next week! 'I heard what I heard. I didn't dream it up!'

'Sheath your claws, *amada*.' He reached forward, placed strong warm hands on her tiny waist and dragged her against the curve of his body.

Desire tugged at her. She resisted it, made herself rigid as a plank of wood, staring fixedly at the painting of a bowl of old-fashioned roses on the opposite wall. One of the blooms had fallen onto a light grey velvet cloth, like a dew-filmed deep red jewel. She told herself that she would never understand him in a million years. Having been found out, he should be making arrangements for her permanent and immediate removal. Not this. Whatever *this* was.

'Had you arrived a few moments earlier, or listened just a little longer, you would have heard what I really said.'

His dark head was so close to hers now. If she turned they would be touching. Her forehead against the side of his jaw...

Keep staring at the painting!

'My uncle can get tedious on the subject of my settling down and raising a family. Not having experienced a loving family life—just a father who could hardly bear to look at me, a series of tutors and then a rigidly strict boarding school—I convinced myself early on that I could stand alone. Besides, I believed I was incapable of wholehearted, unconditional love. I was a complete stranger to such an emotion,' he told her frankly. 'This afternoon I reminded Miguel of what my past and admittedly flippant response had always been, but I went on to tell him that, to his doubtless relief, I'd met a woman who had changed my mind.'

The temptation to believe him was strong enough to have her redoubling her efforts to remain totally unyielding. Until the flaw in his explanation hit her. She turned then, and glared at him, her words fizzing. 'Huh! So what happened to keeping the whole thing a deathly secret until we'd spoken to my family? Written in stone, that was! Forget your own strict orders, did you?'

Utilising the best way he knew to stop her yelling at him, Cayo covered her lips with his own, hauling her suddenly boneless body closer. He was already so hot for her he didn't know what to do with himself, but with aching reluctance he dragged his mouth from the heady invitation of hers and managed thickly, 'I didn't tell him who the woman was, only that I had met her. I still feel your family should be the first to be told. You have to believe me—believe that I love you, that I want you with me for the rest of my life, that I want to give you my children, to wake every morning with you at my side, to the sunshine you bring with you. Tell me you want that, too. Tell me you love me. I can't be happy without you.'

At the first intoxicating touch of his lips on hers she had been lost all over again, giddy and boneless, clinging to his broad shoulders with atavistic longing. And at his final words she knew she could believe him—trust him with her life and happiness.

Lifting one hand, she tenderly laid it against the side of his lean dark face, feeling the incipient stubble on his tough jaw, and spoke the words he wanted to hear through lips that felt swollen and ravaged from the unapologetic urgency of his kiss. She saw his dark eyes glitter with shameless male satisfaction.

He turned his mouth into the palm of her hand, and she loved the feeling so much that she had to reach up and cover the underside of his jaw with delirious kisses—until he gave a feral groan and took her face between his hands, his voice not quite steady as he said, in a tone that coming from any other man on the planet Izzy would have described as pleading, 'You will marry me?'

'Just try to stop me!' Not the most romantic response, as she would be the first to admit—but, hey, she was so ecstatic she hardly knew what she was saying.

When he dropped a kiss on the tip of her nose and said, 'So all is forgiven?' she could only giggle.

'Even the headless chicken insult!' she responded.

'Ah! Such a beautiful head, my Isabella.' Lingeringly, he ran his fingers through her untameable hair, and looked as if he was enjoying the sensation just as much as she was. 'An excusable reaction, under the circumstances. One I can fully relate to. When I read that note and thought I'd lost the one love of my life I was ready, for a few moments that are best forgotten, to do terminal damage to anyone or anything I laid my eyes on.'

'That bad, was it?' Izzy snuggled closer. She was the happiest woman ever to live.

Somehow or other her legs had got themselves hooked over his lap, and his hand that wasn't tucked very snugly around her waist was stroking the curve of her jeans-clad thigh with intent.

'I prefer you in skirts, *mi amada*.' He gave her the smile that always sent her off the planet. 'It is a crime to hide such lovely legs, such warm and generous thighs. But...' He vented a sigh that sounded as if it came from the soles of his feet. 'Tough stuff first.' He swung her to her feet and took one of her hands in his. 'Come. We phone your family, issue wedding invitations, and then break our news to Miguel—who will, understandably but frustratingly, insist on a celebratory dinner.' He lifted her hand to his lips, playing havoc with her ability to stand. 'It will be tough getting through the hours before I can have you to myself. I think, *mi amada*, I might go a little crazy!'

* * *

As the helicopter began its descent Izzy clutched Cayo's hand even more tightly. To take her mind off the tummy-churning sensation, she reflected dreamily on her wedding day.

It had been as perfect as it could get. A simple ceremony in the tiny village church—low key, to keep the paparazzi in the dark, Cayo had explained. He had a high media profile, and he refused to have that mob spoil their day. Then a sumptuous reception back at the castle, with all the staff invited along with what seemed like the cream of high-bred Spanish society.

She hadn't been fazed, though. Everyone had been lovely to her, and the language barrier no longer existed—or not really. Cayo had been proud of her attempts and had helped her with enthusiasm. Now she could converse with anyone, with only the occasional slip, which often gave her the giggles when her error was gently explained to her.

Her dad had looked proud of her as he'd walked her up the aisle, and her mother had beamed as if her hitherto trial of a daughter had done something right for the first time in her life. Even James had unbent sufficiently to give her an awkward hug, and his brainy wife had kissed her on both cheeks.

The four of them were to stay at Las Palomas for a short holiday with Miguel, who had pronounced himself delighted that this day had dawned, and had made a long, erudite speech to that effect, intimating that he'd known all along that she was the perfect wife for his picky nephew.

Even Benji had worn a white satin ribbon on his collar in honour of the occasion, and had been fed so many tidbits that he'd fallen asleep in a snoring heap on Miguel's lap.

The reception had still been in full, enjoyable swing when Cayo had plucked her out of the throng and carried her through the courtyard to where a limousine had been waiting to take them to the airport.

'I have already waited too long to have my new bride to myself,' he had murmured as he'd settled her on the rear seat, slid in beside her and closed the shaded glass partition between them and the driver. 'Now I shall make up for wasted time,' he'd vowed, removing her veil. And he had proceeded to kiss her senseless.

And now, after a night flight to Athens in his private jet and a short helicopter ride, they were circling an island, thickly wooded in places, with a tiny village bunched around a harbour. The rocky coastline admitted a few white-sanded coves, and there was a sprawling white mansion surrounded by smooth lawns and what looked like a really dreamy garden flowing down to meet a fern-covered ravine that led to a beach.

'It's so beautiful,' Izzy breathed as they touched down, entranced by what she saw. She gave her brand-new husband a radiant smile. 'Thank you for keeping our honeymoon destination secret. If I'd known we were coming to a Greek island I'd have been imagining what it would look like. Now it's a lovely surprise.'

'And it's yours,' Cayo supplied with his mesmerising smile as he lifted her out of the craft, setting her on her feet as he turned to speak to the pilot about unloading their gear.

Smoothing down the skirts of her fabulous wedding

dress—layers of the softest creamy lace over ivory silk, with a fitted bodice embroidered with seed pearls and the narrowest of sleeves, ending in a point just above her broad gold wedding band and the frankly enormous diamond Cayo had slipped on her finger after the ceremony—she watched with adoring eyes as he strode back to her.

Dawn had been breaking when they'd left Athens, and now the early morning shimmered, fresh and clear. Izzy, her eyes wide with excitement, told him, 'My own honeymoon island for two whole months—how lovely!'

'Yours for ever, wife!' He swept her up in his arms and began to stride towards the white villa.

Izzy, clutching at her trailing skirts with one hand, the other curled around the nape of his neck, said, sounding stunned, 'This is all mine? I can't believe it!'

'When I left you for a few days I was in Athens, pushing through the details. The owner wanted a quick sale—lock, stock and barrel. I didn't tell you what I was doing. I wanted it to be a surprise.'

'Oh, my!' She kissed him with an enthusiasm that stopped him in his tracks. 'What have I done to deserve you?'

'Simply been your own beautiful, loving self,' he answered on a husky growl.

He carried her over the threshold into a cool marble-floored living space, with gauzy curtains fluttering in the breeze from the high arched windows, delicate apricot-coloured walls and comfy-looking sofas covered in cream linen.

Wide glass doors opened onto a stone terrace overlooking the sea, and the kitchen was a dream. Even the bathrooms were a miracle of marble and glass.

'It's perfect!' Izzy breathed excitedly as Cayo set her on her feet in the master bedroom and kissed her smiling mouth. 'Will we be able to come here often?'

'Often,' he promised, beginning to slip the tiny buttons at the back of her wedding dress from their moorings. 'I can do most of my work from Las Palomas, but here will be our retreat. Our special paradise.' His eyes glimmered as he slid the dress from her slender shoulders. 'A couple from the village come each day to attend to the house and gardens—you will meet them later. But first, we will share a shower, and then…'

He ran his hands over her tingling, luscious breasts and shimmied the dress from her curvy hips until it pooled at her feet on the floor, leaving her in just a tiny pair of silk panties.

'You looked beautiful in your wedding gown,' he said on an audible intake of breath, 'but you look even more beautiful without it.' And he plundered her eager mouth until she was shaking with anticipation.

Her only thought, rapidly dwindling in coherence, was that she had her own surprise for him.

In their late-night discussions he had confided that he wanted children.

And she was pregnant. Their child would be her gift to him. That and her eternal, adoring love.

HIS PREGNANT
HOUSEKEEPER

BY
CAROLINE ANDERSON

Caroline Anderson has the mind of a butterfly. She's been a nurse, a secretary, a teacher, run her own soft-furnishing business, and now she's settled on writing. She says, "I was looking for that elusive something. I finally realised it was variety, and now I have it in abundance. Every book brings new horizons and new friends, and in between books I have learned to be a juggler. My teacher husband John and I have two beautiful and talented daughters, Sarah and Hannah, umpteen pets, and several acres of Suffolk that nature tries to reclaim every time we turn our backs!" Caroline also writes for the Mills & Boon® Medical Romance™ series.

CHAPTER ONE

'WHAT on earth—?'

Daniel paused, thumb poised on his car's remote locking button, and watched the woman in amazement.

She was going to do herself a mischief, struggling about in the dark trying to get that huge mattress into the skip—never mind the fact that it was *his* skip and she had no business putting anything in it, but since she was clearly bent on the task—literally—he had no choice but to intervene.

'Here—let me.'

And shouldering her gently out of the way, he slid his keys into his pocket, seized the mattress and lifted it towards the skip—

'No!'

For someone so tiny, she was surprisingly strong. 'That's the wrong way!' she cried, running round to the other side and hauling on the mattress. 'I'm not putting it *in* the skip, I'm taking it *out*!'

He stopped struggling with it and studied her thoughtfully over the top. It was about shoulder height on her, and he could clearly see her stubborn, defiant chin, tilted slightly up as if daring him to argue. He scanned her face, bare of any make-up, taking in the lank brown hair scraped back into a ponytail, the wide, determined eyes and the firm set of that really very soft, lush mouth. He dragged his eyes from it and met her eyes again. 'Excuse me?'

'I said, I'm taking it out—'

'I heard you. I just don't understand. It's an old mattress. Why would you want to take it out of the skip?'

'Because it's better than the one I've got? For goodness' sake, it's unmarked—or it would have been if someone hadn't put it in the skip. Ridiculous waste. So I'm—recycling it.'

'Re—?' He folded his arms, propping them on the top of the mattress, and met those fiery eyes over the great divide. Not the physical object that separated them, but the light years that divided their understanding. She *really* wanted this old mattress?

'That's right, and we've only got a minute before the security guard comes back round. Either give me a hand, or get out of my way and let me move it, but don't just stand there leaning on it until he's back!'

Daniel glanced over his shoulder towards the door of the security guard's Portakabin, then back to the girl. 'You want me to help you steal the mattress?' he said incredulously, suppressing the urge to laugh.

'Well, it's hardly stealing, it's been thrown out,' she said logically, and he couldn't argue with that. He'd sanctioned it himself. 'So—what's it to be? Are you getting out of the way so I can do it, or are you going to help me?'

He hesitated a moment too long, because she reached out to grab it and move it herself before he could react.

And he couldn't let her do that. What if she hurt herself? She was only a little bit of a thing.

Damn.

'Get out of the way,' he said, sighing in resignation and glancing at the security guard's door again. If he got caught—

He grabbed the handles and lifted. 'Where to?'

'Round the corner—it's really not far.'

It wasn't, but it felt far enough. One end bumped the ground, and he lifted it a bit higher and thought it might be time to take Nick up on his offer of the use of his home gym. His biceps were clearly suffering from lack of exercise—either that or it had been a rather good mattress in its day, which would have surprised him since nothing else coming out of the old hotel was much cop.

But then she stopped, sooner than he was expecting, and fumbled for a key. 'In here,' she said, pushing open a door that led into the derelict rear annexe of the hotel, and leaving him to follow, open-mouthed in surprise, she headed up the stairs. 'Be careful, there aren't any lights— they've cut off the power to this part,' she warned him, then, reaching the top, she opened a door and went into a room.

He paused on the landing to get his breath back, and a smell in the air caught his nose. He sniffed. Damp. Definite, overwhelming damp. No wonder she'd needed a new mattress, he thought, wrestling it through the doorway and wondering if he'd lost his mind.

Yup. Definitely. He shouldn't be doing this, making it easier for her to stay. Nick and Harry would kill him, but—

In the harsh glare of the street light outside, she bent and moved a few things out of the way, then pointed to the space she'd cleared, on a floor scarcely big enough to take the mattress. 'There will do fine,' she said, straightening up, and he got his first proper look at her without the mattress in between them, and it stopped him in his tracks.

She was—pregnant?

Squatting in their hotel, holding up progress on the renovations, screwing up their budget and deadlines, piling on the legal fees, and she was pregnant?

Oh, dear God. It went from bad to worse.

He put the mattress down, just because it was easier than standing there holding it, and she promptly lay down on it, sighed hugely and grinned up at him, her bump sticking up into the air like a little football. Her T-shirt had rucked up to reveal the safety pins holding the bottom of her jeans zip together—or trying to. The baby seemed to have made that impossible, and through the gaps he could see a glimpse of smooth, pale skin, curiously vulnerable in the harsh light.

He had an almost overwhelming urge to reach out his hand and touch it, to trail his fingers over her taut abdomen, to rest his palm against that firm swell and make ludicrous promises—

He dragged his eyes away, to find that she'd tucked her hands behind her head and closed her eyes. She patted the mattress beside her and cracked an eye open, still grinning.

'It's fabulous! So much better than the floor—come on, try it!'

Try it? Lie on it next to her? Was she *mad*? He listed the reasons in his head why this was such a horrendously bad idea, starting with a) it was stolen—albeit from his own skip!—b) it was out of said skip, and c) she was lying on it, their sitting tenant, their *bête noire*, the thorn in the side of their development, looking sexier than any pregnant woman had a right to look, and she was *asking him to lie down with her*?

He backed hastily towards the door.

'Um—can't. I haven't got time. I need to get home and make a phone call.' To Nick and Harry, to tell them that he'd met their squatter. Their *pregnant* squatter!

Her eyes were unreadable in the confusing light, but her actions weren't. She scrambled to her feet and headed towards him, ducking past on to the landing and going into the next room, a woman on a mission. 'In which case, on your way, do you think you could just get rid of this for me, because it stinks.'

'This what?' he asked, his heart sinking as he followed her.

'This old mattress, of course. What else?'

What else, indeed? He closed his eyes, then opened them and studied her expectant face. Not that he could see much of it in the dark, but he knew what he'd find there if he *could* see. He could hear it in her voice, and he was glad he couldn't see her eyes, or he'd go belly-up like a lovesick poodle, and he really, really wasn't going to do this for her.

He really wasn't—

'You want me to dump a stinking mattress on someone's skip?' he asked, feeling suddenly very tired and confused and wondering what the hell he was doing in here with a pregnant woman who had no business living in their hotel and screwing up their schedule with her nonsense.

She grinned, her teeth flashing white in the gloom, and he felt his heart kick against his ribs. 'Well, it's only swapping it, technically. I'm sure, compared to all the other grief I'm giving them, the developers won't care in the slightest about one miserable smelly mattress. I mean, it wasn't great before, but it got soaked in the rain the other night when the ceiling came down.'

On the mattress? The ceiling had come down on the mattress of a *pregnant woman*? He swallowed the panic, tried not to think about the public liability implications and followed her further into the room.

She was right. It did stink. More than that—it was ancient, filthy and covered in lumps of ceiling. And she wanted him to carry it down the street in his home town— a town where he was trying to carve out a reputation that would hold him in good stead for the next thirty-odd years—and throw it in his own skip?

Oh, bloody hell, he thought, and grabbed hold of the handles and hefted it. Even sopping wet it weighed considerably less than the other one, such was its quality or the lack of it. He gave it another heave until it was upright, and wet plaster fell to the floor with a crash. 'Open the door,' he said in resignation, and wrestled it down the stairs and out on to the pavement.

'Gosh, it really does stink,' she said, walking along on the other side of it and wrinkling that pretty little nose. 'All that mould—I was worried it was bad for the baby.'

Not nearly as bad as the ceiling would have been, he thought, but he bit his lip and carried the wretched mattress round the corner. Knowing his luck, the security guard would catch them, he thought, and then the game would be up. Fantastic. He could just imagine that conversation!

She halted him at the gateway and peered round it into the car park. 'OK,' she said in a piercing stage whisper, and he stifled a chuckle and dragged the offending article across the car park and heaved it into the skip just as light spilling from the doorway heralded the security guard.

'Hey! What d'you think you're doing?' he yelled, and the girl grabbed his hand and ran for it.

What could he do? She was dragging him, laughter bubbling up in her eyes and bursting out into the night, and her hand was firm and bossy and surprisingly strong.

So he ran with her, catching her as she stumbled at the corner, and pulling her into a darkened doorway a few paces along the road, his hand over her mouth, the firm jut of her pregnancy pressing into him and jiggling as she tried hard not to laugh.

And all he could think about was the softness of her mouth under his hand, the feel of her belly against him, the strength of her hand in his as she'd tugged him away.

Then the baby kicked, a solid little thump against his gut, and the laughter faded, driven out by an urge to protect her so powerful, so immense, that it nearly took his knees out from under him.

He knew nothing about her, other than that she was claiming some title to the hotel and her right to it was being heavily disputed by the son of the late owner, who'd sold it to them just before he'd died. The son himself had assured them that her claim was totally spurious and he'd have her out in no time.

That had sounded fine six weeks ago, but then she'd refused to move, and now Dan had met her, now he'd discovered she was pregnant, that changed everything. Suddenly he needed to find out more about her, to know everything there was to know. His head was telling him it was everything to do with the hotel and nothing to do with her laughing eyes and the feel of that baby's kick against his gut, but his heart knew better.

For the first time in nearly a year, Daniel Hamilton was interested in a woman, and everything else, including his common sense, paled into insignificance.

* * *

Her co-conspirator and press-ganged mattress-wrestler stuck his head out of the doorway and scanned the street. 'There's no sign of the security guard. I think he's given up.'

'Good. I didn't think he'd bother much. He's too lazy.' She tipped her head on one side, knowing that she ought to move away but enjoying the feel of his hard, lean body against hers rather too much. 'Well, I suppose I ought to go and find something to eat,' she told him reluctantly, trying to summon some enthusiasm for another tin of cold baked beans, but he just eased away from her, dropping the hands that had settled warmly on her shoulders and leaving her feeling oddly bereft.

'Haven't you eaten?' he said, tipping his head on one side and studying her with a little frown. She couldn't see his eyes—it was too dark in the doorway—but the look on his face was kind, and he'd heaved mattresses for her. He couldn't be all bad.

'Well—no, I haven't, or I wouldn't be thinking about food,' she explained patiently, and his mouth twitched, as if he was suppressing a laugh.

He stepped out of the doorway into the light of the street lamp, and for the first time she was able to see him clearly. Not the colour of his eyes, but the expression—thoughtful, curious, a little hesitant, maybe? Then he seemed to make up his mind about something, and he straightened up.

'Fancy a take-away?'

'I thought you had to make a phone call?' she said, and could have sworn he went a shade darker.

'It'll keep,' he said gruffly. 'Anyway, I have to eat, too. We can take it down to the beach—my treat.'

The beach sounded OK. She wasn't keen on the idea of going to his house or flat or whatever, but the beach seemed safe enough. Nice, even, and 'my treat' was music to her ears. And she didn't have to be gone long.

'OK,' she said, unwilling to turn down the offer of food, whatever the source. She'd been hungry for weeks—that was pregnancy, of course, because the baby was stealing everything it needed and her diet at the moment was a little hit and miss, to say the least. She wasn't able to earn anything, and every penny she had was destined for legal fees—

'Chinese, Indian, Thai, Italian…?'

'Not Thai,' she said quickly, not yet ready to revisit the emotional minefield that was Thailand. 'Chinese, perhaps?'

'Sure. There's a good one on the front. Come on, we can walk from here—unless you're not feeling up to it?'

She shook her head. 'I'm fine to walk. I'm fit—I'm just hungry and pregnant.'

'Then let's get you some food. Any preferences?'

'King prawns, stir-fried vegetables and egg fried rice,' she said promptly, not holding back if he was offering to buy. He took out his phone, speed-dialled a number and rattled off the order, adding Singapore rice noodles and chicken in ginger and spring onions. Oh, joy, more of her favourites! It was looking even better, she thought, and tried not to drool.

The restaurant was on the sea front, at the bottom of the steep, winding little hill that led down to the beach. She'd eaten there once, with Jamie, when they'd first come back to Yoxburgh. It seemed a lifetime ago.

Two lifetimes—

'Coming in?'

'Sure.'

She got her first proper look at him in the lights of the restaurant as they waited by the take-away counter, and her eyes widened. Her mattress-heaving benefactor was seriously hot! She'd already known he was tall, but now she could see the perfect geometry of his face—the high cheekbones, the chiselled jaw, the firm, full lips—and a body that even in her 'condition' made her pulse crank up a notch.

He was wearing a white shirt with the neck open and the cuffs turned back, showing strong, lightly tanned forearms and the powerful column of his throat. His shoulders were broad and solid under the shirt, his chest deep, his abdomen flat, his legs long and lean and clad in soft old jeans just snug enough around the hips to hint at things she shouldn't even be considering. Fit, in every sense of the word, and he looked good enough to eat. Or touch, at least. His dark hair was soft and glossy, making her fingers itch to rumple it, and she wondered what her own hair looked like after weeks of washing it in cold water and washing up liquid and letting it air dry.

Dire.

It wasn't speculation, it was fact, and she swallowed hard and dragged her eyes off him. He was so far out of reach it was ridiculous, and she had no idea why he was bothering with her.

Pity, probably, but she wasn't going to walk away from a square meal on the grounds of a moral victory. Not even she was that stupid.

He picked up the bag and led her out of the restaurant and across the road to the prom beside the beach. 'Here?' he asked, pausing by a bench, and she nodded. There was enough light from the street lamps behind to see by, the moon was sparkling on the water, and the food smelt so good she really was starting to drool.

'Perfect,' she said, making herself forget about him and

how far out of reach he was and concentrate on the core business. She sat down with one leg hitched up and tucked under the other thigh so she was facing him, and more importantly the food, while he pulled all the containers out of the bag, laid them out on the bench between them and ripped the tops off, then handed her a pair of chopsticks.

'Sorry it's not a fork.'

'Chopsticks are fine,' she said, stripping the paper off them and piling right in, and the first king prawn to hit her teeth made her sigh with joy. 'Oh, boy,' she said round it, and grinned at him. 'Fabulous.'

It was the last thing she said for ages.

'Better?'

She finally seemed to have eaten herself to a standstill, and her smile was a little embarrassed. 'Oh, yes. I think I'm probably going to burst, but yes, fantastic. Thank you—and thank you for lugging that mattress for me.'

He gave a grunt of laughter. 'Which one?' he asked drily. 'The one you stole, or the one you donated?'

She laughed, and her eyes lit up and sparkled like the sea. 'Both,' she said, then her laughter faded and she turned her head, staring out over the water and catching her full, lush lower lip between her teeth and worrying it gently.

'Penny for them,' he prompted softly after a moment.

She sighed. 'I was just wondering if it was worth it— all the hassle of moving the mattress. I mean, it's not going to be for long, is it? I can't stay there, anyone can see that, but if I don't—well, I won't have any chance of getting anything for my baby, and it's her birthright. She's entitled to it, and I have to stay and fight for her.'

'Her?' he asked, ignoring the rest. There'd be time to

deal with that later, when he'd spoken to Nick and Harry, but for now—

'My baby. She's a girl. They told me when I had the scan. I wanted to know—I mean, it's only the two of us, and I wanted to start getting to know her. That seemed like a good place to start. We can have more meaningful conversations now.'

He didn't even comment on that, just smiled to himself and decided that it was a rather nice idea, if a little wacky. 'Have you got a name for her?'

She laughed. 'Well, it won't be Yoxburgh, that's for sure.'

'Pardon?'

'I'm Iona,' she explained with a smile. 'Named for the place where I was conceived, apparently. It could have been a lot worse. Knowing my mother, I'm lucky it wasn't Glastonbury or Marrakesh!'

He chuckled. 'I have to say Iona's far and away the best of the bunch, but I always did have a weakness for the Scottish islands.' He held out his hand and smiled. 'I'm Daniel,' he said, withholding the rest of his name because he didn't want to spoil this brief interlude. It wouldn't be long before she knew who he was. Time enough to hate him then, he thought, and then stopped thinking for a heartbeat because her hand, slim and firm and a little greasy from the food, gripped his and, like a trip-switch in a power surge, his mind shut down and his body took over.

'So—your daughter, whatever you're going to call her—where will she be born?' he asked, dragging his mind back from oblivion and retrieving his hand, and a shadow crossed Iona's eyes.

'I don't know. It depends.'

'On?'

'Whether I can win my fight.' She sighed. 'It's a long story.'

'I've got time,' he said, shifting so he was facing her and settling back against the bench, his arm propped along the back. He could see her like that, watch her body language, try and get to the root of this problem that was threatening to cause havoc with the development. And he could see her hands, curved protectively over her baby, which wasn't, of course, nearly as important in the great scheme of things as establishing the facts, and yet seemed curiously like the most significant fact at this point.

'It's messy,' she warned, and he nodded.

'I don't doubt it for a moment. It usually is,' he agreed, and waited for her to go on.

She was quiet for a moment longer, then she lifted her head and squared her chin. 'I met Jamie when I was travelling. I'd been dragged round the world from birth—my mother's an anthropologist and a bit of a hippy, and I'd spent my life moving from place to place. I'm not sure she knew who my father was apart from the fact that he was called Rick, but it was irrelevant because he never featured in our lives after I was conceived anyway.

'I'd scraped an education, ricocheting from one international school to another, sometimes taught by my mother when there wasn't a school near enough, which was quite often, and somehow I got enough points in my IB—my International Baccalaureate—to go to university.'

That surprised him, and he sat up a little straighter, intrigued. 'What did you read?'

'Law. I wanted to be a human rights lawyer, but I didn't finish my degree. My mother got some horrible tropical bug midway through my second year and nearly died, and

I went to look after her and never went back. She recovered, amazingly, considering how ill she was for a while, but I'd missed too much by then and if I was going back I had to redo the year. I hadn't had a gap year, and I wanted to travel on my own, to follow my own agenda for the first time in my life, so I did, meaning to go back to Maastricht at the start of the next academic year, only of course I didn't. I went to Thailand, and I met Jamie, and we just started travelling together. We backpacked round the world, and I showed him some of the places I'd been to, and then after a year we came back to Yoxburgh to see his father.'

She stopped talking, a frown pleating her brow, and he waited, watching in fascination as emotions chased each other across her face.

'His father, Brian, wasn't well. He wanted Jamie to stay, to help him run the hotel, but he wouldn't. He wanted to go, and he wanted me to go with him. I refused, so he went anyway and I stayed with Brian, helped him with the hotel and continued my studies part-time. One of the advantages of my upbringing is that I'm multi-lingual, so I've been working as an interpreter part-time and doing translations for a bit of extra cash as well, and I carried on doing that. Brian couldn't afford to pay me, so it was essential, really. Then Jamie came back in November after nearly a year away. I really thought that this time he'd stay, do the decent thing, but I might have known he wouldn't. And if I'd known—well, anyway, yet again he wouldn't stay, not even till Christmas. He blagged some money out of his father and went back to Thailand after a fortnight, caught Japanese encephalitis and died. He never knew about the baby.'

Oh, hell's teeth, Dan thought. This was so much more

complicated than they'd imagined. He didn't say he was sorry. It would have been a lie. If he was anything, he was disgusted at the man's careless and irresponsible behaviour, but it wasn't his place to say so and, anyway, there was no real sign of grief on her transparent face, just acceptance. So he kept quiet and watched her, her thumb stroking rhythmically, soothingly over the curve of the baby—a tender, comforting caress for her unborn child.

He couldn't take his eyes off that slowly moving thumb.

After a small, thoughtful pause, she went on quietly, 'Brian was devastated. He had a bad heart, and the shock of Jamie's death was awful. He had a heart attack, and they told him to sell up and settle down, so he put the hotel on the market. He'd managed to get a really good deal from these developers, considering how run-down the place had got, and he was going to make sure the baby was all right. We'd found a house for the three of us to live in, and he was going to give the other half of the money to his other son, Ian. And then, a month before we were due to move, he died, and Ian, who'd never even been to see him until he was on his deathbed, came up to me at the funeral and told me his father had asked him to look after me, so he gave me five hundred pounds and a week to move out.'

He crushed down the anger brought to life by her stark rendition of the facts. 'What about the will?'

'He said he was going to change it,' she told him, and a sad little smile touched her lips. 'Like just about everything else it was on his to-do list, though, and when he died his will was nowhere to be found. He'd told me that in his original will it was all left to Jamie and Ian, and by then Jamie was dead, which was why he wanted to change it, but he obviously never got round to it, and because the will couldn't be found, under the intestacy laws Jamie's share will go to his brother, of course.'

'Isn't the baby entitled to Jamie's half?' Dan suggested, not sure of the facts but thinking of the justice of the situation.

She shrugged. 'Not necessarily. It depends on the wording of the original will, but, since we can't find it, it's all a bit academic. I thought maybe Ian might give the baby something out of goodwill, knowing what his father's wishes had been, but apparently he doesn't have any goodwill where I'm concerned, so my only hope is to prove that the baby is Jamie's and hope that the will turns up and there's a clause in it about issue—you know, children and unborn children and so forth.'

'Is the will likely to turn up?'

'I doubt it. Ian ransacked the place looking for it, because without it probate takes for ever, but he didn't find it and I think the hotel's been cleared now ready for the builders to move in. And Brian was so horrendously untidy and disorganised that it could have been anywhere. It's probably been thrown out by mistake, but of course I can't go in there and look. I don't have access to the main hotel, only the disused annexe. Anyway, I'm not allowed.'

'Allowed?'

'By the security guard. Site rules. We aren't best friends.'

He made a mental note to organise a search. 'So—what happens now?'

'I stay in the hotel, and I'm a thorn in everyone's side and hold things up in the hope that Ian will give in and help me out for the baby's sake, but I can't have a DNA test done until she's born, and by then I'll have had to move out of the hotel, and that'll be that. And I don't want to move out, because possession is nine-tenths of the law and all that, but I can't have her there. And Ian's refusing to budge without a valid will to force him to give me money. I can't blame him—he doesn't know me from Adam. He'd never met me before the funeral and I haven't seen him since he finished tearing the place apart to look for the will. I've had plenty of threatening letters, though.'

Dan clamped his teeth shut to keep in his thoughts. They were unprintable, and if Ian had wandered into range just then, Dan would cheerfully have hung him out to dry. Lucky for him that he didn't, but Iona's situation was infinitely more complicated than they'd imagined, and the implications of her sorry little account of the events leading up to this point were huge. He needed to speak to Nick and Harry, but it was too late now, and anyway, Iona was yawning her head off and he needed to walk her home.

Home?

He nearly snorted in disbelief that she was living like that, her few possessions scattered around her on the tired carpet, the ceiling down in the next room, the all-pervading stench of mould filling the building. There was a lingering aura of it hanging over them even now, in the sea air—because of handling the mattress, or because her clothes were permeated by it? Whatever, it couldn't be healthy living in that atmosphere.

There was no power in the annexe, no light, although the water was still on. That, apparently, was a legal requirement, and they were still at the point of trying to negotiate her removal with the solicitors.

Or they had been.

What they did now in the light of this new information he had no idea.

'You're tired. Let me walk you back,' he said, and she started scraping all the leftovers into one container, squashed them down and put a lid on.

'For tomorrow,' she said, her words tinged with defiance as if she was daring him to challenge her. 'Unless you want it?'

He lifted his hands. 'Be my guest,' he said, and vowed to sort her situation out once and for all. First thing in the morning, he was contacting the others, and if he had anything to say about it, she'd only spend this one night on her recycled mattress in that dank and dismal room with her leftover Chinese for company.

She wasn't going to let him in, but he insisted on checking that it was safe, that nobody had broken in. Then he went out and listened to her as she closed the door and locked it. There was the scrape of keys and slide of bolts, and he wondered who she was trying to keep out. He stood there, deep in thought, worrying about her, before finally walking round the corner to his car in the car park. The security guard came out of his Portakabin and hailed him as he unlocked his car and the lights flashed.

'You off, Guv?'

'Yup. Everything all right?'

'Fine. Someone put a mattress on the skip, but I chased them off,' he said. 'They were only kids.'

Daniel kept a straight face with difficulty.

'Happens all the time,' he said and, lifting a hand in farewell, he got into his car and drove home.

Home to his newly built, just commissioned house, with

its five bedrooms and guest wing, stunning views of the sea and only one person rattling around in it.

Guilt pricked at him as he walked through the door and turned on the lights. Guilt, and shame. Not because of the opulence, because it wasn't opulent at all. If anything, it was stark and spare, with nothing to detract from the purity of the spaces. The house flowed naturally from one area to another—uncluttered, simple, a perfect symphony of glass and brick and wood and stone working in harmony.

And empty.

Hence the guilt, because all this space, for one person— that was the obscenity. That, and the fact that Iona, alone and without support, was fighting a battle she should never have had to fight, in the squalid environment of that near-derelict hotel annexe. Fighting it not really with them, but with her baby's uncle, and not for herself but for the child.

He'd have to talk to Nick and Harry first thing in the morning and see what they could sort out, because she couldn't stay there, even without the pressing consideration of their refurbishment schedule and the fact that that wing of the hotel was due for demolition in the next couple of weeks.

They'd have to make sure she was all right, find her somewhere safe to go, he thought. He'd get on to it first thing in the morning. At least it didn't look like rain tonight.

His conscience as clear as he could get it, he went up to bed and lay staring out over the moonlit sea and wondered if she was asleep yet on her new mattress, and if she was more comfortable, and if she was safe behind all the locks and bolts, in that dismal room with her scant possessions and her leftover Chinese meal in its little box.

When the rain lashing on the window woke him in the small hours, he lay there listening to it and wondering if the ceiling in the new room was safe or if that, too, was going to fall down on her while she slept.

Two hours later, unable to sleep again and calling himself every kind of a fool, he went down to the kitchen, made a savagely strong espresso and sat sipping it with the doors flung wide while the sky lightened and the pale disc of a watery sun rose out of the sea and sparkled on the water, tranquil and soothing, and wondered what they could do to help her.

CHAPTER TWO

'WE NEED a meeting.'

Nick groaned, and Dan heard the rustle of bedclothes and a sleepy murmur from Georgie in the background.

'Do you have any idea what the time is?' Nick growled.

'Five-thirty?'

'And you think that's *reasonable? On Sunday morning*?'

'I've met our squatter.'

There was a heartbeat of silence. 'And?'

'She's pregnant.'

Another silence. Then something unprintable, and the sound of bedclothes and then footsteps. 'We need a meeting.'

Dan chuckled. 'That was my line. Where? And when?'

'Yours—since you're up, you can cook us breakfast. Give me half an hour. And I'll let you ring Harry. If he's got any sense, he'll tell you to go to hell.'

He didn't. He was actually rather ruder, but since his suggestion was anatomically impossible, Dan chuckled and hung up, then had a quick shower and filled the oven with frozen pastries while he made the coffee, then pressed the button to open the gates.

'This had better be good,' Harry muttered, wandering in moments later in shorts and a T-shirt that he could well have slept in, his jaw dark with stubble and his hair rumpled and Nick hard on his heels.

'Oh, it's good. Hi, Nick. Sorry about this. Coffee?'

'Too right. Can I smell croissants?'

'Yup. Sit down, I'll bring them over.'

He poured three mugs of coffee—slightly weaker this time, since his stomach was still rebelling after the last one—and brought the whole lot to the low coffee table in the middle of the seating area and put it down.

'So—this pregnant squatter,' Harry said round a mouthful of almond pastry and gooey marzipan. 'Is she going to be a problem?'

'Could be.' He picked up a *pain au chocolat* and sat back, studying it intently. 'Apparently the baby is Brian Dawes's other son's child.'

Nick choked on his croissant and dumped his coffee mug back on to the table. *'What?'*

'I said—'

'I heard what you said. I didn't even know there was another son. What are the implications?'

'And how the hell can we throw her out if she's pregnant?' Harry put in, his almond croissant forgotten.

'I don't think we can—and there isn't another son, not any more. He's dead. But she can't stay there, so I have a plan.'

They groaned and exchanged glances, then looked back at him, scepticism writ large on their faces.

'Which is?' Nick prompted.

'We need to get her out of the hotel. Move her some-where appropriate—somewhere where the ceiling isn't going to fall in on her if it rains.'

Harry narrowed his eyes, then his jaw sagged. 'The ceiling fell in?'

'On the mattress. That's how I met her—she was nicking a mattress out of the skip at the hotel to replace it.'

'And you stopped her, and she told you all this?' Nick said, and he ran his hand round the back of his neck and pressed his lips together.

'Not exactly.'

'So—what, exactly?'

So he told them about the mattress-swapping, and once they'd finished howling with laughter and ribbing him about being a sucker, he asked them what they would have done.

They shrugged thoughtfully, and he nodded.

'I rest my case. Anyway, I took her down to the sea front and we had a take-away, and I found out tons about her, and about this situation, and it really isn't cut and dried. If the baby is the dead son's, and she's assured me it is, then I think she—the baby—might be entitled to his part of the estate.'

'You know that?'

'I don't know. I think so. I've been on the net. It's confusing. "Unborn" seems to have several connotations—like already conceived and not yet born, and to be conceived and born at some point in the future, but there's an expression—*en ventre sa mère*. In the womb of the mother. It's not really clear, and without a look at the will it's not possible to know if she would inherit, but there's a slight problem—apparently the will's disappeared. We need to get her legal advice.'

'We do?'

'Yes, we do,' he said shortly. 'We can't mess this up. I can just see the headlines now—PREGNANT WOMAN KILLED BY FALLING ROOF—NEW OWNERS DENY RESPONSIBILITY.'

'I'm surprised you didn't drag our legal team out of bed

at five-thirty on a Sunday morning to ask them to join us,' Nick said mildly, with just a touch of rancour.

Dan rubbed a hand through his hair, embarrassed to admit that if he'd had a home number he might have been tempted. 'We need to take advice on this, guys—it's important. And we need to get her out.'

'I agree,' Harry said, frowning. 'We do—need legal advice, before we move her out and end up responsible for her welfare and incurring huge legal bills for a fight which isn't ours. In fact, none of this is our concern. We should just get her moved out and let Social Services take care of her.'

Dan frowned at Harry. 'Like you'd do that. Harry, she's probably seven months pregnant.'

'Exactly. And there are people professionally employed to deal with situations like that. It's not as if the baby's anything to do with any of us.'

'That didn't stop you before.'

Harry's eyes flicked away momentarily. 'That was different.'

'Was it? And I'm only talking about getting her legal advice, not marrying her—'

'Time out, boys,' Nick interrupted, sitting forward, all business now. 'Dan's right, we need to take legal advice, and we need to get her safely out of there before any harm comes to her. Her presence in the building is irrelevant to her claim, anyway, since we've bought it.'

'Except that she doesn't have a tenancy agreement so we can't legally kick her out,' Dan reminded him. 'And if any more of that ceiling comes down before Monday and injures her, I don't know where we stand.'

'So what the hell do we do?'

'I have an idea.'

'Why doesn't that fill me with confidence?' Harry said darkly, and Dan laughed.

'I can't imagine.'

'Going to share?' Nick suggested.

He shook his head. 'Not till I've thought it through and discussed it with her.'

Harry frowned. 'Don't you think you should discuss it with us first? As your business partners and co-owners of the development?'

'No,' he said bluntly. 'I don't. If there's anything to tell you, I'll report back.'

'You do that. There's a substantial chunk of my royalties riding on this venture,' Harry reminded him.

'You've got till nine on Monday, then I'm phoning the law team,' Nick said briskly, and got to his feet. 'Now, I'm going home, and if I'm really lucky, the kids'll still be asleep and I can go back to bed with my wife.'

He walked out, leaving Harry there watching Dan in a thoughtful silence.

'What?'

'I should be asking you that,' Harry said.

'Don't bother. It's only an idea. It probably won't come to anything.'

Harry stood up slowly and let his breath out on a sigh. 'A word of advice,' he said. 'Don't get sucked in, Dan. It's all too easy.'

'You can talk.'

'Absolutely. I think I'm precisely the person to talk— and I can see you falling into exactly the same trap.'

'Hardly.'

He put a hand on Dan's shoulder. 'Just be careful, eh?' he murmured, and then left him alone to work out the finer details of his plan.

She turned him down.

He hadn't expected it at all, but he probably should have done. When he'd thought it was late enough—bearing in mind her interest in this problem was rather different from theirs—he'd gone round and knocked on the door to the annexe.

He heard her yell something, heard the sound of her running lightly down the stairs, then, on the other side of the door, she stopped.

'Who is it?' she said.

'Dan.'

'Dan?' she said, her voice surprised. 'Daniel? As in last night?'

'Yup—Iona, can I come in?'

There was a rattle and a clatter, the sound of locks turning, and then finally she opened the door, her eyes wary. 'What can I do for you?'

'I've got a proposition for you,' he began, and she started to shut the door. He jammed his foot in it.

'Not that sort of proposition,' he said, feeling inexplicably weary. Although perhaps not inexplicably, since this woman and thoughts of her had kept him awake for the better part of the night. He pushed the door gently open and went in, shutting it behind him. 'You're quite safe with me, Iona,' he said without moving any further. 'I just want to talk to you. May I come in?'

'I thought you had,' she huffed, then sniffed the air and stared at the brown paper carrier in his hand. 'What's that?'

'Breakfast—coffee and croissants.'

She all but snatched the bag from him, shoving her nose into it and inhaling the smell that drifted up from the coffee. She moaned softly and threw him a megawatt smile. 'Come in and mind where you walk,' she said, beaming, and led the way up the stairs past a fresh mess of plaster and wall-paper that had obviously fallen down in the night. Tons of it, leaving a gaping hole in the roof.

Jeez. How much worse could it get?

Her room, he was glad to see, seemed dry still. She sat down cross-legged on the contentious mattress with her back against the wall and the bag in front of her, fished out the coffee cups he'd picked up at the café down the road and handed him one, then, ripping open the bag of pastries, she waded in without another word.

Lord, she must have been starving, he thought, frowning. She looked up and stopped chewing, then rubbed her mouth on the back of her hand and straightened up, ges-turing to the bag. 'Sorry. Never did have any manners when I was hungry. Would you—?'

He shook his head. 'I've had some.' Hours ago, when he'd dragged his friends out of bed to share the glad tidings. 'Why don't I talk while you eat?' he suggested, settling himself on the edge of the mattress, against the wall, at right angles to her so he could see her, and after a second she nodded and carried on, pausing only to rip the top off the coffee and sip it with a groan of ecstasy that made his blood run hot.

'Well, go on, then,' she prompted when she was halfway through the second croissant and he still hadn't said anything.

'Um—I wanted to offer you a job,' he said. 'As my housekeeper.'

She coughed, swallowed and stared at him. 'House-keeper? Me?'

He shrugged. 'You need somewhere to live, I need someone to live in and look after my house and cook me supper in the evenings and keep the chaos under control—and if you were able to keep this hotel running, I'm sure my house would be a walk in the park.'

'I can't,' she said flatly after a nail-biting pause. 'I can't move out. If the developers knew I was out, they'd demolish this bit and I'll lose my home. I hardly even dare leave to get food in case they change the locks. And as soon as I'm out, I cease to be a problem to them and if I'm not a problem, then I haven't got a prayer of getting them on my side to help me fight Ian.'

He contemplated telling her that he *was* one of the developers and he was definitely on her side, but thought better of it. Just for now.

'What if I offer to help you fight the case?'

'Why the hell should you do that? I mean, I know I shouln't look a gift horse and all that, but I've been round the world a few times, never mind the block. I've met people you wouldn't believe, seen things that would make your hair curl. I know all about human nature, Daniel, and, trust me, it's nasty. So forgive me if I'm not in a hurry to fall into your arms and let you carry me out of here on your white charger—'

'I was offering you a job,' he pointed out mildly, wondering what it would feel like if she fell into his arms and let him carry her off, in his BMW if not on a charger, and decided that fantasising would get him precisely nowhere.

'Yeah, right. No strings and all that.'

'Well, no. There are strings. I expect you to keep the

house clean and tidy, to cook me something rather healthier than the average take-away, which is what I exist on at the moment, and to do my laundry. And I'll pay you, and you'll have a home for you and your daughter where the ceiling won't fall in and the lights come on when you press a switch and you won't go to bed hungry and wake up with no prospect of food—'

He broke off, because her eyes had filled with tears and the sight was threatening to unravel him. She blinked hard and looked away.

'Um—why?' she asked.

Good question. He had no intention of giving her the right answer. Either of them. She didn't need to know he was involved in the project, and she *certainly* didn't need to know that she'd haunted his sleep and wasn't doing much for his waking hours, either!

'Supply and demand,' he said instead, sticking to the job angle. 'Why don't you look at the house before you give me an answer?'

'I'll want references,' she said, eyeing him as if she still wasn't quite sure he was for real, and he laughed.

'I don't doubt it. I could return the favour.'

Her smile was sad and a little crooked. 'Brian's dead. He would have told you what you wanted to know. There isn't anyone else, but I don't lie and I don't cheat and I work hard. How about a trial period? Say—a month? That should give us both time to see if we can live together.'

'You haven't even seen the house,' he said, but she just laughed.

'You said it has electricity and the roof doesn't leak. What more do I need to know?'

* * *

'Oh, my God.'

She saw him glance across at her, but she didn't take her eyes off the big iron gates as they glided open at the touch of a button and the car eased past them down a drive between high, clipped hedges. The right hand hedge carried on straight down the boundary, but the left hand one turned sharply and the drive widened out in front of a house.

At least, she assumed it was a house, but it was a house unlike any she'd ever set foot in, and light years from the door-in-the-middle-and-windows-either-side house of convention.

A great white stucco block, much wider than it was high, with a flat roof that projected out into a deep overhang, it had a big, plain black door to the left of centre, three small black-framed windows scattered apparently randomly across the blank white expanse of the elevation facing her, and a single tall window on the left of the front door stretching up almost to the roof. There was a long, low garage block set at the far end at right angles, connected to the main house by a single-storey section that, apart from a lonely door, was featureless.

It should have been ugly, she thought, but it wasn't; although it certainly wasn't pretty, there was a kind of stark simplicity, a rightness about it all that was curiously calming.

Not that it was calming her at the moment. Not a chance, because she just knew that when that door opened, the house was going to blow her socks off, and she could hardly wait.

He pulled up in front of the garage beside a skip half-full of building materials and rubbish, and she realised it was either newly built or in the final stages of a major renovation. She couldn't tell from there, but no doubt once the door was opened all would be revealed.

She glanced across at Daniel. He still hadn't said a word, but he got out of the car and came round and opened her door and helped her out on to the tarmacked drive and, with anticipation fizzing in her veins, she followed him. He slipped a key in the lock, turned it and pushed the door open, and gestured for her to go in.

She took two steps, slowed to a halt and stared in awe. The far wall was glass. All glass, from floor to ceiling, side to side—all of it, a wall of glass, and beyond it, beyond the smooth stone terrace and the manicured emerald lawn that stretched away like a giant billiard table towards the horizon, was the sea.

She took another step forward. She didn't even notice the house. It was irrelevant. The sea was calling her. The sun was sparkling off its ruffled waters today but she could picture it with an oily, flat calm, or a lazy swell, or crashing against the unseen shore in the teeth of a gale—knew it would reflect every mood of nature, every breath of wind and drop of rain changing it, recharging her batteries, renewing her spirit, filling her soul. It was stunning, amazing and awe-inspiring, and she felt the threatening prickle of tears.

She loved the sea. Needed it. It was in her blood— something to do with Iona, with the island where she had begun? And he had this all the time, every time he glanced up or opened his eyes. Amazing. Lucky, lucky man.

She dragged her eyes from it and looked around, and then, finally, the house itself registered, and she felt her jaw sag.

They were in a staircase hall that ran from front to back, empty except for the cantilevered timber treads of the stairs that seemed to grow from the wall beside her on her left, and

a huge canvas propped against the opposite wall—an evo-
cative, swirling abstract that captured the essence of the sea.

She walked past them towards the glass, looking around
her now, taking it all in—the smooth white walls soaring
up towards the roof, the slate-flagged floor, almost black
and honed to a fine, soft finish, which carried on out to the
terrace beyond. There was an opening on the right before
the glass wall—not a doorway, just a wide gap leading her
on—and as she looked through it, she saw a huge open-
plan living room with big squashy sofas grouped around a
low table set in the middle of a beautiful bold woollen rug.
The room was partly divided, so that the kitchen area was
tucked round a corner out of sight, and yet arranged so that
as you were working in it, you could see the sea. And it
was beautiful.

Stunning. So simple, the lines so clean, again like the
frontage almost monastic, and—oh, there must be a word,
just a single word for it if only she could—

Pure.

That was it. It was *pure.* It gave her a feeling of tranquil-
lity and calm that washed away all the stress of the past few
months, as if all that were somehow irrelevant. How amazing,
that a house could do that as soon as you stepped inside.

She turned and looked at Daniel, met his eyes—wary,
watchful, waiting for her reaction.

'It's beautiful,' she said softly, and to her surprise she
saw the tension go out of him, as if her insignificant
opinion actually made a difference to him, which was
absurd. 'Stunning. I thought it would be from the front. It's
like one of those fabulous iconic Modernist houses from
the thirties that I've seen in books—don't ask me who by,
I'm hopeless with names, but—oh, wow, Daniel! It's just

amazing. All that space, light—can you feel it, or is it just me?' she added, suddenly unsure and wondering if he'd laugh at her for going over the top.

He did—a soft huff of laughter. 'I think you could be over-egging the pudding a bit. Not that I'm not flattered, but they were in a different league. But I'm glad you like it.'

She shook her head, sure at least about that. 'Oh, I love it. It's amazing, and it's not in a different league at all. Well, I don't think so, not that I know anything at all really, but I think you're doing the architect a disservice. It's fabulous. I wonder who designed it? I'd love to meet him. Is it new, or did you refurbish it?'

'No, it's new.'

He suddenly looked a little awkward, and then something occurred to her, and she sucked in her breath and tilted her head a fraction. 'Oh, my God,' she said softly, almost under her breath. 'It was you, wasn't it? You designed it! Designed it and built it for yourself.'

The tension was back, and she knew she was right. 'You did, didn't you?' she said, more positively now. 'You were the architect!'

He nodded, his mouth kicking up on one side in a tentative smile. 'I was really lucky to get the plot. There had been a house here, a much simpler and smaller house but in a similar style, but the lady who lived in it couldn't afford to maintain it, and it fell into disrepair. In the end there was a fire and it had to be demolished, and the planners insisted that the new house was in keeping with the original, which suited me down to the ground. I've always loved Modernist architecture, and I've been dreaming about building a house like this for years, but I never thought I'd get the chance. Well, not till I was a lot older, anyway, but I was in the right place at the right time—and I had luck on my side.'

Luck? Try money, she thought, and then another thought came, and she felt the hairs stand up on the back of her neck. 'Oh, good grief. You're seriously rich, aren't you?' she said, staring at him as if his appearance would give her any clues. None as glaringly obvious as the house, but his car and clothes reeked of quality. She groaned. How could she have been so stupid? 'You're probably a millionaire— and several times over.'

He gave a self-deprecating laugh. 'Not several. I've got pretty stonking debts at the moment, but I got lucky in New York—picked up some real estate with potential, took a few gambles that paid off, built on what seemed like a successful formula. I sold up and pulled out recently—nearly a year ago.' A muscle tensed in his jaw, and she wondered why.

She didn't ask, restraining her usually unrestrained tongue for a change. Instead she concentrated on the successful formula bit. 'So—how long did it take you to build this property empire?' she said, scanning his face for any further clues, but there were none.

He shrugged. 'Ten years, I suppose. I bought my first flat when I was twenty-one—that was the start of it. But it was only in New York four years ago that things really started to take off. And because of my connections in the property world I've had opportunities others wouldn't have had.'

And a gift, she realised, despite his modesty. An extraordinary talent. And she hadn't even seen the house yet, not really.

She swung back and looked around again, taking in the detail she'd missed the first time. It was simply furnished. It would have to be, of course, to work, and it did work. It worked in spades, and yet it looked welcoming. The dining table, like the coffee table and the stair treads, was sleek, solid oak, carefully placed between the kitchen and the glass wall and beside the seating area, so that wherever you were in the room you would be able to see the sea and be part of all that was going on.

And something had been going on. There were crumbs and mugs and plates scattered all over the coffee table, and on the worktop in the kitchen was an empty plastic milk bottle.

'Sorry about the mess,' he said, but she just shook her head.

'At least I can believe you now when you say you need someone to look after it.'

He snorted softly, and she smiled to herself and walked over to the kitchen, running her fingers reverently over the slate worktop honed, like the floor, not polished, because that would reflect too much light and be hard to work on, but a soft, silken-smooth matt finish, almost black, contrasting sharply with the flat, high-gloss cabinet doors. They were white, stark like the house and yet curiously understated, and the hob was a featureless sheet of black glass let into the stone of the worktop.

'Think you could work in this kitchen?' he asked, and she laughed softly.

'No. I'd stand here all day staring out over the sea and dreaming,' she said honestly.

'You get used to it after a while.'

She shook her head. 'Never. It's stunning, Daniel. I'd love to see the rest—will you show me?'

His smile was just a flicker, but his eyes—hazel, she realised belatedly, with flecks of gold—were warm. 'Of course,' he said, and led her back to the entrance hall.

She pointed at another opening off the far side, this

time with a sliding partition pulled half across it. 'So—what's through there?'

He pulled the partition closed before she could stick her head in and look. 'My studio. It's a mess. You don't need to worry about that.'

He took her upstairs and showed her the bedrooms, each one facing the sea with that same wall of glass. Even the bathroom in the master suite had full-length glass, so you could lie in the tub and stare out over that wonderful, endless sea.

'Oh, wow!' she said under her breath.

And then found herself picturing him lying there in the water, a glass of wine in one hand, a book in the other and the sea stretched out in front of him, and her eyes were drawn to him.

What would he look like—?

No! She mustn't think like that! Not if she was going to have to live with him, be his housekeeper.

Housekeeper, for heaven's sake!

What a crazy word. It conjured up an image of some middle-aged, dumpy mother figure in a grey serge dress and starched, blindingly white apron, bustling around and keeping the servants in order.

Not an otherwise homeless, pregnant woman of twenty-four with an unfinished degree and no real idea of where she went from here.

She felt her smile fade, and pasted it back in place.

'Very impressive,' she said, scanning the wet-room area of the bathroom and wondering how easy those stone tiles would be to clean. That's it, stick to the practicalities, she reminded herself, and followed him back into the master bedroom, keeping her eyes firmly away from the big, rumpled and deeply inviting bed set opposite the windows.

'No curtains,' she said, suddenly noticing that. 'There aren't any anywhere. Is that because you've only just moved in? I noticed the skip on the drive and a pile of building stuff.'

'I have just moved in, but there aren't any curtains because I don't need them.'

And he pressed a button on the wall and the view disappeared, leaving them in a softer light. He pressed it again, and it went darker, then lighter until the glass was clear once more and the sea reappeared.

'Smart windows,' he said.

She was amazed. 'How do they work?'

'They pass a current across the crystal and it realigns it, cutting out the light.'

She frowned at him, not at all sure she understood. 'So you won't have curtains for insulation? Is that entirely environmentally sound?'

His mouth quirked into a smile. 'Not entirely. If I was being entirely environmentally sound, I wouldn't have a wall of glass, but I've done everything else I can. They're triple glazed with Low-E glass, and by cutting out the light transmission they save energy and keep the heat in in the winter and out in the summer. And they only use a very small amount of energy to change the opacity, then the current goes off. They're as good as they can be.'

'Guilty conscience in the face of all this conspicuous consumerism, Daniel?' she murmured, and had the pleasure of watching him frown slightly.

'Not at all. The whole house is heavily insulated, the roof's tiled with solar panels, the heating's run from a ground-source heat pump powered by solar cells, it's got grey-water and rain-water recovery for flushing the loos and watering the garden, there's a heat recovery system for the ventilation in the winter and because of the design of the windows and the roof it stays cool and doesn't need air-conditioning in the summer—I think I'm allowed the odd toy on top of those impeccable credentials. And it's not really conspicuous consumerism. It's a showcase for my work, and it's what the modern consumer is looking for.'

He looked a little defensive, as if he didn't expect her to believe him. She stared at him, then turned away so he didn't see the smile tugging at her mouth. So he was a closet eco-warrior as well as an architect, was he, juggling commercial pressure and ethics? And a champion mattress-wrestler and provider of breakfast, to boot.

Not to mention thrower of lifelines on the job and accommodation front. And what a lifeline!

She went back on to the landing, past the head of the stairs, and glanced into the other rooms. They were unfurnished, confirming her earlier suspicion that he'd only just moved in, and one of them was stacked with boxes. Boxes he'd been rummaging in.

She looked beyond the mess and saw a doorway to what was probably a bathroom. Another one? 'Are all the bedrooms *en suite*?' she asked a little incredulously.

He lounged against the doorframe and grinned. 'Will you shoot me down in flames if I say it seemed reasonable?' he said, making her wonder about the definition of reasonable. Just now she'd settle for a bowl of hot water instead of cold to wash in!

'As if,' she said, and smiled back. 'So—which one would be mine?'

'Oh, none of these,' he said, sounding slightly shocked. 'Yours is downstairs.'

And he led her down the stairs and along a hallway while she kicked herself for imagining that staff would even conceivably have a room with a sea view, but then he opened a door into another hall that led in turn to a small sitting room. Well, small by his standards, no doubt. Not by hers. There was a bedroom off it, with a brand-new bed still in its wrapper facing the to-die-for view, a comparatively modest but still very generous bathroom, and a little kitchen area with a small table and chairs set to one side.

They must be in the single-storey area beside the garage, she realised—a whole suite of rooms, like a little self-contained flat, with its own entrance from the drive and yet another bedroom behind the first, the only habitable room in the house apart from her kitchen that didn't face the sea

And this would be hers? This whole area?

As if he could read her mind, he spoke softly behind her. 'I thought if you and the baby had this bit, you'd have everything you need. The kitchen's pretty simple, but you won't need it if you're cooking for me anyway, except to do the odd thing on your days off. I imagine you'll eat with me?'

Would she?

Only if she could cook well enough that he wouldn't throw the food at her!

She felt a sudden moment of blinding panic. What if she failed? What if she couldn't do this? What if he hated living with her? She wasn't worried about her reaction to him; she could live with anyone, she'd had a lifetime of doing it. But he might find her baby noisy, or her very presence in his house disturbing. Or her habit of speaking her mind without engaging her brain first. She really ought to stop doing that.

His studio was just next to her, she realised, although the doors were miles apart. What if the baby cried and disturbed him while he was working? Maybe he didn't do much work there—perhaps it was just a home office and most of the time he was somewhere else? She wished she'd had a chance to see it. Maybe it would have told her more about him.

Like whether he could live with her?

'So—what do you think?' he asked, and she thought she could detect tension in his voice again. 'Will it do?'

'Do?'

'You know—for you and the baby. It was designed to be flexible, a guest suite for longer stay visitors, an annexe for dependent relatives, a staff flat, but it wasn't really designed with a baby in mind. I suppose I could carpet it— that might make it more baby-friendly. What do you think?'

'Of the house? Or the carpet?'

'Either. Both. All of it.'

She contemplated teasing him, but relented. Apart from the fact that she not only needed but *wanted* this job more than she would have believed possible, she couldn't lie to him. Not when her insignificant opinion seemed so important to him.

'I think it's the most beautiful house I've ever seen,' she said softly. 'And I'm sorry I teased you about the conspicuous consumerism.'

His mouth twitched and his eyes creased in a smile. 'You do have a valid point, to an extent, even if I try and justify it on work grounds.' He hesitated. 'So—could you live here? *Would* you? Will you take the job?'

She buried her doubts about her abilities and let her

smile bloom. 'Oh, absolutely. I don't know how well I can do it, but I'll do my best and I'm sure I can learn. If you'll give me a chance to prove myself, I can't imagine anywhere I'd rather be. It's stunning. And for what it's worth, I think you've created something far more than just a house here, something utterly exceptional, and I think it's breathtaking.'

Breathtaking?

He smiled to himself, a little wryly. Odd, how much her opinion mattered to him, but it did, and her enthusiasm for it was absurdly uplifting.

'Thank you,' he said, genuinely humbled by her praise. And then he thought about the rest—the job he'd created out of nowhere, the fact that she was moving out of the hotel against her better judgement without being in full possession of the facts about him and his vested interest, and he felt a flicker of guilt for not telling her that he was involved with the project.

Time for that later.

She'd probably be mad with him for not telling her, but by then she'd be out and safe, she'd be getting the best legal advice that money could buy and her future would be on the way to being more secure.

His conscience could live with that.

CHAPTER THREE

IONA demanded references, of course.

'You can't say you weren't warned. Just because you're a fantastic architect doesn't mean you aren't an axe-murderer,' she pointed out not unreasonably.

Dan tucked the 'fantastic' thing in his pocket to massage his ego with later, and let the axe-murderer go. 'So who would you find acceptable as a referee? Bearing in mind that it's Sunday.'

She shrugged. 'Someone who's known you for years? A doctor? Teacher? Vicar?' She eyed him doubtfully. 'Probably not a vicar,' she amended, and he felt perversely insulted.

'How about Harry Kavenagh?'

She frowned. 'The guy on the telly? The foreign correspondent or some such?'

'That's the one.'

'You know him?' she said, disbelief in her tone.

He nodded. 'We've been friends for years, and we're business partners now. He's married to my sister. They live round the corner.'

She shook her head. 'Uh-uh. That's too close a relationship. Try again.'

'Nick Barron—heard of him? He's a mover and shaker in the City—nice guy. He's another business partner.'

'No. He probably has his own hitman,' she said, and he thought of Nick throwing away his bachelor lifestyle to bring up his sister's children, and laughed at the absurdity of her suggestion.

'I don't think so. How about Nick's wife? She's another architect, but she's up to her eyes in nappies at the moment. She's known me since primary school—will she do? I doubt if she's got a hit man. Or is that too close, as well?'

'How close is close?'

He grinned wryly and went for honesty. 'I kissed her once when we were kids. She slapped me. I wasn't tempted to try again.'

Her mouth twitched. 'She'll do. Not ideal, but she'd tell me if she thought you were dodgy. A woman wouldn't lie.'

He snorted softly. That didn't tally with his experience, but he didn't want to go into the sordid details of Kate's litany of lies and deception, so he let it pass. 'I'll call her,' he said, and when she answered, he said economically, 'Hi, Georgie. I need a character reference—for a potential employee. In the absence of a vicar, you're top of her list. Care to oblige?'

'Oh, Dan! What's it worth?' she teased, and he gave a little huff of laughter.

'She's here with me now—her name's Iona. I'll put you on hands-free,' he said, pressing the button that would ensure he got both sides of this conversation, and crossing his fingers in his pocket that Nick hadn't mentioned Iona's name. Don't blow it, Georgie, he prayed, and set the phone down. 'Georgie? Have you got me?'

'I've got you,' she said, her voice clearly audible in the room. 'Hi, there.'

He looked at Iona and tipped his head towards the phone, and she straightened up.

'Um—hi, Georgie. I gather you've known Daniel for a while?'

'Try twenty-five years,' Georgie said with a dry chuckle. 'Man and very irritating boy.'

'Can I trust him?'

'*Trust* him?' Georgie said, her voice slightly shocked. 'With what? Your safety? Your reputation? Your virtue?'

To his surprise, Iona laughed. 'It's a little late for my reputation, and my virtue's long gone. I was thinking of my safety.'

'Absolutely. Well, all of them, really. Put it like this, we trust him with our children, and he's fabulous with them. They adore him, but then they would. He's a sweetheart— a genuinely nice guy. Nothing's too much trouble.'

He rolled his eyes at that. Iona, catching it, shot him a searching look, and smiled. 'Yes. I think you're right. And he has a very nice house.'

'He's shown you the house?' Georgie said, clearly surprised.

Iona, oblivious to his frantic attempts at telepathy, said blithely, 'Oh, yes—well, it was sort of relevant. He wants me to be his housekeeper.'

'*Housekeeper?*' Georgie squealed, and his heart sank. 'Good grief, I thought he wanted a PA or something, Iona!' and he heard a muffled exclamation in the background.

'Is there a problem with that?' Iona asked cautiously.

'Shush, Nick, she wanted to talk to me, not you, you can talk to Dan in a minute. Um—no, no problem, I just didn't know he was looking for a housekeeper, but I can understand it. He's pathologically untidy. Although he's been a neat-freak since he got that house—'

'And I can't cook,' Dan said firmly, picking up the phone and switching off the hands-free before Nick said something to land him in the doo-doo. 'And I'm lousy at ironing. Anyway, the novelty's wearing off.'

'I didn't think it would last. Iona, don't listen to him; you really don't want to work for him in the house, he's a nightmare—'

'She can't hear you now—'

'Tell me she's not our squatter,' Nick said, cutting Georgie off and chipping in.

'*What?*' Georgie was shrieking.

'Thanks for the reference,' he said blithely, and cut them off fast before either one of them said something to put Iona off.

Iona, however, oblivious to the furore no doubt breaking out at Nick and Georgie's house, was studying him like an insect. 'Pathologically untidy? I would have said neat-freak, but then there's the mess in here, and the boxes upstairs, and you hadn't made your bed,' she said thoughtfully. 'And considering the house is virtually empty because you've only just moved in, there's not a lot to make a mess with. So maybe she was right the first time. Or will the neat-freak in you win?'

He gave a grunt of laughter. 'It rather depends on the day of the week, and you haven't seen my studio. The neat-freak's not winning in there, I can assure you.'

She studied him in silence for another second, then smiled back. 'Fine. She sounds nice. Decent. I'll take it.'

'The job?'

She nodded, and he let out the breath he'd been holding and smiled. 'Great. When do you want to start?'

She laughed. 'How about some time in the next five minutes?' she said, and he felt his shoulders drop about a foot. Thank God. He really, *really* hadn't wanted to think about her in that dangerous annexe with the ceiling coming down round her ears for another night.

His smile widened. 'Sounds good to me.'

He stared at her few meagre possessions in horror. 'Is that all?'

'Most of my clothes got ruined when the ceiling fell in, but it doesn't matter much; they didn't fit me any more. I haven't got much else. I've learned to travel light,' she said.

Light? *Light?* 'I take it the rest of your things are with your mother somewhere?' he said, and she gave a brittle laugh.

'I don't even know where my mother is at the moment,' she said, stuffing a T-shirt into a rucksack. 'Egypt, I think, but I'm not sure. She might be in South America by now— Peru, possibly.'

'So—what about your home?'

She straightened up from the bag and sighed patiently. 'I have no home,' she reminded him. 'I told you that.' She examined a T-shirt, sniffed it and rejected it.

'What—not even a base?' He was appalled, but he reminded himself of what she'd told him about her child-hood. Maybe it had been worse than he'd realised. 'You must have some kind of base,' he added, still not able to comprehend what on earth it could be like to belong nowhere.

'Daniel, if I had a base, I wouldn't be living in this hell-hole,' she said reasonably, and he folded his arms, his frown firmly in place, and watched her pack.

If you could call it that. Most of the things were being thrown back on the bed, and he could see the mildew on them.

He swallowed. What an odd, rootless existence. How on earth had she coped? But she couldn't really be surprised if he found it hard to understand her lifestyle. She was the odd one out here, not him.

She tugged the drawcord tight and stood up.

'OK, that's me.'

'Right, let's get you all loaded up and we'll get off.'

They took everything—a rucksack, a battered flight bag and a pair of tired trainers—down to the car, then she straightened up and headed back towards the door.

'I'll just get the cat,' she said blithely, and went back inside.

He followed her. 'Cat? *What* cat?'

'Pebbles. Hotel cat. She'll be about here somewhere. She comes and goes through the window on to the flat roof.'

'So—what's that got to do with you?'

She turned and stared at him in astonishment. 'I feed her.'

'And?' he said, wondering what was coming next and getting a distinct sinking feeling.

'And I can't just leave her. She's old.'

'And if I don't want her in the house?'

'Then I don't come,' she said, quietly but firmly, and he just knew she was crazy enough to mean it.

He sighed and rubbed his hand through his hair. 'Get the cat,' he said, surrendering, and started wandering through the rooms. 'Kitty, kitty, kitty!'

'Save your breath, she's stone deaf. Hence Pebbles. You'll just have to find her—oh, got her!'

And she appeared in the doorway with a scrawny, moth-eaten little tortoiseshell snuggled in her arms.

'Pregnant women should be careful with cats,' he said, and she just laughed at him.

'Don't worry, she's been wormed and she doesn't have a litter tray. Right, that's it. Shall we go?'

He stared at the cat, and she stared back, then turned her head away, dismissing him and snuggling into Iona's arms with a loud and slightly off-key miaow.

Wondering what on earth he'd let himself in for, he gestured to the stairs, and she went down in front of him, got into the car and with one last rattle of the door to make sure it was secure, he got in beside her and started the engine.

'Come on, then, let's go home.'

Home?

Maybe. After the strain of the past few weeks, it seemed like a dream, and she kept expecting to wake up.

He brought her things in through the side door and put them down, her well-used rucksack and flight bag looking horribly shabby in the pristine surroundings of his brand-new and untouched guest suite, and then frowned at the bed.

'I'll give you a hand to make that up, and then I think you should have a shower and a sleep,' he said. 'You look shattered.'

'I'm fine,' she protested. 'I can make the bed, and I need to think about what to cook for you later.'

'No, I'm cooking today. You sort the cat out, I'll get the bedding.'

And no sooner was the bed made than he was gone, leaving her alone with the cat. She had a litter tray now, which he insisted he'd deal with, just until Pebbles was used to the house and could be allowed out; they'd picked it up at the supermarket on the way home, along with some sachets of food, and after christening the litter, eating the food and wandering round for a minute, Pebbles stopped by the bed and miaowed.

Iona sat down on the edge of the bed and sighed. 'Pebbles, I don't know if you're allowed on the bed,' she said softly, but Pebbles couldn't hear her and didn't care, anyway. She miaowed again, her funny, squawky little miaow, and, giving in, Iona picked her up and put her down on the bed.

'No shedding or plucking,' she warned, and felt her eyes drawn to the bathroom door. The lure of hot water was overcoming her, and she went over and looked inside. There were toiletries there, still in a carrier bag—shampoo, conditioner—oh, the luxury!—a toothbrush and tooth-paste, flannel—and hanging on the rail were thick fluffy towels that Daniel had brought in with the sheets, and the shower head was the size of a dustbin lid.

Almost moaning with anticipation, she turned on the basin tap and waited a second to see if it ran hot.

Yes! There was real, proper hot water!

Oh, the joy!

She stripped off her clothes, turned on the shower and stood under it motionless for a second, revelling in the sensation of the hot water pummelling down on her. Then she squirted a dollop of shampoo into her hand and worked it up into a lovely rich lather in her hair.

Fabulous. Then conditioner, and gradually it started to feel like hair again instead of straw. There was even a razor on the side! Oh, bliss. She soaped herself gloriously all over, used the razor—such luxury, a new razor!—and then stood rinsing longer than necessary, until guilt began to prick at her and she turned the water off reluctantly and wrapped herself in the towels.

Two towels—one for her body, one for her hair, and a mat for the floor, all pure white and soft as thistledown.

And there was even a hairdryer hard-wired to the wall!

Minutes later, feeling human again and ready for that nap, she pulled a clean T-shirt out of the drawer she'd put it in, sniffed it and wrinkled her nose. It had that horrible smell of washing that had taken too long to dry, and she could hardly bring herself to put it on. She'd wash it—wash all her things—later, if he didn't mind. She was sure he wouldn't. After all, he wouldn't want her smelling of rotten washing.

She sat down on the bed to pull her jeans on, and ran her hand over the bed.

Oh, bliss.

The bedding was so soft and silky it was like a caress against her skin. The quilt felt like goose-down, the mattress was hard enough to be supportive and soft enough to snuggle her, the pillows would be just the right height.

She could snuggle down in it, close her eyes and let go...

Or she could just look at the sea.

The bed was calling her, soft and smooth and inviting, but so was the view, and just now the view was winning, so she went into the sitting room, slid back the door and breathed in the warm summer air.

Gorgeous.

The guest suite—or staff flat, or whatever it was—was set back slightly from the rest of the house, with its own private terrace. It looked clean enough, so she took one of the cushions and sat on it cross-legged on the smooth, warm slate, and resting her hands palm up on her knees, she closed her eyes and let her mind drift.

Sounds.

Birdsong, the soft drag of waves on shingle, cars. A dog

barking in the distance, and then from somewhere closer she heard a doorbell.

She tuned them out, breathed deeply and let it go, but the voices penetrated, angry and frustrated and getting closer, and then she heard the words and shock held her motionless...

'Are you totally insane?'

Emily stalked past him, and Dan shut the door and sighed. 'News travels fast, doesn't it? I take it Georgie's been on the blower.'

'Too right she has—Nick saw you driving away with her earlier, and she said you'd got some cock-eyed notion of making her your housekeeper! What the hell do you think you're doing, taking some aimless drifter into your house? You must be mad!'

Dan followed his sister down the hall and out on to the terrace where she was pacing up and down. 'Solving a problem. I thought you might all be rather grateful—'

'Grateful?' she ranted. 'Because you've lost your marbles?'

'Rubbish. Because I've got our sitting tenant out of the hotel!' he retorted. 'She's was holding things up big-time—and keep your voice down. She's asleep,' he added belatedly, wondering why Nick hadn't kept his mouth shut, at least until tomorrow. It would have given him a little respite.

But no, Emily was here now, scraping her hair out of her eyes and pacing round the terrace, giving him hell and probably not without justification.

'You're mad,' she said flatly. 'Utterly mad. Harry warned you not to get involved, but you didn't listen. I might have known you'd pull a crazy stunt like this.'

He pulled the door to, so their voices didn't drift down the hall to Iona. 'Em, she's pregnant. The ceiling had fallen in. How the hell could I leave her there?'

'Oh, I've got no problem with that—it's bringing her here and installing her in your house—'

'Like that's so unprecedented,' he said drily.

Emily gave a low growl under her breath and skewered him with an icy glare. 'Well, exactly! You're just as gullible as Harry. What is it with you bloody men and pregnant women? You fall for it every time.'

'Oh, come on, Em, this isn't Carmen, and I've got no intention of marrying her. We aren't talking about a pregnant teenager who'd been raped. Iona's an adult, she's made a conscious decision to keep her baby, she's clever—'

'Clever enough to outwit you, evidently! She's a drifter, Dan—a rootless bit of flotsam that's drifted up on the shores of Yoxburgh!'

'Actually, no. She's an educated, intelligent, mature, funny, brave cosmopolitan woman—she was reading law at Maastricht! And *she* doesn't have a closed mind,' he added pointedly.

'So she's a graduate?'

Damn. 'No. She didn't finish uni. Her mother was sick—'

'How convenient. So she's not just a drifting backpacker, she's a bright and articulate drifting backpacker and sees this as a way of making money off the back of an executor's sale—she was probably working on him to change his will, and he got there before her and popped his clogs!'

He hung on to his patience with difficulty. 'No, she was looking after him because his own sons wouldn't! And apparently before he died he was making plans to secure her daughter's future!' he told her.

'I'll just bet he was. So where's the will?'

'That's what everybody wants to know.'

Emily rolled her eyes and sighed impatiently. 'And in the meantime she's trying to get the other brother, Ian, to cough up. Good grief, I can't believe you men are all so gullible! She's a conniving shark, Daniel! Why can't you see it?'

'Because I don't think it's true—and even if it was, if she's doing it to secure her daughter's future, what's so wrong with that? Carmen married Harry for that reason, and as a result Kizzy's secure, she's loved and she has a good future.'

'Only because I was able to help Harry to look after her when Carmen died, but I'm not helping you to get yourself into the same mess, because I've seen what it's done to Harry, and it's nearly torn him apart. He still blames himself for her death.'

'That's ridiculous,' he said flatly, frowning. 'She's dead because she didn't look before she crossed the road. It's not his fault—but if I'd left Iona in the hotel and the roof had fallen in, it would have been my fault. And I don't want that on my conscience, and you shouldn't, either. Nor should Harry or Nick or Georgie. Anyway, I would have thought you'd be glad she was out. At least this way we can get on with demolishing that wing and getting the building work back on schedule. We aren't running a charity here, and I need to see a return on that investment, and so do you guys.'

Emily gave a short sigh and scraped her hair back again. 'You're going to end up in so much trouble,' she grumbled. 'I can see it now. You'll end up involved with her—

knowing you, you'll fall in love with her, and she'll screw you over just like Kate did.'

'Leave Kate out of this!' he growled. 'This is nothing to do with Kate.'

'No, it's to do with you, and your lousy judgement of character and naïve inability to see the worst in people. Well, when she takes you to the cleaners—slaps a harassment suit on you, or some trumped-up rape charge, don't tell me you weren't warned!'

'Rubbish, you're being ridiculous! I have no intention of getting involved with her. She's pregnant with someone else's baby, and anyway, I couldn't be less interested in her,' he lied, and ignored the little jab from his conscience. 'The housekeeping thing is just a way of getting her out of the hotel, and if she's any good, so much the better. It'll kill two birds with one stone—three if you count getting the baby somewhere safer, which I'm sure you do, being the soft-hearted woman you are.'

'Don't bet on it,' she said, and levelled a finger at Dan. 'And on the subject of this baby, how do you know it's the brother's at all? It could be the chef's or some other random—'

'You haven't even met her,' Dan retorted, cutting her off, 'and you talk about me being a lousy judge of character? At least I've met the girl to *judge* her. For God's sake, she was going to be a human rights lawyer!'

'Nice line. Pity you fell for it. When did she tell you that?'

'In the half-hour I spent getting to know her yesterday,' he retorted. 'Which is more than you've done. And anyway, when did you get to be so cynical and bitter?'

'When Pete walked out on me because he wasn't interested in his own children!' Her voice changed, softening, and he could see the worry in her eyes. 'Dan, please, be careful. She could be a perfect saint for all we know, but what if she isn't? What if she's some twisted, money-grubbing little bitch? I don't think I can bear to watch this.'

'Then don't. I'm prepared to take the risk, because I believe her, but if it makes you happy, I'll get a contract of employment drawn up tomorrow while we're talking to the legal team about her,' he said, going back to the kitchen and the onions he'd been chopping when she'd arrived. 'And now, if you don't mind, I have things to do.'

'Yeah, like cooking for your housekeeper,' she said, her voice ripe with disbelief. 'And I thought I was a sucker!' She rummaged in her bag for her keys and shook her head. 'Just be careful, eh? You're taking a hell of a risk.'

'What about her? She's vulnerable, Em. So vulnerable, so desperate that she's prepared to take a job living in the house of a total stranger, a single man about whom she knows *nothing*. I could be a rapist, a paedophile—anything. She's spoken to Georgie, that's all. How the hell would Georgie know if I have a dirty little secret life? I could be any one of those things, and she wouldn't know. Nobody would know. So how about thinking of it from her perspective? How would you feel in her situation?'

'You're forgetting—I've *been* in her situation.'

He shook his head. 'No, you haven't. When Pete left you pregnant and alone, Mum and Dad were there for you. But what if they hadn't been? What would have happened to you? Em, for God's sake, she's got no one. This isn't her fault. And she reminds me so much of you—'

'OK, OK, I give up,' she said and, throwing Dan a frustrated smile, she headed for the door. 'Just don't say I didn't warn you. I'll see you tomorrow—if she hasn't murdered you in your bed. And lock up your wallet.'

'Yes, Mummy.'

She stuck her tongue out and went, and Dan walked out into the garden and stared out over the sea while he calmed down. The water was choppy now, the sky suddenly dark and menacing, and in the distance he heard the rumble of thunder. There was a band of rain moving in across the water, and it would hit them any time now. Thank God Iona was out of that leaky annexe—whatever Emily and the rest of them had to say on the subject.

He glanced over towards the guest suite and wondered if she was still asleep. Probably. She'd looked exhausted. He'd leave her until she woke up naturally. He could finish the cooking when she got up and came and found him, and they'd eat together. He realised he was looking forward to it.

Emily's words rang in his ears, but he ignored them, as he'd ignored Harry's warning. Harry and Emily hadn't met her. They had no idea what she was like, and Dan had absolutely no intention of getting personally involved with her.

It would just be nice to have a little company, that was all.

The rain arrived, slashing, horizontal sheets racing towards him, bending the trees and shrubs before it, and he went back inside and shut the door just before it thrashed against the glass. He glanced at his watch.

Four o'clock. He was getting hungry. He hadn't had lunch, and breakfast had been disgustingly early.

He found some biscuits, made a cup of tea and went through to his studio, leaving the door open so he could hear her when she woke. With any luck it wouldn't be long…

He'd lied to her!

All that rubbish about needing a housekeeper. He was one of them! One of the developers who'd wanted her out.

He'd lied to her—lied and cheated and tricked her, and his sister had the gall—the *gall*!—to suggest that *she* couldn't be trusted? How *dared* she! How dared any of them?

She was going to be sick.

Heart pounding, nausea rising in her throat and her legs barely able to support her weight, Iona grabbed her few miserable possessions and stuffed them in her rucksack and the ancient flight bag that carried everything of any importance to her.

Except her pride, and right now that was in tatters.

She'd *known* it was too good to be true! Had known it was all going to come crashing down around her sooner or later. Well, it had—in spades. Just rather quicker than she'd imagined. Still, at least she'd had a shower and washed her hair, and it was just as well she hadn't had time to get too used to it. She could go back to being a *drifter* right now!

'Come on, Pebbles,' she whispered, scooping her up, and opening the other door a crack into her little hall, the one which led to the drive, she listened carefully for any sound before she opened the door a fraction further and scanned the front garden.

She froze at the sound of a door opening, but then it closed and she heard the slap of flip-flops.

She peeped carefully through the gap. A woman was getting into a car, dressed in jeans and a T-shirt and the flip-flops. So that was Emily. Taller than her, maybe a size larger, a little older perhaps. She looked harmless, but she'd heard her voice—and her words and Dan's were ringing in her ears, sickening her.

Where was Dan? She'd heard the front door shut, and Emily hadn't looked back or waved, so she thought it was probably safe. And if she didn't hurry, she'd miss the electric gates.

Damn. She hadn't thought of that. Shrugging the rucksack on to one shoulder and cramming a couple of sachets of cat food into her flight bag as an afterthought, she crept out into the front garden, looked around and hurried after the car. The drive was empty, and the gates were starting to swing shut, so she sprinted through them with inches to spare, then paused on the pavement and scanned the road each side.

Nothing. Emily must have turned off.

Good.

She realised she was crying, and she wanted to scrub the angry tears off her cheeks, but her hands were full of bags and cat, so she wiped them ineffectually against her shoulders and set course for the hotel. It wasn't far—maybe half a mile at the most? She could do that. Of course she could—even on shaking legs. And then she could fall apart in private.

It took her only fifteen minutes, and as she turned the corner, her composure hanging by a thread, she was stopped in her tracks by the sight of a workman fixing a sheet of board over her door.

The cry of protest stuck in her throat.

Her bolt-hole was gone, her retreat cut off. Dismal as it had been, she'd hung on to the illusion of safety it had represented, but now even that had been taken away from her.

She'd lost everything—her home, her right to stay there, the only lever she'd had in her claim against Ian for her baby's birthright. All gone at a stroke, and the job she'd foolishly hoped would be her passport out of there wasn't worth the paper it was written on.

She laughed. What was she thinking? She didn't even have a bit of paper with it written on!

She had nothing.

And then, right on cue, as if things weren't already bad enough, the wind whipped up and an icy squall drenched her to the skin…

CHAPTER FOUR

WHERE on earth was she?

It was almost dark outside, the rain still lashing against the glass, and Dan couldn't believe she hadn't appeared yet. She hadn't seemed *that* tired, and he would have thought the thunder and lightning would have woken her.

He glanced at his watch and frowned. Eight-thirty, just gone. Was she really still sleeping? Maybe she was waiting in her room, reading or something, expecting him to call her. What had he said to do? He couldn't remember his exact words. Had it been ambiguous?

He went down the hall to the entrance to the guest suite, and tapped on the door. 'Iona?'

There was no reply, so he eased the door open and was greeted by a blast of fresh air. He frowned. How strange. The outside door leading to the drive swung to with a crash as he came in, and the door from the sitting room to the garden was wide open, the rain driving in. He called her again, louder this time, but there was no reply. There was a cushion on the paving outside, getting soaked.

Why? He went out on to the terrace and picked it up, then glanced across at the other terrace to his right. The terrace where he and Emily had been talking.

About Iona.

He felt a sickening sense of dread. If she'd heard them...

She might not have done. He went back in out of the rain and shut the sliding door, then called again, then went through to the bedroom and stopped dead.

Empty. The whole flat was completely empty, except for the cat's litter tray and the food bowls. Her bags were gone, the cat was gone—Iona was gone, and with hideous certainty, he knew why.

He groaned and leant back against the wall, staring up at the ceiling. She'd heard them. She must have heard them. She must have been sitting out there on the cushion and overheard Emily giving him an earful.

Overheard all of it. She would have realised that he was one of the developers, thought that he'd wanted her out for commercial reasons—misunderstood his motives and, instead of confronting him, she'd run.

Oh, hell. She'd be back in that terrible annexe again, holed up like a criminal in the stinking, crumbling ruin that should have had a closure order on it! And no way was she going to let him talk her out of there again.

But he had to try. He couldn't just leave her there without trying to explain, and at the very least he had to pay for her to go into a hotel.

'I'm going to kill you, Emily,' he growled under his breath, and shutting the side door and locking it, he ran back through the house, grabbed his keys, punched in the alarm code and went out. His car was still outside, and he got into it and gunned it down the drive, paused impatiently while the gates opened and then stared at them.

How would she have got out of the gates? He hadn't had time to show her where the keypad was, and she didn't know the code anyway. So was she still here, in the grounds, waiting for the gates to open, or had she left when Emily did? Hours ago—hell, nearly five hours ago, and the storm had been raging ever since.

No. She'd gone. She must have done, he thought, but he searched the gardens anyway, just to be certain.

No trace.

He left the gates open in case she came back, and drove slowly to the hotel, scouring the shadows for any sign of her, his heart pounding even though he knew she wasn't there. She must have left right after Emily, must be there by now, safely locked away under those collapsing ceilings.

He swore softly under his breath, craning his neck to see, and then turned the corner to the hotel and braked to a halt.

The door was boarded up! Nick must have got on to it the moment he'd known she was out, because of the danger. He'd said he was worried about the public liability angle. He must have got one of the building team to secure it straight away.

And now he had no idea where to find her.

He stared around through the streaming windows, and felt fear for her grip him. She'd be freezing, for all it was June. Freezing and angry and betrayed and all alone.

No, not alone. She had the cat, the poor, ancient, moth-eaten little cat that she'd refused to leave.

Damn!

He slammed his hand on the steering-wheel and growled.

What now? He punched in Emily's number, fear and anger pushing him over the brink.

'Iona's disappeared. She must have heard us talking. Get out there and look for her—and I don't want any damned excuses. This is your fault. You came bursting into my house making unfounded accusations against a person you'd never even met, and if any harm comes to her, I'll hold you personally responsible.'

'Oh, Dan, no! It's vile out there! Where are you now?'

'Outside the hotel. The annexe door's been boarded up. She's got nowhere to go, so she might have gone back to my house. Get round there and search the garden again. I only had a quick look. I've left the gate open, but the house is locked so she might be sheltering somewhere in the garden, at the back of the shrubbery or somewhere.'

'No, she won't be out in the open, Dan, not in this storm! It's filthy out there!'

'I've noticed—and I've no doubt that she has, too, after five hours. And I'm hoping she might have had the sense to come back to the house.'

'Really?' she said skeptically. 'Is that likely?'

He rubbed a hand through his hair. 'Probably not, after what she must have heard, but she doesn't have a lot of options, I don't think. Just do it, Em, or send Harry, and if you don't find her, then drive round and round looking until you do, and I'll do the same round this area. And call me!'

'Hang on! I don't know what she looks like!'

Beautiful.

He cleared his throat, his voice sharper than he'd intended when he spoke. 'Yeah, you do. A pregnant woman with a rucksack and a cat. There won't be many of them. If anything's happened to her, I might just have to kill you.'

He jabbed the phone, cutting her off, and dialled Nick.

'Get out in the car and start looking for Iona. She's disap-peared,' he said, and filled him in, giving him the same pithy description he'd given Emily.

'I'm on it,' he said, and the line went dead.

She was so cold.

Her teeth were chattering, she was soaked right through to the skin and on her lap Pebbles was shaking. The cat might be deaf, but she could feel the thunder, and the poor little thing was terrified. They were huddled in a doorway by the side of a shop, the doorway Daniel had dragged her into—gracious, was it really only last night? It was round the other side of the hotel from the annexe where she'd been living, and at least it was a little shel-tered from the rain, but it was a busier road, and people kept looking at her.

None of them stopped, too busy trying to get home out of the rain, and frankly she was quite grateful for that, because she didn't want to have to move or explain herself. She and the cat were at least sheltered there, and sitting on her rucksack she was reasonably comfortable. Well, that was probably pushing it, but comfort was the least of her worries at the moment.

Where to go next was much more pressing, and with the cat in tow her choices were frankly hugely limited.

What was she thinking? Her choices were negligible anyway, what with having no funds, no friends in the area and probably a good few enemies.

Not least Emily, who for some reason seemed to have a real hatred of her, even though she'd never met her. Something to do with Harry—her husband?—and someone called Carmen, but she hadn't caught it all. And

Kate, whoever she was. Not that it mattered. Nothing mattered except finding somewhere dry where she could lie down, because she was beginning to change her priorities about the comfort thing.

She looked up, wondering if there was anywhere she could sit for a while in the station opposite and get a bit warmer, and there right in front of her was Daniel's car, cruising slowly down the street.

Dear God, he was looking for her! She didn't need this now. Not at the moment, when she was so cold and angry she was likely to say something that would land her in court. She shrank back into the opening, trying to make herself invisible, but it was hopeless. He'd seen her. He swung the wheel, hitched the car up on the kerb and jumped out, leaving the engine running and the door hanging open into the road.

Horns tooted, but he ignored them and ran over to her, crouching down in the doorway so she couldn't see his face. She could hear him, though, hear the tremor in his voice as he gripped her arm and shook it lightly.

'Where the hell have you been? I've been worried out of my mind!'

'Let go of me,' she said clearly, and he dropped her as if he'd suddenly realised what he was doing.

'I'm sorry—Iona, please, come and sit in the car and talk to me. Let me explain.'

'No. I'm not coming with you.'

'I'll give you the keys. That way I can't drive you anywhere you don't want to go. But please let me explain.' He jammed his hand through his hair and water flew from the strands. She looked at him more closely and realised he was soaked. Soaked to the skin and nearly as cold as she was. He'd been out looking for her, she realised, not just in the car, but walking up and down, searching for her in the pouring rain.

But why?

'Explain what?' she asked, her voice curiously flat considering her turbulent emotions. 'Why you lied to me?'

He sighed a little raggedly. 'I didn't lie. I just didn't tell you all the truth.'

She laughed at that, at the absolute absurdity of it. 'All? How about you didn't tell me most of it? Or at least the bit that mattered.'

'I did tell you the bit that mattered,' he said, and his voice was strangely sincere and subdued.

A car horn honked, and there was a screech of brakes.

'You've left your door open,' she reminded him unnecessarily, but he didn't budge.

'Please. Come with me. Let's go somewhere you can get warm and have something hot to eat and drink, and talk about this. We'll go somewhere public—a café or something. You can choose.'

'I've got the cat,' she pointed out, and he sighed.

'Iona, please,' he said again, and because he wasn't moving, because he was starting to shiver and he was getting even wetter, if that were possible, she relented.

'OK, but just in the car. We aren't going anywhere. And you've got five minutes.'

He had to move the car. It was obstructing the traffic, but he just drove round the corner, turned into the hotel car park and pulled up next to the skip containing her old mattress. Then he cut the engine, handed her the keys and shifted so he was facing her.

'I don't know where to start apologising,' he said, knowing he could blow this so easily and drive her back out into the rain.

'Cut the apologies. I want the truth—all of it. And can you put the heater on?'

'Not without the keys.'

She handed them back without a word, and he started the engine and cranked the heating up. They were so wet that even with the climate control on, the windows started to steam up, and there was a definite smell of wet dog and nasty washing. And the cat was shaking.

Poor old Pebbles.

Iona was stroking her, her fingers almost blue with cold, and she needed to get out of those wet clothes.

'This is crazy. Please let me take you home and get you dry and give you something to eat. You must be starving, and you're so cold, and the cat's freezing.'

She looked down at Pebbles, and something dripped on her. It could have been water from her hair, but it could equally have been a tear, and his heart twisted.

He reached out his hand and touched her cheek, turning her to face him, and saw another tear sliding down her proud, angry face.

He brushed it away with his thumb, then met her stubborn grey eyes—beautiful eyes, like a rainwashed sky, wary and defensive and defiant to the last. And disappointed. In him. That hurt.

He swallowed. 'Please let me take you home. You don't have to stay. I'll leave the gates open, you can go whenever you like. I won't hurt you, Iona.'

'No. You'll just lie to me, you and your sister and your friends. I thought I was fighting Ian, but you were the real enemy all the time, and now I'm out and you've won. Well, congratulations. How does it feel, stealing from a baby?' She knocked his hand away, scrubbing furiously at the tears that somehow wouldn't stop falling.

'We haven't—'

'Oh, you have! It's hers, Daniel! She should have her inheritance, and now I'm out it'll be so much harder. I knew it was stupid letting you talk me into leaving, but you were so damn convincing, you and your friends, and it was all just a pack of lies, a way of getting me out. I *knew* it was too good to be true. I even told you that, and still I fell for it. I can't believe I was so *stupid*! But you shouldn't have had the door boarded up. I could have gone back there. I still could. I'll unscrew it—'

'No.' He shook his head. 'It's too dangerous,' he said, and as if to illustrate his point, a sheet of roofing material blew off the flat roof in front of them and tumbled across the car park, coming to rest against the skip.

Her lip wobbled, and she bit it and turned her head away, just as the phone rang. He turned it on, on hands-free so she could hear what Emily had to say.

'Any news?'

'I've got her,' he told his sister, and there was a heart-felt sigh.

'Thank God,' she said, her voice relieved. 'Is she OK?'

'No thanks to you.'

'Oh, Dan, don't, I'm kicking myself. I'm so, so sorry. It's just the Carmen thing—I could see you getting sucked in and I know what you guys are like when you get all pro-tective. It's too close to home for me, and I'm sorry I threw Kate in your face, that was uncalled for. Look, I'll come round, talk to her, explain—'

'I think you've said quite enough today,' he told her. 'Don't worry, I'm looking after her.'

There was a tiny pause, then Emily said, 'Right. Um—tell her I'm sorry, will you? And I'll give you a call tomorrow.'

'Do that.'

He cut off the phone, and turned to her. 'I need to ring Nick. He's out looking for you too.'

'Worried about a lawsuit?'

He gave a harsh sigh and ran his fingers through his wet hair. 'No. He's worried about a vulnerable young woman out on the street in a thunderstorm, with nowhere to go because of his actions.' He took a breath and softened his voice. 'We aren't out to get you, Iona. We're on your side.'

She snorted. 'Well, forgive me if I don't quite believe you,' she said tautly, and then her anger at Emily came rushing to the fore again. 'How dare she, Dan? How *dare* she make those accusations about me? She's never even *met* me! I don't care if she is your sister, it's just unforgivable. I would *never* make snap judgements like that about anyone. Who does she think she *is*?'

She realised she was talking pretty much in italics, and snapped her mouth shut, turning to look out of the window. Not that she could see through it in the pouring rain, but it beat looking at Daniel and wondering if he was a genuinely nice man or just a gullible sucker like his sister said. Or worse. As he'd pointed out, Georgie didn't know what he got up to in his private life. Maybe he was a serial sex offender?

She was about to get out of the car and head off into the rain again when there was an almighty flash and clap of thunder right near them, and the cat shivered and cried out. No. She couldn't do it. Pebbles would die, and she couldn't have that on her conscience.

Daniel was ringing Nick, telling him Iona was safe, saying he'd speak to him in the morning. She was treated to Nick's apology, too, before Daniel cut him off, and maybe it was that, or maybe it was just the cold and the fact that Pebbles was crying pitifully now, but she turned to him, her chin stuck out in that way he was beginning to find rather familiar.

'OK,' she said, her voice like ice. 'But just because of the cat. I'll let you take me back so I can get her dry and feed her, and I'll change, and I want to know exactly what's going on. Then we'll talk about me staying.'

He gave a silent sigh of relief and nodded. 'OK.'

'Where do you want me to start?'

She eyed him warily, not sure she could believe a word that came out of his beautiful lying mouth, but he'd left the gates open, had shown her where the keypad was and told her what the combination was that would open them if they were shut at any time.

He'd also given her a key to the front door and the side door, the code for the burglar alarm, and cash, nearly two hundred pounds, all he had on him, he'd said. And a cash card and his pin.

Really? So trusting? She wouldn't have been. Maybe his sister was right about him. Or maybe it was because even if she went mad with his cash card, it couldn't rival the damage to their commercial enterprise of her squatting in the hotel annexe and holding up their purchase. So—damage limitation, or genuinely decent? The jury was still out.

He'd shooed her into the guest suite, and by the time she'd come out of the shower he'd wrapped the cat in a warm towel and fed her, and unpacked her bag.

'Your clothes are soaked,' he said, frowning, and left her, coming back a minute later with a pair of jog bottoms, a T-shirt and a big fluffy towelling robe that she snuggled into gratefully. They were all far too big for her, but she didn't care; she was warm, and the cat was on her lap, sleeping, her clothes were in the washing machine and she was waiting for him to begin.

He must have showered at some point—probably while she'd dressed—and he was wearing worn old jeans and a soft cotton jumper. His feet were encased in thick sports socks, and he propped them up on the coffee table between them and met her eyes.

'Start at the beginning,' she said. 'When you first realised I was living there, and you decided to hatch this plot.'

'It's not a plot.'

'What would you call it, then? Oh, yes, I remember— "solving a problem",' she said, her voice putting it in quotes. 'I think those were your words, pretty much.'

He swore softly and rubbed his hands through his hair, ruffling the damp strands and perversely, crazily, making her fingers itch to straighten it out, to lift that lock that had fallen over his forehead and ease it back out of the way so she could see his eyes better.

But he lifted his head, so she could see them anyway, and she let her fingers stroke the cat, instead. Much safer, and much, much more sensible.

'It was about a fortnight after we completed—'

'Completed?' she said, sitting bolt upright and staring at him in horror.

'Yes—what, did you think we were just wasting legal fees and making your life a misery for the sake of it? Of course we've completed. We completed the day before

Brian died. We'd made an agreement that he could stay there for up to a month after completion to give him time to clear his debts and find somewhere to live, but to be honest I think he realised he was dying and he wanted the money in the bank before then, so the sale wasn't compromised, so he let us rush it through.'

'And he died before he could do anything with it,' she said softly, sinking back against the sofa, her mind whirling. 'But if you've paid the money—then where is it? Does Ian have it?'

'No, I don't imagine so. The probate office won't release it until probate's been granted. There was a small retention, to be paid over when the property was finally handed over with vacant possession, and we've still got that, because of course we haven't had vacant possession until today.'

'Until you engineered my move.'

He sighed tiredly. 'I didn't engineer your move—well, that's a lie, I did, I suppose, but not for that reason.'

'Why, then?' she challenged.

'Because it was so dangerous! I didn't sleep last night for worrying about you under that ceiling, and rightly, because when I came back this morning the chunk over the stairs was down. The roof's in shreds, Iona. You saw that sheet of felt fly off it. The boards will be rotten, and probably the joists. It's only a matter of time before the lot falls in. And there's the baby to think about.'

She looked down, her hands instinctively curving around her daughter. He was right, it had been dangerous. Last night when the hall ceiling fell down had been scary, but she'd been in the bathroom when the ceiling had come down in the bedroom a week ago, and the potential consequences of that had been even more terrifying. All her clothes had been ruined, the mattress soaked and covered in plaster, the room all but destroyed.

If she'd been in the bed—

She shuddered, and a quick frown flickered across his face. 'Are you all right? Warm enough?'

She squared her shoulders. 'Yes,' she said, although she was very far from all right even if she was warm now, and as if he knew that, he sighed. After a long pause, he spoke again.

'Iona, I know what it must look like, but I really wanted you out of there for the best possible reasons, and if it also suited us that you were no longer in the building, that was just a bonus. If it had been safe, I would have left you there if that was what you wanted and then taken you to see our legal team tomorrow to talk through your claim,'

'So you can sort it out and get rid of me in the shortest possible time?'

'Because I don't want to see you cheated by a man who couldn't even be bothered to visit his sick father until he was dying,' he said tightly.

Could she believe him? He sounded angry enough.

She sighed. She didn't really have an option, she thought. She had nowhere to live, no money to live off and a baby on the way. Soon. She didn't have the luxury of multiple choices, and she was so tired of fighting.

'You know, if I'd realised that you'd completed, that whatever I did couldn't stop the money from changing hands, I needn't have spent all that time there in that horrible place,' she said heavily. 'I thought it was all held up by probate—so why didn't you just get me chucked out?'

He chuckled, to her surprise. 'We have been trying,' he

pointed out. 'That's why we were seeing the law team tomorrow. We were still having difficulty evicting you, and then there was the question of your safety and our public liability to add to it,' he said. 'We're going to demolish that wing, and you were seriously holding up our schedule. We'd got a meeting lined up for tomorrow with the legal team to discuss it.'

'So why did you offer me the job? I mean, if your hotshot team were about to pull out the big guns, why not just let them get on with it now?'

His eyes flicked away, and he looked a little uncomfortable. 'Because we found out you're pregnant,' he said, pointing out the obvious.

'So?'

He looked shocked. 'So, it makes a difference. A huge difference. My sister ended up in a similar situation when she was pregnant, and she came home to live with our parents. She was a little older than you, with a small daughter and another baby on the way, but at least she had our family home to run to. You have nowhere, and however much a bastard you might think me, I couldn't just turn you out onto the street. And I didn't think you'd accept charity, and you have to admit I could use someone to help me keep this place in order. And it's not like I'm short of space.'

She couldn't argue with that, but there was something about the way he wouldn't look at her that made her wonder about his motivation. Something he was hiding from her, or at least not ready to share. Something to do with Kate? Whatever. She'd come back to it later.

'So how exactly did you find out about me?' she asked. 'At the beginning?'

'We were told there was a sitting tenant—some person

who'd been working in the hotel and was making some ridiculous claim—his words, not mine—on the property. They said it wasn't a problem, you'd be moving out within the month. And then the month was over, and you were still there.'

'And Ian told you I didn't have a claim?'

'That's right. Or his solicitors did—although how they could say that without the will, I have no idea.'

'Even without it, there's a chance I can claim for her. There's an ancient piece of legislation involving babies— *en ventre sa mère.*'

He nodded, and she searched his eyes, surprised. It was a pretty obscure thing. Had he been scouring the net?

'I have to be able to prove that she's Jamie's, though, before I can do anything—'

'Is there any question?'

She glared at him, and he just raised his hands. 'Only asking, Iona. It could be relevant. If you only think it's Jamie's, we need to know if we're footing the bill.'

'Does mistrust run in the family?' she asked, and he winced. Actually, even she winced at the harshness of her tone, and she softened it, relenting. 'She's Jamie's. Of course she is. It's not me who needs the proof, Dan,' she added more gently. 'It's the courts. And if Ian gets the money before she's born—'

'But he won't get it. He won't have it yet, and if you make a claim, probate won't be granted until they've proved it one way or another. Our solicitors will go over it with you tomorrow and start things moving—assuming you'll talk to them?'

She was back to that whole choice thing, and it was pretty cut and dried. Go out on the streets and throw herself on the mercy of the local housing department, and try and fight a legal battle without funding—because she couldn't get legal aid for this, she'd checked, and she had no intention of using one of those unscrupulous 'no claim, no fee' firms that advertised all over the place—or she could stay here, in this beautiful, peaceful, sublime house, with a man who, despite her misgivings and the fact that he had no reason to trust her, had been nothing but kind to her, and let him help her fight her legal battle from a position of security.

And that was the word that did it for her.

Security.

For her, and for the cat, and most particularly for her daughter.

'Iona?'

She met his eyes—gentle, concerned—and tried to smile.

'I'm sorry. I think I might have misjudged you. I probably owe you the benefit of the doubt, at least.'

'I think, in view of what you heard, it would have been quite reasonable if you did misjudge me,' he said, his mouth kicking up in a rueful smile. Then his smile faded, and his brow creased into a frown. 'So—can you forgive me? Forgive us? And will you stay?'

She thought about it. They maybe had a little way to go yet before she could forgive him, and she'd have to think long and hard about forgiving Emily, but stay? Maybe. 'You said something about an employment contract. I think that would be a good idea—put it on a proper footing. I don't want anybody making insinuations.'

He nodded. 'Of course. We can do that tomorrow.'

'And you mentioned supper,' she added, and the frown vanished, replaced by a smile that warmed her battered, exhausted heart.

'I did,' he said. 'A chicken casserole—it's all ready in the oven.'

She returned his smile cautiously. 'Then let's start there—and we'll worry about the rest tomorrow.'

CHAPTER FIVE

CHAPTER FIVE

THEY made it through to the morning.

Iona without running away again, and Daniel without lying awake all night and wondering if she was still there.

He'd contemplated setting the burglar alarm so if she opened the outer door it would go off, but he'd thought better of it. He didn't want her feeling trapped, and he had to trust her.

She'd said she'd stay. So he gave her the benefit of the doubt, and in the morning, she was still there.

He knew that because when he got out of bed he saw her standing motionless at the end of the garden, swathed almost from head to toe in his towelling robe and looking out over the calm, tranquil sea, and he felt a welling of something he really didn't want to analyse pushing up through his chest.

He pressed the button to cloud the windows, something he never usually did, and after showering and dressing, he went downstairs to put the kettle on and saw her still standing there, her face tipped up slightly to the sky, soaking it up. He slid the door open and stepped out on to the terrace, and she turned and smiled, the sunlight glinting in her hair.

'Morning,' he said, and she headed back towards the house, her feet bare in the wet grass.

'Morning. I was just soaking up the sea air.'

'You'll be there a while, then,' he said, unable to keep the smile in check, and she smiled back.

'I'll take the risk. It's worth it. It's beautiful here.'

'Did you sleep well?'

She nodded. 'I was tired.'

'Hard day yesterday.'

'Yes.' She said no more, but there was a lingering reserve in her eyes that hadn't been there at first, and it saddened him. 'How enclosed is the garden?' she asked instead after a pause.

'Completely.'

'So would Pebbles be able to get out if I let her out of the house?'

'Only if the gates were open, and they aren't usually. And if you let her into the back garden, she can't get round to the front. I take it she can't climb? There's a wall with a door in it up by the garage, and another wall on the other side, and she can't get down to the beach unless the gate's unlocked.'

'So she could go out through the sitting room door and walk round the garden?'

'She could.'

Iona smiled. 'She'd love that. She used to lie on the roof in the sun for hours and watch the birds; she's probably long past being able to catch anything, but she'd love to see them.'

'I'm sure. Let her out, by all means. It would do her good to stretch her legs.'

Her smile widened and she went, leaving wet footprints on the slate, and he heard her door slide open and waited for her to emerge with the cat. It took a minute, but then finally Pebbles appeared at her side, looking round cautiously, ready to run if anything threatening appeared.

'Tea or coffee?' he asked, and she looked up.

'Tea would be lovely, but aren't I meant to be making it?'

'Only if you're taking the job.'

The pause stretched out forever, until he thought he'd probably blown it, but then she smiled and said, 'I'll make the tea,' and he let out the breath he hadn't known he was holding and grinned back.

'You watch the cat. I'm not sure early morning tea should be in your job description anyway,' he said, and went back inside, humming cheerfully to himself and not allowing himself to consider why he should suddenly feel so damned happy.

'What time's our appointment with the solicitors?'

He frowned. 'Not sure. Ten?'

'Oh.' She looked at the clock and chewed her lip. She'd really meant to go through her clothes last night and sort out something to wear, but what with all the upset—

'What's wrong?'

'My clothes all stink—well, such as they are. I was going to wash them last night. I can't really go to the solicitors in my tatty jeans and that T-shirt.'

The memory of the previous evening's events shadowed his eyes, and he frowned. 'Have you got any maternity clothes?' he asked.

'Baggy sweatpants, a few T-shirts. Nothing respectable, really. My jeans don't fit any more, but they're the best thing I've got and at least they were washed last night, thanks to you.'

The frown deepened, and he ran his eyes over her assessingly. Since she was still wearing his big towelling robe with her bare feet sticking out the bottom, she felt a little self-conscious. She pulled it tighter.

'I could ask Emily if she's got anything.'

She swallowed and felt her chin come up a notch. 'Please don't bother. I'll wear my jeans.'

He dragged a hand through his hair and sighed. 'Look, we'll go shopping straight afterwards, OK? Get you something.'

'And that'll really help with the money-grubbing bitch thing,' she muttered under her breath.

'Rubbish,' he said, his hearing obviously acute enough to catch her words. 'Think of it as uniform.'

She didn't say a word, but her face must have given her away, because he chuckled. 'Not the French maid variety,' he said drily. 'But you need clothes if you're going to help me to entertain. After all, you can hardly hide in the kitchen, can you? And anyway, the ceiling was our responsibility, so technically you could look on it as claiming off us for replacements.'

Logical. And clever of him, and a get-out clause for her pride, on the clothes front, although she panicked a little about the entertaining thing. Entertaining who, for instance? Hopefully not his sister. But he was studying her, waiting for her answer, and she let it go for now.

'Just a few things,' she conceded. 'Just until I've earned enough to buy more.'

He nodded. 'Done. Right, we ought to get on. I'd like to leave in half an hour—is that enough time for you to get ready?'

She nearly laughed out loud. It would take her two

minutes to do what she could do, or days, if she was going to do it properly—the haircut, the new clothes, shoes that weren't flip-flops or dropping to pieces, a facial, make-up—the list went on and on, but that was for later. It seemed everything was for later.

'Half an hour's plenty,' she assured him, and used the time to put her clothes into the washing machine. She was only going to let him buy her a few things. The rest would have to do for now.

They set off for the solicitors right on time, and as they walked into the office, two men got to their feet and came over. Harry and Nick, she realised. She recognised Harry from the television reports that he used to present from all over the world, but Nick's face was also slightly familiar. She realised she'd seen him around the hotel before Brian died, only she'd never realised his significance.

They looked sober, she thought, and a little uncomfortable in her presence—Harry, particularly, presumably because it was his wife who'd upset her last night. She put it behind her, straightened her shoulders and went over to them, hand outstretched.

'Hi, I'm Iona Lockwood,' she said, and made herself meet Harry's eyes.

He shook her hand. 'Harry Kavenagh,' he said. 'I have instructions from Emily to apologise to you on her behalf.'

She found a smile. She wasn't even slightly sure that Emily had said any such thing, but she gave him credit for doing it for her. Although she had apologised to Dan on the phone last night, and she'd wanted to come over, so maybe—

'Nick Barron,' the other man said, and smiled at her as he shook her hand. 'I recognise you. You were working on Reception when I met Brian Dawes.'

'Reception and everywhere else,' she said ruefully. 'It's a good job I can multi-task.'

They chuckled, and the atmosphere eased a little. They were called in then, and the solicitor was very interested to hear her story, so she told it again.

'And you say there's no sign of the will, Miss Lockwood?'

'Not that Ian could find, and I don't know where Brian would have put it.'

'Did he have a solicitor?'

'I don't know. There was a man—Barry Edwards, I think his name was. He might have known something about it. He was dealing with the sale, I think, but I don't know where he was from. Brian kept it very much to himself.'

'I know Barry Edwards. We've been dealing with him. I'm sure if there was a will it would have come up in conversation. We've been talking about your claim on the estate. I'll have another chat to him, see if he can shed any light. And in the meantime, I gather you're happy to move out of the hotel and give vacant possession to my clients?'

She nodded. She'd forgotten the luxury of proper accommodation, and last night was like a dream. She had no urge to return to the nightmare. 'It wasn't safe.'

'It certainly wasn't. The roof fell in last night,' Nick told them all. 'I've been in there this morning. The mattress is buried under tons of rubble. Dan got you out in the nick of time.'

Beside her Daniel closed his eyes and let out a long, slow breath. 'Hell's teeth,' he muttered. 'Really?'

'Really. We're knocking it down today before anything else can happen.'

She felt sick. Her hands instinctively went to her baby, her fingers stroking it, her eyes fixed on Dan's face. He reached out a hand and touched her shoulder lightly, and she smiled.

Whatever anyone else thought, he'd done the right thing, and they both knew it. Nick, too, for boarding it up so she couldn't get back in there.

The solicitor cleared his throat. 'Right, well, then, I think the next thing to do is to get some information from you about this claim.'

'I'm not sure we need everyone for that,' Dan said, looking at the others pointedly. 'Do we?'

They all shook their heads. 'Do you gentlemen have anything further to add?' the solicitor asked.

'A contract of employment,' Dan said promptly. 'To protect Iona and give her proper employee's rights.'

'OK. I'll do that with her, too, and let you look it over and have your say when it's done. If that's all?'

'That's all, I think?' Dan said, and the other two nodded. 'We'll go back to the hotel, then, shall we, and carry on there? Iona, would you care to join us when you're finished? It's not far from here. We'll be in the office.'

'OK. Which door?'

'The side door, by the security guard.'

She smiled. 'Tell him to let me in, would you? We aren't best friends.'

Dan's mouth tightened. 'I'll tell him.'

'She's nice.'

Dan rolled his eyes at Harry. 'I said she was nice.'

'Pleasant, well-spoken, educated—'

He sighed, and Harry pulled a face. 'Em was afraid you were getting involved with some little slapper who was after your money.'

'And Brian Dawes's money—and I think the expression was "conniving shark",' he pointed out, and Harry winced.

'Ouch.'

'Indeed.'

'She needs to meet her.'

'Oh, absolutely, but I'm not sure Iona wants to meet her, and I can't say I blame her. I wouldn't. It's a miracle she didn't just walk off and never speak to any of us again.'

'That may be something to do with a lack of options,' Nick pointed out as they turned the corner into the hotel car park. 'But I have to say I agree with you about her, and I think she's sound. She was fantastic when she was working here,' he added. 'A real asset. It would have gone under long before without her, I suspect, because Brian's health was pretty rough. I'd already started negotiating with him before the son came back from Thailand, and he was more than ready to give up. I think he was only hanging on in case either of his sons changed their minds. If I'd realised she was the squatter, I would have talked to her directly and we could have sorted this out ages ago.'

'Well, we know now, and she's out safely, thank God, and maybe we can help her,' Harry said.

'You could start by convincing my sister that she's not a conniving shark,' Dan said drily, and veered off to the security guard's hut. 'Miss Lockwood's going to be joining us. Don't try and stop her, please,' he said, and the man frowned.

'Miss Lockwood?'

'Our sitting tenant. She says you aren't best friends.'

His face went carefully blank. 'Just going my job, Guv.'

Dan grunted and rejoined the others. 'Right, let's get stuck in.'

* * *

It was odd coming back.

She walked in through the side door and went through to Reception in the big central foyer. The carpeted hush had been replaced by the crashing and banging upstairs and the sound of the wrecking ball demolishing the annexe on the other side of the car park.

It was familiar, and yet not. The carpets had gone, the fittings were all out except for the reception desk, and it was just a shell, echoing strangely with the sound of drilling and hammering, a radio playing cheesy pop and someone singing along with it out of key.

She closed her eyes and saw it as it had been, with Brian smiling at her across the scarred old desk with the brass bell on it, and she felt a now familiar wave of grief. She squeezed her eyes tight until she was under control again, then opened them. The poor old desk. She loved it, bearing as it did all the marks of the hotel's one hundred and fifty year history. She thought of all the people who'd checked in there, the stories they would have had to tell. And now it was going to go. She ran her hand over it lovingly, and it came up covered in fine dust.

Ashes to ashes.

She swallowed and turned away, to find Dan watching her.

'You OK?' he asked softly, and she nodded.

'I haven't been in here since the funeral. It's all so different now.'

'Not as different as it will be.'

No. She'd realised that, and had to let it go. 'So what are you planning? Are you going to gut it and make it all modern?'

He laughed. 'Not at all. We'll restore the old hotel, and the rest is being purpose built. We're turning it into a residential spa and health club, so it will still be a hotel of sorts, but there'll be all sorts of fitness and beauty areas, treatment rooms for massage and physio and aromatherapy, that sort of thing—maybe some reiki or shiatsu. And a swimming pool, steam room and sauna. It's a huge site, and it's grossly under-used, and there isn't a health club for miles.'

'Filling a niche?'

'Exactly. Come into the office and meet Georgie's father, George Cauldwell. He's our builder. I'll show you the plans, and then we need to go shopping. How did it go with the solicitor?'

'Fine. He's getting it all under way. Thanks for leaving us to it—and thank you so much for letting me use him,' she added softly. 'I don't know if anything will come of my claim, but at least I'll know I've done all I can for her.'

'My pleasure,' he said, and his smile did funny things to her heart. Either that or it was indigestion.

She'd put her money on his smile.

Nick was on the phone when they went back in, and he was obviously talking to Georgie.

He looked up and smiled at Iona, and Dan wasn't sure if her answering smile was as confident as it appeared. Probably not, but that wouldn't be surprising.

'No, I don't think we'll be much longer. I think we've just about finished here, haven't we, George?'

George gave him the thumbs up, and he nodded and went on, 'Yeah, he says we're done so we'll be out of here soon. Why?'

His gaze flicked to Iona, and he pulled a thoughtful face. 'I don't know. Dan was going to show her the plans and then take her shopping for some clothes, I think. Hers all got ruined.' He paused, and they could hear Georgie talking, protesting. 'About the same as you? OK, well, I'll see you in a minute. I'll tell them to hang on.'

He turned his phone off and looked up at them. 'Georgie's on her way out with the girls. She's going to pop in—she's got some things for you.'

'Me?' Iona said, looking startled.

'Mmm. Maternity clothes. She said it was silly you buying any for such a short time when she's got hundreds and she's about your size. She's going to drop some in.'

Hell. Dan wasn't at all sure how that would go down. She'd flatly refused his offer to ask Emily, but maybe Georgie was different. Apparently so, because when she spoke, Iona was nothing but gracious.

'That would be lovely. Thank you. It would be useful to borrow one or two things just to tide me over until I get my own.'

Borrow—and for the shortest possible time. Reaching out to touch the olive branch? Not that it was Georgie who'd said anything, but if she was wary of all of them, he wouldn't blame her.

Interesting. And it revealed another facet of a woman he was beginning to find intrigued him more and more…

Ten minutes later, she'd been introduced to George, had seen the plans for the leisure club complex and she had a huge bag of clothes, dropped off by Georgie on her way out with the children. She hadn't come into the hotel, so Iona hadn't gotten to meet her.

Pity. She could have summed her up a little better, but Nick had gone out to get the bag when she'd rung to say she was in the car park, and now she and Daniel were on their way home so she could try them on.

A moment later, alone in her little flat with her emotions, she tipped the whole lot out on to the bed and stared at the clothes in longing. Classy linen trousers, a soft jersey dress, battered jeans, crazy denim bib shorts, T-shirts, a zippy top—the whole shebang, scooped out of storage by Georgie and smelling of fabric softener.

Lovely, after mould and mildew and rotten washing. She pressed her nose into the jersey dress and breathed deeply, and felt herself tearing up again. She put the dress down and lifted the clothes one by one, studying them.

The dress was a beautiful cut, as were the trousers, and the tops looked really useful. There was even a bra. A proper bra, not a flimsy little cotton thing, but a proper, supportive and yet pretty bra with cups the size of melons. It would never fit, she thought, but she tried it on anyway and discovered to her surprise that it did. Not only did it fit, it was comfortable, and pretty, and she felt nearer to sexy in it than she had in ages. And she didn't have four boobs, for a change.

Amazing.

She tried a pair of black linen trousers with a vest top and a loose natural linen shirt, and stared at herself in the mirror. Good grief. She looked almost respectable. No. More than that. She looked as if she could hold her head up in the street again, and after the past few weeks and months, it was enough to bring those wretched tears to her eyes again.

'Don't be stupid,' she muttered, and picked up the jersey dress that she'd buried her nose in.

It was gorgeous. Soft and clingy, and yet elegant. She

looked at the label and flinched. It certainly wasn't a chain store cheapy, that was for sure. No wonder it felt so nice.

And looked so good, once it was on.

There were some flat sandals, and as she pulled them out of the bag, a note fluttered out:

Hope some of these are of use. Sorry you've had such a dreadful time the last few weeks. Give me a ring when you've had a look and we can have coffee and sort through the rest of my clothes. Crazy to buy any, I've got tons! Georgie.

She swallowed hard, and sat down on the bed with a bump. A girly coffee. She hadn't done that for ages. So long that she could hardly remember the last time.

There was a tap on the door. 'Iona? Are you OK?'

'Fine,' she said, blinking back the tears, and went to the door, opening it and walking back to the bedroom. 'They're lovely. It was really kind of her. She's invited me for coffee. What do you think? Should I go? And what do you think I should wear? I don't know her, you do. Not this, obviously, it's too dressy. Any ideas?'

She turned back to him and realised he was staring at her as if she'd committed some terrible *faux pas*, and she stepped back, her new confidence starting to crumble into dust. 'Um—maybe I should just stick to my jeans—'

'No! No—you look great. It's lovely. I'm sorry, I just— it took me by surprise. Seeing you like that. You look—'

He broke off, and for an endless moment his eyes burned into her, then he looked hastily away. 'Um—I need to go back to the hotel. Something's come up. If you want a lift to Georgie's, I can take you, but I need to go nowish. And wear something casual—jeans or whatever. Georgie doesn't do formal when she's got the babies crawling all over her.'

And he backed out of the door as if the room were on fire. Why?

She turned and looked in the mirror, and then it dawned on her. The dress was a wrapover with a low V, and with the new bra there was more than a hint of cleavage. And she had a waist, even though the bump stuck out. She looked—sexy?

Heavens.

She took the dress off with trembling fingers, tried on the jeans and a pretty top, and felt a little better. Now all she had to do was open the door and go back out there to Daniel and pretend that nothing had happened.

Not that she had the slightest clue what had happened, but it *had* rattled her, whatever it was, and she had no intention of going there again.

Beautiful.

That was what she looked like in the dress. Beautiful, and sexy, and all woman, with her hair down round her shoulders, soft and glossy and making him itch to sift it through his fingers...

He went out into the garden and dragged in a lungful of air. Pebbles was lying on the paving soaking up the sun, and he picked her up carefully and brought her inside.

Iona appeared in the doorway, her hair up again, pulled out of the way into a ponytail and then folded into some kind of loose, messy bun the way Georgie and Emily did theirs. She'd changed into jeans and a pink top that was, if anything, even sexier than the dress, and he swallowed. Her eyes were wary, and he hoped his smile was a little more convincing than it felt.

'Ready?'

She nodded. 'I'd better put the cat in my room,' she said, and took it from him, but their fingers brushed and he felt as if they'd been burned. Iona backed away from him, then turned and walked swiftly back to her room, shutting the cat in and coming back, her front a drift of multicoloured fur on the pale pink top.

'Um—you've got cat fur,' he said. All over the bump. Damn. And on those breasts. Had they been that size yesterday? Really? He dragged his eyes off them and went into the utility room, coming back with a sticky roller. 'Here.' He handed it to her. There was no way he was running that over her body!

'Better?'

'Fine,' he said, trying not to look too hard and, putting the roller down on the table, he tossed his keys in the air and caught them. 'I've phoned Georgie and she's in. You're going for lunch. Let's go.'

She had a wonderful time.

Georgie greeted her at the door with a welcoming smile and a baby on her hip, and drew her inside.

'Hi, there, it's lovely to meet you,' she said, and looked her up and down. 'Oh, they're a brilliant fit! I'm so glad.'

'They are. Thank you so much. It's just amazing to have something that fits round the bump! I'm really grateful.'

'You're welcome. Iona, this is Lucie. Say hello, Lucie. Come on in; Maya's drawing on the kitchen table,' she said, and took her through to the kitchen. Lucie must have been about nine or ten months, and Maya was probably two, she thought. She looked up from her drawing and gave Iona a great big smile, and within seconds she was admiring the picture and being offered a drink.

'Want juice? Me having juice,' Maya said, sliding down off the chair and heading for the fridge.

Georgie took the carton from her before she dropped it and poured the drinks, then handed one to Iona. 'That top looks lovely on you. Nick said you were about my size, but I didn't really believe him. Men are usually dreadful with things like that. Was anything else any good?'

'Wonderful,' she said honestly. 'Well, I expect so; I didn't have time to look at much. I tried on the black dress—the wrapover?'

'Oh, that one. Nick always adored it. It's really comfy; I wore it loads. I've got a few more things like that, but I wasn't sure what sort of person you were—girly or practical or whatever.'

Girly? She'd never been girly in her life, but she had the sudden urge to try it.

Although from the look on Daniel's face, maybe that wasn't such a good idea.

'Let's go in the garden. I've made us a picnic—shall we go and have lunch, girls?' Georgie said.

Lucie gave her a big grin and said, 'Mum-mum-mum,' happily.

Georgie looked down at her. 'Actually, Iona, could you do me a favour and take her for me, and I'll bring the cool box? Thanks.' And she handed the baby over.

'Hello, sweetheart,' Iona said, smiling at her, and was rewarded with a gummy grin of her own, complete with three tiny little teeth. And she was going to be a mother?

Heavens. What an amazing thing to come out of such a dreadful year.

She followed Georgie and Maya out to the garden, winding through the centre of the house, through a big playroom smothered in toys and games, and out of the French windows on to a lawn that overlooked the sea.

It was a fabulous house—nothing like Daniel's but a Victorian Italianate villa with a big square tower, set up above the prom and the beach—and over lunch Georgie told her about the restoration of the house and the development of the other buildings on the site two years before.

'Daniel said you were an architect,' Iona said.

'*Were* being the operative word,' Georgie replied, wrinkling her nose. 'I do the odd bit now, but with four children it's a bit of a struggle. I can always go back to it later, and I worked with Dan on his house. That was fun—a bit of a rush. Dad built it for him, and because they wanted to start on the hotel they pushed on a bit and finished it in six months from breaking ground. I don't think Dan minded, though. He was so pleased to get in. You met my father this morning, incidentally. George Cauldwell.'

'Oh—yes. Nice man.'

'He is, but I'm a bit worried about him. It's a huge job—not his usual sort of thing, but he's enjoying the challenge. He had a bypass op two years ago and he had to take it easy for a while, but he's right back in the swing of it now. I'm trying to stop him overdoing it but I'm wasting my breath. Nick drags him into meetings and makes him sit down and chat for a while if he thinks it's all getting too much.'

Yes. Iona could imagine Nick doing that; he struck her as a nice man. And Georgie was lovely. Witty and sparky and full of fun, and the girls were delightful and very cuddly.

Once they'd finished eating Georgie put them both down for a nap while they trawled through her maternity clothes.

Iona tried lots of them on, and even though she felt guilty about it, Georgie's comment that it was pointless buying any when hers were going begging did make sense.

'I'll let you have them back as soon as I've finished with them,' she promised as they packed her chosen items into a bag.

'When's the baby due?'

'The beginning of August. About eight weeks. I can't wait to meet her.'

'Her?'

Iona nodded and stroked her tummy affectionately. 'So they said, at the twenty week scan. Hope it's right. I've got used to her being a girl.'

Georgie smiled. 'Girls are lovely. Not that I don't adore the boys, but the girls are special. Well, they all are, of course they are. You'll meet them later, if you're still here. In fact, as the men are tied up all day, do you want to come to the school with me and pick the boys up, and then we can come back here and maybe everyone can come over for supper.'

Everyone? Including Emily?

She didn't feel ready for that—or the yummy mummies at the school gate.

'I really ought to be getting back,' she said with a certain amount of regret. 'After all, I am supposed to be Daniel's housekeeper and if I don't earn my keep—well, I have to,' she said with a wry smile. 'But thank you, anyway.'

'My pleasure.' Georgie handed her the bag of clothes at the door, then hesitated. 'You know, Emily's a lovely person. I know she said some awful things yesterday, but she loves Dan, and she's worried about him. We don't know what Kate did to him, he won't talk about it, but one minute they were like a permanent feature, and the next he was back here from New York and building a house. Anyway, it's none of my business, and he'll tell you if he wants you to know, but she's just worried he'll get hurt all over again.'

'Georgie, I'm his housekeeper,' she pointed out, and Georgie laughed softly.

'Really? Just his housekeeper? We'll see.'

'I am. And that's all. I don't want to be involved with anybody, and it doesn't sound like he does, either.'

But Georgie just smiled. 'We'll see,' she said again, and then, to Iona's surprise, she leant forward and hugged her. 'Take care. Ring me if you need anything.'

'Thanks. And thank you for a lovely day.'

'My pleasure. I'd run you home, but the girls—'

'It's fine; it's a gorgeous day and it isn't far. I'll enjoy the walk.'

And it would give her time to get her thoughts in order— most particularly the niggling little one that kept wondering what it would be like to be involved with Daniel Hamilton...

CHAPTER SIX

'So HOW was your day?'

Iona smiled. 'Tiring.'

'That bad, eh?'

'Oh, no, it was lovely,' she said quickly. 'But I am tired. Georgie's gorgeous but she made me try on loads of clothes, and the children are quite full on and I'm not used to it at the moment. And then I went shopping.'

'Oh, lucky you. I loathe shopping, it's my all-time favourite pet hate,' he said with a grin.

'Well, I didn't really have a choice. I had a look through the freezer and it was even emptier than the fridge, so I walked into town and bought some things for supper.'

'You walked? And did *food* shopping?' He sounded shocked, and she laughed.

'Well—yes. I don't have a car. What else did you think I was shopping for?'

'God knows. Women and shopping are a mystery to me. You should have rung me.'

'I don't have a phone.'

'Well, there's one here.'

'But I don't know your mobile number.'

He sighed and rubbed a hand through his hair, leaving it rumpled and sexy. Oh, dear. That again. Then he shot her a thoughtful look. 'Can you drive?'

She stopped looking at his rumpled hair and smiled. 'Well, now—are you asking me if I *can* drive, or if I'm *allowed* to? Because yes, I can, and no, I'm not. I don't have a UK driving licence.'

'Oh. Pity.'

'Why? Got a spare BMW lying around?' she asked lightly, and he chuckled.

'No. But I do have a lovely old TR6 in the garage that comes out from time to time, and I could have used that and lent you the BMW.'

'Not the TR6?'

He shook his head and pulled a wry face. 'Sorry. That's my baby. Not even my father gets to drive that, and he was a policeman.' He glanced towards the kitchen. 'So what did you get? I'll start cooking.'

'You? But it's my job—'

'Not tonight,' he said firmly. 'Tonight I'm doing it.'

'But you cooked last night,' she said, her brow furrowing. 'And it is supposed to be my job.'

'In that case,' he said, 'I'll compromise. I'll let you sit there at the table and tell me what to do. You're a woman— that should be right up your street.'

She laughed and shook her head. 'No. I can't do that. It's not fair.'

'Oh, go on, I'm sure you can bring yourself to do it. Emily tells me what to do all the time.'

And then he let out a sigh, his smile fading as he gave her an apologetic look. 'I'm sorry. I wasn't going to mention her.'

Iona found a smile. 'Dan, she's not going to go away. I'm going to have to learn to live with her opinion of me.'

'She doesn't have an opinion of you. She has an opinion of a fictional woman she's never met—but that won't last. She's round here all the time. She's a garden designer and she's doing a bit of landscaping for me. You'll probably meet her in the morning—and, if it's any consolation, it'll be harder for her than it will for you.'

She doubted it.

'I'll cope,' she said. 'So—how about penne pasta with crayfish tails in fresh tomato sauce with a touch of chilli and stirred through with cream, and a side salad?'

He blinked. 'You can cook that?'

'No,' she said blithely. 'You can. And if you're very good, I'll tell you how.'

'Oh, I'm very good,' he murmured, and then the air suddenly changed, becoming almost solid, so she could hardly drag it into her lungs.

For a breathless moment they stared at each other, then he seemed to collect himself and turned away, rummaging in the fridge while she fanned her flaming face and told her lungs how to work again.

He'd been flirting with her? Really?

Really.

Even though she was just his housekeeper?

But in her head she could hear Georgie's voice saying, 'Really? Just his housekeeper? We'll see.'

Why on earth had he said that?

He must be nuts. She was pregnant, grieving for Jamie—although why she'd waste emotion on such a useless example of the human race he couldn't imagine, but there was no accounting for taste—and anyway, he wasn't interested in another relationship. Most particularly not one with so many strings attached.

So why on earth was he flirting with her?

Because she was funny and fascinating and liked the same kind of things he did? Because she teased him? Because she was beautiful? She'd been open and friendly when he'd first met her, a little wary, which was natural, but essentially open, and she was beginning, slowly, inch by inch, to open up to him again, and he realised he wanted that, wanted to get to know her, to find out more about her.

He wanted to spend time with her in a way he hadn't wanted to spend time with a woman since—well, for years. Even Kate hadn't made him feel so curious, so keen to get to know her. Not that he ever really had, apparently.

And he didn't know Iona, so if he had a grain of sense he'd back off and stop being so stupid. What if Emily was right?

No. He *knew* she wasn't right, and Emily would, too, the moment she met Iona. But that didn't mean he should get involved with her.

Even if she was the sexiest woman he'd met in years.

He stopped dead, his fingers locked on the fridge door, and he stared into its depths in confusion.

Sexy? Seven months pregnant, and *sexy*? Really?

Oh, God, yes, his body was telling him. Very, very sexy. Not trivially sexy, not superficially, tartily sexy, but deeply, in a sort of earthy, all-woman way that would endure for ever. Even when she'd lost her looks, when she was old and grey and everything was going south, she'd still have that elemental, almost spiritual sensuality that could bring him to his knees.

And it was a damn shame that he wouldn't be there to enjoy it, but he wouldn't. Wrong time, wrong place.

'So,' he said, letting go of the fridge door and straightening up. 'What am I looking for?'

He was a good cook.

He'd led her to believe that he couldn't cook, but in fact he could, and he cooked well. Under instruction, at least, and he confessed he'd never attempted that dish before, but that didn't mean he couldn't do it. And the casserole he'd made last night had been delicious.

Maybe he just didn't like cooking, or maybe he couldn't be bothered just for himself. She could understand that.

Whatever, it was gorgeous, and they sat down together at the dining table, looking out over the sea with their backs to the mess in the kitchen that she knew she'd have to go and clear up in a minute, and they talked.

He talked about how he'd found the plot, about building the house, and his plans for the garden.

'It needs something simple—there was nothing much here to speak of when I bought the plot, no shrubs or trees except for a few old things down each side and a million brambles, and the retaining wall at the end there was broken and crumbling towards the cliff, so the first thing we did was clear the lot and then make it safe. The end's been remodelled so the top of the new retaining wall's level with the lawn, and then it slopes down to a new wall and fence above the cliff. I was going to plant a hedge down there in the autumn, to give a bit more privacy, but as Em said, it isn't really necessary and she's talking about a sedum bank. Apparently they'll love the dry, free-draining conditions. There's a path down to the beach—did you notice that this morning?'

She nodded. 'I tried to go down, but it was locked.'

'Because it's a public beach. I don't want everyone thinking they can use it as a shortcut to the top.'

'No, God forbid.'

He shot her a look. 'Think of the security aspects—and anyway, I value my privacy—is there something wrong with that?'

'No, of course not,' she said with a little smile. 'I'm just not used to things like security and privacy and I've never had anywhere that was my own, so it's just foreign to me.'

'What about when you were at university?'

She shrugged. 'I shared a flat, and had to share a room, so I didn't even have that to myself. Then I was with Jamie, and we were in youth hostels and sleeping on the beach in Thailand and things like that. You don't get much privacy there.'

'No, I can imagine not,' he said, but he looked as if he couldn't imagine it at all, and she thought he'd probably had his own room in a big house when he was growing up, and never had to share anything in his life.

And now he had this, all to himself. Why?

'Why build something so huge?' she asked, echoing her thoughts without stopping to wonder if it was prudent.

Instead of answering he looked out across the sea and his face was sad. 'I don't know. It just seemed right for the plot. I've wanted to build a house like this for years, and I got the chance. And realistically I had to look at resale and maximising its potential, as well, because I won't stay here for ever.'

'Why not?'

He turned to her with a little frown. 'Well—because it's a family home.'

'I know. So why build it? Just for you? Really purely for economic reasons, and as a showcase? That's what you said before, but it doesn't make sense.'

He looked away. 'Does it have to?'

Was that a tic in his jaw?

'No. No, it doesn't have to make sense. Why should it? Nothing else in the world seems to.'

He threw her a smile at that, and went back to the topic of the garden. 'I had the lawn relaid after the ground source heat pump plumbing was put in underground, and now I want to work on some planting at the sides. Nothing distracting, though. I want the sea to be the main focus.'

'I agree,' she said, not letting herself think about that little jumping muscle in his cheek and the defensive look in his eyes before she'd let it drop. 'I don't think you want colour—nothing fussy or cottage garden. Maybe just white flowers, if any at all?'

He nodded, and his smile was wry. 'That's what Emily said. She's drawn a few designs—want to see them?'

'I'd love to.' Even if she was still halfway to hating Emily.

No, she warned herself. Don't judge her, or you'll be just as guilty as her.

The drawings were interesting, but it was his studio itself that fascinated her more than anything.

It was, as he'd warned, chaotically untidy, and there were boxes everywhere. Boxes of books, boxes of paperwork, all sorts of things.

'Excuse the mess,' he said as they went in. 'I've had everything shipped from New York and I need to go through it. I just haven't had time.'

He moved a box off a chair so she could sit down, and

as he put it down a photo slid out of the top of it and
drifted to a halt at her feet. She bent and picked it up and
handed it back to him, and as she did so she saw his jaw
clench again.

'Who's Kate?' she asked, guessing, and he threw the
photo down and turned away, but not before she'd seen the
flash of hurt and disillusionment in his eyes.

'Nobody,' he said, and her heart ached for him, alone in
his great big house with nobody to share it, no future in
sight, and a girl called Kate with waist-length blonde hair,
who'd held his heart in her hands and thrown it away.

What a foolish woman. Had she no idea what she'd
had, what she'd lost?

Or what he'd lost because of her?

'So—let's see these drawings, then,' she said, and tried
to pretend an interest in something other than the sadness
in his eyes and the scent of musk and citrus and soap drifting
from his body, and the echoing emptiness of his heart.

The doorbell rang the next morning, just after Dan had gone
to the hotel for another site meeting with George Cauldwell.

Iona was getting to grips with her duties, trying to
fathom out the central vacuuming system and giving up in
favour of mopping the floor, when she heard the sound ring
through the hall.

Odd. She'd thought the intercom from the gate would
signal visitors, but this was definitely the doorbell, and the
only other time she'd heard it had been on Sunday.

And that had been Emily.

So she wasn't altogether surprised when she opened the
door and a young woman with long, dark, wavy hair and
troubled eyes was standing there. Even though she'd only

ever seen her from the back, she recognised her instantly, and the car on the drive was the one she'd seen on Sunday.

Oh, help, she thought. She didn't feel ready for this, but then she realised she'd never be ready, and it might as well be now as any other time.

For a moment neither of them spoke, but then she straightened her spine and took the bull by the horns.

'Hello, Emily,' she said. 'I'm Iona.'

Emily stared at her for a second, then swallowed. 'Can we be civilised about this, or do you want me to go?'

'Well, it isn't really up to me, is it?' she said softly. 'It's Dan's house, you've come to do the garden—you've got more right to be here than I have.'

'Actually, I've come to talk to you.'

Iona stepped back. 'Well, then, you'd better come in,' she said, and closed the door behind her. 'Coffee?'

'Not yet.'

There was an awkward pause. It was never going to be anything but embarrassing, but Emily frowned slightly, as if she didn't know where to start, and then, meeting Iona's eyes, she said directly, 'I owe you an apology. I shouldn't have said what I did without meeting you, and giving you the benefit of the doubt, but I know my brother and my husband, and they're soft as lights. They wouldn't see a brick wall till they walked into it, and they're very big on the weaker sex thing. Sometimes they just need protecting from themselves, but I'm sorry you heard it. It wasn't meant to be personal.'

Iona grimaced. 'Well, it couldn't be, could it, since you didn't know me,' she said frankly. 'And I understand where you were coming from, but it felt pretty personal at the time, believe me. It wasn't just what you said that upset me, anyway, it was the fact that Daniel hadn't told me he was connected to the hotel and so everything he'd said suddenly seemed like a lie.'

'I can imagine. But he wouldn't lie to you, Iona. He's not like that. He might not tell you everything—in fact he can be infuriatingly obtuse and guarded, but he doesn't lie and he certainly doesn't cheat. And I'm really sorry you were so hurt, but I meant what I said, and I'll say it again to your face,' she went on, her voice quiet but no less forceful for that. 'Don't hurt him. Don't cheat him, don't swindle him or screw him over, or you'll have me to deal with. He doesn't deserve it.'

Well, that was plain enough, Iona thought, and in a way she admired Emily for sticking to her guns.

'Fair enough,' she said. 'But I can assure you I have no intention of screwing him over or taking him to the cleaners. You don't have to fear me.'

'Good. I love my brother to bits, and he's been through hell. I don't want to see it happen again.'

'Kate?' she said, and Emily blinked.

'He's told you about Kate?'

'No. You said something about her on Sunday, and last night in his studio I saw a photo of a woman with long blonde hair.'

'That would be her.'

She nodded. 'I thought it might be. So I asked him who Kate was, and he clammed right up and said, "Nobody."'

Emily gave a grim smile. 'I couldn't have put it better myself, but it's not my story to tell. You'll have to ask him about her, but don't expect an answer. The rest of us haven't had one yet. And I'm sorry for upsetting you. Can we start again?'

'I think that would be a good idea,' Iona said and, summoning a smile, she held out her hand. 'Hi. I'm Iona.'

Emily smiled back, her eyes soft. 'I'm Emily. It's good to meet you,' she said, and shook her hand.

'So—coffee?'

'I gather you met Emily.'

'Mmm. She's nice.'

He gave a sigh of relief and smiled. 'Funny, she said the same about you. I thought you'd get on.'

'Well, let's not push it,' she said. 'She's left some more drawings in your studio, by the way.'

'Where?'

'I don't know. I haven't been in there. I've been busy.'

'Busy?'

'Oh—you know,' she said breezily. 'This and that.'

This and that? 'Right. Well, I could do with a shower. Something smells nice, by the way.'

'Chilli,' she told him. 'I don't know if you like it, but I've been a bit tied up so I didn't have time for anything elaborate, and you didn't say what time you'd want to eat, so I thought it would keep for another day if necessary.'

'Where did you get the mince? You haven't walked into town again, have you?'

'Emily took me shopping—oh, and she said something about an old bike in the garage at their house. A shopping bike, with a basket or something? It belonged to Harry's grandmother, I think she said. Anyway, she's going to ask Harry if he minds lending it to me so I've got some transport.'

'A bike?'

'Well, yes. What's wrong with that?'

He frowned, horrified at the prospect of her wobbling

about on a bike at this stage of her pregnancy. 'Nothing at all, if you've got a death wish. But an old one—has it got lights?'

She laughed. 'Dan, it's the summer! I'm not going out for a bike ride at midnight! I want to be able to get to the shops, that's all. Go on, go and have your shower, I've got to get the washing in.'

'In?'

'Mmm. I got a washing line at the supermarket. You didn't have one.'

'There isn't a post.'

'I know. I tied it to the trees.'

Trees? 'What's wrong with the tumble-drier?'

She rolled her eyes. 'So much for your impressive eco-credentials,' she said, and he frowned again.

'I hate washing on the line.'

'Don't be silly. You can't see it; it's round the side of the house where nobody need ever go. Emily thought it was a good idea. Oh, and I wanted to ask you about having a vegetable patch there.'

He stared at her for a moment, then shook his head in bemusement. 'Whatever,' he said. 'Get Emily to OK it, make sure she doesn't have plans for the area you want to use.' And he headed up the stairs to the sanctuary of his bedroom, wondering what on earth he'd unleashed.

'Wow.'

'Like it? I used up the fresh chillis from last night.'

'It's good,' he said.

'Too hot?'

'No. It's really tasty. I'm just surprised it's not too hot for you. Emily would choke on it.'

She laughed. 'Dan, I've lived everywhere and eaten everything. Mum and I spent two years in Mexico and Jamie and I were in Thailand for ages. You learn to eat chillis or starve.'

He chuckled and reached for another spoonful from the pot on the side.

'More?' he asked, but she shook her head. Enough was enough, and she didn't want to overdo it. She was running out of room faster these days, what with the baby in the way and everything.

'You OK?'

She realised she was stretching out her side, easing the pressure, and she smiled. 'Just getting a bit crowded in here.'

'I'm sure.' His eyes drifted to her bump, lingering on it like a caress, and then he turned his attention back to the food and cleared his plate. 'That was great. Thanks.'

'Pleasure,' she said, getting to her feet and taking the plate. 'I've made a fruit salad.'

'Ice cream?' he said hopefully.

'I thought you wanted healthy,' she teased, and then got it out of the freezer and waved it at him, and he laughed softly and got up, bringing the rest of the things from the table.

'Witch,' he murmured, reaching past her, and because her bump was getting bigger by the day and she hadn't got used to it, she brushed against him as she turned, and wobbled with the fruit salad in her hands.

'Steady,' he said, his hands on her shoulders, then he let go, taking the bowl from her and putting it down next to the ice cream and leaving her shoulders burning from his touch.

'Why don't you go and sit down and let me do this?' she suggested, suddenly crowded by his big, rangy body in the enclosed space.

'Or I can load the dishwasher while you serve the fruit

salad, and then we can take it out in the garden and sit on the steps at the end and listen to the sea.'

What a silly idea. A silly, romantic, absolutely lovely idea.

They sat there for hours, and when she shivered he went back inside and found her a sweater, a lovely soft cashmere sweater that had a lingering trace of his aftershave on it, and she snuggled into it and sipped the mineral water he'd brought out with him and listened to the sound of the sea, and talked about other beaches she'd sat beside, and Pebbles came and curled up on her lap, and she thought it couldn't get any better than this.

Even if he wasn't hers, even if she didn't really belong here but was just passing through, because that was what she'd always done and nobody had ever said anything about a permanent position.

It was light years from the last few weeks, and she couldn't for the life of her imagine turning back time seventy-two hours, to when he'd found her wrestling with the mattress. It seemed so much more than that. A lifetime ago.

Or certainly a lifestyle.

She had a job, a home, new friends, even if they'd had a bit of a rocky start and things weren't quite comfortable yet. The cat was contented, she was contented and her baby was safe.

'Daniel?'

'Mmm?' His voice was soft, hardly disturbing the night, and she had a crazy urge to lean against him.

'Thank you.'

'What for?'

She smiled in the darkness. 'Being my knight in shining armour. Rescuing me from that awful mess. Taking me and the cat in. Take your pick.'

He chuckled softly. His arm came round her and gave her a brief squeeze, then let go. 'My pleasure,' he murmured, and his voice slid over her nerve-endings and brought them all alive. She could feel the warmth radiating off his body, the heat from his arm around her shoulders, smell the aftershave drifting up from his sweater and from him, and something else, something that did funny things to her insides.

And that probably was indigestion, she thought, and stood up, the cat in her arms. 'I'm going to turn in,' she said.

He got up, too, took her elbow and steadied her on the steps, then walked back to the house with her elbow still cradled in his hand, the glasses clinking in his other hand, and the sound of the surf teasing the shingle beach behind them.

He paused at the door of his studio and, to her surprise, he lifted the hand that had held her elbow and cupped her cheek, his thumb grazing gently over her skin. 'Goodnight, Iona. Sleep well. And thank you for this evening.'

The meal? Or the rest? She wasn't sure, and she wasn't asking. All she could feel was his hand against her cheek, the stroke of his thumb, and she wanted to turn her face into it and press her lips to his palm. But then he dropped his arm and stepped back, freeing her from the spell.

'You're welcome,' she said and, turning on her heel, she took Pebbles through to her little flat, undressed and got into bed and lay there, watching the bright patches on the lawn until the light in his studio went out, and then the hall light, and his bedroom light spilt out into the night.

Then, finally, he turned it off and the night reclaimed the garden. 'Goodnight,' she whispered, and closed her eyes and curled on to her side, her hand tucked under her cheek, where his had touched her so fleetingly.

She could still feel it, she thought, cradling her as she went to sleep…

CHAPTER SEVEN

IONA was a little powerhouse.

Dan came back from the hotel the next evening to find his sheets changed, the towels in his bathroom replaced and the pile of suitcases and clothes in the dressing room next door gone.

And she still had his towelling robe. She seemed to have adopted it, and he wasn't sure he could wear it now without disgracing himself, so he hadn't bothered to get it back. So he had nothing to put on to go in search of her. He contemplated his dirty clothes, and shook his head. No way. They were sweaty and dusty and he'd just got clean. So he wrapped a towel firmly round his hips and ran downstairs.

She was in the kitchen chopping vegetables, and she looked up and her eyes widened, then shut tight and she swore in a very unladylike way and sucked her finger.

'Grief, Dan, you startled the living daylights out of me!'

'Let me see that.'

He took her hand and straightened out her finger, and the blood welled from the deep, clean slice she'd put in it. 'I don't think it needs stitches—'

'Of course it doesn't need stitches! It just needs a plaster, but I don't suppose you've got any.'

'I have. I have no idea where to find them. There are some in the car, though, but I seem to lack clothes.'

'Ah.' Her finger was back in her mouth, so it was more like 'Argh'. She pulled it out and wrapped it in a paper kitchen towel, squashing it firmly. 'In the cupboards.'

He frowned. 'Cupboards?'

'The great run of wardrobes and stuff down the side of the dressing room? Just where the suitcases and stuff were? Except for the stuff that's waiting to be ironed. You don't really do washing, do you? Clothes, that is. You had—well, must be weeks' worth.'

'It is,' he said, pondering on her impact on his life and wishing he had the right to kiss her finger better. No. For heaven's sake, not when he was only wearing a towel! 'Um—I'll go and find my clothes. Then I'll get you a plaster.'

And he went back upstairs two at a time, clutching the towel like grim death and lecturing himself with every stride for his unruly libido. Inappropriate. Pregnant woman. Grieving woman. Beautiful, sexy woman—

Damn.

He opened the cupboards and found everything lined up in neat rows. His socks were paired, his boxers were folded, his shirts were hung in two banks, short-sleeved and long-sleeved, grouped by colour—it was amazing. Like something out of a magazine. He found jeans, his favourite shirt that had been missing for weeks, and some very orderly underwear, threw them on and ran back downstairs and out of the door to get the plaster.

When he came back in she was in the kitchen with her finger trussed up in tissue and sticking up into the air while she chopped.

'I can do it,' she said, taking the plaster from him and

giving him a look when he continued to hover over her. So he went to the fridge and opened it, hunting for a drink while she fiddled with the plaster.

'There's tea in the pot, or I can make you coffee if you don't want a cold drink,' she said.

He shook his head emphatically. 'I've been with builders all day. I never want to see another cup of tea again,' he told her, pulling out a bottle of rosé and un-screwing the cap. 'Want a glass?'

She shook her head. 'Not while I'm pregnant. I'll have fruit juice, though, if you're offering.'

'Sure.' He poured her the juice, handed it to her and peered at the vegetables. 'So what is it tonight?'

'Paella.'

'Rice again.'

She turned, a little frown pleating her brow. He wanted to straighten out the creases with his thumb. 'Don't you like rice?' she asked.

'I love rice. And pasta. I just wondered if you don't like potatoes?'

'I love potatoes, but they're a bit heavy to carry. Oh, Emily says I can have the bike. Harry's going to do it up a bit and drop it round later. They're coming for supper. She wanted to talk to you about the garden.'

'Right.' So now she was inviting his sister round for supper? 'Thanks for sorting out my clothes, by the way. I didn't even think to look in the cupboard. I just hadn't got round to it.'

'Story of your life, isn't it?' she said mildly, and reached past him for the fridge. 'If you've got everything you need, could you give me a bit of space so I can work?' she asked, and thus dismissed, he picked up his wine and moved out of her way.

'I'll go and make some phone calls, then,' he said, and took himself off. God forbid he should be in her way. In his kitchen.

Oh, don't be petty, he told himself. You just want to stand next to her and sniff her like a bloody dog. Get over it.

He slid the partition shut and dropped into his chair and stared down the garden.

She was getting to him. Getting to him in all sorts of ways, and if he was going to be able to cope, he was going to have to distance himself from her. No more finding excuses to steady her, or hug her, or touch her unbelievably soft, smooth cheek—

'Oh, stop it!'

He slammed his wine down on the desk, spun the chair and caught sight of the photo of Kate lying on the edge of the desk. Damn. He picked the photo up, held it over the shredder for a second, then put it down again, propped up against his computer, her laughing eyes mocking him. He'd leave it there, to remind him not to make a fool of himself over a woman ever again.

The bike was wonderful, and supper with Harry and Emily was fun.

She didn't overstay her welcome, though, and the moment they'd finished eating and she'd made everyone coffee and cleared the kitchen, she left them to it. She had things of her own to sort out, clothes to wash and iron, and anyway, eating with them was one thing. Expecting to spend all evening with them was quite another.

So it was ridiculous that she felt so lonely and isolated

and cut off in her little flat. Doubly ridiculous since the moment she sat down, Pebbles came and curled up on her lap and went to sleep. She was having a lovely time in the garden these days. She hadn't been upstairs, as far as Iona was aware, but she'd been in his studio, curled up in a filing tray shedding fur for England.

She'd cleared it up, and had to force herself to leave the boxes alone. Especially the one that had had the photo of Kate in it. It was on the corner of his desk, and she'd looked at it.

Hard. That was what her eyes were like, she decided now. Hard and calculating, even though she was smiling. Iona had disliked her on sight, and found it interesting that Emily hadn't liked her, either. She wondered what had happened, but she wasn't going to ask. He'd tell her if he wanted to.

There was a tap on the door, and she shifted the cat and went and opened it.

'Sorry to disturb you,' Dan said, 'but Emily wants to talk about the vegetable patch. She's got hold of this idea and really likes it—wants to do some kind of formal geometric thing, and she wants your advice.'

'Mine?' Iona started to laugh. 'I know nothing about vegetables. I just want to grow them. I've never had a garden before, and I thought it would be fun.'

He frowned slightly. 'Oh. Well—she wants to talk to you, anyway. Why don't you come and join us since you aren't busy?'

'How do you know I'm not?' she asked, and he smiled.

'Because you've got a circle of cat fur on your front,' he said, and walked away, chuckling. She shut the door and followed him.

* * *

It was amazing.

Two days, and Emily, with some help, had transformed the area beyond Iona's end of the house into a gorgeous courtyard garden, with climbers planned to clothe the perimeter walls, and a little vegetable patch and herb garden in the centre surrounded by little gravel paths. There was even going to be room for a bench, set so it faced the sea and would be shaded by a nearby tree from the midday sun. Emily had dug it over, worked in compost and now it was ready to plant.

And, on her new bike, Iona went down to the garden centre next to the supermarket and bought runner beans for the centre of the circle, and French beans and courgettes and lettuces and spring onions to plant around the outsides, and brought them home carefully stacked up in the basket at the front, ready to plant the next day.

She slowed the bike down as she approached the gates, and noticed two women standing looking through them.

'Can I help you?' she said, getting off the bike and walking up to them, and they turned and smiled a little guiltily.

'Oh, no. We were just looking,' the older lady said. 'I used to live here with my husband, but after he died I couldn't look after it any more and in the end I had to give up. It was just too expensive, and then with the fire…I was just wondering what it had been replaced with, but it's none of my business. I have to let go, but after seventy-five years that's easier said than done,' she added with a little laugh.

But there was a look of longing on her face, and Iona, ever given to impulse, said, 'Would you like to see it?'

'Oh, no, we couldn't trouble you, could we, Mum?' her younger companion said, but her mother was still looking through the gates, and the longing on her face tore at Iona.

'It's no trouble,' she said firmly and, keying in the combination, she pressed the button to open the gates and ushered them through.

'So—do you live here?' the daughter asked.

'Yes—well, sort of. I'm the housekeeper. But he won't mind,' she said confidently, and crossed her fingers behind her back...

Daniel was exhausted.

He'd been working all day at the site, running up and down stairs, backwards and forwards, checking details and making on-the-hoof decisions as the tradesmen had come to him in turn with one problem after another. And in between he'd been looking for the will without success.

He wanted a shower, clean clothes and a glass of nicely chilled wine in the garden.

What he didn't want was to come into his house—*his* house!—and find Iona sitting there with two strange women having a damned tea party at his dining room table! He stopped dead in the doorway, and she looked up at him with a pleading look in her eyes and said, 'Ah, Daniel, you're just in time. Grab yourself a cup and a plate and come and join us. This is Mrs Jessop. She used to live here. Her husband built the original house. And this is her daughter, Mrs Gray.'

He took a slow, steadying breath and walked towards them, his eyes skewering Iona with a look that should have had her running for cover. But she held her ground, and his eyes, and finally he looked away, dredged up his manners and smiled at the older of the two women.

'Mrs Jessop. It's good to meet you.' And he reached out his hand and took her frail, gnarled fingers in his, and met the rheumy old eyes that had seen too much and lost it all, and his anger faded.

'I do hope you don't mind us imposing like this,' Mrs Jessop was saying, hanging on to his hand. 'We didn't want to put you out, but Iona assured us you wouldn't mind, and it's been so wonderful to see it. I asked my daughter Joan to bring me here, just so I could look down the drive, but I never expected that we would be invited in.'

He hadn't either, but he was suddenly ridiculously glad that Iona had made them so welcome.

He pulled out a chair and sat down, still holding her hand. 'I don't mind at all. I'm delighted to get a chance to talk to you. I didn't realise your husband had built the original house or I would have spoken to you earlier.'

'Oh, yes. He built it for us, just after we married in nineteen thirty-four.'

'Nineteen thirty-four? But that's—what, three-quarters of a century ago!'

'Which probably explains why I feel ninety-six,' she said with a smile.

He stared at her. 'Good grief. Well, I hope I look as good as you when I'm three times my age,' he said with a grin, and she laughed and patted his hand.

'Flattery isn't obligatory, you know.'

'Oh, but I believe in giving credit where it's due,' he replied, and she gave a cracked laugh and sat back.

'I like you, young man, and I like your house. My husband would have been delighted to see it. We didn't have the money to build anything this grand, but he would have loved to have done. And you still have the big lawn. Nobody could understand why we didn't plant anything in the middle of it, but why would you need to, with that to look at?'

'Absolutely. I quite agree.' He turned to her daughter and gave her an apologetic smile. 'I'm sorry, I'm ignoring you. I'm Daniel,' he said, and shook her hand. 'So—you must have lots of childhood memories.'

'Oh, yes. Lots of fun on the beach—we had a proper beach in those days, but the coast's changing all the time. We had a look down the garden, and the sea's closer now than it used to be.'

'Oh, it is, but it was lovely to see it again. It's years since I could walk to the end of the garden. Not since Tom died in nineteen ninety. It got so overgrown then without him cutting the grass, and I couldn't afford a gardener.'

'It must have been hard living here all that time without him,' Iona said gently.

'It was. Too long— and I let him down. I didn't look after it, but you've done his vision proud, Daniel. He would have loved it.'

He smiled, a little embarrassed by all the emotion just under the surface, but soft enough to be pleased. 'Thank you. That's the nicest thing anybody's said about it.'

'It's only the truth. You've made a lovely home. You're a nice man, Daniel Hamilton. A good man. There should be more architects like you.'

He realised Iona was watching him, a cup in her hand— one of the espresso cups and saucers, the nearest thing he had to a teaset—and notwithstanding what he'd said the other day about tea and the building site, he took it without a murmur, smiled reassuringly at her and accepted a slice of cake to boot.

His teeth sank into it, and he stopped in surprise and shot Iona a look.

'Carrot cake. It's healthy,' she said, and a smile flickered on her lips and was gone.

He chewed and swallowed, and let his own smile out. 'It's very nice,' he admitted. 'Thank you.'

'Pleasure. I made it for Emily—we were doing the courtyard.'

'Courtyard?'

'You know, the pretty little courtyard garden at the end, by Iona's flat,' Mrs Jessop said, beaming. 'It's where Tom always had his vegetable patch, and it'll grow the most wonderful beans. Iona's going to plant them tomorrow. And the water feature will be lovely.'

'Right.'

Water feature? Well, he'd known the vegetable patch was coming, but a courtyard? With a water feature? And beans? Together? That'd teach him not to pay attention to his garden designer and his conniving housekeeper. He had another bite of the gorgeously moist and tasty carrot cake and hid his smile.

'I've got lots of photos of the house when it was being built,' Joan was saying. 'I was going through them with my grandchildren when it burned down, so they were saved. In fact lots of things were saved.'

'But not the house.'

Mrs Jessop shook her head. 'It doesn't matter. I couldn't stay here alone any more, and it needed so much work. It had served its purpose and, if I'm honest, I'm quite glad it's gone. It was so much *our* house. It wouldn't have seemed right to have somebody else living in it. There was too much of Tom in it somehow.'

He could understand that. There was so much of him in this house that the idea of selling it in the future was untenable. Was that why he'd built such a big house? Iona had asked him the other day, and he hadn't really told her the truth, maybe because he didn't know the answer. But was it because he was secretly hoping that some time in the future he'd bring a bride home, a woman who'd give him children—children who'd bring it to life?

A woman like Iona?

He swallowed, and Mrs Jessop reached out and patted his hand. 'You'll get there,' she said softly, as if she could read his mind, and he met her tired old eyes and found a smile.

'We'll see. Has Iona shown you right round?'

'Oh, no. That would be too much. She showed us her flat and in here, and we've walked down the garden. I wouldn't let her show us any more.'

'Fancy a guided tour?'

'I'd love one, but I can't manage the stairs now.'

He eyed her. She couldn't weigh more than Iona's cat. 'What if I carry you?'

She gave a little crack of laughter. 'Heavens. It's years since a man last carried me up the stairs.'

'So, Mrs Jessop,' he asked, winking at her, 'do you want to come up and see my etchings?'

She laughed out loud and patted his cheek. 'Do you know, young man, I believe I might.'

'I'm really sorry.'

'Don't be. She was delightful. They both were, and it wasn't hard, was it?'

'But they're going to come back with the pictures,' she said, washed with guilt. 'It could go on for ever.'

'Hardly,' he said realistically, and Iona nodded.

'No. You're right.' She tipped her head on one side and smiled at him. 'She was right. You are a nice man, Daniel Hamilton. Kind.'

'And dirty,' he said. 'I'm going for a shower, and then I want a drink of something that isn't tea, and food.'

She touched her forelock and grinned. 'Coming right up,' she said, and went back to the kitchen and cleared away the debris of her impromptu tea party, then put the salmon steaks and new potatoes on to cook, dressed the rocket salad and laid the table again.

Poor Daniel. But he'd been a star, just as she'd known he would be once he'd met them, and really risen to the occasion. She couldn't believe he'd carried Mrs Jessop upstairs, twinkling away at her and flirting right, left and centre. The old charmer.

She grinned and went back into the kitchen to check the salmon, humming softly under her breath, and then as she turned she saw him standing there watching her, an enigmatic look on his face.

'So—what's all this about a water feature?' he asked.

They planted the vegetables after they'd eaten, even though he was wearing clean clothes, because, as he said, she could hardly struggle around and plant things when she was seven months pregnant, and he knew perfectly well she'd give it her best shot if he didn't do it first.

And he had to admit it was going to look nice.

'So where's this water feature going?' he asked, and she pointed to the wall behind him. 'There. Well, that's what Georgie said. My kitchen's there, so the power and plumbing won't be a problem, she said.'

'Did she.'

'Yes.'

'So what kind of water feature is this, that I'm no doubt paying for?' he asked, and she blinked and shrugged.

'Search me. Georgie said you ought to choose it.'

'Big of her,' he said drily.

She chewed her lip. 'Don't blame her. It was my idea. Running water is very soothing.'

'It always makes me want to pee.'

She chuckled. 'Well, that, too, but it is restful. We thought this would make a lovely sheltered area for quiet contemplation. Productive, restful—a good place to come when things all get too much.'

'They're all too much now, and I can't say it's helping,' he grumbled, but his heart wasn't in it and he helped her water the little plants in and then stood back and admired them. 'Right. I want another glass of wine, I've got some phone calls to make and then I'm going to crash. What about you?'

'Actually, I'm tired,' she confessed. Well, he'd known that. That was why he was making himself scarce, so she felt able to retreat to her flat and have an early night.

He left her at the door, went into his studio and stared at Kate. She wouldn't have understood him showing Mrs Jessop round at all. Or the beans and lettuces and things, and she would have tossed the water feature off the cliff. Mrs Jessop too, probably.

He put the photo in the shredder, and felt instantly better.

She was more than tired, she was exhausted.

It had been a really long day, what with helping Emily to do the courtyard garden and making the cake, as well as ironing a load of Dan's shirts and trousers, which she'd washed and dried. And then there had been the trip to town to buy the plants, and Mrs Jessop and her daughter, and then planting the seedlings after supper.

And now she was just ready to fall into bed, but instead of winding round her legs and nagging her for food and a cuddle, Pebbles was missing. And her food dish was still sitting there with food in it, and the litter tray hadn't been used. Not that that was surprising, now she could get outside, but everything together made a picture that worried Iona.

A lot.

She searched the flat, looked around outside in the dusk, and then went through to Daniel and tapped on his studio door.

It slid open. 'Hi. What's the problem?'

'I can't find the cat. I wondered if she was in here with you.'

He shook his head, a frown creasing his brow. 'When did you last see her?'

'I don't know. Earlier. She was in the garden with me and Emily this morning. I haven't seen her since then.'

'Did you leave the side gate open when the front gates were open, too?'

She shook her head. 'No. The big gates were closed.'

'But she might have gone into the front garden and be stuck there, now the side gate's shut. Let's go and look.'

They searched the house together, then he turned on the floodlights and they went out into the garden and looked around, checking under bushes and behind bins and anywhere she might have gone.

And then she looked up and he was standing there, looking down at her, and she knew. She pressed her hand to her chest.

'Where is she?'

'Under the old lilac,' he said softly. 'She lay there a lot, in the sun. I've noticed her, because I can see it from my studio. She loved it there in the evening.'

She got slowly to her feet, dragged down by the weight of yet another loss. 'Show me,' she said, her voice rusty, and he took her arm and led her over to the lilac, and there underneath it, curled up as if asleep, was her moth-eaten little cat.

She knelt down and stroked her, but she was cold, the life gone out of her.

'Oh, God, Daniel, I can't do this again,' she said, and a great sob rose in her throat and she covered her mouth to hold it in, but it wouldn't stay there, and it was followed by another, and then another, and he knelt down beside her and rocked her gently in his arms as she cried.

Finally she hiccupped to a halt, and he sat back and looked at her, his eyes concerned. 'Are you OK?'

She nodded. 'It was just—I don't know. She's the only pet I've ever had, and Brian was the only father I've ever had, and I've never really grieved for him, and my baby will never know her father, and it's all just too much—'

The tears fell again, and he gathered her up against his chest and held her there as she cried for Jamie, and for Brian, and for the poor, deaf, scruffy little cat who'd loved her unreservedly.

'I'm so sorry,' he said at last, and she scrubbed away the tears and reached for a tissue, but she didn't have one, and he handed her one from his pocket, all neatly folded, and she wondered if he'd picked it up because he'd known what they'd find under the bushes.

'Can we bury her here?' she asked, and he nodded.

'Of course. I'll get a spade.'

He disappeared, and came back a minute later with a

shoe box full of tissue paper and the spade, and while she watched he gently lifted the cat into the box, covered her with the tissue and put the lid on, then started digging.

It didn't take long and, when it was done, she stood up awkwardly and stared down at the bare little patch of earth under the bush.

'Are you OK?' he asked softly, and she nodded.

She was. Terribly tired, terribly sad, but she'd felt worse and probably would again.

'I'm OK,' she said.

He drew her into his arms and hugged her gently, then, lifting his head, he stared down at her for a long moment before brushing her lips with his.

As kisses went it was tame, hardly more than the touch of a feather, but it reached right down inside Iona and warmed the parts of her that she'd thought would be cold for ever.

Then all too soon he lifted his head and looked down into her eyes and sighed.

'Come on,' he said gruffly. 'You're exhausted, and you're much too tired to deal with this. Let's get you back inside and make you a drink and get you into bed.'

He wanted to get her into bed? Tired and tear-streaked and seven months pregnant? She gave a slightly hysterical little giggle, and he laughed softly. 'Come on, I didn't mean that,' he said, and she felt a huge wave of regret.

'Sit there and don't move,' he said, depositing her in her sitting room and putting the kettle on, then he disappeared, and she realised he was in her kitchen still, clearing away all the cat's little bits and pieces, and she felt her eyes welling up with tears again.

Oh, it was ridiculous! She'd been ancient, she'd had a lovely peaceful death—it was silly to cry for her, but cry she did, and when Daniel came back into the room he sighed and dropped down on to his haunches in front of her and wiped her eyes.

'Come on,' he said and, drawing her to her feet, he led her through to her bedroom and pushed her gently towards the bathroom door. 'Get ready for bed. I'll be back in a minute with a hot drink.'

And he left her there, standing staring in the mirror at this red-eyed, lost little waif with eyes as old as time, and because she couldn't bear to look into them she cleaned her teeth with her eyes shut, then went to the loo and changed into a lovely nightshirt that Georgie had lent her, and when she walked back out into the bedroom Daniel was sitting there on the bed, a thoughtful look on his face.

'You OK?'

'Do I look OK?' she asked, and he shook his head.

She pulled back the quilt and climbed in, then straightened the covers with meticulous attention before finally looking up and meeting his eyes. 'Stay with me,' she said softly. 'I know I look like Methuselah's mother at the moment and I'm probably the last person in the world you want to be with, but I don't think I can be alone tonight.'

'Oh, Iona.' His sigh was gentle, his hand against her cheek tender. 'You don't look like Methuselah's mother. You don't look old enough to be anybody's mother, and, for what it's worth, I think you're beautiful, but you don't need this tonight.'

God, the rejection hurt. She met his eyes and tried to smile. 'It's OK. You don't have to be kind. Go to bed, Daniel. I'll be fine. And thanks—you know, for the cat and everything.'

For some reason he didn't move. 'I'm not being kind,'

he said gruffly. 'I'm trying to be fair to you. I'm not what you want, Iona. I'm damaged goods. Bad news. And your judgement's right off at the moment—'

'Have I asked you for eternity?' she said, and for a moment she thought he'd go anyway, but then he gave a ragged sigh, stood up and peeled off his jeans and T-shirt. He was barefoot, as usual, and he left his boxers on—to protect himself, or her? She didn't care. Then he flipped off the light, slid into the bed beside her and drew her down into his arms.

'Sleep now,' he said. 'We'll talk later.'

Sleep? Was he crazy?

But the warmth of his body and the steady, even rhythm of his heart soothed her, and with his arms close around her, she drifted peacefully to sleep, feeling safer than she'd ever felt...

CHAPTER EIGHT

SOMETHING woke him.

He didn't know what—a noise? It took him a moment to work out where he was, another moment to work out that he was alone.

And there was the noise again. A sob, muffled by distance and the wind, but triggering his protective instinct even in his sleep. He threw back the covers and went through to her sitting room, and found the door open into the moonlit garden.

Iona was kneeling by the lilac, arms wrapped round her body, rocking as she sobbed, and the sight unravelled him.

It was so unfair. How much more could she be expected to take? He didn't know whether to go to her or not. Not, he thought. She'd waited until she could be alone. He had to respect that.

Dan watched as she stood up awkwardly and walked to the end of the garden, sitting down on the steps overlooking the sea. But then she looked so forlorn, sitting there alone staring out over the sea, that he couldn't bear it any more. He went to her, barefoot in the damp grass, and sat down beside her. At first she said nothing, then with a sigh she turned to him and smiled sadly.

'I'm sorry,' she said softly. 'I know I'm being pathetic, but I've just had a basinful recently, and the cat was the last straw. She was just such a sweetie, and I'm going to miss her.'

'Of course you are—and you aren't being pathetic at all. I think you've been incredibly brave about all of it.' He slipped his arm round her shoulders and pulled her against his side, and with a sigh she leant against him and rested her head on his shoulder, propped in the crook of his neck, her hair tickling his ear.

He brushed it back, threading his fingers through it and lifting it away from her face, loving the feel of it. So soft, like silk. Beautiful. She raised her head and looked up at him in the moonlight, and then suddenly everything seemed to shift and change, as if even the sea was holding its breath.

He felt her slim, cool hand settled against his jaw, and he turned his face into it, pressing his lips to her palm. Then he lifted his head and stared down into her eyes.

'Iona?'

He'd spoken so softly he wasn't sure she'd heard him. For an endless moment she did nothing, then he felt her fingers thread through his hair and draw him down, and as he bent his head he felt the warm sigh of her breath whisper over his mouth, just before his lips touched hers.

Then the world settled back on its axis, and the sea breathed again, and everything just seemed right.

'Oh, Iona,' he murmured and, cradling her head in his hands, he kissed her again, and again, until suddenly instead of tenderness there was fire raging through them.

He stood up and pulled her gently to her feet and led her back to her room, leaving the doors open so they could hear the sighing of the sea in the shingle. Then he turned her in his arms and kissed her gently, cupping her shoulders in his hands and staring down into her face. Her expression was hard to read in the dim light, but when she came up on tiptoe and kissed him back, he didn't need to see her.

He let his hands slip down her arms until their fingers linked. 'Are you sure?' he asked, just to be absolutely certain, and she nodded.

'Quite sure.'

'You'll have to tell me what to do. I've never made love to a pregnant woman before.'

She laughed softly. 'I'll tell you when I've worked it out. Do you want to phone a friend?'

He chuckled. 'I'm sure we'll manage.' He slipped his hands free and took hold of the nightdress, gathering it in his fingers until it was bunched up and he could lift it over her head.

She raised her arms for him, and then slowly let them fall as he watched her, spellbound, breathless. All that woman. Dear God. He dropped the nightdress, reached out a hand and stroked it gently over the smooth, taut curve of her child.

'You're beautiful,' he said gruffly. 'I'm so afraid I'll hurt you.'

'You won't hurt me. It's supposed to be good for you.'

'Really?' He smiled at that. 'Like vitamins and stuff?'

He could see her mouth tipping up at the corners. 'Something like that.' He felt her thumbs in the top of his shorts, easing them down, and he kicked them away and let her look at him.

'Wow,' she said softly, reaching out a hand and running her knuckles down over his ribs before turning it and laying her palm flat against his heart. 'I don't suppose I can tell you you're beautiful, can I?'

He gave a surprised laugh and drew her into his arms, then gasped at the feel of her, warm and firm and all woman against him. Heat raced through him and, with a ragged sigh, his mouth found hers and clung.

She felt amazing.

She'd never felt so loved, so cherished or wanted or beautiful in her life—which was ridiculous, considering she was like a beached whale now. But she didn't feel like one in his arms—she felt glorious. She shifted so she could see him better, lying sprawled beside her with one arm flung up over his head and a knee bent up towards her.

His body was gorgeous. Firm and fit and toned, with just a scattering of hair over his chest that arrowed down to that impressive—

'Do you always watch people when they're sleeping?'

She gave an embarrassed laugh and pulled the quilt up over them both. 'I'm usually alone,' she pointed out, and he rolled towards her and slid a hand round the back of her neck, drawing her closer so he could kiss her.

'Me, too,' he said. 'Well, for a while, anyway.'

She reached up a hand and rested it against his chest, loving the feel of his heart beating just the other side of his ribs, its rhythm steady against her palm. 'Tell me about Kate,' she said, holding her breath, and he went still.

'There's nothing to tell. I don't want to think about her.'

'But you just did. When you said you'd been alone for a while—she came into your thoughts.'

'You're going to nag until I tell you, aren't you?' he said.

'Probably,' she admitted, softening it with a gentle touch to his cheek.

He gave a heavy sigh and rolled on to his back again, tucking her up against his side. 'We were lovers. We worked together for three years on various projects, and for eighteen months she was sleeping with another member of the team.'

She jacked herself up on her elbow and stared down at him. 'Oh, my God—and you were working with them both? Didn't you want to kill him?'

'Her.'

She stared. 'Her?'

'Her. Angie. And how can you compete with that? If it's another man, you're on a level playing field. You have a bigger car, a bigger income, a bigger—whatever. But a woman? Where do you start?'

'So where did you start?' she asked softly.

'I walked away. I sold up, moved out, came back here.'

'And you didn't tell anyone.'

'How do you know that?'

'Because I've asked them about Kate, and they didn't know anything. Emily said it was your story to tell, and good luck to me, because nobody else could get it out of you.'

She rested her head down again and snuggled closer, her hand round his side holding him tight. 'That's so unkind. To sleep with you both, not to tell you, to just—to *lie* to you like that, in that way, for *years*. Horrible. No wonder you ran away.'

'I didn't run. I walked. And she tried to follow me, and I told her to go to hell. And her girlfriend dumped her.'

She tried to feel pity, but couldn't. 'Why didn't she just say what she felt? Why did she keep up the pretence?'

He shrugged. 'Her father was a church minister. Living

with me was bad enough. Living with a woman would
have been the end. She couldn't tell them. And I guess the
cover suited her.'

'So she used you as cover?'

'Sort of, I suppose.'

She stroked his chest, loving the feel of it, the warmth
and strength and beauty of him. How could Kate have
done that to him? 'That's a real bummer.'

'Yeah. Whatever, it's over now.'

Was it? She didn't think so. He'd called himself
damaged goods. You wouldn't do that if you didn't believe
it. And he must have loved her at first.

Mustn't he?

They went shopping for baby things the next day, because
it was the weekend and he didn't have to go to work. She
told him it was too early to think about baby stuff at seven
months, but he was insistent.

'You never know how early it might be,' he said and,
because it made sense, they went—just to look. Only they
didn't just look, they bought.

All sorts. A big proper pram, because she'd always
wanted one, so she could walk to the shops and put her
shopping underneath, and a cot for the bedroom, and a
clever carrycot-cum-pushchair-cum-baby-seat like Emily's
daughter Kizzy's, and clothes. Not for the baby, because
Georgie and Emily had lots of tiny clothes to lend her, but
underwear for her. Bras, like the one Georgie had lent her,
and some new knickers. Something pretty for Daniel to
take off her, she thought, and blushed hotly.

'If you're thinking what I'm thinking, we could well be
arrested,' he murmured in her ear, and she blushed even hotter.

'Stop it,' she hissed, and then got the giggles, and they ended up having to leave before they disgraced themselves.

They went to another shop and tried again, and she emerged victorious with a lovely little string-handled bag with a sticky seal on it and lots of gorgeous underwear wrapped in tissue inside it. She'd protested vigorously about the price, but he'd just grinned wickedly and said it was for him, not for her, and she'd teased him about looking silly in it.

It was a fabulous day. They had lunch out—fish and chips in paper up the coast at Aldeburgh, from an award-winning chip shop, and went for a stroll along the beach and looked at Maggi Hambling's huge and controversial sculpture of scallop shells.

'I love it,' she said, stroking the warm metal thoughtfully.

'So do I. Lots of people hate it—or hate where it's sited. They say it changes the long view down the beach, but I think it's thought provoking and I love the lines of it. Fluid. Beautiful.'

They walked on, beside the marshes, and then they strolled back to the car and drove home again.

Home. Funny, how readily the word tripped off the tongue, she thought. The baby stuff wouldn't be delivered till the following week, but he handed her the bag of underwear with a glint in his eye as they got out of the car, and they got thoroughly sidetracked after that.

He took her out for dinner that night, to the Chinese restaurant where they'd bought the take-away on that first night just a week ago, and afterwards they sat on their bench and held hands and she was stunned to realise that it had only been one week.

It felt like for ever.

* * *

He invited the gang round for a barbecue the next day, and then had to rush out and buy one and screw it all together before they arrived. And she had to shop and cook for them, however many there were.

Lots.

She tried to do a head count and got lost, because the children were running about all over the place like ants. Emily and Harry, of course, and Nick and Georgie, and all of their children, to start with. They were joined by George Cauldwell, Georgie's father, who lived a few streets away, and Nick's mother, Liz, who lived in her own flat behind Nick and Georgie's house, where she had her own art studio. And Juliette and Andrew Hamilton, Daniel and Emily's parents, who she'd never met before. Ten adults, then, and seven children ranging from nine years to nine months, and because she felt a little self-conscious of her role—Dan's housekeeper, as well as, very newly, his lover—and not really a bona fide member of the group, she ended up in the kitchen with the food while the grandmothers supervised the children and the men organised the wine and watched the barbecue and Emily showed Georgie the courtyard.

Her courtyard, she thought, but it wasn't, it was his, and it wasn't her fault they didn't realise Daniel was sleeping with her.

It seemed bizarre that only a week before she'd been huddling in a doorway in a thunderstorm, and now the sun had come out and everything had changed. Except, perhaps, it hadn't. She'd been feeling as if she really belonged with him, but now here she was in the kitchen, with a house and garden full of people and feeling, if anything, even more alone.

Not that Georgie and Emily were anything but nice, but

they didn't know things were different now with Daniel, and she wasn't actually sure how different they were. It was more that she felt she didn't belong, and so she was holding herself back.

Then Emily and Georgie came into the kitchen and started helping without being asked, and Georgie was really enthusiastic about her little vegetable garden, and she wondered if she was being silly.

Probably, because when they were out in the garden again and they'd all finished eating, Harry dropped down next to her chair on the grass with a grin and said, 'I gather you've done a lot of travelling. Tell me where you've been.'

And finally she was on safe ground.

She talked about Peru, and Africa, about Papua New Guinea and Bornco, and he told her about Iraq and Kosovo and Indonesia. She discovered he could speak fluent Malay, to her delight, and she tried to practise on him. Hers was a little rusty, but it was fun to try—until she looked up and found Emily watching her thoughtfully.

Oh, hell, she thought, I hope she doesn't think I'm after her husband! If only Dan would come over and give her a hug, give them all some signals, but Dan seemed to be avoiding her, and only Liz was in range, so she turned to her and asked her about her painting.

'Oh, I just dabble,' she said dismissively, and Harry snorted.

'You're such a liar,' he said benignly. 'Iona, you've seen her work. The seascape in the hall? The triptych in the sitting room?'

'Yours?' Iona said, awed. 'Wow. I wish I dabbled in something like that!'

'I would say you dabble in languages,' Harry said in

Urdu, and she smiled and told him, in Swahili, that he was a show-off, and he threw back his head and laughed.

'What on earth are you two on about?' Emily said, bemused.

Oops. Don't upset the enemy, Iona thought, still not convinced that Emily had totally accepted her, but Harry just grinned at his wife.

'She's a natural linguist,' he said. 'And rather too fluent. She just called me a show-off.'

'Comes from having such a random childhood,' she explained. 'Either I learned the lingo or I didn't speak to anyone. It was a no-brainer, really.'

'Well, you're light years ahead of me; I struggled with schoolgirl French,' Emily admitted with a smile. 'Anyone for tea?'

'I'll make it,' she said, moving to get up, but Emily pushed her back down.

'Absolutely not. You sit there and talk international politics and stuff like that with Harry, because you understand it better than I do, and Mum and I'll make the tea, won't we, Mum?'

So Mrs Hamilton followed her daughter with a laughing shrug, and Iona turned back to Harry and said, 'International politics? Really?'

He laughed. 'What would you rather talk about?'

And because she'd never learned to put a leash on her tongue, she said quietly, 'Who was Carmen?'

She regretted it immediately because a shadow went over his face, but he gave a soft sigh and stared out over the sea, plucking a blade of grass and shredding it thoughtfully. 'My first wife. Well, technically. I married her to save her from an untenable situation, and she died after a stupid accident. She was pregnant, and I ended up with Kizzy. That was when I met Emily again. I hadn't seen her for years.'

'But you've loved her for a long time.'

He shot her a keen look. 'Yes, I have. Did she tell you that?'

She shook her head. 'No. But you've got that sort of confidence in your relationship that comes with knowing each other for years. I envy you that. I've never had that with anyone.'

'Goes with being a nomad, I suppose,' he said, and then tipped his head on one side. 'But I dare say you could settle down?'

She could feel that her smile was unsteady. 'If I was ever in the right place at the right time.'

'And is this it?'

She looked away. 'I don't know. It might be—for me, anyway. I don't know about Daniel.'

'I don't know what happened with Kate, but it hurt him very deeply. Be gentle with him, Iona. He's a good guy.'

'I know that.'

Dan was coming towards them, and Harry smiled and got to his feet. 'I'll go and chase up that tea,' he said, and left her alone with him.

'You OK?' he said, pausing beside her and studying her thoughtfully.

'I'm fine.'

'You sure? You look a little uncertain about that. Are you tired? You can go and lie down if you want. You don't have to stay here with this lot if you've had enough.'

Was that a hint that he wanted her to go?

'No,' he said, hunkering down in front of her and

taking her hands. 'That wasn't a hint. I was trying to look after you.'

Could he really read her mind? 'Making sure I get plenty of rest for tonight?' she said, not entirely joking, but his mouth kicked up in a grin.

'Now there's a thought—yours, not mine, but an interesting one.' He stood up, his fingers trailing over her shoulder. 'You've caught the sun. I'll get you some sun cream.'

But it was Georgie who put it on her shoulders, and Harry who brought her the tea, and Emily who came and sat next to her and took her hand and said, 'I'm so sorry about the cat. I didn't know—Daniel's just told me. You should have said. I thought you looked sad.'

And she hugged her, and Iona closed her eyes and hugged her back.

Would this woman who'd been so wary of her a week ago really turn into a lifelong friend? That would be so nice. If only she could dare to believe in it. In all of it, all of them.

Dan caught her eye across the lawn and winked, and she felt something warm and wonderful bubble up inside.

It felt too good to be true, but maybe it wasn't? Maybe it was her turn to find some happiness.

Then George Cauldwell stood up and called everyone's attention. 'I've got something I want to say to you all. Well, firstly to Nick, because I feel I ought to do this properly.' He grinned, and Nick gave him a puzzled look.

'I've asked Elizabeth to do me the honour of becoming my wife, and she's agreed, so with your blessing, Nick, we'd like to get married.'

Nick's mouth opened, but no words came—just a strangled laugh, and a huge hug for his mother and his father-in-law. 'Oh, you dark horse!' he said at last, sweeping his mother off her feet and whirling her round with a laugh. 'Absolutely.' And he pumped George's hand, and slapped his back, and Georgie was sucked into it, and just when Iona was feeling that it couldn't get any better, Dan came up behind her and bent over, sliding his arms round her shoulders and folding them under her chin, and his lips brushed her temple.

'Well, isn't that lovely?' he murmured. 'I thought they'd never get round to it. I wonder if David'll come home for the wedding.'

'David?'

'Georgie's brother. He's in Australia. He hit me, too, when I kissed her.'

'No wonder you never tried again,' she said with a smile, and he chuckled and hugged her, then straightened up, leaving his hands on her shoulders.

And Harry, glancing across and catching her eye, raised an eyebrow almost imperceptibly and smiled.

CHAPTER NINE

THAT weekend set the scene for the next few weeks.

During the day Daniel either worked at home in his studio, or went down to the hotel, and Iona pottered round the house and cooked their evening meal and kept the laundry under control, and when she had time she'd take a cup of tea outside and sit on the bench he'd had installed in her vegetable garden and watch the beans rushing up the bamboo canes, and turn her face up to the sun.

He caught her there quite often, the sound of his footsteps drowned out by the sound of water running down the wall and into the pebbles at her feet.

Sometimes he'd bring her a drink, sometimes he'd arrive with the others and they'd have an impromptu barbecue or go down to the beach and play with the children, and sometimes he'd fetch her and take her to the Barrons' house and they'd all play in the pool for hours.

She became great friends with Emily and Georgie, and they gave her lots of helpful advice about babies, as well as some that wasn't helpful at all! And lots of equipment, to go with the things that Dan had insisted they buy. She wasn't sure if the girls knew about the quantum shift in her relationship with Daniel, but she wasn't going to be the one to tell them, and nothing was said, but she had a feeling that Emily, at least, suspected something.

'You're good for him,' she said one day. 'I can't believe the change in such a short time. He's opened up such a lot.'

But she didn't say any more, and nor did Iona. If Dan wanted his sister to know, he'd tell her. Until then, she was quite happy for their private time together to remain just that, and it did.

It was a wonderful, glorious summer, and she felt rested and at peace.

Until she went to the doctor for a check-up, and her blood pressure was high.

'Are you worried about anything?'

Not consciously, she thought, but the future was unknowable and that might be preying on her mind. There was still the business of the will and the DNA test to sort out, but she'd been shutting it out.

'Maybe,' she said. 'But nothing major.'

'You have to rest,' she was told, and so even the pottering came to an end. Daniel spent more time at home, and she spent more time in the garden lying on the bench with her toes trailing in the water, feeling guilty for doing nothing and waiting for her baby to come.

And then she did—two weeks after Daniel had built the cot in her other bedroom—bringing their blissful idyll to an end.

It was four in the morning, and the sun was just edging up over the horizon when she felt the first tightening, low down in her abdomen.

She got quietly out of bed without disturbing him and went downstairs. They'd taken to using his room because he had the phone and the radio alarm clock by the bed, but she still used her room in the day if she lay down for a rest, and she went there now and sat up, propped against the pillows with her legs crossed, and watched the sun come up and waited.

By five she was uncomfortable. By six she was pacing. By seven she was in the car on the way to the hospital, filled with regret that she couldn't have the baby at home but accepting the wisdom of it.

'You OK?' Daniel asked when she sucked her breath in, and she breathed through the contraction and gave him a smile.

'I'm fine,' she said.

Fine?

It was the most terrifying day of his life. He'd never knowingly come within a hundred miles of a labouring woman, and he had absolutely no idea what to do.

'Just hold her and talk to her and remind her to breathe,' Emily told him when he rang in a panic after he'd been sent out so they could examine her. 'Do you want me to come and take over?'

He thought about it—thought about missing the baby's birth, and how he'd feel—and said, 'No. I'll cope. I'll be in touch.'

'You can come back in now, Daniel,' the midwife said, and he took a nice deep breath of hospital air and went back into the labour room.

'She's seven centimetres,' he was told, as if that was meant to mean anything, but the midwife must have seen his blank look and she smiled. 'Ten means she can push.'

'Ah. Right. Thanks.' And he wondered why on earth he hadn't read anything about it or thought about this bit at all.

Because he'd been blanking out the baby? Trying not to think about the child put there in her body by another man? A man who, if he weren't already dead, Daniel would have liked to kill with his bare hands for doing all this to her.

He made himself relax then, straightened out his fists, flexed them, reached for her hand and gripped it, and gradually, bit by bit, her body let go and the baby came.

And when she was born, when the squalling, slippery little thing that was her daughter was laid on her bare chest, heart to heart, and he saw Iona's hands curve protectively over the tiny little back and hold her tight, he felt a lump in his throat so big he could hardly swallow it.

'Clever girl,' he said, bending to kiss her cheek, appalled by the blood and the violence of it all and staggered by the fact that his sister had done this—was going to do it again, in fact, apparently—that Georgie had done it, and his own mother, and everybody's mother.

Left up to him, there would only have ever been one child before the whole process got referred back to the designer for a thorough review. He let his breath out on a long sigh, ran his hand round the back of his neck and met her tearful, happy smile with an unsteady one of his own. 'Are you OK?'

She laughed a little shakily. 'I'm fine. Say hello to Lily.'

'Lily?' He smiled. 'Lily. Hello, Lily. It's nice to meet you,' he said, and touched her tiny hand with his finger. Immediately she gripped it, the strength of those tiny fingers startling, and he swallowed hard and stroked them with his thumb, afraid he'd break her because she was so small.

He was sent out while they cleaned them both up, and he phoned Emily. 'She's had her. She's called her Lily,' he said, his voice cracking, and Emily shrieked in his ear and called to Harry, and then Harry was on the phone congratulating him.

'Me?' he said, giving a shocked laugh. 'She's all Iona's work; she's nothing to do with me.'

And even though it was true, it hit him like a sledgehammer. Lily wasn't anything to do with him, no matter how magical, how beautiful, how utterly perfect she was. She was Iona's, and he'd do well to remember it.

She was amazing.

Tiny, perfect—and everything was like a dream until Daniel took them home that evening.

To her flat.

He'd changed the sheets, made up the cot and put the pram in her room with new little sheets and blankets on it.

The midwife came and made sure everything was all right and that she was settled, said she'd see her in the morning and left. And after he'd brought her a hot drink and tucked her up in bed and made sure she was all right, he, too, headed for the door.

'Where are you going?' she asked, wondering if he could hear the note of panic.

He stopped and turned back. 'Next door. I don't want to disturb you. I won't be far away if you need me.'

She wanted to say, I need you now! You won't disturb me, but something in his face stopped her, so she nodded numbly. 'Thanks,' she said instead, and he left the room, pulling the door to.

She stared at it. Not shut, not quite, but almost. Shut enough so he couldn't see her, but not enough that she could cry in peace. And she wanted to cry, because they hadn't slept apart since that first night together, and she missed him!

Well, that was stupid of her, wasn't it? He'd told her he was damaged goods. Clearly he'd meant it, or he would have realised that she needed him beside her more than she needed not to be disturbed.

Which was a joke in itself, because Lily had decided that being awake and able to make noises was great, and that was what she was going to do. All night.

Iona had no idea what to do for her. Was she hungry? She wasn't crying, but if she picked her up, would that wake her so she had to feed her? And she wasn't sure she could get her to latch on without help. She'd struggled in the hospital, but she was adamant that she was going to breast-feed and now she was face to face with the reality of single parenting.

Alone, in the night, with a very new baby and not a single parenting skill to her name.

She swallowed hard and sat up, easing herself carefully back against the pillows. She hurt. Everything hurt, but especially *there*, and she found herself longing for a bath. Could she do it? On her own? Because she could hardly ask Daniel to help her, in the middle of the night.

She ran the water and eased off her nightdress, the same one Georgie had lent her, the one she'd been wearing the night Pebbles had died. The one he'd taken off her that very first time.

He'd thought she was beautiful, but she looked down now at her stomach, hanging like a bag of jelly on her front, and she had to fight back the tears. It was temporary, she told herself. It would soon firm up and go back to normal.

If she could only remember what normal was.

She had one foot in the bath and the other on the floor when Daniel knocked on the door.

'Iona? Are you OK?'

'I'm fine,' she lied, wincing as she lifted the other foot in. Now all she had to do was sit down. Hah. 'I'm in the bath.' Sort of.

'Can I come in?'

She opened her mouth to say no, but he was coming in anyway, his eyes concerned, and tutting under his breath, he came and held her under her arms and lowered her gently into the water. The lovely, lovely, warm water.

It felt fabulous.

Wonderful. Now if only Daniel wasn't standing there looking at her trashed body, she could lie back and enjoy it…

'I'll leave you in peace. Give me a shout when you want to get out and I'll give you a hand.'

He closed the door and she lay back with a sigh of relief. Oh, that was better. So soothing.

She closed her eyes and let herself drift away to a safe place, a quiet, gentle place, tranquil.

She was in the courtyard, her feet on the edge of the water, the sound soothing her and blanking out all the chaos in the world. Brian was there with her, watching her, a smile on his face, and Jamie was behind him. He looked at her—no, through her—and turned and walked away.

She let him go. She had no way of holding him, and she didn't want to. He needed to be free, and so did she. Wonderfully, marvellously free.

She opened her eyes, to find Daniel sitting there on a chair, watching her. 'Oh,' she said, surprised and yet not. She had felt someone was watching over her. She'd thought it was Brian, but maybe it had been Daniel she'd sensed. And where had the chair come from? She stifled the ridiculous urge to cover her body with her hands. He'd been watching her for however long, and sayings about stable doors and bolting horses came to mind.

'How long have you been there?'

'Ten minutes? You've been in there ages. You fell asleep, and I didn't want to leave you. The water must be cold now—do you want a hand out?'

'I need to wash, first,' she said, and expected him to leave, but he didn't. He ran more hot water into the bath, took a new flannel from the shelf and soaped it thoroughly, then, sitting her up, he washed her back, his hands gentle and yet thorough. He slid down her arms, under them, over her breasts, down her legs—even between her toes. And then he rinsed her just as carefully, and helped her out.

His hands were strong and sure, and the moment she was on her feet, there was a warm towel to wrap her in, and he helped her over to the chair. 'Give me a call if you need me,' he said, and tactfully left her alone to do the things she needed to do after giving birth.

She slipped her nightdress on and went back into the bedroom, to find him standing there with Lily in his arms.

'She was crying,' he said softly, but she wasn't crying now. She was lying staring up at him, her eyes wide open, locked on his, and she felt a huge lump in her throat. He looked so comfortable with her, so natural. Of course he'd had Kizzy and Lucie to practise on, and with all the blatant fecundity of his close circle of family and friends he was no stranger to children.

What a terrible shame that he wouldn't be there for Lily, too. Because he wouldn't. She knew that. She was just his housekeeper, and he was way out of her league. He might be kindness itself, and he might have diverted himself with her, but that was all. And the moment the

DNA test had been done and her claim for Lily had been proved, she'd be out. The only light at the end of the tunnel was that there had been no sign of the will. They'd torn the place apart now, and there was nowhere else it could be, really. Her last chance, Brian's office, had proved a barren hope when they'd moved their site office out into a Portakabin and gutted the room.

Nothing. Not under the floorboards, or tucked under the carpet—nowhere.

And without it, there was a chance she'd get nothing.

Foolish woman that she was, she was almost clinging now to the hope that it didn't turn up, that she did get nothing, because, given enough time, maybe Daniel would realise that he loved her as much as she loved him.

She felt her legs go weak, and sat down abruptly on the edge of the bed. She loved him?

Well, of course she loved him. She knew it. It was just that the words had popped into her mind and shocked her. They were just so—so *significant*.

'I think she's hungry,' he said, bringing the baby over to her, and she settled herself back against the pillows, pulled up the quilt and took the baby from him.

'I can manage now,' she lied, clinging to the remnants of her pride, and he nodded abruptly and walked out, pulling the door to again.

She opened the front of the nightdress, pushed it aside and turned Lily towards her. Now. Brush her nipple against the baby's cheek—so. Then as she turns, push her head—done it! The crying stopped, replaced by a surprisingly loud, rhythmic sucking noise that nearly made her laugh out loud.

And she stopped worrying about the will, stopped

thinking about Daniel, and settled down, comfortable at last, to enjoy her beautiful little girl.

The next few days were a time of adjustment, but to his untutored eye, at least, Iona seemed to be taking to motherhood like a duck to water.

Daniel made sure he was never far away, and if she missed him at night, she didn't say so.

After that first night, she never once asked for his help. After a week, when she was clearly all right without him, he moved back up to his own bedroom with a strange sense of regret. If he'd just slept with her the night he'd brought her home—held her in his arms, or lain beside her holding hands—maybe they would have still been close, but there was something distant about their new relationship, something remote, that saddened him, because he knew their little interlude was over.

She was a mother now, and the time for dreams was over. She settled into a sort of routine with Lily, and Emily and Georgie were amazed at what a good, easy baby she was.

She had so many cuddles it was a wonder she knew who her mother was, he thought, and because he didn't want Iona to feel that she had to do anything except spend time with Lily, he was trying to keep the place clean and tidy.

'You need a housekeeper,' Harry teased one day when he'd dropped in with Emily and the kids on their way back from the beach. He just shot him a look and carried on scrubbing the sink.

'It's only for a little while, but if I don't do it or get someone in, she'll feel she has to, just because she's like that.'

Harry propped himself up against the wall and studied

him thoughtfully. 'So how long are you going to go on kidding yourself that she's just a housekeeper?'

Dan threw the scourer back into the sink and straightened up, staring down the garden to where the girls were sitting on the grass with all the children. She was feeding Lily, and his heart contracted. 'Well, what the hell else is she?' he growled.

Harry shrugged, following his gaze down the garden to the happy little group. 'I don't know. Your girlfriend? Your companion? The woman you love?'

He swallowed hard and turned back to the sink. 'I don't love her,' he said. 'I don't do relationships.'

'Well, it looks to me like you do relationships. You just don't know what to call them.'

'Hazardous,' he growled. 'Complicated. Unnecessary.'

'Oh, I'm with you on the first two, but unnecessary? No way.' Harry's voice lowered. 'You need her, Daniel. And she needs you. Don't close your mind.'

'This from the man who was telling me not to get involved?' he said incredulously, and Harry gave a wry laugh.

'Yeah, well, that was before I met her.'

'So what's changed?'

'You have,' Harry said quietly. 'You're happy. Contented. You've let it all go—all the Kate stuff.'

'What Kate stuff?' God, he'd kill Iona if she'd told him—

'Whatever happened. I have no idea. I guess she cheated on you. God knows why; she wouldn't find a better man.'

He gave a soft snort and rinsed out the cloth he'd been using to wipe down the cupboards. Funny, when Iona did them, they had a wonderful streak-free shine. Now, they looked as if a two-year-old had been let loose with a grubby rag. They'd been better before—

'OK, don't talk about it,' Harry said with a sigh. 'But think about it. Think about Iona, and what she means to you. And don't let her slip through your fingers, Dan. She's a darling. Clever, funny, intelligent, well-read, provocative, generous to a fault—'

'Leave her alone,' Dan snarled, turning on him with a glare. 'You're married. Don't forget that. And if you mess my sister about, I'll kill you.'

Harry held his hands up in surrender. 'I have no intention of messing your sister about. I love her to bits. That doesn't make me blind and insensitive, though, and if you've got any sense, you'll open your own eyes and pay a bit of heed to what's right under your nose. Iona's the best thing that's ever happened to you. Don't let her go.'

And, without another word, he walked out of the door and down the garden to join the others,

Daniel snapped his jaw shut and turned back to the cupboards. God, they were awful. He got the cloth out and tried again.

CHAPTER TEN

THE days turned to weeks, and Dan couldn't justify hanging around for Iona any more. She was well, she was fit, and anyway she had Emily and Georgie if she needed any help or advice.

Both of them were much better equipped in that department than he was, so with a strange feeling of redundancy, he went back to work at the hotel.

And not before time.

He'd really taken his eye off the ball, he thought, when he walked into the foyer and found the old reception desk—the central feature of the foyer, the desk that Iona loved so much—had been ripped out to leave a yawning void.

He found George in the area where the annexe had been, supervising the setting out. 'Where's the desk?' he asked, trying to keep a lid on his boiling emotions.

George frowned. 'It's outside. The boys only took it out this morning, but you said you wanted the fittings all cleared and it was the last thing.' He tipped his head on one side. 'I did wonder if you meant the desk, but the boys had done it before I realised. It's still in one piece. It's a lovely thing, actually. Very heavy. It's solid mahogany. Seems a shame to chuck it out. The shelves are there, too. We thought you might have plans for them.'

He felt his shoulders drop a little. 'I do. We're going to get it restored. It needed to come out, but carefully.'

George looked insulted. 'They took it out carefully, Dan. Go and have a look at it—it's just by the site office.'

So he went and stood behind it, where generations of staff would have stood to welcome their guests, placing his hands flat down on to it. The top was battered, scarred by the passage of many keys, the old wood gleaming even through the dust, and he ran his hand over it, feeling its history with his fingertips. He'd seen Iona doing that, touching it lovingly. That was why he wanted to keep it, he realised. Not because the hotel needed it. In fact working it into the scheme would be a bit of a nightmare.

But Iona loved it, and that was good enough for him.

He dropped down on to his haunches, peering up underneath the inside, into the recess formed by a shelf that was set about nine inches down from the top, to see if he could work out how the top was fixed. Maybe they should just keep that bit…

He couldn't really see. The September sun was so bright it threw the recess into deep shadow, but there was something stuck on it. Something white—a long rectangle taped to the underside. He reached up, feeling it with his fingers. An envelope?

Peeling it away, he stood up, the envelope in his hands, and stared at it.

'Copy of The Last Will of Brian Henry Dawes', it said on the outside, and the date was the tenth of March. Six months ago, and just a few weeks before Brian had died.

And the original will, it stated, was lodged with Cooper,

Farringdon, Solicitors, 29 High Street, Yoxburgh. Not Barry Edwards. Which was why he'd had no knowledge of it.

Dan was standing there with it in his hands when Nick pulled into the car park and came over to him. 'What's that?' he asked, and Daniel held it out to him.

He took it, read the outside and blinked. 'Right,' he said slowly. 'Where did you find it?'

'Sellotaped under the desk,' he said.

'Well, why on earth would he put it there? And why use a solicitor who wasn't his usual one?'

'Because he didn't trust Ian? Because he knew it would be found when the hotel was refurbished? Or because he wasn't sure about it?' Dan didn't know, but he knew one thing. He had to tell Iona, and they had to open it and read the contents.

'I think we need to contact our solicitor,' Nick said, reading his mind. 'Leave it with me. I'll take it there, we'll get him to see us now. You go and get Iona—tell her to leave the baby with Georgie, if she doesn't want to bring her.'

Dan drove home, the tension making his muscles tight and his heart pound. What did the will contain? And what would the significance be for Iona and Lily?

And for him?

'You're home early.'

He looked worried—no, not worried. Cautious. As if he had bad news. She'd seen enough of those looks recently to last a lifetime, and she sat back down on the bench in the courtyard and stared at him, her heart starting to pound.

'Daniel, what is it?'

He frowned slightly. 'We've found the will.'

Her hand flew to her chest, holding down the surge of

emotion that rushed through it, and she closed her eyes and counted to ten.

'Have you got it?' she asked, her voice rusty with shock.

'Nick's got it. He's taken it to the solicitor. We thought it should be opened officially.'

'Oh. Right. Yes—yes, of course. So—will he tell us what's in it?'

'I don't know. It's only a copy. He needs to contact the solicitor who's got the original.'

'Barry Edwards?'

He shook his head. 'No. Not Edwards. It's apparently with Cooper, Farringdon.'

Light dawned. 'Mike Cooper—of course! He was there a few times a couple of months before Brian died, but then I didn't see him again. He retired a while ago. He used to come in and see him from time to time. He was a friend, I think. We used to put up clients for him on occasions, but I thought by the time Brian died, he'd been retired for ages.' She shook her head to try and clear it. 'So—where did you find it?'

'Under the reception desk, taped under the top.'

She closed her eyes, wondering how she could have been so stupid. 'On the right?'

'Yes. Why?'

She laughed, because it was so obvious. 'He said something to me in the hospital, just before he died. He told me he'd taken care of me, and said "Check it out". He said it two or three times, but he was so unwell I didn't want to press him, so I told him not to worry. I didn't understand the significance at the time, but when people were checking out, that was where we put the paperwork—on the right-hand side of the desk, on the shelf underneath. Hence "check it out". Oh, I can't believe I didn't think of it!'

She stood up, her legs trembling. 'Can we go and talk to him? To Mike Cooper?'

'I think our solicitor's setting it up.'

'Good.'

Then she would know, one way or the other, what her options were. She was very much afraid they didn't include Daniel.

Since she'd had the baby, although he'd been kindness itself, he hadn't been near her. He hadn't held her, hadn't touched her, hadn't kissed her—OK, her body wasn't ready for more than that yet, but it didn't have to be all or nothing, did it? And if he was keeping such a distance from her, it could only mean that he'd been looking for a diversion and she'd been available—and now she wasn't, he didn't want to know. Oh, well, she'd told him she wasn't asking for eternity, and he'd obviously taken her at her word.

The knowledge was bitter, and the will that only a few weeks ago she had been dreading, now seemed like her way out of an impossible and painful situation.

Not that she expected much. A few thousand, hopefully? Enough to put down a deposit on a little house, so she could work and pay a small mortgage and give Lily some kind of lifestyle. That was all she wanted. Just enough of a leg-up to give her some security. Then she could stop worrying about the future and get on with their lives.

They couldn't see Mike Cooper until late that afternoon, to give Ian Dawes time to come from London. The fact that he was prepared to come in such a hurry was interesting, as was his face when he saw Iona there in Mike's old chambers with the baby.

'It's born,' he said blankly, as if he hadn't expected there to be a child. Or had hoped there wouldn't be? Well, tough, Daniel thought, and hoped Iona would be up to dealing with his hostility. Apparently so.

'It's September, Ian,' she said, and Dan wouldn't have been surprised if she'd rolled her eyes. 'I got pregnant when Jamie was home in November. I'm not an elephant. Lily, say hello to Uncle Ian,' she added pointedly.

The man frowned, and Daniel wanted to kill him. He still obviously didn't believe that Lily was his brother's child, but the DNA test was under way—at least Lily's part of it. Ian had refused to co-operate until there was a need proved by a valid will or a court of law. Dragging it out to the bitter end.

And now there they were, in Mike Cooper's old office, and Cooper was straightening out the document and smiling at Iona. 'So this is the baby? Well, hello, little one. Goodness, she's the spitting image of her father,' he said with a smile, and then resumed his seat, steepled his fingers over the will on his desk and ran his eyes over them all.

'First, let me apologise for the delay in revealing the contents of the will to you. Because I'd retired, I was unaware of my client's death until I received a call from my office earlier today, and he obviously hadn't made the whereabouts of the will known to you all. Still, we're here now, so if we're all ready?' he said, and then started to read.

It was gobbledegook. Well, to most people it would be. To Iona, who'd studied law, it was just legal jargon.

But it was legal, signed and witnessed, and as Brian had promised, he'd taken care of Lily.

Mike Cooper read:

'To my son Ian I leave the sum of ten thousand pounds. Of the balance of the residuary estate, the Trustees shall hold one half in trust equally for such surviving child or children of my late son James, whether born or *en ventre sa mère*. Subject to that—'

She didn't hear the rest, because Ian was making such a noise he was drowning Mike out.

He took off his glasses, looked up at Ian and said, 'Mr Dawes, I would appreciate it if we could conduct this in a proper and formal manner, without interruption.' Then he carried on reading, but she'd tuned him out, staring down at her baby in a state of shock.

She swallowed. Half? He'd really left Lily half? And Ian only ten thousand pounds? Not that she knew how much half was, but surely that couldn't be right? It must be more than ten thousand, unless Brian's debts had been absolutely enormous. Which was quite possible—

On the other side of the room Ian was fulminating, but all she could do was stare down at Lily in her arms and shake her head in disbelief.

He'd done it. Dear, darling Brian, who'd never got round to anything, had found time, even when he'd been so ill, to ensure Lily's future.

'Will there be enough to put down a deposit to buy her a little house?' she said, and Mike Cooper chuckled.

'I should think so, my dear. The hotel sold for in excess of one and three-quarter million pounds. Once the debts are cleared and the inheritance tax paid, I understand from Barry Edwards that there will be a little over a million pounds, of which half will belong to Lily, and you and I have that in trust for her, for you to use as we see fit, until she reaches the age of eighteen. The other half, of course, is yours to do with as you wish. So, yes, you can buy a house. A very nice house.'

Now he really was talking gobbledegook. She stared at him. 'Mine?' she said, puzzled. 'Why mine?'

'Because those are the terms of the will.' He read it again, and this time she heard it.

'—one half of my residuary estate I leave to Iona Lockwood, for her care and compassion and unfailing consideration of me; in the event that there is no surviving child of my son James, then the whole balance of the residual estate to go to Iona Lockwood.

'He's left ten thousand pounds to his son, and of the rest, half to Lily, in trust, and half to you, my dear. And if anything should happen to Lily, then you inherit her half.'

'Me?' She turned and stared at Daniel, who was looking as stunned as she felt.

'Only if she's James's daughter,' Ian said, finally finding his voice again. 'And that's yet to be proved. If she's not James's daughter, then it should come to me! Dammit, it should all come to me! What the hell was the stupid old bastard thinking about—'

'Mr Dawes!' Mike Cooper roared, lumbering to his feet and making Lily stiffen with shock. 'I will not have this language in my chambers! During the course of the preparation of this will, I had lengthy discourse with your father, and through it all he had nothing but praise for Miss Lockwood and concern for her future. She asked for nothing, she worked for no salary, and she was tireless in her care of him. All he ever said of you was that you had been a selfish, vindictive little boy and you'd turned into a selfish, vindictive little man. And there is no provision for the money to come to you. The wording is precise. No surviving child. If this child is not that of your brother James, then there is no surviving child, in which case the whole would go to Miss Lockwood anyway. All you are entitled to is the ten thousand pounds stipulated by the will.'

'I'll contest it!'

'You are, of course, at liberty to do so, but I have to tell you that your father was in sound mind when this will was made, and it was written with great consideration and after much thought. Your chances of winning are so slight I would say they do not exist, but if that is how you wish to spend your legacy, it's your prerogative, but I haven't come out of my retirement to listen to any more of your nonsense.'

He turned to Iona, who was still sitting there in stunned silence, staring at him and shushing Lily on autopilot. 'Miss Lockwood, I have here a copy of the will for you to study. I'm sure, being a law student, you'll understand its ramifications, but if you require any clarification, give me a call. I'd be delighted to explain it to you. Mr Dawes? Your copy,' he said, handing it over without volunteering any explanation, and Iona had to bite her lip.

Ian was furious, and getting crosser by the minute, and she had to remind herself not to feel sorry for him.

'You'll be hearing from my lawyers!' he yelled, leaving the room and slamming the door behind him.

Or attempting to. It was on a closer, though, and all he did was hurt his hand. He swore, threw them all a furious glare and strode off down the corridor.

'Oops,' she said softly, and Mike Cooper smiled.

'Indeed,' he said. 'Now, is there anything else I can help you with, or can I get back to my golf?'

'I can't keep it.'

They were sitting on the steps at the end of the garden, staring out over the moonlit sea, and Iona was mulling over the afternoon's events and toying idly with a glass of champagne.

Just the one, because of feeding Lily, but they were supposedly celebrating. Daniel, not being restricted by motherhood, poured himself another one and set the bottle down on the step beside them.

'Why can't you keep it?'

'Because I ought to give it to Ian.'

'Ian?' He nearly choked on the champagne. 'Iona, are you nuts? He's a nasty piece of work. Even his own father recognised that. That's why he gave him such a token pay-off.'

'No,' she said, shaking her head. 'I've worked it out. He gave him ten thousand because that's what he'd given Jamie over the previous few months before his death, and he was nothing if not fair and even-handed. But I just feel guilty—as if everyone's looking at me and thinking I wormed my way into his affections and conned him into changing his will—'

'Rubbish. You were wonderful to him when neither of his sons could be bothered to lift a finger. Nick said the place wouldn't have been running without you. You know he said he thought of you as a daughter?'

She stared at him. 'Really?'

'Really. That was how he described you to Mike Cooper, apparently. He genuinely loved you, Iona.'

'Gosh.' She swallowed the sudden lump in her throat

and stared down at her hands. 'He was wonderful to me. I really miss him.'

'Well, you'll be able to think of him every time you walk up to your front door and put the key in it and let yourself into your very own home. That's a fitting legacy, don't you think?'

Oh, God, how lonely. Even if she'd have Lily for company. *I don't want to do that! I don't want my own front door! I want yours—I want you to ask me to stay here with you, to tell me you love me. Not tell me that moving out into a house of my own would be a fitting legacy, for heaven's sake!*

'Yes, it would, wouldn't it?' she said, throwing him a probably very unconvincing smile. 'If I keep it.'

'Well, you'll have to keep Lily's half, you don't have a choice, and as a long-term investment, property has out-performed all other forms of investment substantially over the past thirty-odd years, so buying a house with it would be the only sensible thing to do. And, as for your half, what would you do with it? Apart from give it to Ian. I might have to kill you to stop you doing that,' he said mildly. 'The man's a waste of a good skin.'

The bit of her that wasn't screaming inside about out-performing investments actually managed a laugh. 'So what else would I do with it?' She shrugged. 'Give it to charity? Nick does a lot for charity, Georgie says. I could ask him.'

'You could finish your degree,' he suggested, more seriously now. 'Get qualified, and set up a foundation to help with legal fees for people who can't afford to fight for their rights. You wanted to be a human rights lawyer—here's your chance. You could call it the Brian Dawes Foundation in his memory.'

What a wonderful idea. 'I could,' she said slowly. 'That would be a better use of it. He'd approve of that. Thank you.'

She rubbed her temples. She had a headache, probably brought on by the stress of the afternoon and Ian's vitriolic outburst. She stood up and brushed off her skirt, and it billowed round her ankles in the light sea breeze. 'Daniel, do you mind if I have an early night? I'm feeling a bit shell-shocked.' *And I need to go and cry my eyes out, because all you seem to be able to talk about is me going, and I don't think I can bear it...*

'Sure.' He stood up and walked back in with her. 'Can I get you anything?'

She shook her head. 'No, I'm fine. Thank you for coming with me today.'

'You're welcome.'

She hesitated, gave him a chance to hug her, to kiss her goodnight—dammit, anything at all—but he just stood there and waited, so she turned on her heel and walked down the hall into her flat, closed the door and started to cry.

'So what the hell is this about Iona moving? I thought she was going to buy some kind of investment property?' Emily asked, plonking herself down on his sofa and rubbing her hands over her gently expanding middle while she interrogated him.

He looked startled. 'No. Of course not. Well, only incidentally. She's going to buy a house and move into it. What's so odd about that? It's the obvious thing to do, I should have thought.'

'Really?' Emily looked stunned. 'But what about you two?'

'What about us two? What us two? And anyway, there are three—'

She growled and rolled her eyes. 'God, you're so obtuse. For heaven's sake, Dan, I thought you loved each other.'

He blinked. 'What the hell gave you that idea?'

'Oh, dear. I've seen you together?' she said, as if he was a slightly dense toddler.

When? Because certainly since she'd had the baby he'd kept himself as far away from her as he could without actively ostracising her. 'You're imagining it,' he said flatly.

'Am I? I don't think so. You're really close. Or you were before she had the baby. Lots of lingering glances and little touches—it was obvious. A blind man on a galloping horse could see you were in love.' She frowned. 'Although since then you've been a little distant—'

'She doesn't love me, don't be ridiculous—and anyway she's had a baby!'

'Well, it's not exactly some foul disease, Dan! And why is it ridiculous? Just because she's had someone else's baby doesn't stop her loving you, and it shouldn't stop you being nice to her. You can still cuddle her. And you haven't,' she said accusingly. 'I thought she was looking a bit glum. I thought it was the will thing, but when I spoke to her earlier on the phone, she didn't sound too happy, and I've been thinking about it.'

'Oh, God help us,' Dan said, rolling his eyes, and she gave a tiny little scream of frustration.

'Dan, I'm serious,' she said. 'She loves you to bits. And you love her. You do love her,' she said again, when he opened his mouth to argue. 'You know you do. So when are you going to admit it?'

He swallowed hard and rested his head back on the sofa, closing his eyes. 'She doesn't love me, Em,' he said gruffly. 'She's still in love with Jamie.'

'Oh, rubbish! She's no such thing! She outgrew him years ago, Dan—he was little better than his brother. Nicer, but just as idle and unhelpful. She loves you, Daniel, and she needs a real man—one who's grown-up enough to love her back. A man like you—kind and thoughtful and safe.'

'Oh, God, damned by faint praise,' he said, and Emily rolled her eyes and dropped back against the sofa.

'Is that what you think? Faint praise? Look at her life, Dan! Those are the most important things you could give her. That and your love. So when are you going to tell her you love her? When are you going to tell her you don't want her to move out, you want her to stay here and marry you and spend her life with you, so you can be part of Lily's life and watch her grow up and give her brothers and sisters—?'

'Enough! For God's sake, Em, that's enough!' he said, panicking, his palms breaking out in a cold sweat. 'I can't do that.'

'Why?' she asked, relentless. 'Because Kate cheated on you? Iona isn't Kate. Kate was a real piece of work. She never loved you, but Iona does; she loves you with all her heart, and she'll never cheat on you or lie to you or hurt you, and she needs to know you love her back.'

He sat forward. 'You really think that? That she loves me?' He shook his head. 'She's still grieving—'

'No! No, Dan, no, no, no! She's over him! It's you she loves. You have to tell her.'

He swallowed, remembering Kate, when he'd found out about her and Angie, when he'd said he loved her, thought she'd loved him, and she'd just laughed at him. Thrown back her head and laughed—

'What if I tell her all that and she laughs at me?' he said, his voice uneven.

Emily frowned. 'She won't. But what if she did? So what? What have you lost? Just pride. What's that, compared to a lifetime of loving her?' She sat down beside him, sliding her arms round him and hugging him. 'Give her a chance, Dan,' she pleaded. 'Give both of you a chance. Go and talk to her now.'

He shook his head. 'She's asleep. She wanted an early night.'

'So why's she standing at the end of the garden looking at the sea as if she'd like to throw herself in it?'

She stood up, kissed his cheek and left him sitting there staring out of the window at Iona.

The woman he loved. The only woman he'd ever really loved, he realised. Please, God, she wouldn't laugh at him.

He got to his feet and walked slowly, mechanically, to the door and slid it open, going out into the night. It had been a warm day, but now there was a chill in the air—or was it fear making him cold?

He swallowed, took a deep breath and started walking down the lawn.

She didn't hear him coming, but she felt his presence and turned as he reached her.

'Hi, there,' he said, and she scanned his face. He looked grave, and she gave him an unsteady smile in the moonlight. Was this it? The grand goodbye?

'Hi,' she managed.

'I thought you were having an early night?'

'I couldn't sleep. I just needed to hear the sea.'

'Want me to leave you alone?'

She shook her head, wondering if he could see the tears on her cheeks or if they'd dried in the wind. 'Not really. I was just thinking about Brian.'

He sat down on the top step and patted the stone beside

him. After a long pause, she sat down, and he took her hand and rubbed it softly, his thumb grazing over the back of it, slowly, back and forth. 'You really miss him, don't you?' he murmured. 'You've had a tough year.'

She nodded, thinking back over it. Tough? It had been momentous. 'What with watching Brian fall apart over Jamie's death, and then seeing him die just when he was about to retire and put his feet up and have the rest he so badly deserved—' She shook her head, remembering his awful, bitter disappointment in his sons, the shocking deterioration of his health, his death. 'If only Jamie had helped, or Ian, but they were as bad as each other. Neither of them cared about him, and he was such a good man. He deserved better from his sons.'

His thumb stilled, and he turned his head and looked at her. 'I thought you loved Jamie?' he asked quietly, and she shrugged.

'Did I? I don't know. Maybe once, or maybe he was just fun and I was bored of travelling alone and it was good to have company. If I'm honest, I think I was just lonely, and if I hadn't met him I would have gone back to Maastricht as I'd planned. But then I came here and met Brian, and he made me so welcome, and for the first time in my life I had a proper base. Somewhere I could call home—even if it was a shabby old hotel with a derelict annexe and an even more derelict cat—'

She gave an unsteady laugh and looked towards the lilac. 'He was the only father I've ever known, and he gave me my first real home, my first pet. Poor little Pebbles. Still, at least she got to die here, under a bush in the sun, without pain. I can't think of a more beautiful place to die.'

'Or live?' he said tentatively, and she looked at him, hardly daring to hope. 'Is it a beautiful place to live?'

'Here?' She turned and stared at the house, wondering what he meant. Not that, surely. He was talking about the out-performing damned investments again. She sighed. 'It's a beautiful place to live, but I could never afford something like this, and anyway, I couldn't justify it. I can't possibly keep all that money and spend it, Dan. I'm not like that. I find it really hard to cope with Nick and Georgie having so much money, and the fact that you're a millionaire and Harry's got such huge advances for his memoirs, and everything's such big numbers, you know? When I met you, I said I had to go out and find some food. I didn't mean it literally, not quite, but Ian had given me five hundred pounds at the funeral, and I was going to have to make it last, but with the power off, I could only eat things that didn't need cooking—so no cheap pasta. I can't tell you how sick I was of cold baked beans and tuna sandwiches. That Chinese take-away was the first hot food I'd had in six weeks.'

He looked shocked. Shocked and horrified, and she wanted to slide her arms round him and tell him it was all right, she'd survived, but he was looking at her oddly, as if he didn't quite know what to say, and she turned away, looking back out over the sea and wishing she could just tell him how she felt…

'Marry me,' he blurted out, and she turned and stared at him in astonishment.

'What?'

'I said marry me,' he repeated, but this time in a calmer, surer voice, as if having said it out loud, it suddenly seemed like the most sensible thing in the world. 'Marry me and let me love you. Because I do love you, you know. I've loved you since I caught you dragging that mattress out of the skip, and I know I've been a bit slow on the uptake, but I really thought you were still in love with Jamie, and it was Emily who told me not to be so dense.'

Emily? Bless her heart. She was a good friend.

She thought back to the time after the baby's birth, to her loneliness and isolation when he'd been so remote. 'Really? You love me? Then why've you been keeping me at arm's length since I had the baby, Daniel? Why didn't you stay with me? Why didn't you *tell* me?'

He shrugged, as if he was looking inside himself and finding the awkward truth. 'I think—I felt that Lily was Jamie's, and it was as if you were with him then, because you were with her, and she's a part of him. And I felt as if I didn't belong, as if I was intruding on something private.'

She started to smile, a slow smile that lit up the depths of her eyes as she stared up into his beautiful, beloved face.

'Oh, Daniel,' she said softly, reaching up and touching her fingers gently to his cheek. 'Of course you belonged. You were there for me when I was at my lowest ebb, and at my highest high. You've been my rock, the only thing that's got me through. You've rescued me from falling ceilings, buried my cat, washed me when I had Lily, changed her nappies, cooked and cleaned and done the laundry so I didn't feel guilty—'

'Did you feel guilty? I didn't want you to feel guilty.'

'Well, I did, but only because I felt it was my job. If I'd thought you were doing it for love, I would have treasured every gesture.' She reached up and pressed a tender, loving kiss to his lips. 'Ask me again, Dan. Ask me to marry you. Ask me to live here with you.'

He swallowed hard, then, taking her hand, he stood up, walked down a few steps and went down on one knee just below her, stared up into her eyes and said, his voice gruff and sincere and steady as a rock, 'I love you, Iona. And I love Lily. Stay with me. Marry me, and live here with me, and turn this ridiculous great house into a home. Help me fill it with children—fostered or adopted, preferably, so I don't have to watch you going through that awful thing all over again, but somehow, some way, help me turn us into a family. A proper family. For ever.'

'Oh, Daniel.'

As she reached for him and lifted her face to his, she could feel the tears tracking down her cheeks—tears of joy, of happiness, and a love so profound she thought her heart would burst from it.

'Of course I'll marry you,' she said softly. 'I'd marry you and live with you and give you children wherever we lived. This house is just that—a house, but it's a beautiful house, a wonderful house, and I can't think of a better place to make our home. And we'll fill it with children. As many as you want. So long as I'm with you, I couldn't ask for anything more. But I do want to finish my degree, and I want to set up that foundation in memory of Brian, and when Lily's old enough, I'll tell her about her grandfather. Maybe she'll even get to meet her grandmother, if I can ever persuade her to come back to England. She'll love you, by the way.'

'Tough. I'm taken,' he said, wrapping his arms round her and drawing her closer. 'Maybe you could buy a house for Lily as an investment for her, and your mother could live in it?'

'A base?' She laughed. 'Not her thing. I told you, she's a hippy.'

'Even hippies grow old.'

She tipped her head back and looked at him. 'You try to fix everything for everybody, don't you?' she murmured, and kissed him. 'I love you, Daniel Hamilton. You're such a good man. Brian would have liked you, and Mrs Jessop thinks you're wonderful. She'll be really pleased to hear we're getting married. We'll have to invite her to the wedding. She won't be at all surprised.'

He thought of Mrs Jessop, and the knowing look in her wise old eyes as she'd said, 'You'll get there.'

And he smiled down at Iona and feathered a gentle kiss over her lips. 'You know, I don't think she will.'

He kissed her again, and then again, and then in the distance they heard the baby cry.

He lifted his head and gave her a wry smile. 'This may have to wait,' he murmured ruefully, and she smiled back.

'There's no hurry. We've got the rest of our lives,' she said.

And, arm in arm, they walked back up the garden to their home, and their daughter, and their future...

* * * * *

THE MAID AND
THE MILLIONAIRE

BY
MYRNA MACKENZIE

Dear Reader,

All right, I'll admit it. I am a sucker for a wounded hero, especially if he's a loner who tries to hide his battle scars. But I know that heroes of that type are bound to be trouble. A guy like that never follows the rules. He never does what you or the heroine wants him to do.

So when Donovan Barrett walked into my subconscious and refused to leave, I tried to ignore him. I did my best not to notice his pain or the way he fought to be tough and untouched.

Of course that didn't work. He had already won me over before I could even say no. So I allowed myself to daydream. Maybe he'd go away eventually.

No such luck. Instead, Anna Nowell stepped onto the stage. She was everything a lot of us would like to be. Strong, stubborn, and determined to win the key to her dreams while keeping her heart intact.

Now I had trouble. These two people were swirling around in my imagination together and neither of them wanted to get involved. They'd been hurt and needed some space. What neither of them *needed* was a romantic entanglement—especially since they both had other issues that made a relationship impossible. What neither of them *wanted* was to be attracted to the other one. And yet…

I could see the disaster approaching. A war was about to begin in my imagination. You'd think that it would be panic time, wouldn't you? Instead, I smiled. A story—a twisting, turning love story—was about to unfold, and I would have a front row seat…

I reached for a pen.

Best wishes and happy reading,

Myrna Mackenzie

"Lake Geneva is a bit of a magical place. There's a wonderful blend of yesterday and today that appeals to the romantic in me. The historic mansions that ring the lake, the stories of the wealthy Chicago families who retreated here after the Great Chicago fire, the beauty of the lake and the surrounding area, all combine to create a bit of a fairy tale setting. I find something new and unique and lovely every time I'm there."
—Myrna Mackenzie on *The Maid and the Millionaire*

Myrna Mackenzie, an award-winning author, was recently asked what, as a child, she had wanted to grow up to be. At first she was thrown by the question. At eight, she'd been too busy playing (and reading) to think about wanting to be anything except maybe…a princess? That was it! She'd wanted to be a princess. Years later, she hasn't yet made it into the royal ranks, but she's found that getting to make up stories on a day-to-day basis suits her perfectly, and is probably even more fulfilling than the princess lifestyle—even if she doesn't get to wear a tiara, silver slippers and a frothy pink dress.

Myrna lives in the Chicago area in her own little (compact) castle with her prince of a husband. They have two wonderful sons. She loves to hear from readers, and those who still love to daydream, so all other former princess wannabes (or anyone interested in contacting Myrna) can visit her online at www.myrnamackenzie.com

To my mother, Virginia Mackey, who
introduced me to the joy of reading.
Thanks, Mom. You're a great role model!

CHAPTER ONE

ANNA NOWELL stared at the telephone receiver she had just hung up. "Okay, don't panic," she told herself. "This is just a little bump in the road. Nothing to worry about."

But even as she whispered the words, she knew there was everything to worry about.

For two years she had been house-sitting Morning View Manor, the Lake Geneva, Wisconsin, mansion belonging to Donovan Barrett, Anna's wealthy employer and absentee owner. In all that time, Mr. Barrett had never once stepped foot on this beautiful lakefront property. With the exception of the gardeners who showed up to take care of the manicured grounds, Anna had lived here alone, playing at being lady of the manor.

Now Donovan Barrett was coming here. What was that going to mean for her?

A lump formed in Anna's throat. She knew what it meant. It meant that a house sitter was no longer necessary. She was going to lose her job.

She ran one hand over the rich golden oak of a nearby table and stroked the lush dusky-blue upholstery of a chair. Her days of pretending that she belonged here, that she had been born to privilege, were over, but not being able to pretend that this fantasy house was hers was the least of her worries.

All the time she had worked here, she had lived rent free and had been able to save a significant portion of her income. This job had paid better than most positions that were open to a woman without a university degree. Working here had not only allowed her to live a fantasy, but it had put her closer to being able to afford her dream of adopting a child.

Closer, but not close enough. She had saved some money but she could still not support another person for any significant length of time, not in the way she wanted to. And she would not bring an innocent baby into the poverty she had grown up with, the kind that had driven her father to abandon his family and had led to a painful and lonely existence for Anna. She would never subject a child to that kind of life. Not ever.

Her throat ached at the thought that she might have to postpone something she had wanted for so long, a child she could lavish with the kind of love she had never known. But truth was truth and she had grown used to meeting it head-on when she had to.

Anna swallowed. "Face it. Things have changed."

The woman on the phone had been Donovan Barrett's Chicago assistant. Tomorrow morning Mr. Barrett would move from his home base to his Lake Geneva estate.

It was less than a two-hour drive by car and yet that distance would be life-changing in so many ways.

Anna took a deep breath. She had been hired to do a job and she had done it. Donovan Barrett had needed a house sitter and now he wouldn't. It wasn't the man's fault that she wished he was staying in Chicago. Now she had to get the house ready for his arrival. She wasn't jobless yet.

"And I'm not beaten yet, either," she said, though her fear was still there. She knew little of Donovan Barrett other than what his assistant had reluctantly told her and what the area gossips had read on the Internet and shared. Born to wealth, he had been a renowned physician until the tragic accidental death of his young son. Dr. Barrett had given up his practice and become a recluse. In the eighteen months since his son's death, Donovan Barrett had become difficult. He disliked closeness; he disliked people. He craved darkness and quiet.

Anna loved light even though her upbringing had been filled with darkness. She loved conversation and music and company, perhaps because she'd had little of that in her life growing up.

She sounded like just the kind of person Mr. Barrett disliked, but…

"He'll need at least a skeleton crew," she told herself. "A cook?"

If she'd been in the mood to laugh, she would have laughed until tears rolled. She was a terrible cook.

"Okay, a maid, then." A house with ten bedrooms, six bathrooms, and a kitchen the size of a small city needed lots of cleaning.

Could she realize her dreams on a maid's pay?

Anna frowned. None of this worrying was getting her anywhere. The truth was that much of the house had been closed off for two years and now it had to be opened up, gotten ready. In less than twenty-four hours. If everything wasn't perfect, if the house didn't glow, if it didn't meet the exacting specifications that a man like Donovan Barrett was undoubtedly used to, she would appear incompetent. All hope of securing another position here would be gone. She would be jobless, homeless. She would have to dip into her savings until she found another place to work, and her hopes of becoming a mother…

Anna closed her eyes. She resisted the urge to smooth her palm over the empty place on her abdomen where other women could carry children and she took a deep, energizing breath. Self-pity wasn't allowed. It was pointless.

"Get a grip," she told herself, standing taller. "Get to work."

Maybe if she did a good job of preparing the house for its owner, she and Donovan Barrett might come to terms.

"Miracles can happen," she whispered as she set off to clean what needed cleaning, to take the dust covers off the furnishings in the rooms she had not spent much time in and to do her best to impress the man who held her fate and the fate of her unknown child in his hands.

She had to try to win the man's favor, and from what his assistant had implied, he wasn't a man particularly interested in doling out favors.

* * *

Donovan Barrett was on his way to a destiny he wasn't interested in. But he had his reasons for being in Lake Geneva, and it was here he intended to stay.

For now.

Having only visited once, he barely remembered the picturesque resort town set midway between the metropolitan areas of Chicago and Milwaukee. He did know that the lake was a summer retreat for many wealthy Chicago families and had been ever since the Civil War. His ex-wife, Cecily, was the one who had chosen the house. In retrospect, he supposed she'd wanted to get him away from his practice long enough for him to pay attention to his family, but it hadn't worked. He'd shown up once, to sign the closing papers, and had gone straight back to his patients. He'd never returned.

Driving past the shops now, he passed a long, low Frank Lloyd Wright-style building, the library, overlooking a grassy park, a beach and the east end of Geneva Lake. In the bay were small boats, sailboats with rainbow-colored sails, and a cruise ship with a paddlewheel and an open second deck filled with passengers. For a moment Donovan imagined how much Ben would have loved riding on the historic-looking vessel.

If only he'd brought his son here once. Just once. Ben had only been four years old when he died.

Donovan gripped the steering wheel and drove on toward Morning View Manor, cursing himself for all the ways he had failed his child, including not being able to save his life despite the fact that Donovan was a doctor. Rage rushed through him, and he remembered why he had come here.

Not to forget.

"That's never going to happen," he promised himself as he drove down the snaking road that led to his estate.

He would never forget Ben, but he couldn't be the man he'd been anymore. At least at Morning View he could leave his old life behind. He had to. He'd spent the first twelve months after Ben's death in a fog, but these past six months, well-meaning friends and colleagues had started to urge him to move on. Gently, at first, then more urgently. They didn't understand why he wasn't going back to his career as a successful physician or why he had to get away from a world that was a constant reminder of all he had lost.

He didn't want to hurt or disappoint those people anymore but he couldn't do what they wanted him to do.

Donovan fought the dark tide of anger that threatened to overtake him. There was no going back to his practice and there never would be. There wasn't going to be a slow slide past the pain back to meaningful relationships. His neglect had been the cause of his son's death, on more than one level. He had to live with that, but he'd do it on his own terms. He would give himself no opportunities to fail anyone else. Here, where people came to escape the reality of their worlds for brief weekends, where no one knew him, he would immerse himself in mindless diversions. He could disconnect without the sad, expectant looks from old friends.

"Here, I can pretend I never heard the words

'Hippocratic oath,' and no one will care." A grim glimmer of satisfaction greeted the thought, but Donovan had barely uttered the words when the house, a wide white building with a wall of arched windows and a fountain courtyard, came into view. Twin towers framed the house. There were five chimneys. Ten bedrooms, if he recalled the description. If he had brought Cecily and Ben here, she might have been happy. They might have stayed married. Ben wouldn't have been crossing that street at the same moment the car had gone hurtling down it.

Hot, dark agony threatened to overcome Donovan. He pulled up in front of the house with a squeal of tires and shoved his way out of the car.

Keep moving. Don't think. It was a mantra that had gotten him through many days. He angled toward the house, dug out his key and inserted it into the lock. Pulling back the wide double doors, he strode through the entrance, nearly colliding with a woman who was halfway up an old wooden ladder. An exceptionally tall ladder.

The ladder shook. Instinctively Donovan reached out. The woman swayed on her precarious perch, twisting so that her weight stopped the ominous tipping. His hand came down on the wooden frame two rungs beneath her feet.

"What in hell are you doing?" he bellowed.

He looked up into startled wide gray eyes.

"Oh, darn, I've made you angry. I didn't mean to start this way. There was just—the light needed changing." She held out the bulb. Her face was pale, and Donovan realized that he must be glowering. He recalled the explosive tone of his voice, made far worse by the disturbing thoughts he had been running from when he had opened the door.

As if he hadn't hurt enough people.

He took a step back. "I'm not angry," he said, beating back as much emotion as he could muster. He had gotten good at this skill lately. It had been necessary when friends arrived, but it was a skill he had hoped to abandon here at Morning View. He supposed he should have expected to run into someone here. He'd given his accountant free rein to make sure the place didn't fall into disrepair. He just hadn't remembered to ask the man who was working or what to expect.

It was too late to ask questions now. She was coming down the ladder. He watched as her denim-clad legs slid past him, the curve of her rear, the slope of her back. She stopped her descent when she was at eye level with him, and a brave smile lit her face. "You *are* angry," she said simply. "And why not? No doubt you weren't expecting to find someone right inside the doorway. Yet, here I am."

Yes, here she was. Donovan studied her. Her face was slightly round, slightly plump. Her hair was an unremarkable shade of brown and curved slightly, brushing her cheeks before ending just beneath her chin. She was, he supposed, a decidedly ordinary looking woman. Except for those gray eyes that seemed to stare a bit too intently, see a bit too much.

A sliver of awareness of himself as a man ran through

Donovan. Inappropriate, he thought. Meaningless. It had simply been a long time since he'd looked directly into the eyes of a woman. His reaction wasn't her fault. None of his problems were her fault.

"Who are you?" he asked, his voice more gentle this time.

Her smile grew, showing even teeth and the faint trace of a dimple in her right cheek. She pushed out one hand, the warmth of her body brushing his arm where it still rested on the frame of the ladder.

"Anna Nowell, your house sitter," she said.

He raised one brow. "I have a house sitter?"

A delicious and far from ordinary laugh slipped between her lips. "Didn't you know?"

"'Fraid not. This house and I don't have a history. My accountant handles the bills, and I let him."

"But you'll be living here now. You'll make a history. You'll need to hire more people in addition to me."

"In addition to you?" He raised a brow. She had said she was the house sitter, but now that he was here, he wouldn't need a sitter.

A faint hint of rose suffused her cheeks. "And in addition to Clyde," she added. She had a nice, low voice.

"Clyde?"

"Your gardener."

He gave a curt nod. "Any others I should know about?"

She shook her head. "Not yet. But you'll need a cook, probably a maid and a housekeeper at least."

More people. He wanted to be alone. In his penthouse in the city, he had gotten by with a cleaning service.

"I'd like to make do with a skeleton staff. I'm not used to having a lot of people around," he said.

Something flickered in her eyes. He wasn't sure what it was, but her smile faded and she looked suddenly vulnerable. Slowly she descended the last few steps of the ladder, placed the used lightbulb on one rung and looked up at him.

"I know everyone around here. I'll help you find what you need."

Somehow Donovan stopped himself from groaning. He didn't want to need anyone or anything.

"I'm sure my decision to come here caught you off guard," he said, suddenly realizing that must be true and that a job house-sitting must not pay particularly well. She probably needed the money. "I'll give you two weeks to find a new position and I'll provide a generous severance package."

Her look was so crestfallen he felt as if he'd hit her. Donovan looked to the side, but he refused to back down. The thought of he and this woman interacting on a day-to-day basis was…

"Impossible," he whispered.

"I beg your pardon?" Her voice was strained.

"Leave the ladder," he said. "I'll take care of it. And in the remaining time you're here, do not go climbing on it again. I don't want your neck broken."

I just want you gone. But he kept those words to himself as he strode past her and into the bowels of his house.

CHAPTER TWO

Two weeks. She only had two weeks to make herself indispensable to a man who just wanted to be left alone.

"So I'll become the invisible superwoman," she whispered as she laced her shoes, snatched up a clipboard and headed for the main part of the house.

For two years she had taken care of Morning View and done odd jobs on the side, but during all that time she had been the only inhabitant. Caring for this house, big as it was, hadn't been an involved process. Her needs were simple.

But Donovan Barrett was practically royalty, or at least as close to royalty as she was ever going to get. He was used to better, and she intended to give him the best.

For starters, he would need breakfast. Not exactly the job of either a house sitter, a caretaker, or a housekeeper, but for now there was no cook. While she wasn't handy with a stove, she could at least manage the basics.

She rushed down the stairs as quietly as she could just in case he was still sleeping, then picked up her pace when she heard movement, sliding into the kitchen and opening a cabinet.

For half a second, she thought about the fact that she and Donovan Barrett had slept in the same house last night. Different wings, but still more or less alone. A vision of that dark hair against a pillow hit her.

She slipped and clanged the pan in her hand against the stove.

"Stop it," she told herself. The man was miles above her in social class, wealth, education…everything, and anyway, she didn't get involved with men. She'd been foolish enough to trust her heart to at least three men, including her father. And all of them had failed her, hurt her, shredded her ego and danced on the pieces. How much more foolish to start daydreaming about someone so obviously not meant for her as her boss?

"Just make the coffee, toast and eggs, Nowell," she told herself. "Pour the orange juice." She did.

Minutes later she slid the omelet onto a Tiffany dinner plate, loaded the food upon a tray, and went in search of Donovan.

He was in the sunroom, staring out the window at the lake and the long green lawn sloping down to the water.

Anna cleared her throat.

When he turned, she tried not to notice how handsome he was. His black hair had a streak of white. His brown eyes held a touch of pain.

Stupid, she thought. Don't notice. Concentrate on staying. Adopting means jumping through hoops and having enough money. That's all that can matter. Don't try to analyze Donovan Barrett. Just get him to hire you.

"Breakfast," she said, setting the tray down on a small table flanked by white rattan chairs.

He raised one aristocratic brow. "I thought you were the house sitter, not the cook."

"House sitting involved cooking. For myself at least."

"But not for me." He gave her a long, assessing stare, and Anna felt awkward, transparent in her eagerness to please. She was thankful that she wasn't a blusher.

"You gave me two weeks, but my job of making sure the house is secured from intruders and that the pipes don't freeze in winter is essentially ended now that you're here. I'm just improvising during the interim. I can take the food away."

"No." He made a slashing movement with his hand. "You made it. It would be a shame to waste it. I'm…appreciative, but perhaps I *should* make arrangements for my meals."

Anna looked down at the slightly lopsided omelet. "It may be unattractive, but I promise you it's not poisonous."

She glanced up and thought she caught the ghost of a grin on his face. "I believe you," he said. "I'll risk it, but my point was that I didn't hire you to be a cook."

She wanted to blurt out that she could do that, but it would soon be obvious that she couldn't.

"I'll find someone," she said, her voice softer than she liked. Disappointment lanced though her. Stupid. She had known from the start that she couldn't be the cook, but with the advent of his hiring a cook, her employment options were narrowing.

"*I'll* find someone," he said. "Or at least my assistant in Chicago will. It's not your job to do extras." He stared at her, a frown forming between his eyes. Anna realized that she was twisting her hands nervously.

"Don't do that," he said. "I won't hurt you." His words were emphatic, louder than necessary.

Anna took a deep breath and raised her chin. "I never thought you would."

But he was still frowning. "I can pay you for the two weeks. You don't need to stay."

No, no, no, her mind screamed. *I can't go yet, because if I go, I can't make myself indispensable.*

She stared straight into his eyes. "I have experienced charity, Mr. Barrett, and I'll never go that route again unless I'm totally desperate. I'm not wealthy, but I'm not desperate. You said I could work for two more weeks, and I intend to work."

"It wouldn't be charity. It would be…a bonus for a job well done."

"It would be charity to me." Okay, she was pushing it here, being a bit too self-righteous when she could see that he was just trying to do the right thing. "I'd like to stay, and I intend to work at whatever tasks are necessary to the successful running of the household. I'll call your assistant and help her locate a cook."

"Ah yes, you know the town."

"I do. There's no place like it on earth, I don't believe." True, she had experienced painful moments here, but she had also found acceptance and friendship and roots. "Even though the population of Lake Geneva swells with tourists, especially on the weekends, there are really just over seven thousand people who live here year-round. They're wonderful, for the most part. I know them, and I promise you that I'll find someone talented for the position."

"I don't need much. I may not be at home all that often."

Anna was reminded once again that Donovan Barrett was from a different world. He was used to parties filled with wealthy guests, jewels, bright gowns, the scent of money, the aura of those who could have—or buy— anything they wanted.

Even babies.

The thought came unbidden. She fought her frown and kept her face impassive. It had been an unfair thought. Donovan couldn't be held responsible for her own barren state or her struggle to raise enough money to achieve her goals.

"I'll take care of everything," she promised.

She turned to go.

"Are you always this accommodating?" she heard him ask. She looked over her shoulder to see that he was frowning at his plate.

"Excuse me?"

"You've just volunteered to do extra work, and you haven't even asked for extra pay. Do you always let people take advantage of you this way?"

She didn't. It was just that she was concentrating so hard on staying here and getting paid.

"I never let people take advantage of me," she assured him, holding her head as regally as possible given the fact that she had egg yolk spilled on her apron.

His gaze locked with hers. "Good. I'm not known for my sensitive ways. I'm assuming you'll let me know if I'm too demanding an employer."

"I will." But the truth was that he couldn't demand enough of her during these next two weeks.

As for the money for extra work…

I'll cross that bridge if I manage to secure the position, she promised herself when she had left the room and returned to making a list of tasks.

She tried not to hope too hard about the future.

That kind of thing could only get a woman in trouble, and the last thing she wanted was to be in trouble with Donovan Barrett.

Donovan finished his breakfast and tried not to listen for the sound of Anna working elsewhere in the house. Even though the place was palatial, there was something about the woman that made him too aware of her. Maybe her tough I'm-a-survivor attitude, or the fact that she seemed insistent on staying and giving him his money's worth.

Or maybe the fact that now and then during that last conversation, he'd thought he saw a hint of vulnerability in her expression.

"Ridiculous," he told himself while wandering the house and getting the lay of the land. The rooms here were huge, with golden oak floors that clicked underfoot. But despite the sound of his footsteps, he could hear Anna in another room. It sounded as if she was moving furniture. He almost wanted to demand that she stop doing whatever she was doing. She was far too small to move anything heavy without hurting herself.

He clenched his hands at his side and managed to stop himself.

As he entered a long, gold and blue and white kitchen with a massive island in the center, he could hear the sound of thudding and pounding, followed by a metallic tap.

"What on earth is the woman doing?" he wondered, irritated that he was even wondering. Thudding? Pounding? That might mean messy repairs, wrestling with nails and splintering wood, getting puncture wounds, cuts and bruises.

When he heard the unmistakable sound of a hammer against wood and then a distant "ouch" he turned toward the sound and started up the stairs.

Her laughter followed, melodic feminine stuff that spun through his senses and made his blood heat.

Donovan halted. Obviously Anna wasn't hurt badly.

His concern turned to anger. Anger at himself. He had come here to disengage. He'd come here for mindless pleasure, to lose himself. Consorting with the hired help wasn't what he'd had in mind and it wasn't acceptable in the least. As the one holding the power and the money, he had to watch out for his employees and hold himself to a higher standard when dealing with them. Getting close wasn't smart and wasn't allowed.

She laughed again.

Donovan growled and turned back toward the sunroom. He pushed open the French doors and stepped onto the two-level deck, following the steps down to the lawn.

He needed to get away from Anna. Remembering her eyes, he winced. A man like him could easily hurt a woman with eyes like that.

Immediately, he realized how ridiculous his thoughts were. Just because he had hurt Cecily and Ben and others by his single-mindedness, he was starting to imagine that he was a danger to everyone. Which was idiotic. Anna Nowell wasn't even going to be here that long.

He breathed in the fresh scent of mown grass, summer blossoms and open water as he continued down the lawn toward the lake. To his left, most of the town was hidden by the curve of the shore, but on the East Coast was a huge and impressive white stone building.

Lost in his thoughts, he nearly walked into a man bending over a bed of red and yellow zinnias.

"Stone Manor," the man said.

"What?"

"That's what it's called. Stone Manor. The original owner made his fortune by buying up land on State Street after the Great Chicago Fire. I've lived here all my life but I'm still impressed whenever I look at it."

Donovan nodded. "Are you Clyde?" he asked.

The man smiled. "You must have talked to Anna."

His words sent Donovan looking over his shoulder. He could see Anna at an upstairs window. She must have finished whatever she had been doing. She was on a ladder again, dusting a high shelf.

He frowned. "I told her not to do that."

Clyde chuckled. "Telling Anna 'no' doesn't do much good. If she thinks something needs doing, she does it."

"I'm sure that's beyond the job of a house sitter."

"She wants to earn her way. You should hire her for something else."

It occurred to Donovan that his gardener was giving him advice…and that he was listening. He frowned at Clyde.

The man coughed. "Sorry. Anna's almost like a daughter. I feel protective. She needs steady, good paying work."

"I'll give her a recommendation."

"Why not keep her on here?"

Good question. He had just asked her to find him some workers. But what he had meant was find me some invisible workers, workers I won't know or care about. Not someone young with eyes that spoke to him and reminded him that he was still a man.

"I don't think that will be possible."

"That's too bad. Anna needs the money for her baby."

Donovan's breath caught and stuck in his throat. Pain lanced through him like a heated sword. "She has a child," he finally managed to say.

"She *wants* a child, and Anna will do almost anything to get one."

Donovan's chest felt tight. He was still having trouble breathing. An image of Anna begging a man to give her a child invaded his thoughts and he tried to ignore it. He fought to get back to the matter at hand.

"She needs work because she wants a child?"

"So she can *afford* to have one."

And she would risk having her heart broken, shattered, lacerated. The thoughts tumbled through Donovan's consciousness. Visions of Ben filled his head. Emotion assaulted him and he nearly stumbled.

Anna wanted a baby. She would do whatever she could to get a baby, which meant, in time, she would have one.

Being around her had just gotten more uncomfortable.

"Thank you," he said to Clyde as he turned and left. Donovan knew the man didn't know what he was being thanked for. He also knew Clyde would hate to discover what Donovan intended.

He veered toward the house, slammed through the door.

"Anna," he called, pounding up the stairs, directed by what he had seen through the window and by the sound of her humming. Her voice was low and husky.

That thought only fueled his determination. Right now they were going to end this. He would insist that she leave here.

Today.

CHAPTER THREE

ANNA was humming a favorite song. She had finished
dusting the top of the high bureau and was down on her
hands and knees, peering beneath the bed when she
heard Donovan bellow.

She raised her head quickly, bumping it on the metal
rail that held the mattress in place. Blinking back tears,
she was kneeling, rubbing her head when Donovan
came through the door.

"What are you doing?"

She gestured toward the bed. "Dust bunnies. You
have some. I need to get rid of them."

"You need to stop climbing on ladders."

She tried not to look guilty, but didn't succeed. "You
saw."

He gave her an accusing look.

"It was necessary," she argued.

"You could have fallen and hit your head. Killed
yourself."

The words hung between them. Anna knew he must
be thinking of his son.

"I'm always careful, and the ladder wasn't that high. Mr. Barrett, I need to do these things."

"Because you want to feel you're earning your money."

"Yes." She refused to say more.

"Clyde tells me that you want to have a baby, that you need the money to have one."

Anna blinked. "Clyde is a traitor." But she couldn't manage to sound mean. She loved Clyde like a father. "And anyway, he didn't mean…what it sounded like. I'm—" she didn't want to say it "—I'm trying to adopt a baby. I'm incapable of having my own. An accident long ago followed by surgery."

To her relief, while Donovan looked horrified, he didn't ask any questions.

But he was going to let her go. She could see it in his eyes. She knew it was because of the baby. Of course, it would hurt him to even think of children after his loss. She cared about that, she worried about that, but it didn't change her own situation.

"Please," she said. "I need the work. Let me stay. I won't mention my reasons, ever. I'll work harder than anyone you've ever known. I'll be the perfect employee. You'll get results and I'll be invisible."

She hated to beg, but Clyde was right. She needed the money and would do whatever was necessary to get it.

"Please, this job pays better than any I've ever held."

He raised his head. "I could get you work in Chicago. The pay would be good."

A deep pain went through her. She had been to Chicago once. With Brent, her fiancé, the man whose betrayal had hurt the worst. She didn't want to go back there and leave the life she had made behind. Lake Geneva was her home. She had friends who cared about her and would love her child. She was not alone.

"I don't want to leave. If I had to, I would, but I'm hoping I don't have to."

Her words were a plea.

Donovan blew out a breath. "All right, we'll try. It's obvious that you've taken good care of the house and that you're attentive to details. But when I'm home I need to be alone."

Anna gave him a grateful smile. "I'll be completely invisible."

One corner of his mouth lifted in disbelief.

"All right, I'll *try* to be invisible," she amended. Despite the hammering of her heart at Donovan's smile and his low "thank you, Anna," Anna told herself that she had gotten past the biggest hurdle.

But that was before the doorbell and the telephone started to ring over and over again. The neighborhood women had discovered that there was a new single male in town.

And all that stood between this reclusive man and them was Anna.

Donovan was in the dining room having lunch when he noticed the golden bowl in the middle of the table. Anna had obviously hired a talented cook. The food was delicious, but the bowl didn't contain food. It was filled to overflowing with envelopes.

He dragged it toward him and picked up the first one. Heavy cream-colored vellum, he held it in his hand and breathed in some expensive scent. He broke the seal.

You are cordially invited, it began.

He picked up the next and the next and the next. All invitations. All addressed to him.

He hadn't met a soul in town yet outside of Anna and Clyde and Linette, the cook. But obviously his neighbors knew that he was here. They were extending their hospitality.

For half a minute, he was tempted to pitch the whole batch in the garbage, but hadn't he come here for mindless escapism? And hadn't he been here for three days in which he'd done nothing but explore his immediate surroundings and try to ignore his—for lack of a better word—housekeeper?

That hadn't been working all that well. Donovan was constantly aware of Anna. That had to stop.

He looked at the invitations spread out before him, then picked up the first one. A family picnic, the pale script said.

"No." He placed it to one side.

The next was for a cocktail party at a neighboring mansion. "Yes." It went in another pile.

He was reaching for the third invitation when the doorbell rang. For the past couple of days Anna had been answering the door. He'd heard her light step as she moved from the stairs to the wooden floor to the marble entrance. But today she'd left a note that she had to run an errand, some piece from the hardware store that she needed to pick up.

Donovan blew out a breath and walked to the front door. He swung it back.

A woman stood on the doorstep holding a plant. When she saw him, she smiled, revealing teeth too perfect to be natural. She had blond hair that curled precisely at the curve of her jaw, flawless makeup, and she wore a tasteful gold rope at her throat that was echoed in a matching bracelet.

Donovan saw all these things in an instant, his physician's tendency to assess a situation kicking in. This woman was of his world. He had met hundreds like her over the years. Tanned, perfectly coiffed and dressed, and wearing just the right amount of scent. If she had come in a box, it would be an expensive one.

"Dana Wellinton," she said holding out one slender hand.

"Donovan Barrett," he answered automatically, shaking her hand.

"I'm your neighbor," she said. "Two lots over. I've been trying to reach you, but you haven't been home."

"I'm home now," he said, perfectly at ease. Dana Wellinton was, as he'd thought, like a copy of many other women he'd met in his lifetime. Her smile was practiced; her eyes were unreadable; her beauty was partially owed to money. She posed no threat whatsoever to his sanity.

Until she held out the plant. That's when Donovan saw that she was pregnant. A child was growing inside her, an innocent. He struggled to keep breathing normally.

It wasn't as if he hadn't seen many pregnant women

in his time. It was just that since Ben's death he hadn't been this close to one. The desire to go back in time to when Ben had still been waiting to arrive was almost overwhelming. He would do so many things differently if he could be where this woman was today.

Donovan forced himself to keep functioning. He took the plant, not looking down.

"Thank you. That's very nice of you."

"It's an orchid. Delicate. Exotic. I refused to leave it with your housekeeper."

He almost said that he didn't have a housekeeper, but for now he guessed he did.

"I'm sure Anna would have taken good care of it," he said.

"But then I wouldn't have had an excuse to meet you."

Out of the corner of his eye, he saw Anna's little white car turn into the driveway. He wondered if she had seen the woman's pregnancy or if the plant had hidden it from her as well.

Anna wanted a baby and she couldn't have one of her own. Being with pregnant women must be excruciating.

Ignoring his own reaction to the woman, he smiled at her and stepped to one side. "Come in," he said to her. "I'll ask Linette to get you something to drink. We'll sit in the sunroom."

Anna wouldn't come back there. She had, true to her promise to become invisible, been avoiding him completely. And once she was securely ensconced in another part of the house, he would politely escort his neighbor back to the door. Anna need never even see her.

* * *

Anna was pacing the floor wondering what she should do. Dana Wellinton had finally made it past the defenses she had erected and had wormed her way into Donovan's house.

The woman, who had divorced husband number two several months ago, was clearly angling for husband number three, and Donovan was a decent prospect.

"Doesn't she have any heart?" Anna muttered. Everyone had heard about Donovan's little boy and that he had still not recovered. Did Dana think her pregnancy would be a draw? A child was irreplaceable, not a toy. It was hard enough for Anna to be around the woman, knowing that Dana didn't appreciate the children she already had while other women would kill for even one baby, but for Donovan

"I can't leave him to deal with her alone." The woman had been terribly persistent the past two times she'd come here. Donovan had probably felt that he had to be polite.

If Anna had been here, Dana would have been sent away. Taking a deep breath, Anna scooped up the first piece of paper that came her way and headed for the sunroom.

"Mr. Barrett," she said, waiting in the doorway.

Both Donovan and Dana looked up. Dana's ever present smile seemed a bit forced. "Look, Anna, he was home this time," the woman said. "I guess I got lucky at last. But then I was bound to meet him sooner or later. We *are* neighbors and fellow homeowners."

What a not-so-subtle dig, Anna thought. Clearly the hired help was being put in her place.

"Of course," Anna said. "Mr. Barrett, I hope this isn't a bad time, but I have a rather important matter I need to speak to you about." She looked down at the blank piece of paper she held in her hand. "It's about the plumbing emergency in one of the guest baths. I'm afraid it's rather urgent, but if you're busy I'll try to tend to it myself." She added that last as an afterthought. Maybe Donovan wanted to visit with Dana.

"I'm sure you can handle it, dear," Dana agreed. "Donovan and I are just getting acquainted."

But Donovan rose to his feet. "I believe in being a hands-on owner," he told Dana. "After all, I just moved to Morning View, and I need to know all its quirks and charms. These old mansions are fascinating, aren't they?"

Dana blinked. "Yes, of course, they are, but—"

"Thank you for dropping by," Donovan said. "And for the housewarming gift. I'm sure that Clyde will find a special place in the house for the orchid."

He was slowly but subtly moving Dana toward the door. The woman clearly didn't want to leave but was helpless to stop Donovan, especially when he was smiling at her as if she fascinated him.

Anna wondered if Dana did fascinate him? Did he really believe the story about the plumbing? Maybe he would be upset with her when he discovered that she had fabricated it. Perhaps her attempts to shield him had been overreaching her authority. After all, she really was just the hired help. Dana, annoying though she was, came from old money. Her ancestors had been leaders of industry. She was of Donovan's world.

As Donovan escorted Dana to the door, said his goodbyes and let her out of the house, panic began to seep through Anna. Living here for two years really had addled her brain and made her start acting like the lady of the manor when she was only here because she had begged Donovan for work.

She heard his footsteps as he turned and started heading her way, and a thousand inadequate excuses began to flit through her head.

I shouldn't have done that. I'm just the housekeeper. Turning away his neighbors wasn't what he meant when he said he wanted to be alone. He meant you, you idiot. He didn't want to be bothered by people like you.

"Interesting list you have there," she heard him say just as she felt his warm breath over her shoulder. He had stepped onto the carpeting and come up behind her while she was berating herself.

Anna tried to take a deep breath and failed as she turned to face her employer and found herself inches away and staring up into his fierce eyes.

"Now tell me, Anna, just how many of my neighbors have you turned away from my door these past few days?"

CHAPTER FOUR

DONOVAN knew what the face of guilt looked like, and Anna had guilt written in those expressive gray eyes of hers. To her credit, she didn't try to look away, but worry lines creased her brow, marring her pretty, pale skin.

"A few," she admitted. "Not many, but then…even one would be too many. I've overstepped my boundaries, haven't I?"

Her voice was stricken, penitent. She was reminding him of their employer/employee standing when only a few moments ago he had been worrying about her reaction to his pregnant visitor. Was that the way a man viewed his hired help?

No, but still…he didn't want her to feel guilty. Guilt meant pain.

"Overstepped your boundaries? That depends," he said carefully. "Why did you turn them away?"

"You said you wanted to be alone."

"I *did* say that, didn't I?"

She blinked and stood up straighter. "You don't have to let me off the hook. I made a mistake, a ridiculous one.

I should have known that when you said you wanted to be alone, you weren't referring to your neighbors but merely to those of us who share living space with you."

He did his best not to think of the fact that he and Anna lived in the same house. It wouldn't be right to allow his mind to wander down the wrong roads, wondering where she slept, what she wore, what she did with her free time. Those things were private. She might work for him but…

"Those who work for me are no less deserving of respect than anyone else," he said.

The guilt left her face. She tilted her head, a concerned look in her eyes. "Yes, but you can't think of us in the same way as your neighbors. There has to be some distance."

The faintest of smiles lifted his lips. "Giving me lessons in how to be a boss, Anna?"

Her eyes opened wide. "No, of course not. But your neighbors do occupy a different sphere than your employees. I should have asked you before assuming you meant everyone when you said you wanted to be alone."

He shook his head. "I *did* mean everyone. I needed some time to get settled in."

"But now you're settled."

"Yes, I'm settled." At least he was as settled as he was going to get.

"So I'll stop screening your visitors."

A vision of Dana with her expectant, predatory look and her pregnant belly came to him. He wasn't ready for that, and he never would be. But he wouldn't hide behind Anna.

"I'll have to meet everyone eventually. Perhaps…"

She waited.

"Perhaps you could help me sort through all those invitations. I started, but I'd appreciate your expertise."

"You'd trust me to give you advice on which parties to go to and which ones to turn down?"

He gave her a long look. "I trust you more than I trust myself. You know much more about the locals than I do, so let's at least give it a try. If there was an invitation from Dana and I asked for your thoughts…?"

She tilted her chin up. "I would advise you to stay home and read a book."

"Because?"

Anna hesitated, not sure how much she should say.

"There must be a reason," Donovan prompted.

"She wants a husband. I don't think you're looking for a wife yet."

"Very tactful," he said.

She didn't deny that she had hedged, avoiding the real issue. But the truth, the real issue, was an elephant in a closet. And it was Donovan's elephant. She wouldn't intrude by bringing up the topic of his son.

Anna waited.

Donovan's expression was grim. "Thank you, but if you're going to help me, we need to be honest." It was something he'd found to be true as a physician, and though his doctoring days were over, the basic tenet still held.

"I don't want a child ever again," he said. "You don't have to shy away from the topic. I don't." He simply shied away from *memories* of Ben as much as he could.

"All right. No pregnant women or ones with children. Women on the prowl?"

He shrugged. "I'm not looking for a wife, but I know how to keep my distance without offending." Donovan realized that he was standing very close to Anna. *Not exactly keeping his distance.* But he wouldn't be so obvious as to step away now. At least that was his reasoning for why he remained right where he was. It had nothing to do with the way her fresh womanly scent made him want to step closer still.

"No family gatherings," he added, to hide his sudden physical awareness of her. "Does that help?"

"I think so. You're looking for adults-only events. There will be plenty of those. How many do you want to accept?"

None, he wanted to say. He was content just to be standing here talking to Anna with her forthright manner and no hidden agendas. When he didn't answer, she glanced up directly into his eyes, and he could tell that she was trying to read him.

Donovan stepped away. He didn't want anyone reading his mind, and if she knew what he'd been thinking…well, the point was moot. He would monitor his thoughts more carefully from now on.

A man like him? A woman like Anna?

Improbable. Disastrous. Impossible.

"I'll accept as many invitations as I can," he said suddenly.

The more he was away from home in the next two weeks, the better off both he and Anna would be.

* * *

Anna sat at the long oak table with the golden bowl in front of her and Donovan at her side. She picked up the first invitation. Cream vellum slid through her fingers, rich and crisp to the touch. The invitations to this event probably cost more than she spent in a month on all her living expenses.

Ah, well, she couldn't eat vellum. A smile lifted Anna's lips.

"What?" Donovan's low voice slid in, that voice that reminded her of forbidden subjects. And why not? Donovan might not be looking for a bride but that didn't mean he wasn't looking for a woman.

Anna frowned. Well, he would most likely find plenty of them at one of the events represented by the cards in the bowl. "I was just admiring the...tastefulness of this invitation," she said lamely.

Donovan raised one brow. "Looks pretty much like all the other ones to me."

"That's because you're a man," Anna said, even though he had merely spoken the truth. She certainly didn't intend to tell him that she'd been thinking about what he might be planning to do with the local women.

A twinge of something that felt a bit like regret slipped through her.

Not acceptable. What he did with the local socialites was his business, not hers. He was her boss. That was all. He had asked her to do a task.

She read the invitation. It was from Kendra Williams, who was rich, beautiful and available.

Anna stared at the card.

"What do you think?" Donovan asked. "Yes or no?"

Clenching the invitation just a bit too tightly, Anna took a deep breath and placed it on the table. "Yes," she said and let out her breath.

"You seemed uncertain."

"No, I'm not. This is exactly what you wanted."

Before he could ask her any more questions, she moved quickly to the task before her, sorting the invitations efficiently into two piles. She wondered what Donovan's neighbors would think if they knew that a mere housekeeper was passing judgment on their social affairs.

Her hand shook slightly.

"Anna?"

She turned to him. He was scowling. "This was probably a mistake. I'm sure this isn't in your job description. You don't have to do this if you'd rather not."

She'd rather not. It had been easy when she was turning *everyone* away. That hadn't been judgmental. This was, and it was uncomfortable. These people might someday be potential employers. Moreover, she knew who many of them were, but she didn't really know them. They traveled in different circles than she did. Who was she to warn Donovan away from their parties?

Anna turned to tell him that he was right, this task wasn't for her. And then she remembered how he'd looked when he mentioned his son. His life had, no doubt, been a horror these past eighteen months.

It was important that he reenter the world, but she

didn't want him to be exposed to needlessly difficult or painful situations.

"I'll just look over these one last time." She reached for the yes pile and started to pick up the top one. "Just to be sure these are the ones best suited to your purpose."

Donovan looked slightly amused. "What do you perceive as my purpose?"

Anna froze in midreach. "I'm…not sure. I guess I was assuming that you wanted to ease back into the social world, to take your place again."

Donovan stared at her hand, which was still suspended. He reached out and touched her, lowering her hand to rest on the table. His fingers brushed her skin as he took the card from her.

She jerked, and her body bumped up against his. When she looked up, Donovan was closer as he stared at her intently.

"Taking my place in the world? No, I'm afraid it's nothing so lofty."

His sudden scowl caught Anna by surprise and she breathed in. The scent of his aftershave filled her senses.

"A man has to fill his days. I'm looking for mindless entertainment. That's all." He said the words as though they were a warning, then nodded toward the pile of yeses. "I assume these fit that description?"

Anna could barely think with Donovan this close. She could almost feel the echo of his words through her body. Mindless entertainment? She felt particularly mindless at the moment. If she leaned closer to him…

She took a deep breath as she realized that her thoughts were headed down a path that could only bring heartache. And worse than that, disaster. A woman in her position couldn't afford to get a reputation as someone who entertained romantic or sensual thoughts about her employer. If she did that, she'd be...unemployable.

Her dreams would be dashed forever. Panic rushed through her. What was she doing? What was she thinking?

She jerked, her chair squeaking against the oak floor.

Immediately Donovan moved away. "I'm sorry," he said, tilting his head. "I didn't mean to crowd you. I'm afraid my social skills are somewhat out of commission. That's not a good reason for startling you."

She shook her head. "You didn't. I'm fine. Really. Yes, these will do."

Getting up quickly, she moved away from the table to the sideboard.

So, Donovan was in search of mindless pleasure. She understood the why. It was a mask for his pain, a way to fill the hole that had been left by the loss of his child.

The practice of masking pain behind meaningless activity was something Anna understood. She'd learned how to do that a long time ago. She'd also learned how to fantasize, she reminded herself. About this house. And now, it seemed, about Donovan.

Anna felt sick at the thought.

"Anna, are you sure you're all right?"

"Yes. Of course."

"You've rearranged the candlesticks three times."

Anna glanced down and saw that he was right. She

was fidgeting. Because she was afraid he might have noticed her reaction to him earlier.

"That's better," she said, stepping away from the candles. Her voice sounded calm enough. She even managed a shaky smile, but inside she was appalled that he'd noticed her distress. She prayed he was unaware of where her thoughts had been heading earlier.

Those kinds of thoughts had to stop right now. Letting Donovan know that she was attracted to him in even the smallest way would be a mistake. For both of them.

He would hate himself…and he would let her go.

And she? Well, it would be the worst kind of disaster for her. Fantasizing about a man from a different social class? Very unwise. Daydreaming about a man who couldn't bear to look at a child when she hoped for one every day? A one-way trip to heartache. She almost moaned at the thought.

"Anna."

"Yes?"

Taking an energizing breath and digging for courage and control, she smiled again as she looked up at Donovan. He had risen to his feet.

"I'm sorry I made you uncomfortable," he said again, his voice even and careful. "I touched you and I can see that I've upset you. That was unforgivable. You're in my employ. I want you to feel safe. You need to know that I would never intentionally do anything that might hurt you."

Anna shook her head. "I never thought that." And she realized that she hadn't. It was her own reaction that had alarmed her. "You didn't even want me to stay. Why would you think that I would be afraid of you? I'm the one who pushed the issue of my staying. I'm just—I'm leaving because…well, I suppose because we're done here. I have work to do."

Pasting on one more brilliant smile, she waited. Thank goodness the man would soon be entering the social whirl. No doubt once Donovan took his place alongside the elite of the area, her thoughts would settle down.

I'll lose my exclusive right to him, she thought. I'll learn to do this job the right way. I will *not* fantasize about what touching Donovan would be like.

Her smile nearly faltered. "Are we done?" she managed to ask, holding her trembling hands behind her back.

Donovan frowned, still watching her closely. "We're done," he said softly.

She made her escape. What a mess! What kind of housekeeper acted like she did? None. "And ones who did probably get fired," she told herself.

Well, that wasn't going to be her. She was going to be the best housekeeper Donovan had ever known.

Two days later Donovan woke to the scent of flowers and lemon and—

"Anna," he said out loud.

A groan nearly escaped him. It was unacceptable that he had already learned her scent. What was that about?

"Inactivity," he reasoned as he got dressed and left the room. Since he'd been here he'd spent too much time in the house with no one other than his employees, and Anna was simply the employee he saw the most.

And an exemplary one at that. That lemon scent…she was polishing the furniture. He supposed she did that on a regular basis. Everything shone. The hardwood floors gleamed. Not a speck of dust or a smudge was to be found, even though this was a very large house. There was a vase of yellow roses in a cut glass vase on a sideboard in the dining room. There were flowers in almost every room.

At the moment he could hear her humming in the distance. A clank sounded, followed by an "Ow!"

Donovan frowned. He moved off in the direction of the sounds and found her tucked half-beneath a bathroom sink, a red pipe wrench almost the length of her forearm in hand.

"Anna?"

She scooted out and sat up, just missing banging her head on the hard porcelain of the sink above her.

"Yes?" Her gray eyes were wide. There was a smudge on her cheek. She looked adorable.

Donovan frowned harder still. "What are you doing?"

She looked down at the pipe wrench. "Just repairing a small plumbing problem."

"That's not necessary."

"Yes, it is. The drain was a bit slow."

"I have money. There are people called plumbers who make their living fixing drains."

She shifted her gaze to the side. "I know that, but I can do it. I have a book from the library. I've read articles on the Internet. I'm capable of handling this."

"I see." And he did. He had given her two weeks, but she needed more time, more money. For the baby she wanted.

Donovan nearly winced at that. The smartest thing to do would be to send her away, but he had promised her two weeks, and it was becoming increasingly clear that she was going to push herself to her limits in those two weeks trying to prove to him that he should keep her. Were those dark circles of exhaustion beneath her eyes?

He wanted to swear, but he didn't. As a father he had learned to watch his tongue most of the time. The thought cut into him. He ignored it. He forced himself not to think about the fact that very soon Anna might be a mother learning all she needed to know about babies instead of plumbing.

"All right," he said suddenly.

She blinked. "All right?"

"You're hired. As my housekeeper, if you want the job." He turned away, not wanting to see the eagerness in her eyes. Those eyes could unwittingly tempt a man, even a man who didn't want to be tempted.

"Yes. Thank you," she said in a quiet, grateful voice that nearly killed him. She was grateful? He didn't deserve her gratitude. She was damn good at what she did. She would be good at a lot of things. Like motherhood.

The pipe wrench clinked against metal, and he turned back. "You're hired, on one condition."

She froze, those too-innocent, grateful eyes gazing up at him. For half a second he wanted to walk back, pick her up and kiss the gratitude from those fresh berry lips, to show her that, as always, he was a bit of a selfish jerk. He would not have her thinking he was more than he was.

"I appreciate your expertise and your work ethic. You're an exemplary employee, but hire someone for the tough jobs. I don't want you hurting yourself on my watch. That's an order, Anna." He practically growled the last few words.

For a minute her lips tightened and he almost slipped up and smiled. She didn't like orders? Good. That was something he could use to keep his own inappropriate thoughts of her at bay. If she resented him, there was no danger.

He forced himself to glower at her. "I mean it."

She smiled then.

Donovan sucked in a deep breath. "What?"

"You hired me," she said simply. "I won't let you regret it."

But he already did.

CHAPTER FIVE

"OKAY, the truth has finally hit. I'm still here and by all rights I should be ecstatic, bouncing off the walls," Anna muttered to herself two days later as she prepared to make Donovan's bed. She had a good job and she didn't have to worry about losing it.

Why was there still a part of her that was worried days after she'd been given what she wanted?

Donovan had shown no signs of changing his mind. Actually, she'd hardly seen him. He'd given her the task of RSVPing to the invitations and then he had closeted himself in the library and gym. Now and then she heard the clink of weights being lifted. She tried very hard not to think about what Donovan would look like, shirtless, his muscles gleaming from the exertion.

The thought brought her up short.

Maybe ideas like that are what's worrying you, she thought. Maybe you're afraid that your gratitude to Donovan goes beyond gratitude?

"Ridiculous. He's just easy to work for," she told herself.

That must be it. He trusted her to do what needed doing and other than insisting she call in experts for the big jobs, he didn't make any rules. What woman wouldn't be overjoyed to have those kinds of workplace conditions?

Anna took a deep breath, finished the bed and headed off to do the next job on the long list of tasks she had assigned herself to do. She had more than enough to keep her mind occupied and off of her employer.

Later, however, as she worked in the big open sunroom, running a cloth over the shutters, she heard a noise, a strangled curse and all thoughts of the task at hand slipped away. Donovan had been out on the deck, reading a newspaper. Now he was on his feet, the paper on the ground, pages flying away in the breeze.

But it wasn't the escaping pages of newsprint that had caused his curse, Anna saw. His face was turned to the side as he watched something in the distance. His jaw was rigid, his hands were tight fists at his side. He held his big body so still that he might have been a statue.

She looked in the direction of his gaze. A family was on the shore path that curved around the perimeter of the twenty-one-plus miles of Lake Geneva. The path was seldom crowded, but a family out enjoying a hike here wasn't all that unusual, and Anna realized that Donovan must have surely seen other families on his section of lake frontage. It probably was painful under the best of circumstances, but this had to be worse. These people were different.

The family trailed out over the narrow path, a young

girl of about ten leading the way, followed by her mother, but it was the man and the young boy bringing up the rear that caught Anna's attention, and, she was sure, had also brought Donovan to his feet.

The child was about five or six at the most. He was painfully frail, obviously ill, and his father had stopped to lean down and speak to him, the words so soft that they didn't carry, even through the open screens of the sunroom.

The boy, however, in the way boys had, replied without regard to any listeners who might be nearby.

"I'm mostly okay," he said, when it was clear that he wasn't. "I don't want to go back inside yet. It's been so long since I've been out."

His father looked worried, uncertain, as if he'd been pushed to his limits. When he turned, Anna could see the fatigue in his expression even from here. He reached down as if to pick up the boy and carry him.

A noise on the deck, the clatter of footsteps brought Anna's attention back to Donovan. He was coming inside, and as he did, he looked at her with a dark, unreadable expression. He had shut off his emotions.

"Let them sit on the deck," was all he said. "And…if they need a ride, I would appreciate it if you would find someone to take care of that as well."

Anna nodded. "I will." She knew what he meant. There were a limited number of public access points to the shore path, and Donovan's house wasn't that close to any of them. It would be difficult for the father to carry his child the necessary distance to get back to the nearest access point.

"You don't have to handle things yourself."

She shook her head. "I want to." And there was the difference between them. Pregnant women made her uncomfortable, but children? She adored being near them, whereas they brought shadows to Donovan's eyes.

"Thank you." Donovan's voice was terse, his brows drawn together in a frown. He moved into the house.

She headed for the path. An hour later she was back at work. The parents had been grateful. They'd tried to give her money when she pulled her car up in front of the opulent resort where they were staying. When the mother had taken the children inside, the father stayed behind to talk to Anna.

"Eric has had the best doctors money can buy, and he's getting better, but it's been a tough year. He only got out of the hospital recently and we wanted to give him a special day. Thank you for sharing your deck and giving us a lift."

Anna shrugged. "I'm only the messenger. My employer owns the deck and the car that brought you here."

"I'd like to send him a thank-you."

Anna took a deep breath. She was one hundred percent certain that Donovan wouldn't want her sharing his personal information with anyone.

"I promise I'll give him your thanks," she said. She wanted to say more, but what could she say? Donovan Barrett lost a child not much older than yours? He can't be near children? Your thank-you might only remind him that he used to help children just like Eric and now he can't do it anymore?

The man looked at her as if she weren't quite as nice

as he had at first thought, but she just shook her head. "He was concerned for your family, but he's a very private man."

The dawning of understanding slid into the man's eyes. "The curse of the wealthy," he said. And Anna supposed he was partially right. She reminded herself that there were many layers that separated her from her boss, and money was one of them.

When she came back into the house, she found a grim Donovan waiting for her. "I'm sorry about that," he said.

She blinked. "It was no problem."

"You're not here to run interference for me. At least not in this way."

"I'm the housekeeper. That covers a multitude of tasks." She tried to keep her tone light and pretend she hadn't noticed Donovan's discomfort regarding the boy.

"Your job doesn't cover this, and I shouldn't have asked you to handle this situation."

"Why not? We both know that while you hired me as a housekeeper, you were doing me a favor."

He crossed his arms, raising one brow. "You're a great housekeeper."

"I don't have a clue what housekeepers are supposed to do. Well, not much of one anyway."

He glanced around. "You must be doing things right. I don't see anything wrong."

"I'm just playing things by ear." And sometimes doing it badly. She was pretty sure that most housekeepers weren't as frank with their employers as she was. "Maybe I should try wearing a uniform."

A trace of amusement crossed Donovan's lips. "If it makes you feel more official, go right ahead, but I'm fine with you as you are." He looked at her then, starting at her T-shirt and traveling down her jeans to her tennis shoes, as if he hadn't really noticed what she wore most of the time.

Awareness ripped through Anna, and her T-shirt suddenly felt too tight. She glanced down at the Live For Today emblazoned across her chest in blazing hot-pink.

"This is probably not very professional," she admitted.

But when she looked up and saw that the shadows had flown from his eyes, her concern about her clothing fled.

"I like the sentiment," he said. "It suits you." He started to turn away, then turned back, his lips tight.

"They're all right?"

She didn't have to ask who "they" were. "Yes," she said, "and the little boy's health is improving. His father sends his thanks."

"He should have been thanking *you*."

"He did."

"Good." Donovan's voice was clipped. He was studying her intently. Anna felt too aware of herself in a way she never had before.

Somewhere in the house, a clock chimed softly. Six o'clock. Like Cinderella startled by the knowledge that she had to run, Anna realized that she had been staring into her boss's eyes for too long. She also realized something else.

"You're due at the Williams's party in an hour."

Donovan frowned and swore.

Anna blinked. Donovan never swore.

"I'm sorry," he said. "I'd forgotten about the party."

She shook her head, confused. "You don't sound as if you really want to go."

He looked into her eyes and her stomach flipped over. Darn this man for making her suddenly wake up to her own femininity. She didn't want a man. She certainly couldn't want this man. She had heart-deep dreams that clashed with everything Donovan was and would be, and even if that weren't true…

She ran her fingers purposely across the rip in the thigh of her jeans. She wasn't wearing them to be fashionable but because she couldn't afford to buy new ones and she hadn't had time to patch these yet. The women Donovan would spend his time with tonight would never be in that kind of situation. Someday she might be cleaning the house of one of those ladies.

Donovan was studying her carefully. She prayed that he couldn't read her thoughts or know how much he affected her.

"I want to go to the party," he said. "It's why I came here. To play."

Anna nodded. "Then you'd better go play. You'd better get ready. I'll just get back to what I was doing."

Slowly, he shook his head. "No."

"No?" She frowned, not sure what he meant.

"It's six o'clock. Go home, Anna."

But they both knew that she lived here. She would be here when he left and she would be here when he got back.

And in the hours in between? she asked herself.

She would *not* think about what he was doing. Not at all. She most certainly would not allow herself to do anything so foolish.

So she waited, pretending to be up in her room reading but really just trying not to think about him getting ready, forcing herself not to go say goodbye. Only when he was out the door did she allow herself a quick peek out the window. He was dressed in black and white, his broad back impressive as he walked toward his car.

Most of the functions he had been invited to were informal due to the nature of the resort atmosphere of this area, but this party had been black tie. His suit was immaculate. He looked good in black. Even the starkness of the material couldn't hide the fact that he was muscled and fit.

"The women are going to love you, Donovan Barrett," Anna whispered.

And then, cursing herself for even thinking such a thought, Anna marched downstairs, picked up her list of things to do and started working again. Employee or not, she was not going to allow a man to dictate how she spent her free time.

Not even a man who was her boss.

Not even a man with eyes that made her consider things that could never be.

Or a man whose pain made her ache to help him, when she knew that she was the last person on earth who could do that.

"I'm not going to think of you at all tonight, Mr. Barrett," she muttered to herself as she scrubbed a spot on the wall for the third time.

* * *

The Williams mansion was aglow with what looked to be a thousand lights. Donovan parked his car and strolled up to the door, bracing himself for the night ahead.

He nodded to the black-clad servant who opened the door and led him to the back of the house where the sounds of chatter and clinking glasses could be heard.

As he entered the huge room filled with men in stark black and white, and women with perfect hair, perfectly made up faces and teeth so straight and immaculately white that it appeared as if a dentist magician had been at work here, Donovan relaxed slightly.

This was a world he knew, one he had inhabited in what already seemed like another lifetime.

He accepted a glass of champagne from a white-uniformed servant and moved toward the mass of guests.

A woman dressed in pale peach with auburn hair separated herself from the masses and moved toward him, holding out her hand. She looked at him appreciatively. It was a look he recognized. "You must be Donovan."

He tilted his head in acquiescence. "Are you Kendra Williams?" Although there was no real question of who she was. Besides the obvious fact that she was the one greeting him, there was the fact that Anna had told him that his hostess was a petite, dark-haired, beautiful green-eyed woman. Heir to this house, Mannion Way, and all of her family's fortune, she had been divorced for three years.

The woman tilted her head in a queenlike manner. "Yes, I'm Kendra, and I must say that getting a magnificent man like you here was a coup. Absolutely everyone wants you. Thank you for choosing me first."

The room behind her had gone amazingly silent, so this comment was heard by all. The silence didn't surprise Donovan. He was a stranger, a new toy. The old toys needed to know if he would fit in.

He laughed. "Well, I've taken some time to acclimate, but I'm enjoying the opportunity to finally meet my neighbors. Thank you for inviting me. Great old house. Superb wine. Wonderful company." Which said absolutely nothing but did the trick. The other potential hosts and hostesses had not been slighted but Kendra had not been put in her place, either.

The evening began in earnest, a steady din of meaningless chat and drinks and food that could drown out more serious thought.

It was what he had come for, Donovan thought. He would fit in here and pass the time. He smiled at those who smiled at him, ignoring the speculative glances of the women, married and otherwise, who were giving him obvious come-to-my-bedroom-later glances. When the conversation threatened to get personal he sidestepped and steered it back into more mundane topics about local tourism, the stock market and real estate.

He'd been raised to this kind of talk. He could rattle off such conversations in his sleep and it almost seemed as if that was just what he was doing. His mind began to go numb after a few minutes, but then that was a good thing. It was what he wanted. If, when a woman named Olivia Simms engaged him in a conversation about pier parties, he kept noting that her hands looked as if they had never been used for work, that was a glitch. If that thought was followed by a vision of Anna's pretty but useful hands, sending heat spiraling through him, it was a mistake, and an unkind one at that. Olivia was who and what she was, and he was of the same cloth. He shifted away from such thoughts.

Only once did he falter. To his right, he heard a small male exclamation, a female shriek and the crunching of glass beneath something heavy.

He turned to see Kendra, her dark eyebrows drawn together, her face a mask of fury, reprimanding a male servant who appeared to have dropped a glass, sloshing wine on a female guest. The woman was demanding reparation and the flustered servant was apologizing profusely.

Kendra's voice was low, but Donovan had excellent hearing, so he didn't miss her swift dismissal of the man despite his attempts to offer to pay for the guest's dry cleaning.

Other guests turned to look, then turned back to their conversations as if this wasn't an unusual occurrence.

The woman Donovan was talking to sighed. "Poor man," she said. "That dress was a Versace. He could never afford what it would cost to replace it." She took a sip of her own drink and placed her hand on Donovan's arm. "Now what were we discussing?"

"Something riveting, I'm sure," Donovan assured her as he made an effort to bring a smooth, controlled end to the conversation. Less than two minutes later he smiled at her. "Please accept my apologies, but I'm afraid I have to leave. I have an early appointment."

"So suddenly? It must be important," she said with a raised eyebrow.

"It is," he admitted, but he didn't want to think what that appointment was going to be. Recounting the evening to Anna?

No, he wouldn't do that. But he really did have to go. The memory of Kendra firing her servant nagged at him. Anger was churning in his gut. Smiling was no longer an option.

He excused himself to Kendra, saying all the right and polite things, bid the other guests goodbye, then hurried out the door.

Breathing in the clean fresh air, he tried to clear his mind, hoping for luck. He fought against analyzing what he planned to do next.

Sprinting beyond the area where the guests' cars were parked, Donovan found a few older and considerably less sleek automobiles. He hoped his guess was right and that he had timed things properly and would find the person he was seeking. If he missed his chance, he would have to do detective work, and his most likely source of information was Anna. He didn't want to talk to her about this.

Glancing around, Donovan made a quick visual inspection of the area. There were only a few dim lights out here. The sky was clouded and moonless. Visibility was limited.

No luck.

He waited for his vision to adjust to the darkness, listening for the sound of a car door or an engine. Finally, he began to make out shapes more clearly and this time he saw what he had missed. A man sat on a rock next to a rather battered pickup truck. His head was in his hands.

Donovan approached him.

The man looked up, wary.

"I just came from the party," Donovan said, gesturing toward the house.

The man faltered, looked scared. "I didn't mean to make such a stupid mistake. I looked away just for a minute and…well, it was clumsiness, pure and simple."

Donovan ignored him. "I'm looking for help at my house. Can you use some work?"

The man's eyes lit up, but he didn't jump. "Doing what?"

Donovan almost smiled. "Nothing illegal," he promised, although he didn't have a clue what he was hiring the man for. He already had a gardener. "Do you know anything about plumbing?"

The man looked despondent. "Not really."

"Electrical work?"

"Only a little bit."

Donovan frowned. "Can you lift things?"

The man smiled. "Sure. I'm strong."

"Good. Show up at Morning View Manor the day after tomorrow at 9:00 a.m. sharp."

"What will I be doing?"

"Grunt work. Greeting guests. Assisting my housekeeper. A little bit of everything." Donovan made it up as he went along.

"All right, yes. Thank you, Mr…."

"Barrett. And there's no need to thank me. Just do a good job."

The man nodded. Donovan wanted to stipulate one more thing. *Don't tell Anna how I hired you. She already thinks I'm better than I really am or ever was.* But that would have been too bizarre, even more bizarre than the fact that he had rushed after the man to offer him work.

What was that about?

But Donovan knew. When Kendra had been firing the man, Donovan had only been able to think about how he would have felt if it had been Anna who had been called on the carpet for spilling a drink on a guest's dress. And there was something about Anna that made him want to be a better man.

"You're an idiot, Barrett," he told himself as he headed home.

That was all right. He could deal with being an idiot. He just couldn't deal with guilt. His life had been filled with guilt these past few years, and Anna made him feel even more guilty.

He had the awful feeling that he was going to somehow hurt her, and that there was nothing he could do to stop that.

What a ridiculous thought. He was Anna's boss, nothing more. Nor would he ever be more. Thank goodness.

CHAPTER SIX

ANNA woke that morning, groggy. She had done just what she'd planned to do the night before, finished her work and then gone to bed.

Yet she had been perfectly aware that Donovan had returned home at two in the morning. The party must have been a hit.

That was good. It made it that much easier to remind herself that Donovan was her boss, a man born to mingle with the rich and famous. Now she could get back to her life and think only of her child, her dream.

At least, those were her thoughts in the middle of the night. But in the morning her head ached and she was glad that this was her day off. Still, she took the time to tell Linette, the cook, to make something that would keep since Donovan would most likely be late to breakfast.

Anna prepared to plan her day, fighting the headache that had resulted from her lack of sleep. It was obvious that the day wasn't going to be one of her finest. And that was before the phone rang, its piercing and insistent din sending her flying to answer it.

"Barrett residence."

"Anna, it's me," her friend Bridget said. Bridget worked in one of the gift shops in town. "Did you hear what went on last night? Did your Mr. Barrett tell you?"

The possibilities immediately ran through Anna's head. Visions of Donovan with a beautiful woman, with several women draped over his arms or pressing up against his chest came to mind. The possibility that he might have slept with one of them presented itself.

Anna closed her eyes and ran a hand over her forehead. "I haven't seen him yet."

"Good. I get to do the honors then," Bridget said as she launched into a tale of how Kendra Williams had fired John Jessup on the spot at the party last night and then Donovan had hired him.

"What do you think that's about?" Bridget asked.

Anna tried not to feel relief. Her mind was suddenly a tornado of speculation, but as good a friend as Bridget was, Anna wasn't going to gossip about Donovan with her. "Donovan probably just needed some help, and John was there."

"But he ruined Meredith Talbott's dress. She's probably spitting mad at him."

"That probably won't matter. John won't be interacting with any guests. Donovan doesn't entertain."

Bridget snorted. "He will. Wait and see. Now that they've seen him, the women will be rushing your house. I've already heard one or two in here whispering about his broad shoulders. They'll want to see what else he has to offer. Like property. Sooner or later, he'll have to open the doors of Morning View and let them in."

And she would be the one serving the drinks this time, Anna knew, while the local heiresses and wealthy divorcées did their best to entice her boss to their beds.

"Then I'd better make sure the house is in top shape," she told her friend just before she hung up the phone. After all, who was she to criticize the women of the town for wanting Donovan? He was an attractive and intelligent man.

"And a kind man," she reminded herself, thinking of how he had hired John.

What's more, just because Donovan had said that he didn't want to marry didn't mean that he might not change his mind. Lots of the women he was meeting now would be willing to give up motherhood to have him. Maybe he could be happy again.

Despite the fact that something dark and unacceptable ran through her at the thought of him marrying, she stopped herself cold. Because she did hope that he could be happy again. She wondered how he felt about last night.

But of course, she couldn't ask.

Donovan braced his feet on the floor, lay back and lifted the weighted bar, pressing upward slowly, exhaling, then inhaling as he lowered the bar to his chest. His muscles tightened, his body strained as he tried to push himself harder and concentrate only on what he was doing.

A short time later he sat up, admitting that while the exercise might be good for his body it wasn't doing anything to quell his restlessness. Furthermore, the incidents of the last evening had left a bad taste in his mouth. He needed fresh air.

After taking a quick shower and dressing, Donovan fully intended to head for the lake. He might even take a walk partway down the shore path. For half a second he thought of the family Anna had driven home, the little boy. Then, shaking his head, he headed toward the door.

A feminine giggle stopped him cold.

An unknown feminine giggle. It wasn't Anna's. He knew Anna's voice. Sometimes he dreamed Anna's voice.

Donovan turned. A woman several years Anna's senior was standing on the stairs looking down at him.

Almost immediately Anna appeared, a frown on her face. "I'm sorry, Donovan. Some friends have dropped by. We didn't mean to disturb you."

"You didn't. And…"

She waited.

He shrugged. "It's your day off. You should feel free to have your friends over."

"Oh, I like him," the other woman said. "The John Jessup thing wasn't just a fluke."

Donovan frowned, not understanding.

"The man you hired last night," Anna explained. "Didn't he tell you his name?"

Donovan smiled sheepishly. "I didn't ask."

A look of concern came over Anna's face. "You didn't even ask? You hired him without knowing anything about him?"

"I knew he needed a job."

And he had known something else. He'd known that he wouldn't have wanted Anna to face the humiliation of being fired because she had made a simple mistake.

Right now she was looking at him with soft eyes. "Did you eat breakfast?"

"Not yet."

"Oh, good," the other woman said. "We have food. Anna always feeds us when we come over. Maybe you'd like to join us."

Anna was looking horrified. "Nan, he's got better things to do with his time than eat with us."

"No, I don't." The words surprised even him.

"Well, then," Nan said. "Anna?"

Donovan waited. He should let her off the hook, claim to have other plans. Yet he didn't. He tried not to wonder why.

Anna stared at Donovan and bit her lip. Already the day was getting away from her. Nan and Paula had both shown up unannounced, probably driven here by Bridget's tales. She adored both of them. Together with Bridget, they had saved her sanity when her sanity had needed saving, and they never questioned her baby plans even though she knew they wanted to. But there was no question in her mind that they were here to check out Donovan.

She didn't want anyone trying to decide if he was good or bad. Hadn't he gone through enough?

"I'm not sure this is a good idea," she said.

"Of course," he said, studying her intently. "It's your day off. These are your friends."

And he was her boss, she reminded herself.

"I'm not worried that you're going to fire me because of anything that goes on today. It's not that you're intruding. It's just…"

She paused, flustered, her hands gesturing as she tried to find the right words.

He grinned. "It's okay, Anna. I'm gone." He turned to head back into the other part of the house.

"Don't pay any attention to Anna, Mr. Barrett. I know what the problem is. Anna's just afraid we'll interrogate you," Nan said with a laugh.

Donovan turned and raised a brow, studying Anna.

She squirmed and gave Nan a dirty look. "Nan's a sweetheart but she's right. She and Paula will ask you all kinds of questions. You're a bit of a celebrity, especially after the John Jessup thing."

He swore. "I didn't want you to know about that."

Anna stopped fidgeting. "Why not?"

"Because it makes me look like I was doing something noble. I wasn't. It was an impulse, a knee-jerk reaction."

"Which won't win you any points with Kendra Williams, either," Nan offered.

Anna gave her a warning look.

But Donovan laughed. "You might be right, but that's okay. I didn't come to Lake Geneva to earn points with anyone. Opinions don't matter to me. And I'm not looking for a woman or a relationship, so that's not a problem."

Nan looked a bit surprised. "You're not even interested in the women who'd like to get you in bed?"

"Nan!" Anna's voice actually squeaked.

"Well they are," her friend said. "People are talking."

Anna scowled at Nan. "*We're* not talking."

She felt Donovan's light touch on the small of her back. "It's all right, Anna. Newcomers are fair game for gossip. It's to be expected. And no, Nan, I'm not in the market for a woman of any variety right now."

Nan shook her head and shrugged. "You are definitely not a typical man, Mr. Barrett."

Anna smiled at her friend's look of disbelief. Nan was a large, curvy and very earthy woman. She liked her pleasures and thought everyone else should feel the same. Anna was a constant trial to her.

"Come have lunch," Anna told Donovan. Now that he had made his complete indifference to her as a woman clear and she had shown no concern about his indifference, Nan and Paula wouldn't worry and they would most likely behave themselves. Besides, she knew that if Donovan left he would end up kicking around the house avoiding his demons. Nan and Paula weren't exactly angels, but they weren't demons most of the time, either. They just watched their friends' backs, as she did.

Anna wondered who watched Donovan's back, but then she already knew the answer to that, didn't she? No one did.

Glancing at him, she realized that she must have been silent too long. Donovan was giving her that speculative, I-can-see-through-you look that always made her too self-conscious. She would just bet that his former patients couldn't hide anything from him. Remembering his reaction to the little boy on the shore path and his reaction to John Jessup, she had no doubt that he had been a wonderful, caring doctor.

But he didn't want that anymore. And he was waiting for her to take the lead now. He wouldn't appreciate her delving into his business.

"This way," she said softly and nodded toward the stairs just as if this wasn't his house and he didn't know where she stayed.

They all turned toward Anna's room. Nan led the way and Donovan brought up the rear.

Anna tried not to feel self-conscious; it was all but impossible. She was wearing her usual faded jeans, and they fit a bit snugly over her butt. The realization that Donovan couldn't help but end up staring at that part of her anatomy whether he wanted to or not made her heart start to do terribly acrobatic things she wasn't used to. She wanted to rush up the stairs and end the sensation, but she resisted the urge, trying not to let her hips sway. He already had Dana Wellinton swinging her belly in his face. She didn't want him to think she was trying to get his attention, too.

When she got to the top of the stairs, she turned to the left where her room was located. Like all the rooms at Morning View, it was large and airy. She had, of course, left the basics of the room alone, but she had tried to make it her own.

The room was done in jade and white, and she had set out touches of sunflower gold here and there. There was a vase she'd gotten at a garage sale, a thrift shop scarf she'd draped halfway across the mirror. The room had always looked cozy to her in the past, but today, despite the table she and Paula and Nan had dragged in for their lunch, the bed seemed enormous.

Anna did her best to ignore it.

"You need a bigger room," Donovan said.

She turned and saw that he was staring at the bed, too.

Nan laughed, and Paula, who was crossing the room to meet them, joined in.

"I love this room," Anna insisted as she hurriedly introduced Paula to Donovan.

"I have others," he argued.

"I'm well aware of every room in the house," she answered, a bit haughtily.

Donovan's lips turned up slightly. "Of course. You're the housekeeper."

Paula hooted at that. "Anna, I can't believe you're playing housekeeper. She was always the poet in school," she explained to Donovan.

He raised a brow. "A poet. And I have you washing windows?"

Anna frowned at Paula and raised her chin when she turned back to Donovan. "I happen to love washing windows."

He grinned at that. "Well then, I'm happy to be providing you with an activity you love."

For half a second, Anna thought about Dana and Kendra and half a dozen other socialites who would adore doing something they loved with Donovan. That activity certainly wouldn't be washing windows. Heat filled her and she did her best to tamp it down.

"Thank you," she told Donovan. "You know I appreciate the work."

And that was all there was to say. He knew. She had all but begged for this job. So, Anna trotted off to get an extra chair. When Donovan started to get up to help her, she gave him a quelling look.

"It's my day off. I get to call the shots."

Apparently the man didn't hear well. He followed her and was there beside her when she found an armchair and started to wrestle it down the hall. Immediately he took hold of the chair, stopping her momentum and bracing the weight against his body. "I'm the guest today, and I was taught that a hostess didn't tell a guest no. That's heavy. Give it to me."

Anna started to argue, but only the width of the chair was between them. His large hand was braced near her own slender one. The comparison made her feel feminine, a sensation she wasn't used to. His nearness made it difficult to breathe…or think…or know where to look without looking into his eyes or staring at his mouth. And arguing would prolong the discomfiting proximity. At least that was what she told herself.

In the end, she let him take the chair from her and walked beside him. Was this how it had been with his wife? she wondered and then was immediately appalled.

As soon as she was able, she slipped away to the kitchen to get their lunch.

"Oh, Linette is a dream," Paula was declaring as

Anna came in with the food. "You certainly know how to hire the best," she told Donovan.

"Anna," was all he said, and Nan nodded.

"Anna knows who's the best at everything around here," she agreed.

Donovan's eyes turned brighter. "You should give tours."

"I have," Anna admitted.

"Sounds enjoyable."

"Yes, but this pays better."

She immediately regretted her comment, because she knew what would follow. She looked at her friends, but it was too late.

"Anna really wants a baby, and no one works harder than she does to achieve her goals," Paula said.

Immediately a silence fell into the room. Anna knew that Donovan had been caught off guard. His eyes turned suddenly dark.

"Paula," Anna said softly, but Donovan was already squaring those broad shoulders and turning toward Paula and Nan.

"And how about you? Are you like Anna? Have you lived in Lake Geneva all your life?"

"All," Nan agreed.

"Most of it," Paula countered. She looked a bit uncomfortable and when Anna looked at her, she mouthed an "I'm sorry."

Anna nodded, but Donovan had gone on to his next question, asking Nan and Paula about their favorite places in the area. By the time the two of them got ready to leave, they had scribbled down a list of "must sees" for Donovan and pressed the pieces of paper into his hands.

"He's gorgeous," Nan said as Anna saw her out the door.

"He's charming," Paula agreed.

"Be careful," they said together.

"I thought you liked him," Anna said, wide-eyed.

"We do," Nan said. "That's the problem. What woman wouldn't like him? And you're sharing the same space with him. When he takes a shower don't you just…imagine him?"

"Oh, yes," Paula agreed. "That man is hot. How could you not imagine him naked?"

Anna suddenly felt a bit faint. She had tried her best *not* to think of Donovan that way. "Donovan is my employer," she emphasized. "I clean his house. I wash his walls. He's appeared in the society pages. He goes to parties at the local mansions."

She stared at her friends.

"You're right," Nan said. "He makes it easy to forget that he's got money and connections and that he gets invited to the best parties."

She could almost forget, Anna thought when her friends had gone, if his upcoming evenings and days weren't booked with events at the houses of people she would never socialize with in her lifetime.

When she turned to go back upstairs, Donovan was waiting at the bottom, his arms crossed as he leaned on the wall in a casual pose.

Anna took a deep breath.

"Your friends are very nice," he told her.

She nodded.

"They're worried about you," he added.

Her gaze grew wary. "Sometimes they worry, but they forget I can take care of myself."

"Nan told me to be nice to you."

"What? When?" Anna frowned, her mouth open.

"When you went to get the food."

"I'm sorry. They've both known me a long time, and they're some of my closest friends, but they had no right to say something like that."

He shook his head. "They did. They know how much you want a child. They know that we spend our nights alone in this house."

"Mr. Barrett," she stammered.

"Donovan," he said. "We've moved beyond formalities. Call me Donovan."

Anna swallowed nervously. "Donovan, don't worry. I would never even consider that you would think of me that way. I—"

He pushed off the wall and stepped close to her. Pushing one finger beneath her chin, he bent and touched his lips to hers.

Her eyes fluttered shut. Her breath caught. She fought not to react, but his lips were so warm, his touch so compelling, she couldn't help tipping her head and kissing him back.

"Let's have honesty between us," he said. "I do desire you and I have from the beginning, wrong though that may be."

If she were totally honest she would say that she desired him, too, but that would leave her too vulnerable. She'd been that before, and she couldn't do it again.

"Don't," she said.

He let her go. "I won't. I just wanted you to be aware that your friends were right to be concerned. There's something about you…something vibrant. You're an incredibly desirable woman, Anna. I should hire someone else to be here at night."

"That would be foolish. I trust you. And what would you tell the person they were being hired for?"

He smiled at that. "You're right. There's no need. I would never hurt you, and touching you would hurt you."

She knew why. Because there could be no future between someone like him and someone like her.

"I shouldn't have invited you to lunch with me and my friends. We're not the same."

He shook his head. "I liked them. They say what they mean. They wouldn't let me get away with anything."

"You're right about that," she said with a laugh. "Paula and Nan are direct."

"And you?" he asked.

She stared up into his eyes. "I'm direct, too. You're an amazingly attractive man, and I've wanted to know what kissing you would be like."

His eyes darkened. His gaze honed in on her lips. "What was it like?"

Anna tried to keep breathing normally. She touched her lips. "It was something I enjoyed far too much."

Donovan groaned.

She held up a hand. "But not only do you and I come from different social classes, we want different things. We could never meet halfway and I wouldn't do anything to risk my job here." She didn't repeat her desire to have a baby, but she didn't have to.

"You want a man who'll give you a child," he agreed.

"I *need* a child, not a man," she said.

Donovan brushed his knuckles across her cheek. "Be careful what you wish for, Anna," he said. "I don't want you to get hurt."

"I'm very careful," she said, even though she wished she could be more careful with him.

He smiled then, faintly, and stepped away. "Go enjoy the rest of your day off. Maybe you should take an extra day off, too, since so much of this one is gone."

"Thank you, but I'll be back at work tomorrow."

He turned to go and she noticed the pieces of paper sticking out of his pocket. Nan and Paula's suggestions for things to do in Lake Geneva.

Anna held out her hand. "I'll recycle those."

He put his hand over his pocket. "No, I might try some of these. Maybe even today."

Alone, she thought. He spent so much time alone, except…

"You have another party later today," she reminded him.

He grimaced. "Yes, I remember. Would you like to go with me?"

She froze. Surely he was joking. He'd already offended a few people by hiring John after everyone had seen Kendra fire him. What would happen if he turned up at an affair with his housekeeper?

Probably nothing. The women would still fall all over him. It would be Anna who would feel completely uncomfortable.

"Thank you, but I can't," she said.

It seemed "I can't" were two words she uttered a lot. I can't find a good man. I can't have a baby. I can't spend any more time alone with Donovan Barrett.

And she wouldn't, either. No more tea parties. No more responding to his touch. From now on she would be completely professional in every way.

CHAPTER SEVEN

WHY had he done that? Donovan was still asking himself the next day as he listened to Anna's footsteps in the hallway, watched her endangering herself by climbing on ladders to dust the tops of bookshelves and heard her singing a recent rock song as she tackled the grout in the bathroom.

He'd kissed her, and he could still feel the imprint of her warm lips on his own. His fingers itched to slide over her skin again, to gather her close.

"Insanity," he muttered. He had gone to another party last night, an informal picnic on the grass with torches lighting the night and all the women wearing slinky sundresses.

They weren't all like Dana and Kendra. In fact, most of the guests were fine people with intelligent minds. They obviously had come to this area because they loved the beauty of the scenery. One woman in particular had thanked him for hiring John the other day.

"The rest of us were too shocked to say anything," she said. "We didn't want to embarrass him further.

We're all well aware that the town of Lake Geneva would cease to function without the people who work in the shops and restaurants and who clean our houses and keep our gardens and make the town hum. We'd be lost without them. Most of us wouldn't have successful businesses without their patronage, and they deserve our respect and fair working conditions as well as a decent wage, but we weren't thinking about that the other night. You, on the other hand, actually did something about the situation. You offered John work and repaired his damaged ego."

"I just reacted," Donovan had told her. And if he'd been thinking at all that night, he had been thinking about Anna more so than John, but he couldn't say that here. It would be unkind to her. It would bring her attention she didn't want.

He'd continued his conversation with the woman who had been very beautiful with a lush body and gorgeous blond hair. But all night he kept thinking of serious gray eyes and a voice telling him that she needed a child, not a man. He remembered her walking down to the shore path to meet the man with the little boy...

The doorbell cut into Donovan's thoughts. It rang once, twice, three times.

Anna was running the vacuum cleaner.

He started toward the door. The whirring of the vacuum stopped as the doorbell rang for the fourth time.

Donovan reached the hallway just as Anna swung the door open.

A boy stood on the threshold.

"Frank," she said, and though Donovan couldn't see Anna's face he could hear the smile in her voice. "Is it that time already?"

"First of the month. Time to do your part to keep the news coming," he joked with a big grin on his face.

Donovan fought to keep breathing. The boy was about twelve with flyaway longish brown hair, green eyes and an infectious smile. He waited politely for Anna's response.

"Well, we definitely don't want the news to stop coming," she agreed. "Wait right here and I'll be back."

She turned and noticed Donovan standing there and the smile on her face froze.

"I—this is Frank," she said, her voice sounding a bit weak. "Frank delivers the newspaper."

Frank smiled more broadly. "Are you Mr. Barrett?"

Donovan struggled to fight the tightness in his chest. He fought not to think about the fact that Ben might have been much like this boy one day had he lived.

"Yes," was all Donovan could manage.

"My mom told me that if I should ever see you I should tell you that she hopes you're enjoying Lake Geneva."

"That's very nice of her, and…yes, I am, thank you," Donovan said.

The boy chuckled and the sound of it shot right through Donovan's soul. "Hey, don't thank me. I'd never have thought to ask you somethin' like that. Maybe I'd ask how fast your Jaguar can go. Have to obey Mom, though. She hears everything, and if she found out I'd met you and hadn't remembered to ask…well…"

"She wouldn't hit you?" Donovan asked.

The boys eyes grew wide with shock. "Mom? Hit me?" He laughed. "No, she'd just put on her disappointed face, probably give me a lecture about my manners. I'd end up feeling like a jerk." He blew out a breath. "I hate feeling like that, so if you meet her, could you tell her that I remembered to ask?"

Donovan couldn't keep from smiling even though the pain in his chest grew worse. What a great kid and how hard it was to keep breathing and smiling and just standing here when Ben's memory and thoughts of all that Ben might have turned out to be were assaulting him. He managed a nod. "I'll tell her your manners were great."

Donovan's voice wasn't as steady as he would have liked. He felt Anna's touch on his sleeve. Her eyes were dark with concern. Somewhere in there when he and Frank had been talking she had gone and got some money to pay the boy. She handed Frank a check along with a tip.

"Thanks, Anna. You're the best. You never make me come back later."

"I wouldn't do that, Frank. You're very dependable at your job," she said.

The boy practically glowed. "Hey, if you see Mom…"

"I'll repeat the compliment," she promised with a smile.

The boy said his goodbyes, then turned and loped out to the end of the walk where his bike was waiting. "Nice meeting you, Mr. Barrett. See you, Anna." He waved, and so, of course, Donovan waved back.

But as soon as the boy was out of sight, Donovan turned to go. He needed to be alone, to shut his eyes, to block out the memories and the ache of lost hopes.

"Donovan," Anna said, and he felt her arm on his sleeve again.

He looked down at her. "Don't worry. It's fine," he said. "I can't go through my whole life never meeting boys who will remind me that my own son died before he reached that age."

"But this time was unnecessary. I should have thought about the fact that Frank was coming by today and either met him at the street or at the very least warned you ahead of time so you could prepare yourself."

As if he could ever do that. She must have been thinking the same thing because her eyes looked suddenly anguished. "Next month Frank and I will make other arrangements. I can mail the bill. It's what most people do. I just—"

He knew what her hesitation was for. She didn't pay the bill by mail because she liked Frank and it was a chance to talk to him.

"He's a great kid," Donovan said.

"Yes, he is."

"Glad I met him," he said, and he was glad in a way. But he was also sorry as well. "I have a few things to do," he told her and he started to walk away, but...he knew she was worried. Donovan didn't want that. And he didn't want her to feel guilty in the least.

He turned back.

"Anna, I hope you have a child just as nice as Frank

someday. Hell, what am I saying? You will. Any kid you raise will turn out well." Somewhere he found a smile.

Somewhere she found one, too, although it was a sad one. Her lips…he wanted to touch her lips and turn her smile into one of gladness, but that would be unfair. He could never give her what she needed.

Donovan let her go, but hours later he was still thinking of Anna's sad smile. He realized that for the first time in a long time, he had encountered a child and ended up spending the next few hours thinking about something other than Ben.

He listened for Anna and heard her humming to herself as she worked. She said she loved being a housekeeper. He knew she was loyal to her friends and inspired loyalty in others. Plus, she had brought homey touches to this huge building and was obviously well-liked by Frank, who was of an age when boys often didn't want anything to do with adults.

In other words, Anna was perfect mother material. She longed for a child with all her heart, just as much as he shied away from the thought of ever having another.

Surely at least one of the two of them should have what they wanted. Maybe it was time to stop avoiding painful topics and ask a few important questions.

Anna was setting the table for Donovan that evening, trying once again to make a single table setting look somehow interesting rather than lonely. She moved the salt shaker out a bit farther, replaced the tall vase of flowers with a long low one that was less overwhelming. She was considering the effect and thinking about adding a couple of candles when the sound of footsteps made her look up.

"It's occurred to me that I've been an insensitive male who probably doesn't appreciate your efforts nearly enough," Donovan said, standing in the doorway, the light filtering in behind him.

She shrugged. "People enjoy a meal more when the table looks better even if they don't think about it. This one seems a bit sparse."

"No problem. I can fix that." He went to the china cabinet, pulled out another place setting and arranged it on the table. "Have dinner with me."

Anna's eyes widened. She took a deep breath. Had he thought she was angling for something like this?

"No, I'm fine. I just—"

"Anna, sit," Donovan ordered. He was frowning, his eyebrows dark slashes.

She sat. But she wasn't happy.

"I won't bite," he promised.

"I know that."

"And I won't kiss you again."

She squirmed on her chair. "I know that, too." But now that he'd mentioned it, her lips—and his lips— were all she could think of.

"You're not supposed to eat dinner with your housekeeper," she said suddenly, trying to get her mind off kisses and back on the topic at hand.

"Ah, I see. Rules." He smiled.

She managed to glare even though her heart wasn't really in it. "Rules have a purpose."

"Do you always play by the rules, then?"

Anna thought back to how she had all but forced him to hire her for this job, and immediately dropped her pretend glare. "You know I don't."

"Don't look so sad, Anna. You haven't broken any laws."

"I know. Why?" she asked.

"Why?"

"Why did you ask me to eat dinner with you?"

He leaned back in his chair and blew out a breath. "I have something I want to discuss with you."

"A job evaluation? Or…maybe there's some problem. Or…something you need me to do. Or…"

He held up one hand. "Nothing bad. Nothing that should concern you. Let's just have dinner and then we'll talk."

It was a reasonable suggestion, but waiting made eating difficult. Anna had never been good at waiting.

"Does this have to do with the parties you've been going to? Your social situation? Maybe something that happened at lunch with the girls yesterday? Another employee? Do you need me to talk to Linette or John or even Clyde?"

Donovan put down his fork. His lips lifted slightly. "Let's go sit on the deck," he suggested. "I just have some questions. Not bad questions and nothing that would require you to admonish another employee. I don't have any problems with the staff."

Taking a deep breath, Anna studied his expression. Maybe this had to do with one of the women he had met recently. Bridget had told her a woman at the shop yesterday wanted Anna to ask some questions about Donovan's likes and dislikes. He was obviously fresh meat and the interested women were looking for artillery. Maybe, in spite of his assertions that he wasn't interested in getting involved, he'd met someone he liked. He was a normal man, after all. At least, he certainly kissed like one.

No, that was wrong. He kissed like no man she'd ever kissed before. He'd made her flare and burn and melt like a birthday candle.

Anna cleared her throat and forced herself to rise and stop—please, stop—thinking about Donovan's physical talents. "Fresh air would be nice," she agreed, and followed him out onto the deck.

A breeze blew off the lake and lifted strands of her hair, brushing them against her cheeks. She turned to Donovan, waiting.

"You were good with Frank today," he said.

She ducked her head, wondering where this was leading. "He's easy to talk to."

"I'll bet you were good with that little boy the other day, too."

"Why are you saying these things, Donovan?" Her voice came out shaky and scared. At least that was how it seemed to her.

"You want a child. You want to adopt. Why?"

The question was like a lightning bolt slashing through the air on a sunny day. It caught her by surprise.

"Why do you ask?"

"I'm just wondering how important it is to you, what your rationale is. It's prying, I know."

She took a deep breath and shook her head. "I'm not fond of discussing my past, but it's not a secret. My friends and plenty of my acquaintances know, and since I twisted your arm to get this job, you deserve to know something of my motives, too. I didn't have a glowing childhood. My father deserted us. My mother…wasn't kind or loving. Fortunately, other people were. Neighbors. Friends. But they all belonged to other people, really. They weren't mine in the way a parent should be." She looked at him to see if he understood.

His expression was unreadable. She suspected this subject was hurting him, but he wasn't backing away. "Your parents weren't there for you. I'm familiar with that kind of nonexistent parenting. I was a workaholic and seldom available for my family."

An ache went through her. "It's not the same. You cared about them. My father didn't care at all. My mother resented the fact that she had to raise me, so much so that she once told me she hated me."

Anger flashed in Donovan's eyes. "That's criminal."

She shrugged. "It's the way things were. I survived."

Donovan shook his head.

Anna raised her chin. "What?"

"You amaze me, Anna. It takes a strong and special person to get past something like that and not turn out bitter."

"I'm not a saint or an angel. I *am* bitter, but as I said, I was lucky enough to have other parent figures."

"And now you want to raise a child to attempt to stamp out the past?"

"No, not at all. The past is what it is. It's gone, done. But there are children out there who need love, and I know better than many the importance of love to a child. I can give that. I *want* to give that kind of unconditional love." She struggled to keep her voice steady.

Looking up, she saw that Donovan was studying her. He put down his glass and stepped closer, taking her hand.

"More prying," he said. "May I ask…what steps you've taken to achieve your goal?"

She took a deep breath, tried not to think about how his hand felt, curved around hers. His fingers were long, his skin was warm. She felt protected. She felt that what she had to say mattered.

"I've done research online, at the library and by talking to adoption agencies."

"But you haven't taken the next step."

"No. I'm not going to do this halfway. I want my child to feel secure, and that includes feeling financially secure. I'm saving every penny I can. I have to know that if I got sick for a while, I'd still have enough to cover our expenses. And…I don't want to take a chance of the agency thinking that I might be a bad risk."

He lifted her hand, turning it so that her work-roughened palm was visible. For one breathless second she thought he was going to press his lips to her skin.

Instead he looked directly into her eyes. "I can't see anyone thinking of you as a risk. You're obviously dedicated and driven and giving."

She laughed. "You only think that because I was so pushy about getting this job."

He laughed, too, and she felt the sound echoing through her fingers as he brushed his thumb across her palm, his skin sliding against hers. Heat spread outward from where they touched, radiating throughout her body.

As if Donovan felt it, too, he released her suddenly. "All right, I've interrogated you enough. I should let you go."

Automatically she turned. She was, after all, an employee and she had been dismissed, but one thing kept her from leaving.

"It wasn't just idle curiosity, was it?" She looked back over her shoulder.

He pressed his lips together, then shook his head. "No. It wasn't. A child is such a big responsibility. They feel so deeply. They need so much. I just needed to know how much you wanted this."

She bit her lip. "You were worried that a child might be shortchanged."

"Another child," he corrected. "I shortchanged my child, and I can never go back and fix that. Ever. As you said, the past is gone." His words were low. His voice was tight.

Somehow Anna blinked and held back any response to what he'd said and what he was obviously feeling. He was flailing himself, and there was nothing she could say that wouldn't sound trite or pathetic or wrong. So she gave a tight nod. "I understand. That makes sense." Again she started to leave.

But he touched her, ever so lightly on her shoulder. Sensation slipped through her.

"I was wrong," he said. "I was wrong to question your motives. I already know that you're the right kind of woman for motherhood."

She turned back to him then and touched his sleeve. What she wanted to say was that he was the right kind of man for fatherhood, too. She was sure that she was right, and yet…she was also wrong. He had once been the right kind of man for fatherhood. It was evident in everything he said, all that he did and the way he treated people. But he had left fatherhood behind. He didn't want it anymore, and she couldn't blame him.

"Thank you," she whispered. "Very much," she added, a bit more primly.

He smiled then. "You're welcome. Very much so." And the smile traveled from his lips to his eyes. "But I wasn't fishing for gratitude. That's not what I want."

Donovan's smile relieved Anna's concern, but it didn't put an end to the tension sliding through her. She looked into that golden-brown gaze and instantly became aware that she was still touching him, linked to him. The heat of his body warmed her fingertips. She had a sudden and intense need to rest her palms against his chest. She remembered how his mouth had felt against her own and she wondered what it would be like to have his arms around her.

Her body jerked. She couldn't think straight. "What

were you fishing for? What *do* you want?" she asked, recalling his words. Her hand flew over her mouth. "I can't believe I said that."

He touched her cheek. His smile turned to a grin. "I can't, either. And no, I wasn't fishing for that, but I want it very much. You'd better go."

She stood there, still frozen.

"Anna. Now. Please. For your own good, go."

She fled and didn't stop until she was in her room. Once there, she dug out every magazine she owned. No books. She didn't have enough concentration for books. But turning the pages of the magazines, she saw black hair with a silver streak she wanted to touch. The too-pretty male models made her think of someone a bit more rugged, a man with eyes of golden-brown and fingers that…

Her heartbeat sped up. She flipped the page. A man held a woman in his arms, molding her body to his.

Anna let out a muffled cry, then threw down the magazine and lay down, pushing a pillow over her head.

Darn the man for being who and what he was. And as for herself, she was turning out to be every bit as bad as Dana Wellinton. Her heart's desire might be a child of her own, but right now her body wanted Donovan Barrett's touch.

Tonight was going to be long and tense, and tomorrow, when she would have to face him again…

"Don't think about tomorrow," she whispered to herself.

She did her best. She lay there, trying to get back to

normal. Then a part of her realized that she was half-buried beneath a stack of magazines with a pillow over her head. The situation would be laughable if it weren't so pathetic.

Slowly she sat up. She stacked the magazines and turned off the light. She took a deep energizing breath and forced her thoughts as far away from Donovan as she could.

"There. Almost better," she said, but she knew it was just a matter of seeing the man again, or heaven forbid, touching him again, and she would go back to being a mess. This had happened before. She'd started having feelings for a man and she'd lost. But those times she had at least thought she might win. She'd had justification for hope of a future.

With Donovan there could never be any future.

Anna groaned at her own stupidity. Wanting a man to kiss you when there could be no tomorrow was just asking to have your heart trashed.

She closed her eyes, filled her lungs, tried to think logically.

Work, she thought. I need work. Lots of it. Far, far away from my too wealthy, too handsome, too not-for-me boss.

She might be the housekeeper, but tomorrow she just might add a page to her duties and help Clyde do some weeding in the garden. Surely if she was away from the house she would be safe from this ridiculous ache she had for her boss.

CHAPTER EIGHT

DONOVAN stared out the window, trying to decide the right thing to do. Anna wanted a child, and every day children were born to mothers who either didn't want them or couldn't afford to raise them. But adoption was still a long and complicated procedure, especially for someone struggling to get through it on their own.

She'd said that she'd done her research and he believed her. Anna was a determined woman. When she wanted something she went after it.

"No question about that," he said to himself, remembering how she had rushed around the house from one task to the next trying to prove herself to him.

Anna was definitely dedicated to her dream of adoption, but she didn't have access to all the information that was available. She wouldn't be able to unearth all the private avenues there might be the way someone could who had access to primary sources.

Donovan ran one hand over his jaw. Some of those primary sources were doctors, ones he'd worked with, ones he'd been friends with. Those he'd left behind and hadn't thought ever to see or talk to again.

He was no longer a member of the medical community and he didn't want to be. He couldn't be.

But Anna wanted to adopt a child. And she was alone.

For several moments Donovan just sat there, staring at the ripples on the lake. Boats skimmed over the surface. Birds glided and dipped on the breeze. The pristine-white of piers connected the green of the lawns and trees to the blue of the water. The tranquility should have been soothing, and it would have been if not for the step he was poised to take.

You don't have to do this, he reminded himself. It's interfering. That's not your way.

But he remembered Anna's smile as she spoke to Frank, the softness of her voice, the rightness of it all. Some people weren't meant for parenthood, but some were.

He took a deep breath and plunged onward.

No matter her physical limitations, Anna was born to be a mother. It could happen. It should happen. If a constant source of money was all that was standing in the way…

He reached for the telephone. Money wasn't all. Adoption could be a painful, twisting maze, fraught with disappointment, frustration and setback. Information was what was needed.

Punching in the numbers that would connect him, he waited for the past to rush in.

Ben. His practice. His home. Ben. His patients. Ben.

"Hello." A young woman's voice told him that Dr. Chez was in. Would he like to leave a message?

No, he wouldn't. If he didn't do this here and now…

"I know he's otherwise occupied, but could you tell him that Donovan Barrett is on the phone."

"I—I'm sorry," the woman said. "But—"

"I'm a colleague." A lie. He wasn't that anymore.

She went away. In a moment the phone clicked to life.

"Don?" Phil's voice was incredulous.

"Hello, Phil, how are you?" What inconsequential nonsense. He and Phil had gone to med school together. They had danced at each other's weddings. He had thrown Phil out of his house when his friend had tried to get him to come back to work. Donovan had sent him a curt and formal apology in writing and had received a written acceptance in return. They hadn't spoken since.

"I'm fine. Great, Don. And…you?"

Donovan felt a lump form in his throat. "I'm fine, Phil," he said, trying to inject enthusiasm into his voice. "Really. Thank you for asking."

He could almost hear Phil expelling a sigh of relief. "It's good to hear you."

"Same here, buddy. But hey, I know it's a workday for you. You've got patients, and I have questions."

"You're coming back to the hospital." The hope in Phil's voice hit Donovan. How many people had he harmed or disappointed these past few years? He didn't know. He knew he had raged. He remembered yelling, pounding things, throwing things, cursing fate. He remembered telling Phil to get the hell out of his business and out of his life.

"I—no, I'm afraid I can't come back," Donovan said suddenly.

A pause. "Is there a medical problem, Don? Do you need help?"

Donovan took a deep breath. "Not medical, no, but yes, I could use help. By that, I mean that I know someone, a friend, who is considering adoption. I want to make sure that things go smoothly, that the details are tended to. I need avenues, information, someone who's kept on top of the latest legislation and knows the ins and outs and can help me help her."

"Adoption, Don? You said this was for…"

"For a friend," Donovan clarified. For a minute he was sure that Phil thought he had lost it, that he was going to try and adopt a child to replace Ben who was…utterly irreplaceable.

"She's my housekeeper, Phil, and yes, she's a friend. I'm not interested in adopting any children. I can't, but maybe I need a cause, a chance to do something good."

"You spent years doing good, Don."

"Yes, I did. But I took it too far. It cost me too much. I can't go there again, Phil. Don't ask it. Just…can you help me with this? Open some doors, find out a few things. I guess what I'm asking is…would you? I don't deserve your help but I'm asking."

Phil laughed, a harsh, barking laugh. "Shut up, Don. You think because you threw me out when you were going through total hell that I would hold that against you? I've missed you. I've worried about you, and I've only stayed away because I thought that was what you wanted."

It *was* what he'd wanted. Going back in any way was a danger to his sanity. He'd only called today because of Anna, but…

"I've missed you, too," Donovan said, and he realized he meant it. Looks like he owed Anna more than she knew.

"As for the info, I'll see what I can come up with. I haven't had much experience with adoptions over the years."

"Me either, but I thought you might know someone who had."

"I'll see what I can do. I'll give you a call if you tell me how to reach you and give me some information on the prospective adoptive parent."

"Thanks," Donovan said as he rattled off his number and address and gave Anna a glowing recommendation. "I owe you, Phil."

"You don't. We're friends, Don. Right? Still?"

"Still," Donovan agreed as he said his goodbyes.

He hung up the phone and looked out the window once again at those piers connecting water and land. A bridge, just like Anna. If she hadn't come into his life he would never have called Phil.

Of course, given the fact that he had no intention of going back to his old life, he wasn't sure if this process of reconnecting was a good thing or a bad thing.

But maybe the way she got him to do things even

when she wasn't trying to was just an Anna thing, something unique like her sunny ways, her concern for others or her lips that made him crave another taste.

Donovan slammed his palm down on the desk. He regretted that last thought. One slip regarding Anna's lips had him recalling how it had felt to touch her and to have her mouth opening beneath his.

"Damn!" Donovan stood up, pushing away from his desk and, hopefully, away from the direction his thoughts had been roaming. He was getting far too interested in his housekeeper. If he continued in this manner, he was bound to set off another disaster.

His relationship with Anna had to be a professional one. There were lines he couldn't cross.

"Set up some barriers and create some distance," he ordered himself. That task would at least keep him occupied with thoughts of something other than Anna's pretty lips. He hoped.

Her life here with Donovan was turning into a tango, Anna thought a few days later. When he entered a room she all but waltzed backward from it. When they ended up in the same space, they circled each other warily. The sheer physical energy of the two of them in the same place practically made the walls vibrate.

"I saw Donovan in town the other day," Bridget had told her just that morning. "Somehow I kept myself from salivating, but, Anna, he's even hotter than I thought. How can you be in the same room with him without bursting into flames?"

"It's not like that with us," Anna had said. "Donovan and I have a professional relationship."

But just this minute she had walked in on him reading the newspaper in the library and she knew that her words were a total lie.

Halting just inside the room, her duster in hand, Anna started to excuse herself and leave. The newspaper rattled and she noticed the way his fingers splayed over the pages. He had such wonderful hands.

Heat rose within her even though the day wasn't all that warm. "Excuse me," she said. "I'll come back later."

"No."

She stopped and stared at him.

He raised a brow, a hint of a smile playing over his lips.

"No?" she asked.

Shrugging, he stepped closer. "Forgive me. Make that no, please. I didn't mean to be so direct."

And she hadn't meant to stare at him as if she wanted to do more than dust the room. Anna stared at the feather duster. "This can definitely wait," she said as much to herself as to him.

"I need to talk to you. Why don't you have a seat?"

Uh-oh. She swallowed nervously.

"Don't look like that."

"Like what?"

"As if you think I'm going to devour you or fire you."

Anna sat. She waited, wishing she could figure out something productive to do with her hands. She hated being this way. Nervous. Indecisive. She raised her chin.

"Maybe you'd better just tell me what you want. I like men who are direct."

He looked slightly taken aback, but then a slow smile came to his face. "Okay, let's be direct. I've been making the rounds of everyone else's parties. It's time I reciprocated. I'd like to invite a small group of people over this weekend. Can we handle it?"

No, she wanted to say. Being a housekeeper was one thing. Organizing an event designed to impress people who belonged in a world where she would always be a servant was something a million times different. But she had practically begged Donovan to give her this job. She couldn't quit now.

"How many?" she asked.

"A dozen?"

"No problem." Those were her words, but her thoughts were something more akin to *oh, no!* "I'll just need to get some information from you. Linette and Clyde and John and I will take care of everything. Have you already issued invitations?"

Those slashing brows nearly joined when he frowned. "You think I'd ask people without first making sure you were prepared to do this?"

She couldn't keep from smiling then. "Donovan, you're the employer. I'm here to do your bidding. I'm sure that a man who has grown up with servants knows that."

"It's not the same."

Now she was the one frowning. "Because I'm inexperienced."

"Yes."

Anna got up and began to pace. "Do you have any complaints about my job performance?"

He stepped up beside her, matching his gait to hers. "Absolutely none."

She executed a quick turn. He stayed right with her. "Do you anticipate that I might not be up to seeing to the needs of a dozen people, even if they're rich and used to the best?"

"No, I don't. I known damn well that if I asked you to fly you would somehow manage to do it."

She started to turn again.

Donovan placed his arm around her waist and spun her around so that she was facing him. Because she had been moving when he caught her, her momentum sent her tumbling against his chest. She gazed up into his eyes, feeling his heart beating against her skin.

"I wasn't insulting you, Anna," he said, his voice low. "I would never do that. But the truth is that you and I have never sat down and ironed out your job description. I've been thinking about that. I know how much you need the work and why. And I don't want to inadvertently take advantage of you by asking you to do too much, because I'm pretty sure that whatever I ask you'll do your best to comply. That's a bit too one-sided. You need to be protected."

"From you?"

He loosened his hold and she took a visible breath. "I didn't mean in that way," she said. "I wasn't implying that you were taking advantage of me."

"And yet I have." His eyes darkened.

She shook her head. "No. Are you afraid you've asked too much of me as an employee, because if that's the case, you'd be wrong. You haven't asked. I've taken the initiative."

"I know that, but I haven't stopped you."

She had to smile at that. "Do you really think that you could?"

Donovan crossed his arms. He studied Anna for such a long time that she felt dizzy. "I think I could," he finally said.

He was right. She'd known all along that he was the one with the power. "But you haven't," she said slowly, "because you know how much I need this job."

"That wouldn't excuse me for letting you do too much. How about if we agree to this? I'll promise that your job is secure. You agree that if you're ever feeling overwhelmed, you'll let me know."

"And what will you do then?"

"I'll hire someone to help you."

"I couldn't let you do that."

Donovan stepped closer. He placed one finger beneath her chin, tilting her face up so that she was staring into his eyes. "You wouldn't have a choice, Anna. I'm the one in charge here."

His gaze was almost overwhelming. She wanted to lean closer. But then the meaning of his words shot through her.

Donovan was her boss. He *was* in charge. She was only his employee, and he had just made that abundantly clear.

"Do you understand, Anna? I won't let you sacrifice yourself." He let her go then, and took two steps backward, but he continued to study her. "Anna?"

She raised her chin. "I understand. You're the employer. I will, of course, let you know if I require help in order to do my job correctly."

"Good." His voice was harsh. He turned on one heel and left the room.

Anna let out a breath. She somehow found the wall and leaned against it. Her body sagged as reality hit, and she realized that ever since Donovan had come here, no matter what she'd told herself, she had not truly allowed herself to accept the chasm that stood between them.

He *was* her employer. He lived in a different world than she did. She was his to direct, and even if there was a physical attraction between them, there would always be a gaping cultural divide as well. A career divide. A life divide.

Donovan had made that clear.

Shame rushed through Anna. Somewhere inside, like it or not, she had harbored fantasies about him. She had dreamed about him. Even though she had known that there could never be anything between them, she had given in to those fantasies, however reluctantly. Now, even that had to stop. Allowing those dreams to continue could only hurt her and harm the future of her child. Her only goal right now had to be fulfilling her duties. She had a party to organize. It was imperative that she keep her mind off the man who was giving the party.

"It's for the best," she whispered to herself. Someday,

once some time had passed, Donovan might end up married to one of the guests at this party. She needed to start acting accordingly. From now on her attitude toward him would have to change. In every way.

With great effort, she tried not to think about who might be on Donovan's guest list. Instead she simply waited.

CHAPTER NINE

IF HE hadn't already felt like a jerk, his latest behavior with Anna would have cemented the title, Donovan thought. He had wanted to set up some barriers so he wouldn't be tempted to give in to the desire he felt for her, so he'd come up with the idea for this damned party. He'd thought it might create distance. Then, to keep her from running herself ragged planning the event, he'd pulled rank on her.

That had been totally unfair and arrogant. Because even if she was his employee, he had never really thought of her in those terms. He had plenty of employees, but Anna was different. From the minute he'd met her he'd known she was different. That had always been the problem.

"So, you acted like a pompous idiot and now she's playing by the rules you've set."

Ever since their conversation several days ago, Anna had been unfailingly professional. She had smiled politely; she had cleaned; she had organized and had treated him just the way any housekeeper would treat her employer. With distance and deference and respect and not an ounce of nosiness or stubbornness or spontaneous sunshine.

There had been no more humming or singing, no cute T-shirts, no acts of random impulsiveness like the time she had washed his car last week and had ended up totally and adorably soaked but triumphant. She had eliminated all the little things that had inadvertently, but constantly, brought her to his attention.

A frown drew Donovan's brows together. He supposed he should be ecstatic. In other circumstances, he would be, but he knew that Anna's natural tendency was to hum and sing and enjoy her work. He had silenced her, and she'd voiced not a word of complaint. She still seemed to like her job. So why was he feeling so ill-tempered?

He probably didn't really want to know the answer to that question. It might be incriminating. It would probably lead him to thoughts of Anna's lips. Still, he hated the fact that he'd somehow squelched her brightness.

"So go apologize—tell her you were wrong," he ordered himself.

But then…

Donovan blew out a breath.

"Every time you do something personal like that, you end up touching her." And if he gave in and touched her again, he might take things too far. Right now she was silencing her songs because she felt it was what the job required, but if he lost his self-control with her when he had nothing to offer, he'd end up hurting her for real. He might silence her songs for good.

There wasn't a way out of this that wouldn't be bad for Anna. Tonight was the party. After that…

Maybe he should start thinking of moving elsewhere, for Anna's sake, giving her permanent work here and a set of rooms so she could have space for her child. The place would need a caretaker if he wasn't here.

If he left, her life could get back to normal.

And he…

Could live anywhere. It didn't matter.

He only hoped that was true. He already had his memories of Ben haunting him. He couldn't have Anna haunting him, too.

Donovan was still reminding himself of that hours later when he descended to the first floor to greet his guests.

The uniform made her nervous, Anna conceded, as she and John circled the room handing out drinks and hors d'oeuvres. She couldn't remember ever having worn a uniform in her life other than for gym class, but it had just seemed like the right thing to do. She didn't want any of Donovan's friends noticing her or questioning him for being too soft on his employees.

The man had dared look askance when she had come up to him wearing the black skirt, white blouse and apron.

For the first time in the past few days she had frowned at him. "It's important to set the right tone," she reminded him. "You're trying to impress your guests."

For the first time in the past few days a hint of a devilish smile had played about his lips. "I am?"

She tried to frown harder. "Yes," she said firmly,

refusing to say more. If she took this further, he might end up not only smiling but laughing as well, and both his smile and his laugh did awful, wonderful things to her insides.

Anna refused to think about Donovan's smile. She went to the kitchen, gave Linette and John last minute instructions and tried to keep busy herself so that she wouldn't hyperventilate. If she hadn't done this right, if things didn't go well...

The correct next thought was *I might be fired,* but she wasn't really worried about that. For all that Donovan had been forced to remind her of their positions, she knew he wasn't a vindictive man. No, it was him she was worried about. He was starting a new life here. If she goofed things up for him, he would be hurt.

"Let's do this right," she said out loud.

"I promise not to drop anything or spill anything."

She blinked and turned around. John was standing there. She couldn't help smiling. "Believe me, John, I'm much more worried about doing something wrong myself. You're the experienced one. You have to lead the way and I'll follow."

A look of gratitude brightened his face. "You and Mr. Barrett are the best. He already found me today and told me not to worry." He laughed.

"He did?"

John nodded. "He also told me that if I had to spill something, I might consider aiming for Ms. Williams."

Anna widened her eyes.

Immediately John blushed. "Not that I would, Anna.

I wouldn't do a thing to embarrass him, not after he took such a risk hiring me."

Anna patted his sleeve. "I'm sure he didn't feel that he was taking a risk, John."

"I know. He said so, but still…I'll do my best by him."

And so will I, Anna promised herself after John had gone.

She put her best, maid-of-the-moment face on, picked up a tray and followed John out into the high-ceilinged room where Donovan was entertaining his guests.

Anna had decorated the gold room with white candles and yellow roses. The candlelight flickered off the walls, playing against the brass and crystal chandelier and highlighting the carved molding of the beautiful, spacious room.

The room, lovely though it was, was nothing compared to the guests. The men all wore crisp black and white and the women were mostly in black or white as well. Like beautiful marble chess pieces, Anna couldn't help thinking and then instantly felt awful. These people lived in a world different from her own, but that didn't mean they didn't have feelings and dreams and desires.

She held out her tray to an elderly man.

"Thank you very much," he said, taking a glass.

Anna mumbled a "you're welcome" and moved on, serving guests and being thanked at times. It seemed as if things would go all right, after all. Everyone seemed to like Donovan and he was being the perfect host.

She noticed his glass was empty. John had gone back

to the kitchen to refill his tray. Realizing that she would have to do the honors, Anna's breath caught in her throat. She had served Donovan many times in the past few weeks but somehow sidling up to him in this company seemed different. It made her feel exposed, as if anyone might look into her face and see that she was attracted to her employer.

Ridiculous. She was no longer attracted to Donovan. At least she didn't intend to allow herself to be. And she had a job to do.

She walked up to him and held out her tray.

"Thank you, Anna," he said, taking the glass and looking directly at her.

Oh, wasn't it just like him to do that? He wouldn't want her to feel like a piece of furniture and so he would call her by name and look at her. Didn't he know that wasn't the way it was done? At least she didn't think it was. He probably knew much more about the process than she did.

"You're welcome, Mr. Barrett," she said, starting to move away, but she was still distracted by her thoughts and Donovan's nearness. For a second, her foot caught on the shoe of the person standing behind her. For what seemed like forever, Anna teetered.

Donovan's arm shot out. He steadied the tray, and with his other arm he steadied Anna, his hand at her waist.

She sucked in a breath. To her own ears it sounded loud, like a gasp. She knew her eyes widened.

"Are you all right?" Donovan murmured.

Quickly she righted herself. "Yes, I'm fine, thank you,"

she murmured and somehow gave away the rest of the glasses of wine and found her way back to the kitchen.

She had lied. She wasn't fine. The instant Donovan's hand had rested on her waist, she had felt positively dizzy in a way she hadn't when she was merely trying to get her balance.

"That must have been some grip you had on her, Donovan," she heard a woman's voice murmur. "She looked as if you had just invited her into your bed. What's that about?"

"Oh, shut up, Kendra," another woman said. Anna recognized the voice as that belonging to Susannah McGraff, a gorgeous and intelligent woman whose family had made a fortune in department stores. "Anna was clearly just embarrassed because she knew everyone had seen her stumble. You would have felt the same. Any of us would have."

"Absolutely," another voice said. Anna recognized it as the elderly man's. "Thank you, John," he continued, and Anna was glad that John, at least, was surviving the evening.

But she couldn't hide in the kitchen forever. Linette was putting food on the trays and John had just told Donovan it was time to go into the dining room.

Anna waited to give everyone time to get seated. Then she and John picked up their trays and prepared to serve. With a little luck the evening and her ordeal would be over soon.

CHAPTER TEN

DONOVAN'S heart flipped when he looked up and saw Anna standing in the doorway carrying a tray that looked as if it weighed almost as much as she did. He'd been aware all night that she was nervous, and he was pretty sure she was afraid she'd somehow spoil his party.

Damn him for not making it clear that this party didn't matter. The only point of this affair had been to stop spending so much time thinking about Anna.

He'd wanted to remind himself that he and Anna couldn't be together. This party had merely been a diversion. But, somehow, he'd messed up the message, and here she was struggling to create the appearance that she'd been hauling heavy trays around all her life.

She took a step into the room.

He should stay seated. She wouldn't thank him for calling attention to her.

She took another step, her head high. He knew she was strong, but the tray was completely laden. Her body wasn't meant to take this kind of punishment.

Muttering beneath his breath, Donovan stood. He rose to meet her.

Her eyes widened. He saw her mouth the word *no*.

He frowned and leaned close enough to take the tray. "You promised you'd get help if you needed it," he said, his voice pitched low and meant for her ears only.

"I'm fine," she said.

"You're trembling."

"This doesn't look good for either of us."

"Too bad. I'll fix it. You just smile," he commanded, taking the tray and carrying it the last few feet to the table.

"Can't lose the woman who keeps this house running, can I?" he asked his guests. "The gears would stop turning without Anna. My gardener says the flowers bloom just for her."

Her eyes widened. She gave him a shocked and flustered look. When she leaned in to take the first dish, he could almost swear that the word "liar" came to him on a breath of air, but that might have been his imagination.

Or maybe his conscience. Clyde did think Anna made the sun rise and set, but that last had been a bit of obvious exaggeration designed to make his actions seem understandable.

Not that it had worked. Kendra Williams was smiling knowingly and it was obvious that she would be spreading petty gossip tomorrow. He probably shouldn't have invited her. He might have done it just so John could gloat a bit. Even Susannah was looking at him with a question in her eyes. As well as a hint of admiration.

She *was* an attractive and intelligent and good-hearted woman. A man would be a fool not to try to win at least her lust. But he looked at her and saw only a friend. His heart didn't flip.

Still, he made an effort to smile at her and to engage the rest of his guests. For Anna's sake he didn't call attention to her again that evening. She stayed away, and they didn't speak to each other except in the most necessary of instances.

The minute the door closed behind his last guest, however, and John and Linette had gone home, he headed for the kitchen. Anna was there putting things away, bent over a cabinet, her beautifully rounded bottom in the air.

Donovan groaned.

Anna whirled. "I didn't know you were there."

"I'm here," he said simply. He didn't try for more, because what he was thinking was that he was glad the guests were gone and he was alone with her. She wouldn't want to know that any more than he did.

She fiddled with the handle of a cabinet. "I think it went well tonight. Your guests seemed entranced by you."

"It went well," he agreed. "Thanks to you."

"You don't have to say that."

"It's true. You organized the whole thing. All I did was talk."

"And be yourself. People like you. That's important."

Probably it was to most people, but to him it wasn't anymore. He hadn't cared one bit what anyone in the room thought of him. All his thoughts had been focused on this lady.

"Thank you," he said.

She turned aside slightly, her hair brushing the curve of her jaw. "You shouldn't have helped me with the tray."

"It was heavy."

"You're not supposed to do those things. I am. You know that." She looked at him, taking a step forward. Her eyes flashed. He loved that.

"Are you lecturing me?"

Anna froze. He knew what she was going to say.

"I'm teasing, Anna."

"Maybe, but I *was* lecturing you. That can't be right."

He laughed. "It feels right."

She raised her chin. "You told me that you were the boss, that you were in charge, and you were right."

"I was a pompous jerk."

"Then go on being a jerk."

He shook his head. "You don't sing anymore."

"It seemed unprofessional."

"Then be unprofessional. I don't want you to change to fit some mold you think you should fit just because I tried to bully you."

She laughed at that, then. "Are you sure you were really a doctor?"

Her words stopped him cold. "Why?"

"Don't doctors have to give a lot of orders? To their receptionists and their nurses and their patients?" Her voice was soft. She gazed at him. "Don't answer that."

"Why?"

"Because you never talk about your past. It must hurt."

"It does and yet…yes, I gave orders, but only when

they were necessary. It doesn't seem to be necessary for you, Anna."

"Why not?"

He smiled sadly. "Because you have a tendency to do more than I would ask."

"Do you miss it? Being a doctor?"

Donovan thought about that. "I miss it, but I can't do it anymore. I don't want to. I gave everything to medicine and not enough to Ben. When he needed me most I wasn't there for him as a doctor or as a dad. I wasn't even with him the day that car came out of nowhere and took his life. I was working. He'd been visiting me but I sent him home with a friend instead of taking him myself. So, medicine is over for me. In a way, it robbed me of Ben. I can't help wondering what would have happened—or not happened—if I'd taken him home myself. Does that make sense?"

She nodded. "Yes. I suppose I can see why you would feel that way, anyway. I'm sorry about your son. Terribly sorry."

He took her hands. "Thank you. Me, too."

Anna looked down at her palms resting in his. For a minute she seemed to lean closer to him. Then she quickly pulled away.

"I'm sorry," she repeated, and he was pretty sure that she was apologizing for something else. Maybe even for wanting a child when he had lost his.

"It's okay," he said as she excused herself and left the room.

But it wasn't. It wasn't okay that he had lost Ben and

it wasn't okay that he was starting to ache for a woman who needed a child.

And he did ache. All night long he thought of her.

He wished he had done more than hold her hands. Yet he was grateful that she'd had the sense to pull away.

Next time…

"Don't let there be a next time," he warned himself. He hoped he would heed his own good advice.

The last thing Anna thought of when she went to bed that night was Donovan. The first thing she thought of when she woke up was Donovan, and she thought of him all day.

"Stop it!" she ordered herself, as if that was really going to help. The man had been in her thoughts since the moment she'd met him.

And last night…he'd looked like a dream. She'd wanted to warn the other women in the room away.

Ridiculous thought. Clearly he belonged to those women. He was one of them.

But when he'd taken the tray from her, his hands had touched hers for the briefest of seconds, and she'd thought the trembling in her knees would send her tumbling. How silly. Despite the fires that sprang to life when they got together, he had just been trying to help her.

She'd watched him last night. It was as if he had been untouched by what was going on around him. He had laughed and talked and charmed everyone. Yet he'd left his guests to help his housekeeper carry in a heavy tray. He wasn't as invested in the party as he should have been. She hadn't fully understood until they'd had that talk later. Then she realized what the problem was. There was nothing real in his life anymore. He'd left it all behind.

"There's no fixing that," she reminded herself. "It's his choice."

But she burned to do something to help him, to bring a little life and happiness back to him. Just for a short time.

"And you know what that means?" she grumbled to herself. "It means you're in too deep. You need to back away, to keep your distance from him."

Yes, and that was just what she intended to do. Keep her distance.

Three days later, Anna was starting to feel as if her nerves were completely shot. Because she didn't want Donovan to feel bad she had gone back to her usual methods of keeping the house under control. She'd resumed her humming and singing, but in truth, it was hard. If she sang too loudly, the man might slip into the room and if he did that, she wasn't completely sure she could trust herself to behave normally and not reveal the fact that she wanted to beg him to kiss her again.

The final straw came when she was scrubbing the tiled floor of the hallway. She worked her way down the hall until she found herself in the doorway of the sunroom.

A sound caught her attention. She looked up to find herself staring straight into Donovan's eyes.

"I thought you were in the library."

"I was." But obviously he wasn't anymore.

Anna tried not to think about the fact that she was on her hands and knees, that her clothes were damp and clingy or that she was staring up into Donovan's eyes.

He frowned. "I don't think I pay you nearly enough to do that."

She gave him "the look," the one that brooked no argument. "You pay me plenty."

"You never said you were going to turn yourself into a scrubwoman. There's got to be a better way."

"There are numerous ways. This one works best. The grout needs cleaning."

"Then we'll get rid of the grout."

She sat back in a kneeling position, her hands on her hips. "That would be a waste of money and this beautiful tile."

"The tile is immaterial. Get up off your knees, Anna." His eyes were dark.

Her heart skipped a beat. Oh, who was she kidding? Her heart skipped so many beats that had she been in a doctor's office, he would have called for an EKG.

Anna's first instinct was to argue. She knew what cleaning a house entailed, and it was her job. "Donovan, I—"

She had barely opened her mouth when he was across the room, reaching for her. His big hands found her waist and he easily tugged her to her feet. Dropping the cloth she was holding, Anna stumbled, falling farther into Donovan's grasp.

"You're very bossy," she whispered weakly, embarrassed by her awkwardness and by her reaction to him.

"I know," he said, slipping one hand beneath her hair and cupping her head. He gazed down at her, studying her as if he'd never seen someone like her before. "It's my job."

Then he lowered his head and covered her lips with his own.

Anna's reaction was immediate and involuntary. She pushed her hands up his back and rose on her toes. Straining against him, she tilted her head to give him better access to her mouth. As if he needed help. Donovan was kissing her over and over. Nibbling, biting, licking.

"You make me crazy," he said, his voice harsh. "I think about you too much, all the time. I imagine other men touching you because I know I shouldn't be touching you at all."

He kissed her again.

"Yes," she said on a breath. She returned his kiss. "No. I mean no. I shouldn't be kissing you like this. We don't belong. We don't fit."

She pressed her palms against his chest to push away but ended up leaving them there, breathing in his scent, turning her head to feel more of him as he nibbled his way from her lips to her jaw, down her neck.

Anna shivered in his arms. "I'm not like this," she said, whether to Donovan or herself, she didn't know. And yet she *was* like this. With him.

"I know. I know. Do you think I don't know that?" His lips scorched the side of her neck, made her ache. She twisted, trying to get closer to him. "I know darn well I should stay away from you, for your sake. I don't want to hurt you. I really don't want to hurt you, Anna."

And, as if the truth of his words finally struck home, Donovan took a long, shuddering breath and set her away from him.

He studied her with dark, tortured eyes. He had done things and failed to do things in his life that filled him with regret. Anna knew that. Now she was one of those things, and she hated that, even though he was right about the fact that he could hurt her.

"It's okay," she finally managed to say, struggling to raise her voice from a weak whisper to a firm and affirmative and somewhat normal sound. She failed. "I'm all right," she reiterated, succeeding a bit better this time.

"How can you be all right?" he asked angrily. "This isn't the first time we've done this. It's not what any woman should have to accept from her employer."

Anna blinked, her eyes opening wide. "You think that was what I was doing? Accepting and fostering the advances of my employer because I need work?"

He made a slashing movement with his hand, cutting her off. "Of course not. I think I know you better than that. What I meant was—"

Now she was the one stopping his speech by holding up her hand. "I know what you meant. You meant that you hold all the cards, the power, the money and I'm at your mercy. You're suggesting that I might be unwilling."

His brows drew together and he didn't respond.

Anna sighed. "You're not saying anything because

you know that I wasn't at all unwilling. I've told you that I'm attracted to you."

"Yes, and knowing that, I should never have taken advantage. A good employer doesn't do that."

"You don't get to define being a good employer. I'm the employee. I get to decide."

He let out a groan. "I hardly think that you were looking for a boss who would back you up against a wall and put his hands and lips on you."

As worried and chagrined and afraid of her own emotions as she was, Anna couldn't keep from smiling just a little. "No, I don't think that would have been on my list of desirable attributes, but…it happened."

"Because I stepped over the line."

"And because I followed you eagerly."

Donovan stared directly into her eyes. "It would be best if you refrained from revealing such things to me right now. I don't trust myself."

"But I do," she said softly. "At a time when you wanted to move ahead to the next step, you stopped, and if I'm not mistaken it was for my sake more than for yours. Thank you."

Donovan leaned back against the wall. "Don't thank me. It's all I can do to keep my hands to myself right now. It's very important that I do that, too. I can't hurt you, Anna. I can't."

"I know that," she admitted, softly. "And you're right. It's wrong for us to touch. I trust you, and I haven't trusted a man in a long time."

His eyes came open. "Why?" He looked suddenly

alert in a way he hadn't been before. The agony was gone from his eyes. This was the man who cared about people so much that he forgot his own needs and hurts.

Because he was that kind of man, Anna opted to tell him some things she had told very few people in her life. "I may have mentioned that my father deserted my mother and me when I was little. There's nothing all that unusual in that. It happens all the time, but it did affect the way I thought of men. I think I was a bit too eager to be liked, perhaps less discerning than I should have been. Several times I got involved with boys or men who turned out to be less interested in me than they had pretended to be. They wanted more from me than I was willing to give and they lied to obtain my compliance."

Donovan swore.

Anna shook her head. "I was naive, but not that naive. When it became obvious that I was being used, I walked away. Less trusting and less rosy-eyed but unscathed physically. At least until I met Brent. He was intelligent and funny, and he didn't rush me. I fell like a rock. I loved him. We were supposed to be married. I was honest with him about the fact that I couldn't have children. I moved to Chicago to be with him. At first, he seemed happy, but as the wedding grew closer, he began to withdraw. He started to say cruel things to me. Eventually he threw my childlessness in my face. It seems that while I was planning my move to Chicago he was busy meeting someone else, someone who could give him the children he had suddenly decided he had to have. At least that was what he said. I'm not sure the truth had anything to do with my childbearing abilities. I think…I think he just used that as an excuse and I think he knew he wanted out before I ever made the move. His lies and defection…I guess it was the last straw."

Total silence greeted her words. A clock ticked loudly in the next room.

"So you came home."

She looked away, unable to continue to meet his gaze. The truth made her sound so pathetic.

"Yes. Where else would I go?" There had been nowhere. No one, but she couldn't say that.

"Anna," Donovan groaned. "Come here."

No, she was too vulnerable right now. She should never have told. He was probably pitying her. She shook her head.

"Anna. Please, I won't touch you if you don't want me to."

But, of course she did want him to touch her. Still. Even after remembering how foolish she had been in the past. That was the awful thing.

She sighed and moved closer. He kept his hands at his side. "I wish I had known you then," he said.

Anna raised her chin. "Why?"

"So I could beat up that scumbag for you. You should have had a champion."

"I did. I had myself."

Donovan smiled then. "So you did."

"I didn't tell you this so you would feel sorry for me."

"I don't feel sorry for you. I admire you. You got kicked in the heart but you came away from it and made something of yourself. You turned things around. I've always admired you and now I have one more good reason."

She smiled and shook your head. "I told you," she said, as if he hadn't spoken, "so that you would know that you can't hurt me that way. I've been hurt by unfeeling men. That's not you."

He opened his mouth.

She pressed her fingers against it, struggling to ignore his warm breath on her fingertips. "You've touched me," she said, "but you've always been truthful with me. You never led me to believe there could or would be anything more than desire. I appreciate that, because you and I both know we could never have a future. If you'd promised me rainbows or happily ever afters I would respect you so much less."

He raised one dark brow. "You wouldn't believe me, then?"

Her heart sighed but she smiled. "No, I wouldn't. I've learned a lot since the days of Brent. Actually I suppose I owe him a debt of gratitude, since he greatly simplified my life."

Donovan scowled. "He turned you off of men."

Anna removed her fingertips from Donovan's lips and gave him a quick kiss that sent sizzles straight down to her toes. "No, he turned me off of wanting to get seriously involved with men. I still like to kiss them now and then."

She started to spin away. Donovan caught her wrist and pulled her to him. "Do you kiss a lot of men?"

Just you, she wanted to say. *You're the only one I want to kiss.*

But almost immediately Donovan let her go. "Forget I asked that," he said. "It's none of my business."

His eyes still smoldered, and Anna realized her mistake. She hadn't wanted to hurt him, but her flippant comment had done so. Because he was trying to do the right thing, and she was only making it more difficult. For both of them.

"Forget I said that," she said. "It wasn't appropriate, and it wasn't really true. I should get back to business."

Donovan gave a quick nod and let her go. Anna had the terrible feeling that she would never feel the touch of his lips again. She should be happy about that.

But instead she knew that she would dream about his kisses for a great many years to come. Starting tonight.

CHAPTER ELEVEN

When Donovan emerged from his bedroom the next morning, he heard a voice at the front door. Whispering. Or what might pass as whispering to a boy, he supposed. He recognized the voice immediately. Frank. And since the voice was followed by what sounded like silence he assumed that Anna was there, too, talking too quietly to hear.

The fact that she was talking that quietly concerned Donovan. Anna wasn't a whisperer. If she had lowered her voice, then something was worrying her.

Immediately Donovan turned toward the front of the house. His first instinct might be to shy away from contact with children, but if something was worrying Anna, then he was going to see if he could help.

He quickly made his way to the top of the stairs, his feet silent on the thick carpeting. But there he stopped. Downstairs Anna and Frank were seated cross-legged in the front hallway staring at something Frank held in his hands.

"See, I just ride the thing. I don't know how to fix it," Frank was saying, the frustration apparent in his voice.

"Shh, you'll wake Donovan," Anna said, and Frank immediately blushed.

"Sorry, I forgot."

She stopped looking at what she was holding and turned to Frank. "It's okay. I didn't mean to embarrass you. I just…it's just…"

"I know. Everybody knows about Mr. Barrett's kid. My mom says I have to learn to be more sensitive, but I don't know. If I had a kid and he died, I wouldn't want everyone to act like he had never even been born."

Donovan's heart clenched. He had to concentrate on making sure he didn't gasp or worse. Frank's words, low as they had been, echoed in his ears.

"I know, sweetie," Anna was saying softly. "It's hard to understand, but that's the way adults are at times. The pain of losing a child is so great that it's almost unbearable. Not thinking about it is the only way of coping."

Forcing himself to keep breathing as normally as possible, Donovan thought about what he'd heard. That this child and this woman should be trying so hard to protect him…that they were so concerned they tiptoed around him…

Donovan closed his eyes and took a deep breath. He was half-tempted to slip backward into his room. That would be the sensitive thing to do. It would save Frank and Anna embarrassment and distress. But it would also allow their attempt to wrap him in protective cotton to continue. That wasn't fair to either Anna or Frank. They shouldn't have to be nervous about saying the wrong thing in front of him for fear it would bring up bad memories about Ben.

As if the very thought had been too much, Donovan's next breath conjured up a memory of Ben's ready smile. He could almost feel his little boy's fingers enclosed in his hand as they walked down the street together. Ben's birthday was coming up soon. His child had loved birthdays.

Intense pain swirled with a warm and sweet sadness.

"If you had a kid, what would you do if it died?" Frank was asking.

"I don't know," Anna said sadly. "I guess, like Donovan, I have some things I almost can't bear to think about."

"My mom says that even if I'm a lot of trouble, she couldn't get along without me," Frank said. "And that's why I need to be sensitive with Mr. Barrett."

This was the wrong time to step in, Donovan knew. The boy was going to be horrified, but if he didn't…

Donovan descended the stairs, making as much noise as possible.

Frank looked up, his big eyes round, his mouth a hollow O that emitted no sound. Red crept up beneath his T-shirt, coloring his neck and his face and especially the tips of his ears. Immediately the boy looked down.

Donovan almost reached out a hand to console him even though he wasn't anywhere near Frank yet. He clattered down the last of the stairs, turning his attention to Anna.

Immediately she rose to her feet, her mouth open, although she didn't speak. No doubt she was trying to come up with something soothing to say. More likely she was going to say she was sorry.

Something hot and dark and red and very much like anger slithered through Donovan. He didn't want her to speak, not if she was going to apologize. He suddenly hated all the things that stood between them, most especially her position as his underling that seemed to demand she be submissive and careful and distant.

"It's fine," he said quietly. "It's all right."

"I'm sorry," she said. There, she'd done it. He wanted to rant, to rave, to kiss the "I'm sorry" right out of her.

Donovan sighed. Telling her he was fine obviously wasn't going to do the trick and make her feel less terrible. And it wasn't going to make Frank feel any better, either.

"Look," he said. "It's beyond tough losing a child, but friends shouldn't have to pretend Ben's death didn't happen. It did, and nothing will bring him back. And Frank is right. Despite the fact that it hurts like hell to think of Ben, pretending he never existed is worse. It's only natural for you to talk about what happened."

Donovan didn't know if what he was saying made sense or even if it was true. All he knew at the moment was one thing. "I don't want either of you to feel bad for talking about the fact that I once had a son and I don't anymore."

Frank raised his head slightly, but he still looked horribly uncomfortable. Of course, there was no reason for him to feel comfortable. Donovan was a total stranger, and death was never a comfortable topic. A man couldn't expect a boy to break the ice, no matter the circumstances.

Donovan dropped to a squat. He held out his hand. "That looks like a bike chain. Mind if I have a look?"

"You know how to fix bikes?" Anna asked, a surprised look in her eyes.

A chuckle escaped Donovan, but before he could speak Frank let out a loud whoosh that lifted his bangs. "Anna, he fixes people. Probably bikes are easier."

"Sometimes they are," Donovan said, taking the greasy chain Frank held out to him. "Not always. I'm not an expert on bike repair, but this looks like something I can handle. One of the links needs to be bent and oiled. I doubt there's a chain tool here, but if I'm careful, a hammer, nail and a block of wood will do the trick and allow me to separate the chain so I can fix it. Come on. Let's go see what's in the garage."

"You're going to get all greasy," Anna admonished.

Donovan flashed her a grin and tweaked her nose with his thumb. "I know. Grease is part of the deal when you're taking a bike apart. If you don't get dirty, what fun is it? Right?"

He looked at Frank.

"Oh, yeah," Frank agreed. "It's a guy thing, Anna."

Anna squealed and looked as if she'd just swallowed the chain.

"Uh-oh," Donovan said. "That probably wasn't the best thing to say, Frank. Anyway, Anna's no slouch with tools herself, you know?"

"You mean like an honorary guy?"

Anna crossed her arms. "I am not an honorary guy, I'll have you know."

Frank was starting to get that flustered, red-faced look again. Donovan knew he had to take pity on him. By the look Anna flashed him, he was sure she felt the same.

"Let's just say that Anna's a woman who happens to be talented in many areas. Fixing bikes is not a guy or a woman thing," Donovan told Frank.

Frank gave Anna a sideways tentative glance.

"That was very tactful of you," Anna told Donovan. "A good thing to keep in mind when dealing with girls, Frank," she said. "We don't like to be put in boxes."

Frank looked disgusted. "I'm not ready to start *dealing* with girls, yet, Anna," he told her. "Especially not Mitzi Ronberg."

Anna stopped in her tracks. She gave Frank a speculative glance, like a mother who hadn't realized her baby was growing up. Donovan did his best not to laugh. He had no idea who Mitzi Ronberg was, but he was willing to bet the young lady in question had her heart set on Frank.

"Well, of course not," Anna said, as they resumed their walk and opened the door of the garage where tools and a workbench were kept. "I meant down the road. No rush at all, and anyway, thank you for even thinking that I could be an honorary man. It was very thoughtful of you."

Frank shrugged and smiled. "No problem. I'll remember about the 'no-boxes' thing, though. My mom would probably agree. Can you fix it?" he asked, turning to Donovan and making a swift change of subject.

How quickly young people moved on, Donovan thought. He envied Frank his ability to rebound as if nothing had happened. Despite the boy's obvious youth and that comment about Mitzi, he was, in some ways, wiser than many adults.

"We'll do all we can," Donovan promised.

Fortunately it didn't take long to fix the slightly damaged chain and get it back on the bike. Donovan wiped the grease off his hands and stood.

"I think it'll do," he said.

Frank tried it out, riding in a small circle. "Works great. You're the best, Mr. Barrett! Wait till I tell Mom that you were the one who fixed my bike. I think she has a crush on you. Of course, she says all the women do. I mean…you know what I mean."

"Even Anna?" Donovan couldn't resist.

Frank looked up. He stared at Anna as if such a thing could never have occurred to him. "Well, of course not. Anna works for you. You're her boss. She probably hates you sometimes. I hate my mom sometimes. I mean, not really, but still…I mean…"

"I know what you mean," Anna said, managing a smile. "And you're right. A woman can't have a crush on her boss. That would be a big mistake. How's the bike?"

"Perfect."

"So…don't you think you'd better deliver the rest of your papers before it gets late and your mother wonders where you are?"

"Guess so. Thanks, Mr. Barrett. See you, Anna."

Frank pedaled away.

"Thank you," Anna said softly.

Donovan turned and looked at her. "I didn't do much. It was a simple repair."

"You made him feel comfortable. And you didn't make fun of him, even after that comment about Mitzi."

"She have a thing for him?"

Anna shrugged. "She's a fashion doll wannabe. Nice, but pretty focused on boys right now. And Frank's a sweet kid."

"That's what girls want nowadays? Sweet kids?"

Laughing, Anna started to walk toward the house. "Okay, he's a bit of a bad boy. Gets in trouble at times, but he's not mean."

"Ah, bad boys. I see the world hasn't changed. Women are still chasing the ones who are all wrong for them."

The two of them stopped in their tracks. His comment had been flippant. He'd said it without even thinking, but it had been the wrong thing to say.

"Forget I said that," he said.

"Can't," she said. "Anyway, it was true. No need to be sorry." She continued moving toward the house.

"Going back to work?" he couldn't help asking.

She turned and walked backward, a big grin on her face. "I'm going to get your reward for being so nice to Frank and making his day."

"You're going to give me a reward?" he asked. Unbidden, a vision of Anna in his arms, in his bed, came to mind.

"Cake," she said with a look acknowledging the fact that she knew his thoughts had wandered into the forbidden. "You get chocolate cake. Linette makes the best."

Regret trickled through Donovan even though he knew she was right. Getting close was just prolonging the torture when they'd both agreed there wasn't any future for the two of them.

In fact, if he stayed in Lake Geneva, he might one day have to deal with a painful truth. Sooner or later some man might teach Anna that he could be trusted and that she could risk loving him.

There would be a man who could raise her child with her.

You'll have to see her with that man all the time, he told himself. Exchanging loving glances, maybe even touching. When that day comes, it's going to drive you out of your mind.

He took a deep breath. "I'm sure Linette makes great chocolate cake," he told Anna. "I'll be right in."

He would—somehow—manage to eat a slice of cake, smile and thank Anna and Linette. Then he was going out.

It was impossible to stay here today. He had to escape the confines of this house. Now that the raw truth was in the open, he needed some space, some time.

And in the long run?

Maybe Lake Geneva wasn't big enough for both Anna and himself. If one of them had to go, it would be him. This town was her world.

It was time to start thinking of what his next world would be.

CHAPTER TWELVE

ANNA slid her little car into a coveted parking space near the edge of town and walked toward the shop where Bridget worked. She couldn't stay in the house anymore, not when every thought of Donovan was making her crazy and achy. Fortunately she had errands she could run in town, and Bridget and some friends had agreed to meet her for lunch.

Donovan had told her he was going to Williams Bay hours earlier, so maybe she could have a brief respite from pretending to be the perfect housekeeper when she was obviously so bad at it. Anna was pretty sure kissing one's employer or lusting after him was grounds for instant disqualification in the housekeeper hall of fame.

She really did not want to think about kissing or lusting now.

Breezing into the gift shop, Anna saw that Paula and Nan were already waiting. They greeted her with hugs.

It was a busy day at the shop, and all too soon Anna and her friends had eaten their lunch. Bridget would have to be getting back to work soon.

"You've been so quiet today," Nan told Anna. "You didn't even admonish me for any of my gibes about what you were doing with Donovan."

Anna managed a smile, but it wasn't a prizewinner. And obviously not very convincing, either.

"Oh," Paula said.

"What?" Anna couldn't control the quaver in her voice. Paula had a knack for seeing things a bit too clearly.

Her friend studied her carefully. "Nothing. We don't have much time left today. Let's walk. Have to burn the calories."

They started down the street and had gotten as far as the cruise line docks when Anna felt a twinge, a sense of heightened anticipation and awareness. She started to glance to the right…then quickly glanced away again. If she was right, and her friends saw what she thought she'd seen…

"Let's go this way," she said, attempting to turn in a different direction.

But her voice and actions had obviously given her away. Paula pivoted to the right. "Isn't that Donovan?"

"Probably not. He was going to Williams Bay," Anna said, but her mouth went dry as she looked up. Donovan was there, buying a ticket for one of the cruises.

"Looks like he's back from Williams Bay," Nan said. "Come on, let's go say hello."

"What? We can't do that," Anna said. "He's alone. By choice," she stressed. "Besides, Bridget has to get back to the shop. And you—"

"Have a few hours before work. Paula, too. Bridge?"

Bridget groaned. "I'd love to stay, but Anna's right. I'm gone. That doesn't mean I don't want a complete rundown of what happens here today. Anna, go on. Say hello. The man is a newcomer to our town and you're acting as if he's poison. That's just not right. Now, go over there and be pleasant."

"That's right, Anna. We should be extending our hospitality," Paula said. "Let's go. He looks lonely. Doesn't he, Nan?"

"It's a crime for a man like that to even walk down the street unaccompanied," Nan agreed.

Anna frowned. She looked from Bridget to Paula to Nan. "That's enough. Would all of you just stop? You're not fooling anyone. I see what you're trying to do, so let me tell you something. If Donovan wanted company, he would ask for it, and he'd have plenty of volunteers. You know that. Now I need to get back to work. I have duties."

"Yeah, well I think the house will manage to stay in one piece for a few hours even if you're not there to hold it together. Looks like Donovan is taking the full lake tour on the Walworth. He's alone. That can't be fun," Nan said, sweeping Anna along. "I'll bet he would like company."

Anna was pretty sure he wouldn't. He'd probably wonder why his housekeeper and her friends were crowding him when he was having some alone time.

"Absolutely not," she said, digging in her heels.

"Donovan," Paula called, waving her arm.

A groan escaped Anna's lips as Donovan turned around. For a second he frowned as if he couldn't understand what was happening. Then he started their way.

"You're going to pay," Anna muttered, quietly jabbing Paula in the back. "The man was alone because he wanted to be alone."

"But he's smiling." Nan said the words between her teeth.

"He smiles a lot. He has manners, unlike some people I know," Anna declared, stepping forward to meet Donovan.

"I'm sorry we disturbed you," she told him.

He shook his head. "You say that too much. Don't."

"Ooh, commanding. That's sooo sexy," Paula whispered.

Anna rammed her elbow backward slightly, surprising an oomph from her friend.

"I know, but you were just about to board. We shouldn't have interrupted you."

"You're not. I was just…looking for something to do, getting to know the area."

"A cruise is a great way to do that," Paula agreed. "Of course, so is a local."

Her friends were loyal and she loved them to death, but none of them was particularly subtle and it was obvious that they had gone beyond mere curiosity about Donovan to deciding that Anna needed to be matched up with him.

Somehow she managed to hang on to her teetering, pasted-on smile. "The tour is very thorough and a great way to see the community from a different perspective," she said. "I hope you enjoy it."

Donovan's eyes held a trace of amusement. "You

don't think I'm going to let this pass, do you? I have three locals here and you think I'm going to miss out on the opportunity to hear the secrets the other passengers don't get to hear?"

He tugged on her hand. She didn't budge. "Donovan, don't tell me you're not being pushed into this. Stop being so nice."

His grip tightened. "I'm not being nice. The truth is that after this morning, I did need some time alone. I went over to Williams Bay, had breakfast and spent some time at the water's edge watching the boats. It was only natural to segue from that into actually wanting to be out on the lake. I've heard it's calming."

It was, but Anna felt anything but calm right now.

"You don't have to do this, Donovan."

He gazed down at her and took her hands. "And you don't, either. This isn't a command or an order. It's not part of your job, but I'd like you to come along."

Anna studied his expression for several seconds. "Better decide soon," he urged. "The boat is leaving."

Reluctantly she agreed. She tried not to notice that Paula and Nan were all but high-fiving each other. Anna squirmed. She'd discuss this with her friends later. For now, she followed Donovan onto the boat.

"Inside or outside?" she asked, turning to him.

He held out his hand, motioning for her to lead the way. "After you. You're the expert."

"Upstairs, then. It's open air."

Together they moved up to the top level of the boat. "Anna," someone called out. She turned and saw

Thomas Liddell, a local real estate agent. He was with a young couple, probably showing them the sights, trying to close a deal.

"Hi, Tom," she said with a smile.

He nodded slightly to her right and she got the message. "Tom, this is Donovan Barrett, my boss. He owns Morning View Manor. You know where it is. Tom and I went to school together," she told Donovan.

"We worked at a local restaurant together, too," Tom reminded her. "For more than one summer."

For half a second, Donovan's hand tightened on her arm, but then he let her go.

"I understand you have a way with a bicycle chain," Tom said with a grin.

"You know Frank?" Donovan asked.

"Everyone knows Frank," Tom agreed. "He's got a big case of hero worship. I guess it's not every day that someone of your stature stoops to fixing a kid's bike."

Donovan held out his hands as if to ward off the praise. "No stature here. And the bike thing was mostly luck. I know one or two tricks."

"You bike?"

Anna felt rather than saw the way Donovan jerked slightly. "I used to. Now and then."

From his reaction, she wondered if he'd ridden with Ben in tow.

"Some great trails around here. I could use a companion. My wife doesn't like anything with less than four wheels," Tom said.

Anna turned to look up at Donovan and saw that his

expression had turned thoughtful, even surprised. "I might want to try that," he agreed.

Tom nodded. "Well, better get back to my clients. Nice meeting you, Donovan."

Tom moved away and Anna followed Donovan to a seat near the front of the boat.

"You're handy to have around," he said.

She blinked.

"I meet a lot of nice people when I'm with you," he said.

"Oh, that. Tom's just very friendly."

He hesitated for a second. "He wasn't one of the ones who hurt you, was he?"

"Tom? No, we were never like that with each other."

She looked up at Donovan and saw that he didn't believe her. "We weren't."

"*You* weren't," he corrected. "He would have gone out with you."

Well, she wasn't going to deny that. Tom had asked her out once, but it was right after she'd been hurt badly by another boy and she had told him no. Thank goodness he'd never held it against her.

"Tom's very nice, and he's devoted to his wife," she said, a bit primly.

A laugh escaped Donovan. "All right, I believe you, and he did seem like a great guy."

"You should take him up on his offer. You need some guy time." Donovan didn't answer, so Anna looked up to find him studying her a bit more solemnly than she had expected. "What?"

"You're going to make a great mother," he said quietly.

Her heart lurched. She hoped she would be a good mother, but she was absolutely sure that no matter what Donovan had said, he had been a good, even if often absent, father. His ways with her friends and with Frank showed her that he cared about people. He didn't differentiate between rich and poor. Young as he was, Ben must have known that his father adored him.

"You're missing him a lot today, aren't you?" she said, even though it was the last thing on earth she had planned to say. She gasped.

He placed one finger to her lips. "Don't say you're sorry."

She shook her head. "I didn't even think how that would sound. And with people around to hear, too."

"No one's that close to us," he told her. "Your friends stayed downstairs."

Which only made her feel even more guilty. Her friends had gone beyond the bounds of friendship into matchmaking. Donovan wasn't blind. He would know that, and yet he was still being unfailingly polite.

"Anyway, I *am* missing him a lot today. Ben would have loved this," he told her. "He was crazy about the water, the beach, boats. I think that was part of why Cecily chose a house in Lake Geneva. The first day I drove into town, I couldn't help thinking that he would love riding on one of these boats and yet, until today, I hadn't even ventured near one. I haven't really even gone out on the water. This morning with Frank…well, it was time to do this."

He should have been allowed to do it alone, Anna couldn't help thinking.

Silence crept in. The sun was bright today, the water and the view of the shore with its gorgeous historic homes was stunningly beautiful, but Donovan was here to face a few demons and this couldn't be a pleasant experience for him.

"I should go sit with the girls so you can have some time to yourself." She rose.

He clamped down on her arm. "I'm asking you as a friend, don't go just yet," he said. "Talk to me. Give me the Anna Nowell tour."

She nodded. "All right. That tower that you see is four stories tall. It's part of Black Point Mansion, which was built in 1888."

Donovan let go of her, and she understood. He needed to do this, but it couldn't be easy. Connection with another person, any person, could help. She placed her hand over his and quietly continued with her speech, even though many of the things she was telling him were things he could get from the tour if he listened.

"That's my favorite," she said suddenly, veering away from the standard tour fare.

He turned her hand and rubbed his thumb over her palm, sending a tremor through her. "It's pretty but so are many others. Why this one?"

"It's unabashedly unpretentious," she said, and she wanted to add, *like you,* but she wouldn't. Her friends were trying to set them up. She couldn't do anything that would sound as if she had gotten some foolish ideas into her own head.

"I like that interpretation," he told her with a laugh.

"You're making this much easier for me. I'm enjoying myself. I want you to know that. Now…tell me what you think of the others. You've got a fascinating perspective on things."

So for the remainder of the tour Anna poured out her secret feelings about these stately old buildings. "I've always thought of that one as the playground. See how all the parts kind of turn and fit together in curves and stairs and arches. It looks like a great place to explore."

She continued on in a rush, keeping her voice soft and low and not waiting for Donovan to reply, hoping her mindless chatter was cocooning him without interfering with his thoughts.

When the boat finally docked again, she rose immediately. He stood beside her, towering over her. For a minute she thought he was going to bow over her hand like some gentleman from the Regency era.

"Thank you, Anna," he said, his eyes filled with warmth.

"Was it…okay?" she asked, hoping he knew that she meant his experience and not her performance.

"Yes. It was what I needed. I haven't really said goodbye to him yet, I guess. I think it's going to be a slow, gradual thing. Today was a start. I'm glad you stayed."

He led her downstairs, only reaching out to touch her when she nearly stumbled and then immediately letting her go. When they finally met up with Nan and Paula, both of them were able to act as if the excursion had been just another sightseeing tour.

"You ladies enjoy the rest of your day," he told Anna's friends. "It's been a pleasure seeing you again."

Anna could see that Paula would have liked to stay around and ask questions, but Nan tugged on her arm. "Have to go help my sister. She called me with a work emergency," she said. "I'll call you," she mouthed silently to Anna as the two women turned to walk away.

"You're parked close by?" Donovan asked. "I'll walk you to your car."

"Oh, that's not necessary. Really," Anna said, feeling as if she had reached her limit of being alone with Donovan.

The truth had dawned on her while she was on the boat. She wanted to sit beside him forever. She was in over her head, and her heart was in grave danger of being broken. This time she couldn't even say that he had betrayed her like Brent had. He hadn't. They'd both been painfully honest with each other, and the truth was that they liked and desired each other. They enjoyed being together, but they couldn't ever have more. "It's close," she lied, "and I have things I need to do."

At first she thought Donovan was going to insist on being gallant, but then he told her he would see her back at Morning View. They were about to go their separate ways when the sound of a woman's voice calling Donovan's name made them both turn.

Dana Wellinton was coming down the street. Her stomach was even more rounded than the last time Anna had seen her, but she was still incredibly beautiful.

Rushing up to them, Dana flashed that perfect smile.

"Donovan, you're just the man I've been looking for. Come have coffee with me." She turned as if Donovan would just follow her. Anna assumed most men would, so she gave a brief wave to Donovan and turned back to her car.

"Dana, you remember Anna, don't you?"

Dana stopped walking. She reluctantly turned around. "Oh, yes. She's your housekeeper." Her expression and tone indicated that her view of housekeepers hadn't improved since she and Anna had last met.

"Yes, she is. It's a fascinating, demanding profession. But Anna's also my friend," Donovan said pointedly. "Unfortunately we were just going home, so I'm afraid I'll have to take a rain check on the coffee. It's been nice seeing you again."

"But…"

"I'm sorry," Donovan said.

"But I just heard from someone that your son's birthday would be coming up in a few weeks and I wanted to be the very first to offer you my condolences. You must relive every moment of that accident every day."

Donovan froze in his tracks.

Anna felt her heart turn to stone. She hadn't known. At least she hadn't known the exact date of Ben's birth. No doubt Donovan knew but hadn't wanted to think about it yet. And now he'd been forced to think not only about the fact that Ben wouldn't be here for his birthday but about the horrific way he'd died, just because a selfish woman was trying to score points with him. It was all Anna could do to keep from screaming at Dana.

She wouldn't. She would not make a circus of Donovan's pain in the middle of the street and in front of this insensitive woman.

And yet…Dana seemed confused, even forlorn, clueless. For a minute Anna felt sorry for the woman and her children. Some people just didn't get it, and maybe they were to be pitied. If it weren't for the fact that her words had surely hit Donovan with something he hadn't readied himself for, Anna might have felt a hint of sympathy.

"Thank you, but I have to go," Donovan said, his voice rough, his lips stiff.

He took Anna by the arm and started to lead her away. She knew he had no idea where they were going, but she said nothing until they were out of sight of Dana. Then she stopped. She turned to him.

He glared at her. "If you're thinking of telling me that you're sorry again I warn you I'll be forced to kiss you and keep kissing you until you stop talking," he said, his voice pitched low.

Anna shook her head. "I wasn't going to say that. I was going to say that your son's birthday shouldn't be a cause of condolences. He lived and he made people happy just by being here. His birthday should be a cause for celebration."

Donovan stared down into her eyes, his eyes dark and agonized. Then, without warning, he placed his hands on her arms and pulled her toward him. He drew her close and kissed her. Slowly. Thoroughly. He tasted, he savored, he drove her insane.

Then he let her go and started walking. "You're an amazing woman. It's going to be hard to walk away from you," he said.

But he did. He took her to her car, made sure that she was safely inside and then he walked away.

Anna could barely control her trembling. Donovan's kiss had taken her completely by surprise. It had made her realize just how pathetic she had become where this man was concerned. While he was touching her she hadn't had one thought for anyone else who might have been walking down the street.

Now, however, she worried that someone had seen their embrace. She didn't want anyone to misunderstand him or criticize Donovan for kissing his housekeeper. Mostly, though, she wanted to run after him.

Instead she drove home. She tried not to think about the fact that her friends were trying to pair her up with Donovan. She tried not to think about what she had discovered when Dana had said the words that had ripped Donovan so badly.

But her efforts failed.

I'm in love with him, Anna thought.

And that made staying with Donovan impossible, even if leaving meant putting off her dreams. If she stayed, he would discover the truth. Then he would feel not love but guilt.

That wasn't going to happen, because she was going to leave here and find a new job.

"I will," she whispered to herself, "just as soon as I

can find someone to help him. Someone dependable and honest and…"

Not in love with him, she wanted to add, but she didn't. The truth was that any woman who worked for him would eventually fall in love with him, but not all of them would have children or want children or remind him daily of his loss just by her very existence.

There must be many women who would be perfect for this job, Anna acknowledged. Too bad she was no longer one of them.

The next few days were going to be difficult, but for now…

She began to go through her list of friends and coworkers, searching for someone who would fit.

CHAPTER THIRTEEN

IT WAS late by the time Donovan came home. He'd spent hours pacing, walking the shore path and wondering how he could have behaved so abominably.

He knew Anna desired him just as he desired her, but he also knew that she had grown up here. She cared what people thought. How utterly callous of him to practically maul her on a public street. Her eyes had been shocked when he'd let her go. He owed her so much more…

Beginning with a call explaining why he was late and letting her know he had a few more errands to take care of.

Anna had listened carefully. Her voice had betrayed nothing. Over the phone he couldn't get a handle on how she was feeling, and it drove him nuts. He wanted to be face-to-face with her.

Of course, that was the problem. He wanted to be face-to-face with her all the time these days. He had tried to stay away, tried to keep his hands off her, tried to keep from thinking about her and worrying about her and wanting to be with her. None of it was working.

She deserved a man who would agree to all the babies she wanted, a man who could be a good father and a good husband. She deserved a normal life. Now, not later. Not someday.

Soon he was going to have to leave Lake Geneva. He'd grown to like it here. He was even beginning to feel more like a man and less like a complete disaster, and so much of that was because of Anna and the people she'd brought into his life. But he owed her the chance at a normal life, and she couldn't have that if she kept running into him, a man who was apt to grab her without warning.

Anna would find a man like Tom someday. She would find love, because of course men would love her. Then she would discover that not all men were idiots.

Donovan could barely breathe. His chest felt tight.

"But some men *are* idiots," he muttered. He was one of them. Of course, he had to leave. This was her town, her home, the place where she would find love and raise her babies.

"So do something, Barrett. Finish it. Make her happy," he ordered himself.

He pulled out his telephone and dialed.

Phil picked up on the third ring. "Donovan?" he asked when Donovan had said hello and apologized for calling him at home. "Hey, buddy, don't apologize. I'm glad you felt comfortable doing that. We used to talk all the time."

"I know. I remember. I'm truly sorry I haven't been a better friend," Donovan said suddenly. A part of him wanted to smile. It was the kind of thing Anna would have said.

"Don't," Phil replied. "Maybe *I* wasn't the best of friends. I shouldn't have pushed you when you weren't ready." Donovan could tell that Phil wanted to ask if he was ready now, but his friend refrained.

"I probably would have pushed, too, if our positions had been reversed," Donovan said. "I suppose you know why I'm calling. I wanted to wait, but…"

Phil laughed. "No one wants to wait when adoption is the issue. Actually, I was planning on calling you in a couple of days when things gel a bit more. I've put some feelers out. There are a couple of possibilities." He explained the cases. "I can't promise anything. Nothing is firm as of yet."

Donovan sighed. "That's all right. I haven't told Anna yet, so nothing's firm here, either."

"It's touchy," Phil agreed. "Both sides have to be sure. And everyone has to know the lay of the land going in. These cases can be wonderfully fulfilling and successful, but they also have the potential to be filled with land mines."

"But there's hope for something soon?"

"I think I can say there's an excellent chance. Even if this case doesn't work out, from what you've told me, your Anna sounds like she'd be an exemplary parent. We'll find something, but you have to talk to her, Donovan. I haven't done much beyond asking questions of some colleagues, scouting out possibilities. Without Anna, that's as far as we can go."

"I know. I just wanted to test the waters. I'll get back to you soon." He started to say goodbye.

"Donovan, do you think you'll ever come back?"

Donovan knew that Phil meant more than just to Chicago. He was talking about medicine.

"I don't have any plans right now," he said. "None."

Beyond making sure that Anna had what she needed and wanted. That was the next step. Then he would see to himself.

Anna was trying to keep herself busy the next morning and keep her mind off of Donovan when he showed up in the hallway beside her. She'd been taking inventory of a linen closet even though she already knew exactly what and how much was in the closet.

Turning to meet him, she tried to figure out how to tell him that she was going to leave him without making him feel bad about kissing her and without revealing that she had somehow gone and done something stupid like falling in love with him.

He looked so serious. Staring up into his intense eyes, with his hair falling over his forehead he was like a dark lord ready to tell her that something terrible had happened.

"What?" she asked, not knowing why she asked.

"I need to talk to you. Outside would be best. Seated would definitely be preferable." Gently he took the cloth she was holding and, with her hand in his, he led her out to the deck and beyond. There was a bench midway between the deck and the shore, shaded by a willow. It was private. No one from the house or the shore would hear them here.

Anna wet her lips nervously. She wondered if she

should give him her resignation now along with the list of possible candidates she'd stayed up all night making.

But he surprised her by reaching out and gently smoothing his thumb over her cheek. "You didn't sleep well. You have circles beneath your eyes. That's my fault."

"No," she said, even though it had been him who had kept her awake.

"I'm sorry I kissed you in the middle of the street yesterday. I seem to have made a habit of that. I know it has to stop. Cold turkey this time."

Her heart fell even though he was only telling her what they'd already discussed. "Yes."

"I don't know how much longer I'll be in Lake Geneva," he said quietly. "Not long, I don't think. I came here to get away from things that were destroying me, and I think I've done that. You've helped me. I want to help you before I go. I have connections in Chicago. Private adoption is a possibility. I hope you don't mind but I've made some calls. You could have your baby sooner than you might have thought."

He was leaving. He was leaving. The words ran through her mind and her heart hurt and her eyes ached and she wanted to cry but if she did, she would hurt him. Anna swallowed.

"I can't afford the medical fees."

"I can."

Mutely she shook her head.

"Yes, Anna. Let me."

"I can't take your money."

"You can. You have to."

Don't think about him going. Don't think about anything sad, she ordered herself. "Why?" she managed to say.

He shook his head. "Why do you have to take my money?" He hesitated. "Consider it a severance package. I promised you one once, remember?"

"A severance package couldn't be nearly as much as you're offering," she said. And then she could no longer avoid thinking about what all of this meant. He was going and…

"You're firing me," she said, her voice a whisper. Her heart was breaking at the thought of his leaving, but the other thought—that he was dissatisfied with her—was wrenching her soul apart.

"No." The word was like a shot. Loud. Emphatic. Even angry. "Damn it, no, Anna. I can't believe I gave you that impression. I—"

He leaned forward, cupped her chin and placed a kiss on her cheek. "No." He kissed her forehead. "No. I just want you to be happy."

She couldn't be happy. Donovan was leaving.

"I understand," she said, her voice weakened by the tears she refused to let fall. "You feel bad because you're leaving me without a job. You feel sorry for me."

"That's not it at all." Donovan cupped her face then and forced her to stare into his eyes. "You're a strong, vibrant, admirable woman. I don't feel sorry for you, but your happiness matters to me. More than you know."

His voice was harsh, and Anna felt as if she were somehow making him miserable. She wanted to tell him that his happiness mattered to her, too. That was the only reason she was working to hold her tears back and trying so hard not to beg him to stay. She didn't know how to make any of this right. Taking the money seemed wrong, but if she took it, that might free Donovan. He wouldn't feel guilty. He could leave here satisfied and with no regrets.

"I want you to be happy, too," she said.

He groaned. "Then take the money. Let me help you make your dreams come true."

Anna knew she hadn't earned that money. Taking it didn't even seem honorable, and yet she knew she had to say yes. She could never tell Donovan that he couldn't make all of her dreams come true. She would have her child, and she would be eternally grateful, but she would never have Donovan, the man she now realized she loved more than she had ever loved anyone.

"Anna, please," he said.

A low, whining sound split the air. The sound of a harsh yell and a scream froze Anna's blood. Then a crash, loud and metallic and terrible followed.

She and Donovan turned to each other in shock. The scream had been male. Young. Familiar.

Then Anna ran, with all her might. Her heart screaming, the tears already flowing, Anna turned toward the place where the crash had sounded. Well over a block away. When she made it to the street and had run a full block, Donovan passed her up.

A small sports car sat halfway off the road at a skewed angle, tire tracks showing the path it had taken.

The driver was trying to crawl out the door, but a bicycle, Frank's bicycle, lay partially under the car, up against the door, its frame bent.

Anna scanned the scene, looking for Frank. *Please, please, please be okay,* her mind chanted, even though she knew he couldn't be okay. She couldn't even find him. He'd obviously been thrown.

"Frank!" she cried.

"There," Donovan said, already moving to a small stand of bushes across the road.

Following him, Anna saw what Donovan had seen. A loose tennis shoe, an arm, the small mass that was Frank's body. There was blood. Oh, so much blood. Frank's body was twisted, his legs sprawled, his left arm at an awful angle.

Anna struggled for breath. She fought blackness as she tried to get to Frank.

"He turned out of the driveway like a flash," the driver was saying, limping over. "I didn't see him at first. I tried to swerve. Is he—"

The man didn't finish his sentence, and no one answered him.

Donovan dropped to his knees heavily. He stared at Frank. Then he looked at his own hands.

Anna saw they were shaking. Seconds were ticking away, and fear ripped through her. She didn't know what to do to help Frank.

"Donovan…"

He didn't answer at first.

"Donovan…"

He still didn't look at her.

"Donovan," she begged.

He took a deep, shuddering breath. "Call 911," he said. Then he moved to sit behind Frank's head.

"We're here, Frank," Donovan said, even though Frank hadn't moved. "You've been in an accident, but you're not alone. Help is on the way." His voice was low and almost robotically calm. It betrayed none of the shakiness that Anna had seen in his hands.

"He's breathing. We'll leave the helmet on. It's very important that we not move his head until the EMTs arrive and can stabilize him. His leg is bleeding. I need something to stanch that," Donovan said, looking up at Anna. His eyes were dark, anguished.

Then things started happening very fast. Donovan started barking orders. "Lie down," he told the motorist who was crying and swaying. "If you faint and hit your head, things will be worse. Get off your feet."

The man complied.

Within minutes Donovan had mobilized all of his staff. He had asked for and gotten cloths to stanch the blood flowing from Frank's leg. He had cut away Frank's clothing and examined him, trying to ascertain if there might be any internal injuries. He kept Frank's head immobilized, continuing to check his vitals.

Anna was vaguely aware of a murmuring, of the sound of neighbors and bypassers gathering, stopping to stare. But her heart and her mind were on the man and boy in front of her. Donovan was dark-eyed and tense, completely focused on what was happening beneath his hands. And Frank was lying so still. Too still? Was this as bad as it looked?

Anna bit her lip. The thought of Frank never smiling again, never being…here was too terrible to even consider. And the prospect of Donovan losing a child he'd tried to save after what he'd been through…Anna's heart felt like a bird trying to flutter its way out of her chest. She felt sick. So very sick. Perhaps she swayed.

"Don't do that. Don't lose it on me, sweetheart." Donovan's voice reached her. "Talk to him, Anna. Softly. Sing to him, hum to him. We can't tell if he can hear or not, but he may be able to. If so, it might help."

Anna talked; she sang. She told Frank a story about the first time she met him. She watched Donovan working over his patient and casting fleeting glances toward the driver in the grass.

Once, when the man groaned, Donovan looked down at his hands as if he wished that he had more than one pair. There were people around, some who were talking to the driver but none who appeared to know what to do if the man warranted medical attention. Anna could see the agitation in the glances Donovan gave the man, but he never left Frank. Frank who was so pale that he looked almost—

She couldn't even think it. Anyway, it wasn't true. He was breathing. Donovan was checking his pulse, touching his skin to see if shock had set in.

"Stay with me, Anna," Donovan said. She did. She kept talking to Frank.

Sirens sounded in the distance. Donovan spared a

glance for his watch. He'd done it before. She knew what he was thinking. Getting trauma patients transported to a hospital quickly was of incredible importance. The Platinum Ten Minutes. She'd seen it on a news program.

"Donovan," she began, but then Frank stirred and whimpered.

"Son, can you tell me your name?" Donovan whispered urgently. "Don't try to move your head. Don't try to nod. Just talk to me. Tell me your name," he said as Frank's parents drove up in their car and ran over to their son.

Anna nodded to them. They looked so lost. They nodded back and moved away slightly to let Donovan take care of their child. Anna noticed that Donovan didn't look at them. His concentration was completely on Frank.

"Can you tell me your name?" he coaxed again.

"I—yes." When Frank managed both first and last names in a raspy, disjointed voice, Donovan closed his eyes.

Immediately he opened them again. He looked directly at Anna as he asked Frank a few more questions. For a few seconds it felt as if all three of them were connected, Anna couldn't help thinking. But now that Frank was coming to, he was in pain and he was scared. He started to buck.

"Frank," Donovan said. "I know you hurt, but don't move."

"I—Donovan, my arm—"

"I've got you, buddy," Donovan's voice soothed like

cool medicine. "The ambulance is on the way. Better than a bike, even. A big, fast, red car? You'll be the talk of the school."

Frank stared at Donovan, his eyes glazed but completely trusting. Anna's heart flipped.

"Okay, big guy. The ambulance is almost here," Donovan said as the sirens grew louder. "You hang on and lie still and we're going to take you out of here. These guys tend to be very good. They know their stuff, and they're fast, too."

His words were low. He continued to monitor Frank, but he was so unobtrusive about it that Anna doubted Frank was even aware that Donovan was tracking every beat of his heart and every breath he took.

"Frank?"

"Yes?"

"What day is it?"

"Wednesday."

"You got it. Where are we?"

Frank started to try to shake his head. Donovan soothed him, leaning close to whisper encouragement.

"By Anna's," Frank whispered back. He moaned.

"You're doing great, Frank. That was an excellent job. Keep holding on and listening to me. What kind of sports do you play?"

"Baseball," Frank managed to say, his voice thick.

"Pitcher?"

"Catcher." She knew what he was doing. Trying to monitor Frank for shock and trying to keep the boy's mind off his pain and fear.

The exchange only lasted a moment. The emergency vehicles arrived. Donovan and the emergency workers moved into action, getting Frank on a cot, his neck in a brace. They put him in the ambulance and Frank's mother climbed in.

Anna rushed to Donovan who was starting to look ragged around the edges now that he was no longer the sole person in charge. She wanted to ask if Frank would be all right, but she couldn't ask that of Donovan. If the answer was no…

He was getting ready to climb into the ambulance.

"I'll meet you at the hospital," she said.

Donovan stopped. "Have someone drive you."

She opened her mouth to protest. "Anna, please. You're upset and…if you're not careful…"

"I'll have someone drive me," she promised. She would not argue this time, and she wouldn't cause Donovan to worry about her as well as Frank. He'd had too many personal experiences with auto accidents and their victims.

As he moved into the ambulance, the commanding presence he had been for the past few minutes seemed to disappear. His shoulders sagged. He looked beaten. He hesitated for just a second. Then he took a visible breath, squared his shoulders and moved in to see to Frank.

Hours later, at the hospital, after Anna had talked to a woozy Frank and found out that Frank had suffered a mild concussion, had a broken arm, several gashes and cuts and many bruises along with a broken rib, but that he would be back on his bike in time, Anna finally felt as if she could breathe.

People had been coming and going the entire time she was here. So many people knew and cared about Frank. Tom had shown up. He'd pressed a copy of a flier into her hands.

"They were handing these out at the office. Frank is on the school paper and even though it's summer, some of the kids managed to get a notice out about Frank's accident. Everyone was worried about him, and this seemed like a good way to pass the news along."

Anna read the copy, its words bringing tears to her eyes.

"Thank you," she told Tom.

"I thought the Doc might want to read it," he said, looking a bit sheepish. "Hey, it's only a school rag, but how often do you make the papers?"

It was a lame excuse, but Anna was grateful. She clutched the piece of paper and made her way to a room where one of the interns had told her that Dr. Barrett was resting. The door was open, so she slid inside.

Donovan was on a couch, his big body taking up the whole space. He lay on his side, his lashes resting on his cheeks. Even with his eyes closed, he looked exhausted. He looked wonderful, Anna thought.

She stepped forward. The temptation to just stand here and watch him breathe was too much for her. She took another step. A hand reached out and looped around her wrist. She gasped and looked into Donovan's eyes.

He started to sit up.

"No, don't," she said. "You're tired."

He ignored her and sat up anyway.

"You should be home," he told her.

"You, too."

He shrugged. "I heard that Frank is going to be fine," she told him.

"I know. I'm…glad." His voice was thick with emotion.

"You were pretty wonderful, you know."

Donovan frowned. He looked down at his hands as if he didn't know what they were and then he looked at Anna. "I didn't save him, Anna. He would have survived had I not been there."

"Not everyone feels that way." She held out the flier. It was a childish recounting of how Frank had been hit by a car and how Donovan Barrett had saved his life. She explained why Frank's friends had written the missive. "You're a hero to them," she said.

"Go home, Anna," he said wearily.

She shook her head.

"Anna, I balked. I froze. When we heard that crash, I knew it was Frank. You ran. I didn't. For a good ten seconds, maybe more, I didn't even move. And when I got to the scene, I couldn't do a thing. My hands were like stones. My mind wouldn't function. At all. If you hadn't called my name, if you hadn't been there, if the situation had been worse…"

He shoved one hand back though his hair. "Go home, Anna."

"Donovan, I—"

"No. Don't."

She looked into his eyes and knew there was nothing she could say. Her mind was screaming at her to say something, do something, to stop the tragedy that was happening.

Donovan was drawing back into himself. He was telling her that he had failed Frank, but she didn't think that was the whole of it. More likely, he wasn't seeing Frank lying on the street, but Ben, while Donovan froze and let him die.

"Come home," she said. She touched his arm. She lay a hand on his chest.

Donovan sucked in a deep breath and then he grasped her. He pulled her against him, resting his chin on top of her head.

"I can't be what you need me to be, Anna. And I won't be anything less. Go home, sweetheart."

Anna's heart broke on the endearment. Donovan was at it again. Protecting her. As he'd protected Frank, even as he'd protected the man who had hit Frank, by making the man lie down and remain still. Anna was equally sure that Donovan had given pieces of his soul to many people, trying to help them, to save them.

He'd probably even lost a time or two, but he'd kept trying...until Ben's death had turned everything inside out.

"I'm no hero," he whispered.

She nodded. "You don't have to be." She kissed him. But she knew he was so very wrong. He was *her* hero. He had been from the word go. But he wouldn't want to hear that. She didn't intend to tell him.

A chasm stood between her and the man she loved. One that seemed impossible to bridge. It had always been there. She had always accepted it. But as she'd watched Donovan with Frank today, as she'd seen him doing the work he'd been born to do, she'd learned something. Or maybe she'd simply opened her eyes to something she'd already known.

Life would always be full of dangers, frightening situations, the possibility of failure or even death. But if a person didn't try, failure was a given. Death would win. Life had no chance. Donovan could have walked away from the accident and simply waited for someone else to take charge. He'd probably wanted to, but like it or not, he wasn't built that way. People like Donovan gave life a chance, and even if they sometimes lost, the fact that they tried mattered.

She couldn't blame Donovan for quitting his practice. He'd lost the ultimate. He'd lost a child. He'd outlived his baby. That was a life-changing situation. It made trying so much harder, seemingly impossible.

And yet…when it had counted, when there had been only him or no one to help, he had tried. He had given. If he found himself in that same situation again, he would do it again. Because of Ben, it would hurt. Ben would always be the one he hadn't been able to help, but in the end he would still do what needed doing.

Anna took a deep breath and thought about where that left her. The chasm, the distance between herself and Donovan. She'd thought it was impassable, but just as there would always be chasms in life, there would always be bridge builders, too. Without people making an attempt to cross over, the chasm would remain forever.

Right now Donovan was on an island, separated from her and from life. What he needed was a bridge builder.

Anna closed her eyes. What if she failed?

She could damage him.

But he was already damaged. If she didn't try, he would be alone forever on his island.

Anna picked up the phone. She said goodbye to her dreams and prayed for hope.

CHAPTER FOURTEEN

DONOVAN was alone in the library. He was making lists of things that had to be done before he left Lake Geneva. And he had to leave. He was hurting Anna. He could see it in her eyes.

He had disrupted her life when all she had ever wanted was a child. Now she was worrying about him. That had been clear at the hospital yesterday.

Her friends were trying to match her up with him. He'd known that and he'd allowed it to go on, even encouraged it when he'd known he had nothing to offer a woman like Anna.

You love her. The words seemed to sizzle in the air. He couldn't deny them. He loved Anna. Desperately. He'd told her he wasn't a hero, and he wasn't. Only years of experience had kept him going yesterday when he'd thought Frank's life might hang in the balance. Yet he wanted to be a hero for her.

She needed a hero. She needed a child.

He intended to see that she got at least one of those.

It was time to talk to Phil again and set things in motion at last.

The sound of the doorbell ringing broke into his thoughts. Anna was somewhere in the house, but the doorbell rang again. And again.

"She must be outside," he muttered, amazed that he didn't know exactly where she was. Ever since he'd come here he'd been constantly aware of her. The fact that he didn't feel her presence now made it seem as if a piece of him was missing. She had to be outside.

He swung the door open. A couple was standing on the doorstep. He recognized the woman as Frank's mother.

"Come in," he said, motioning them inside.

The man shuffled his feet, looking slightly uncomfortable, even as he stepped over the threshold. "Thank you. Okay." He held a baseball cap in his hands and was twisting it around and around. "We just…we wanted to thank you."

Donovan froze. He frowned and opened his mouth.

"Don't say you didn't do anything," the woman said. "Anna told me that you were denying that you made a difference, but, Dr. Barrett, we were there. Frank was really busted up. Maybe it wasn't life or death, but it felt like it at the time. You cared, and you knew what you were doing. We could see that. Everyone could see it. Frank was afraid and hurting. You calmed him. You calmed us. You can't know how much that meant."

Anna walked in, then. She was accompanied by a man. Donovan recognized him as one of the EMTs from the other day. "Dr. Barrett," he said. "I just wanted to tell you that it was an honor working alongside you yesterday. Most of the time, it's just me and my crew, and we're usually there in a heartbeat, but it was a bad day for accidents and we were running a couple of minutes slower than I would have liked. I can't tell you how glad I was to see that someone already had things in hand. Anna tells me that you had quite a reputation in Chicago, but I would never have known it."

Donovan blinked and the man turned red. "By that, I mean that you didn't get all high-handed just because you're a Chicago physician. You helped us do our job and you *let* us do our job without throwing your weight around. I'd be happy to work with you again."

"I—" Donovan didn't know what to say. "Thank you. Same here." He shook the man's hand. Now was not the time to tell the man he had hung up his stethoscope for good.

Anna smiled and spoke quietly to the man, leading him into the kitchen where Frank's parents were already ensconced. It seemed that there was a buffet in the kitchen.

"What's this about?" Donovan asked Anna.

"It's about truth," she said. "It's about heroes."

He frowned. "I told you—"

She placed her hand over his mouth, then replaced her fingers with her lips. "I know what you told me. But today I want you to listen, to hear, the way you used to hear your patients. You were known as a sympathetic doctor. I know. I've looked up everything I could find about you in the newspapers, on the Internet, in blogs."

"You're kidding, right. Blogs?"

"Well…I might have posed a question or two. Someone might have written an oratory about you as a result. Your patients and their families loved you, Donovan. Let that happen here."

"I can't do that again, Anna. I can't try to be a hero."

"Then don't be. You don't have to be that if you don't want to. Just be an ordinary man, one who cares. Because you do care. Be a doctor who uses his skills. Because you do have skills. Ones that make a difference."

He didn't know what to say to that. Anna was looking up at him, her eyes shining. And he couldn't help himself. He kissed her. "I care. Very much," he said.

"I know." She smiled again. He knew she didn't understand that he was talking about his feelings for her, not general feelings about the world or his former patients.

But he lost his chance to tell her. A steady stream of people began to file through his house. Parents. Frank's friends. People who had been there on the roadside watching that day. The man who had been driving the sports car.

"You gave me hope when I was half out of my mind," he told Donovan.

"I want my baby to have a doctor like you," a pregnant woman said.

A man and woman with a little girl came up. "You helped Frankie," the little girl said. "Frankie's my friend."

Another little boy tugged on his sleeve. "Frankie says you have a cool car."

Donovan couldn't help grinning. "You like cool cars?"

"Yup."

He ended up taking the boy out to the garage. People streamed out of the house, the men and many of the women exclaiming over Donovan's cool car, others strolling through his gardens.

"Thank you for being there," some said. "Thank you for having us here." They came; they smiled; they talked; they ate; they began to file out.

"Welcome to the area," one elderly woman said, taking Donovan's hand as she readied herself to leave. "I live in Chicago. I've heard of you. I know your reputation and I know what I saw the other day. You were given a gift. Not just the gift of healing, but the gift of caring and of soothing those who are hurting. It's a difficult job, I don't doubt that, but...to walk away from the gift...please don't. We need people like you."

Donovan felt his throat tighten. The woman was smiling at him. He remembered all the people who had come through here today. He remembered Frank. He remembered his patients back in Chicago...and Ben. Could he have saved Ben had he been there? He didn't know. He would never know, but standing here today, he realized this much. He could help some people, save some children. Not all, but some.

It was a truth he had been hiding from. He looked around, trying to find Anna. Damn woman. She wouldn't leave a man alone. She never had. Thank goodness.

Donovan smiled at the woman who had been talking to him. He thanked her. He took a deep breath and faced the rest of the truth.

The road back to life was going to be painful and

scary, and he might need time to ease back in, but he saw now that he couldn't really back away. He'd tried and he'd failed to quit. That was something to think about.

Then, suddenly, the last person left. The room went quiet. Donovan and Anna were alone. She'd been smiling at him all day but now she looked nervous. Tense. Uncertain. She walked across the floor, away from him, her heels clicking on the marble.

"Why?" he asked, but she didn't turn around.

He went to her, slid his arms around her and turned her to face him. She looked down. He placed a finger under her chin and tilted her face up to look at him.

"Why did I invade your privacy and force you into a position like this?" she asked.

He smiled. "Maybe the question I should ask is how? How did you know that I needed this? How did you know that it was inevitable that I would go back to medicine, that I couldn't walk away?"

She bit her lip. She took a deep breath. "Because I know you. Because I love you."

He closed his eyes, tightening his hold on her, pulling her so close that she was almost a part of his body. His lips came down on hers. "You wonderful, crazy, stubborn, amazing woman."

"It's all right that you don't love me," she said. "The truth is that, like it or not, what I saw yesterday was…you need to be a doctor. You could never walk away from an injured child. That's not the way you're made. And I—I just wanted you to have what you needed."

Donovan pulled back. "And you know what I need?"

She nodded slowly. "Yes. To go back to Chicago and take up your practice again."

Anna stared up at Donovan, her heart both rejoicing and breaking at the same time. Donovan was going to have some semblance of happiness and sanity and serenity again. He was going to be a doctor once more. She was pretty sure of that.

And she? She was going to lose him forever. She tried to keep smiling. Why had she admitted that she loved him? Because it was the truth and because it was, indeed, why she understood his needs.

His eyes were dark. He swept her closer. "What if you're what I need, Anna? What if I love you?"

Her heart beat faster. She placed her hands on his chest and tried to read his expression.

"You don't. Desire isn't love."

"No," he agreed. "It isn't, and I do desire you. But I've loved you from the day I met you, even if I didn't want to admit it. How could I not? You stirred up my world, drove me crazy and insisted on doing what was best for me. I came here, recklessly running from my life and ran right into you. It was the luckiest day of my life, Anna."

Donovan brought his lips down on hers. He tasted, he took, he gave back everything until Anna was shaking so hard she could barely stand.

Leading her to a sofa in the sunroom that overlooked the lake, Donovan pulled her close. "I've been running away for too long," he said. "Now I want to run to something. To you, Anna. Love me. Marry me?"

"You can't be sure." She frowned.

He smiled. "I'm positive. I don't want to live without you in my life."

She smiled up at him. "Yes, but…"

Alarm flashed in his eyes. "But what?"

She leaned closer. "I don't have to have a child. I don't want you to worry about that."

"It's been your dream."

"My dream was to have someone to love unconditionally." She kissed him again.

When she pulled back, he was smiling. "I think we have enough love to spare for a child."

"You don't have to do that."

He shook his head. "When Frank was hurt, a part of me knew that I couldn't hold back and still help him. I couldn't shield my heart without freezing up. And you know something? I dreamed of Ben last night. Maybe it was because his birthday was near and you told me that it should be celebrated. Maybe it was because of what happened yesterday, but…he was smiling. And I think Ben would have loved Frank, too. He would be glad I was with him in the ambulance. If they were the same age they might have become friends. So, I'm betting my son will understand that I'll never stop loving him even if I have other children to love."

"He loves you still. And always," she told him. "It flows from heaven to your heart and back again."

Donovan's kiss was gentle, reverent. "You had dreams when I met you."

"I still do. You're in every one of them."

"You've taught me how to dream again. And I do. Of you. Every day," he said, kissing her eyes. "Every night." He kissed her nose. "Sweet dreams," he said as he kissed her on the mouth.

Anna smiled up at him. "Donovan, do you realize you're kissing your housekeeper again? What will people say?" she teased.

"I imagine they'll say that I'm a very lucky man," he told her, amusement lighting his eyes.

"You're a wonderful man, my love," she said.

Then neither of them said anything more, for she was in his arms and that was all that mattered.

* * * * *